William and Mary: a rare double portrait of the Dutch king with his Stuart wife.

HENRI AND BARBARA
VAN DER ZEE

1688
REVOLUTION
IN THE
FAMILY

VIKING

VIKING

Penguin Books Ltd, 27 Wrights Lane, London w8 5tz (Publishing and Editorial)
and Harmondsworth, Middlesex, England (Distribution and Warehouse)
Viking Penguin Inc., 40 West 23rd Street, New York, New York 10010, USA
Penguin Books Australia Ltd, Ringwood, Victoria, Australia
Penguin Books Canada Ltd 2801 John Street, Markham, Ontario, Canada l3r 1b4
Penguin Books (NZ) Ltd, 182–190 Wairau Road, Auckland 10, New Zealand

First published 1988

Made and printed in Great Britain by
Richard Clay Ltd, Bungay, Suffolk
Filmset in 11/13pt Baskerville

British Library Cataloguing in Publication Data

Van der Zee, Henri
1688: revolution in the family.
1. William, *III, King of England*
2. Great Britain—History—
Revolution of 1688
I. Title   II. Van der Zee, Barbara
942.06′7   DA460

ISBN 0–670–80820–2

BY THE SAME AUTHORS
WILLIAM AND MARY

CONTENTS

LIST OF ILLUSTRATIONS

William and Mary: the Dutch king and his Stuart wife
(*BBC Radio Times Hulton Picture Library*) *frontispiece*

Between pages 128 and 129
James II confronts his bishops (*Photo Jean-Loup Charmet*)

James flees Whitehall, 22 December 1688 (*Photographie Giraudon*)

Henry Compton, Bishop of London (*National Portrait Gallery, London*)

Dr Gilbert Burnet (*National Portrait Gallery, London*)

John Churchill (*National Portrait Gallery, London*)

Hans Wilhem Bentinck (*Peter Ellis Photography,
Courtesy Lady Anne Bentinck*)

Queen Mary II (*National Portrait Gallery, London*)

James II (*National Portrait Gallery, London*)

William at Brixham (*Photo Jean-Loup Charmet*)

A caricature of Mary Beatrice and Father Petre, James' Jesuit advisor
(*British Museum*)

William III (*National Portrait Gallery, London*)

Mary Beatrice of Modena (*Conway Library*)

Louis XIV (*Photo Jean-Loup Charmet*)

Princess Anne, Mary's younger sister (*National Portrait Gallery, London*)

For Bibi and Ninka

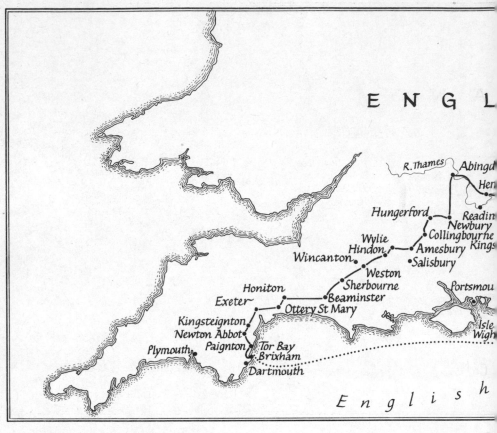

E N G L

R. Thames • Abingd
Hen
Hungerford • Readin
Newbury
Collingbourne
Wylie • Amesbury Kings
Hindon
Wincanton • Salisbury
Weston
Sherbourne
Honiton • Beaminster Portsmou
Exeter • Ottery St Mary
Kingsteignton
Newton Abbot Isle
Paignton Wigh
Plymouth Tor Bay
Brixham
Dartmouth

E n g l i s h

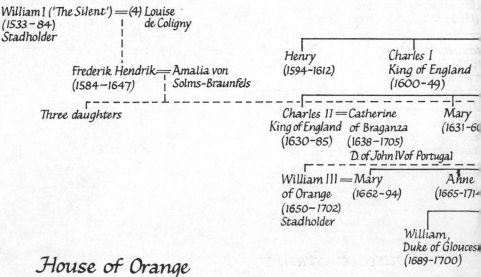

William 1 ('The Silent') = (4) Louise
(1533–84)   de Coligny
Stadholder

Frederik Hendrik = Amalia von
(1584–1647)   Solms-Braunfels

Three daughters

Henry   Charles I
(1594–1612)   King of England
               (1600–49)

Charles 11 = Catherine   Mary
King of England of Braganza (1631–6
(1630–85)   (1638–1705)
            D. of John IV of Portugal

William 111 = Mary   Anne
of Orange   (1662–94)   (1665–171
(1650–1702)
Stadholder

William,
Duke of Glouces
(1689–1700)

House of Orange

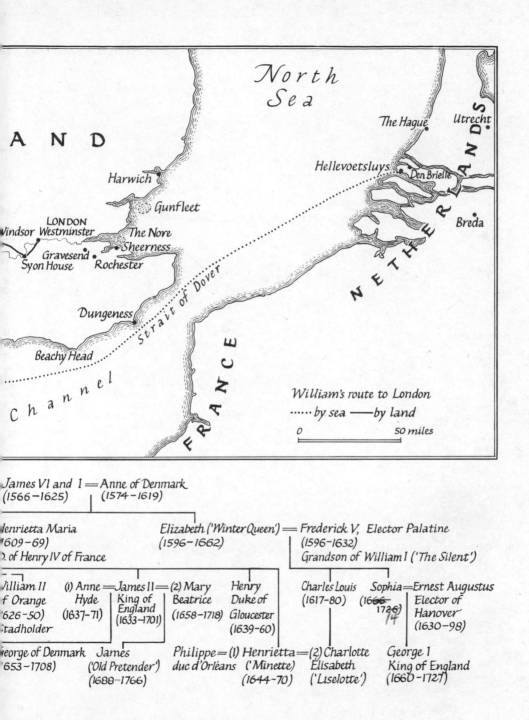

North
Sea

The Hague   Utrecht

Hellevoetsluys   Den Brielle

ENGLAND

Harwich

Gunfleet

LONDON
Windsor Westminster   The Nore
Gravesend   Sheerness
Syon House   Rochester

NETHERLANDS

Breda

Dungeness

Beachy Head

Strait of Dover

FRANCE

Channel

William's route to London
······ by sea —— by land
0   50 miles

James VI and I ══ Anne of Denmark
(1566–1625)   (1574–1619)

Henrietta Maria   Elizabeth ('Winter Queen') ══ Frederick V, Elector Palatine
(1609–69)   (1596–1662)   (1596–1632)
D. of Henry IV of France   Grandson of William I ('The Silent')

William II   (1) Anne ══ James II ══ (2) Mary   Henry   Charles Louis   Sophia ══ Ernest Augustus
of Orange   Hyde   King of   Beatrice   Duke of   (1617–80)   (1666–   Elector of
(1626–50)   (1637–71) England   (1658–1718) Gloucester   1726)   Hanover
Stadholder   (1633–1701)   (1639–60)   (1630–98)

George of Denmark   James   Philippe ══ (1) Henrietta ══ (2) Charlotte   George I
(1653–1708)   ('Old Pretender') duc d'Orléans ('Minette) Elisabeth   King of England
                    (1688–1766)   (1644–70) ('Liselotte') (1660–1727)

House of Stuart

INTRODUCTION

'Individuals, not arguments, are the real units of history,' A. L. Rowse has remarked. The arguments of the Glorious Revolution, the great issues on which it turned, have lost much of their relevance for Britain and the Netherlands today. Our monarchs, shorn of real power, no longer pose any threat to our Parliamentary democracy: they are seen instead as its figureheads and its guardians. We worry about nuclear missiles more than about standing armies. And religious toleration has for many years been taken for granted in our fortunate countries.

But the human drama at the heart of the 1688 revolution has lost none of its poignancy and fascination. The leading roles were played by people closely related to each other: King James II was driven out of his kingdom by his nephew, closely abetted by two daughters whom he loved and trusted. His folly recalls the tragic King Lear as much as does his fate. But even Shakespeare could hardly match the pathos of the luckless king's defeat and flight, or his agony on discovering that his own daughters were part of the conspiracy against him.

Whig historians saw the revolution of 1688 in black and white terms: William the daring, resourceful champion of liberty pitted against James the bigotted tyrant. Real life seldom offers such clear-cut heroes and villains. And an astonishingly rich haul of personal letters, diaries and memoranda, written by the leading actors of the 1688 drama, has survived to tell a different story, and give us a close-up view of each one of the actors in those weeks and months of crisis. Mary's private diaries and her letters to James and Anne; James's wooden little notes to William and his long effusions to his admiral, Lord Dartmouth; Mary Beatrice's guileless letters to William and her 'dear Lemon', Mary; Anne's venomous outpourings; William's letters to his right hand, Hans Willem Bentinck; letters to and from the leading conspirators; detailed reports from William's spy at Whitehall during the tense months leading up to the crisis of June 1688; and dozens of other letters, journals, private or public papers are among the records which cast their light from a dozen different angles on the central figures of the drama.

None of the principal players, it must be said, emerges with much credit from this close-up view. The blinkered James rushing headlong to disaster is a painful spectacle; and however much justified by the event, there is something repellent in the cool gamesmanship of William, or in the tough line that devotion to William compelled Mary to take. Equally chilling is Anne's vindictive jealousy of her attractive stepmother.

Perhaps the only one of the *dramatis personae* we feel to be truly deserving of our compassion is James's pious and unfortunate queen, Mary Beatrice, who behaved with regal dignity throughout, and seems never to have grasped till much too late the depths of duplicity to which her stepchildren and son-in-law were prepared to descend. But before she is cast as innocent victim, we must remind ourselves that her advice to her husband may have been as fatal to his cause as any folly of his own.

Three hundred years after the events of 1688, readers will make up their own minds. What we have assembled here is evidence from the leading witnesses.

In researching our account, our major debt is to the dozens of experts who have already published books and articles on various aspects of the 1688 revolution. It seems invidious to single out any of them, but we feel bound in honour to acknowledge a particular debt to John Carswell's masterly work, *The Descent on England*; to F. C. Turner's comprehensive biography of James II; to Maurice Ashley's *The Glorious Revolution of 1688*; to J. R. Jones's *The Revolution of 1688 in England* and other works of his; and to the various books and articles by J. P. Kenyon and John Miller listed in the bibliography. Inevitably, too, we have drawn heavily on our own previous work, *William and Mary*.

Since this is a work for the general reader rather than the historian, we have not encumbered it with notes, which would make plainer still the extent of our indebtedness. But if readers are stimulated by our book to greater curiosity about this momentous period in history, the bibliography at the back may be a useful guide for further reading.

We are very grateful to Douglas Matthews, Librarian of the London Library and, as always, a fount of knowledge, encouragement and useful suggestions. As we followed the trail of William and his armies from Brixham to London, we also had the pleasure of consulting at every stage the company of experts on England's local and national history to be found in County Record Offices, in public libraries, in private collections and in numbers of amateur societies. Their enthusiasm and helpfulness made an already pleasant task a delight indeed. We should like to thank them very warmly, and we hope they will enjoy this chronicle to which their own contribution has been so important.

Among those to whom we should like to say a special thank you are: Mrs Glenys Downes, Librarian at Brixham; Michael Dowdell, Reference Librarian at Torquay; Ian Maxted, in charge of West Country studies at Exeter Reference Library; K. H. Rogers, County Archivist at the County Record Office, Wiltshire County Council; Joanna Hyde of Newton Abbot Library; Mrs Margery Rowe, County Archivist at Exeter Record Office; Mrs Kay Vince, Librarian at Axminster; Andrew Davey, Librarian at Crewkerne; David Bromwich, Local History Librarian at Taunton; Mrs Ruppersbury at Wincanton Public Library; Nina Sutton at Henley Public Library; Peter L. Smith, Keeper of the Archives, Salisbury Cathedral School; Ms Suzanne Ewart, Librarian at the Cathedral Library in Salisbury; Ms Pamela Colman of the Wiltshire Archaeological and Natural History Society. Other thank yous are due to Joyce Packe who generously shared with us her comprehensive knowledge of the local background to William's invasion; and to Puffy Bowden, industrious chronicler of Wincanton's history. Thank you to Francine Swart for research in Holland; and to Barrie Iliffe, initially Secretary of the William and Mary Tercentenary Committee.

Thank you to Drs B. Woelderink, Directeur van het Koninklijk Huisarchief, Dienst van het Koninklijk Huis, 'S-Gravenhage. Thank you to the staff at the British Library; the MSS Department of the British Museum; and the Koninklijke Bibliotheek in The Hague; to the Curator of the Portland papers at Nottingham University Library; and to the librarians of the Catholic Central Library in London and Lambeth Palace Library.

Thank you to KLM, who made journeys between London and Holland a great deal faster and more luxurious than William's crossing.

Thank you, finally, to Tony Lacey of Viking for his patience and much constructive help; to Judith Flanders who steered our book calmly and knowledgeably through the hassles of editing; and to Richard Simon for his cheerful encouragement throughout.

A NOTE ON THE DATES

Throughout the seventeenth century England, following the Julian calendar, was ten days behind the Continent, where the calendar reforms introduced by Gregory XIII were observed. Thus 12 February New Style on the Continent was 2 February Old Style in England. Contemporaries travelling or corresponding between England and the Continent appear to have sorted out the complexities of this situation without much trouble, switching easily from one calendar to the other. Occasionally, to avoid confusion, they dated their letters both ways – 2/12 February. Historians and biographers, on the other hand, have not always found it so easy to avoid confusing themselves and their readers. We have followed their standard practice by dating events happening in England according to the Old Style, and events on the Continent according to the New Style. When events are viewed from an English perspective, similarly, the dates are in Old Style; when viewed from the Continental, in the New. To simplify matters, we have occasionally given both dates.

ONE

'THE QUEEN'S GREAT BELLY ...'

On 1 January 1688 King James II of England looked forward to a happy New Year. His second wife Mary Beatrice d'Este of Modena had escaped a miscarriage. The striking twenty-nine-year-old Italian queen, whom James had married in 1674 when she was a devout convent-reared teenager, had borne four babies since marriage – not one of whom survived infancy – and had four miscarriages. But this time the pregnancy seemed assured.

'Yesterday morning she was not very well,' James wrote on 30 December to his Dutch son-in-law Prince William of Orange, in The Hague, 'and was for some time afraid she should have miscarried, but now, God be thanked, she is very well, and that fear is at present over ...'

Henry Hyde, Earl of Clarendon, the brother of James's first wife, had braved the 'cold blustering north winds' to be present at the king's levee on New Year's Day, and heard the good news confirmed. 'I'm sure all honest men wish an increase of the royal family,' he wrote in his diary.

The outspoken Clarendon, whose loyal services to his brother-in-law had been spurned when a year earlier he was replaced as Lord Deputy of Ireland by a loud-mouthed Catholic adventurer, Richard Talbot, Earl of Tyrconnel, ought to have known better. Since his conversion twenty years earlier, James had been an ardent Roman Catholic, whose Romanizing policies had already alarmed and alienated most Englishmen, and the pregnancy of Queen Mary Beatrice was being seen as part of a plot to establish in England a Roman Catholic and absolute monarchy, such as neighbouring France already had under Louis XIV. A flood of scurrilous pamphlets and cartoons hinted that she wasn't pregnant at all, and many people were beginning to believe them: a fact noted by Clarendon two weeks later when, after a day of thanksgiving and prayers 'upon the Queen being with child', he wrote that '... the Queen's great belly is everywhere ridiculed'.

Rumours that the queen was pregnant had first begun circulating

the previous October. By early November nobody at Whitehall –
Catholic or Protestant – could talk about anything else. And by the
middle of the month it was official. The French ambassador, Paul
Barillon d'Amoncourt, Marquis de Branges, at once sent the news to
his master Louis XIV that while Mary Beatrice had spoken of it in
doubtful terms up to then, 'she now says that she believes herself
pregnant . . . she is fairly uncomfortable.'

The young queen, as usual, suffered from recurring nausea. Thomas
Bruce, Earl of Ailesbury, James's devoted Gentleman of the Bedchamber, who played cards with her almost every day, was concerned for her: 'Very frequently from a most cheerful (countenance)
and quick eye she turned pale as ashes, and was obliged to go to her
bed chamber.'

The Queen's stepdaughter, Princess Anne, felt no such sympathy.
'No words can express the rage of the Princess of Denmark at the
Queen's pregnancy, she can dissimulate it to no one,' the Tuscan
envoy in London, the Abbé Terriesi, reported. It was a very human
reaction. The stout, dull and rather plain second daughter of James's
first marriage, married to the tedious Prince George of Denmark, had
had a particularly unhappy year herself. In January 1687 she had
miscarried; she had lost two baby daughters in February – victims of
the century's killer-disease, smallpox – and just when the first rumours
of Mary Beatrice's pregnancy had begun to circulate, she had miscarried again.

As second in line to the throne, Anne was naturally not pleased by
the prospect of a male heir who would supersede her eldest sister Mary,
wife of William of Orange, and herself, but there was another reason
for her resentment. A staunch Protestant, deeply attached to the
Church of England, she blamed the devout Italian queen for her
father's religious fanaticism.

In this sceptical age, it is hard to grasp the fear that 'popery' aroused
at that time even in intelligent and educated people, while the 'mobile'
– as the general public were known – readily swallowed the most lurid
rumours about what had once been the faith of their fathers. Catholics,
it was thought, would stop at nothing, not even murder, to gain their
perverted ends, egged on by those sinister black figures, the Jesuits.
Only God's providence had saved the kingdom from any number of
dastardly Catholic intrigues, starting with Guy Fawkes' Gunpowder
Plot. Effigies of the pope blazed annually in commemoration of this
plot on the bonfires of 5 November, and more went up in flames on
another popular anniversary a few days later: 17 November, the date of
the accession of Good Queen Elizabeth.

Catholics already suffered under the Penal Laws passed in Elizabeth's reign, though by Charles II's time, these were seldom if ever enforced. But in the 1670s, to allay the fears raised by the prospect of a Catholic king when James succeeded to the throne after Charles's death, Parliament had passed two further anti-Catholic measures. The first Test Act of 1673 – 'for preventing dangers which may happen from Popish recusants' – effectively barred Catholics from public life, since it required all those holding civil or military office, or places at Court, to produce a certificate that they had recently taken Anglican communion, to make a public denial of belief in the central Catholic doctrine of transubstantiation and to swear oaths of allegiance and supremacy to the king, which were worded in terms deeply objectionable to Roman Catholics.

The second Test Act, of 1678, closed Parliament to them. It was passed in response to national anti-Catholic hysteria, at a time when the nation was rocked to its foundations by the sensational Popish Plot – allegedly the attempt of a group of Catholic conspirators, masterminded by the cunning Jesuits, to assassinate Charles II and overthrow Parliament. As was later shown, the plot was almost entirely the fabrication of an unscrupulous and disreputable ex-clergyman, Titus Oates. But his first 'revelations' initiated a new reign of terror for Roman Catholics, and priest-hunts on a scale unknown since Elizabeth's time. Hundreds of Catholics were flung into prison, twenty-four were executed – among them nine Jesuits, the special targets of Oates's ravings – and even James and Mary Beatrice were at one point believed to be implicated.

At the height of the hysteria, no rumour about the Catholics was too improbable to be believed. 'The credulous all over the kingdom were terrified and afrighted with armies landing, of pilgrims, black bills, armies under ground and what not,' wrote Lord Ailesbury. 'The Countess of Shaftesbury had always in her muff little pocket pistols, loaded, to defend her from the papists . . . and most timorous ladies followed her example.'

Even though Oates was later convicted of perjury, and the complete innocence of many of his victims proved, the damage was done. Fear of popery and paranoia about Jesuit plots once more became rooted in the English mind. James himself had to sue for libel – winning £100,000 damages – a Mr Pilkington who spread stories that the Catholic duke had started the Fire of London of 1666. And Princess Anne genuinely believed – or so she said years later – that Charles II had been secretly done to death by Jesuits so that her father would succeed him.

If Roman Catholics went in terror of the mob as a result of these plots and rumours, the Anglican clergy had anxieties of their own. Should England ever return to popery, how many of their wealthy sees and plump benefices would be handed back to Rome? What of the hundreds of well-endowed abbeys, monasteries and convents, and their thousands of acres of land, seized by the Crown at the Dissolution of the Monasteries under Henry VIII, which had now been in new secular and Protestant hands for three or four generations?

By the time of James's accession, in February 1685, the extreme anti-Catholic hysteria of the Popish Plot had died down, and a reaction had set in. Greatly to his own surprise, James's proclamation as king was greeted by cheers and loyal rejoicings throughout the country, instead of triggering the general insurrection he had half-expected. And at his first meeting with his Privy Council, he went out of his way to allay Protestant fears. 'I know the principles of the Church of England are for monarchy,' he told them, 'and the members of it have shewed themselves good and loyal subjects, therefore I shall always take care to defend and support it.' The delighted councillors asked for this in writing – and James rather reluctantly agreed to have the royal promises printed: they were read out in the nation's pulpits the following Sunday.

Parliament too was reassured by the promises James had made, and at its first meeting the new House of Commons, carefully packed with docile and ultra-loyal Tories, voted him a handsome income for life – more than they ever did for Charles – as well as £800,000 to fit out the navy of which he had once been the proud High Admiral.

After the indolent regime of Charles, the new king brought an unfamiliar air of purposefulness and activity to Whitehall. An energetic fifty-five-year-old, James at first impressed everyone with his dedication and administrative ability. Admittedly, he lacked Charles's easy charm and his great talent for handling people, but he appeared to have other admirable qualities. 'Infinite industry, sedulity, gravity and great understanding and experience of affairs,' noted the writer and courtier John Evelyn approvingly, adding optimistically, 'I cannot but predict much happiness to the nation.'

The new king had at least one trait in common with his brother: a voracious sexual appetite. But unlike the mistresses of Charles II – the indolent, sumptuous beauties immortalized by Lely, notable for their wit, their charm and their personality – the women James found irresistible were almost invariably a plain lot. 'I wonder what he sees in us all,' remarked one of them candidly, 'for none of us is handsome, and if we have wit, he hath not enough himself to find it out.'

Even after marriage to a warm-blooded young Italian, James could not break himself of his old habits, and continued to sneak off regularly to his current mistress Catherine Sedley. Terrible scenes with Mary Beatrice – jealous, deeply hurt, affronted – and expostulations from his priests produced only temporary reform. But whereas Charles openly flaunted his many mistresses, James was desperately ashamed of his sexual misdeeds, for which he actually used to scourge himself in an agony of remorse. A Catholic king should set a better example, as his priests often pointed out to him. And it was generally – and probably accurately – believed that his failure to obey his confessors in this matter gave them a moral ascendancy and an influence over him which they would not otherwise have had.

There were other disturbing traits in his character. James had been nine years old when he rode behind his father Charles I on to the battlefield of Edgehill, to be fired on by Parliamentary troops, and he was an impressionable fifteen-year-old when he learnt of his adored father's execution by his subjects. As a result he had grown up, in the words of a contemporary, 'with strange notions of the obedience due to princes'. It was noted that 'he thinks everyone a rebel that opposes the king in Parliament'. Even the French ambassador, used to Louis's high-handed ways, was startled by James's ideas about how his people should be governed. 'I know the English,' he told Barillon after his coronation. 'You must not show them any fear in the beginning.' And some time later the same ambassador remarked, 'he is very pleased at being complimented on bold displays of power.'

It was not only in Parliament that James saw rebels. Dissenters in his eyes were almost as bad as republicans, and what he admired about the Church of England was its great loyalty to the Crown. It was the absolute authority of the pope, and the unquestioning devotion of his flock, he told his daughter Mary, that had particularly appealed to James and finally won him over to the Catholic Church.

Among the new king's less attractive characteristics was a mulish obstinacy, which always made it difficult for him to admit – even to himself – that he had made a mistake, and back out gracefully once he had committed himself publicly to a particular course of action. Since he came to the throne with one overriding ambition – to secure the full emancipation of his fellow Catholics – his reign was on a collision course from the outset. Given his astonishing insensitivity to political reality or public opinion, disaster was certain.

The French ambassador was the first to know of his plans. 'This prince has thoroughly explained to me his intentions with regard to the Catholics,' Barillon reported to Louis soon after James's accession, 'which are to grant them entire liberty of conscience and the free exercise of their religion.'

James was still realist enough to grasp that given the strength of national prejudice on the subject, he would have to hasten slowly. 'This is a work of time,' he told Barillon, 'and it can only be brought about step by step.'

But discretion was not a word in his vocabulary, and he soon forgot his own advice. The cynical Charles II had sized up James years earlier in a characteristic *bon mot*: 'My brother will lose his kingdom by his bigotry and his soul for a lot of ugly trollops.' Only a few months after the auspicious opening of his reign, James zealously set about making the first of these predictions come true.

From the beginning of his reign, he had mass celebrated openly at Whitehall with splendid ceremony. On one of these occasions, the Duke of Norfolk, carrying the sword of state, pointedly stopped at the chapel door. 'My lord,' said James, 'your father would have gone further.' 'Your Majesty's father would not have gone so far,' retorted the duke. When he publicly received at Whitehall six Benedictine monks in their habits, even Louis XIV remarked that this was 'more likely to distance Protestants from our religion than to attract them to it . . .' But monks and friars in their habits were soon a common sight in London. There were Benedictines in the Chapel Royal of St James's, Jesuits in the Savoy district, Recollet friars in Lincoln's Inn Fields and Carmelites in the City. A newsletter reported that the king had ordered that the Benedictines should 'walk abroad without any guard, and whoever shall offer them affront shall be severely punished'.

The Spanish ambassador, Don Pedro Ronquillo, was amazed to see so many priests at Whitehall openly wearing the habits of their order, and commented on the fact to James. 'But isn't it normal in Spain,' asked James, 'for kings to consult their confessors?' 'Undoubtedly,' replied Ronquillo, 'and that's why our affairs are always in such a mess.'

Many of James's Catholic subjects were appalled by such goings-on. As early as 1685, Barillon noted that 'rich and established Catholics feared the future . . . [and] were ready to be happy with quite moderate advantages such as the revocation of the Penal Laws.' They were appalled by James's reckless disregard for public opinion, and lived in dread of the inevitable Protestant backlash.

In the first summer of his reign, however, James was able to demonstrate that he was firmly in control. In June 1685 the dashing young Duke of Monmouth, the popular bastard son of Charles II, and a great Protestant favourite, made an ill-fated bid for the crown by landing in the west of England with a small army. Thousands of illiterate country-people flocked to join his advance on London, and for a time near-panic reigned at Whitehall. Toasts were drunk to the new Protestant 'king': 'A health for the King, late Duke of Monmouth, for the land is all Popery and Popery is now at the door.'

But Parliament voted unanimously to stand by James with their lives and fortunes, and moved an immediate grant of £400,000 for the cost of suppressing the rebellion, while energetic action by the royal army – brilliantly commanded by the young John Churchill – saved the day. Monmouth was defeated and executed. In line with his well-known horror of rebellion, James followed up this victory by what he described as his 'campaign in the West': a programme of savage reprisals. In the Bloody Assizes at Taunton, James's Chief Justice Jeffreys ordered dozens of the rebels to be whipped through the local market-towns; 849 were deported; a few of the gentry were beheaded; and over 300, most of them illiterate country-folk, were sentenced to the ghastly ritual of hanging, disembowelling and quartering. Their quartered remains were strung up in villages throughout the West Country as a grisly reminder of the fate rebels could expect.

Meanwhile, since the local militia – troops of barely trained, part-time reserves – had proved utterly useless, James seized the chance to increase his standing army from 6,000 to nearly 20,000. He was delighted by this pretext for raising troops, the French ambassador observed, 'and he believes that the Duke of Monmouth's enterprise will serve only to make him still more the master of his country'.

Superficially, this appeared to be true, but for James in fact it was another step down a slippery slope. To English Protestants, the prospect of an absolute monarchy, fortified with a large standing army, was an ancient bugbear. And never more so than at this moment, when another Roman Catholic monarch, Louis XIV, was sending shockwaves through Protestant Europe by his treatment of his Huguenot subjects.

Since 1598, these French Protestants had enjoyed a freedom of conscience and worship guaranteed to them in the reign of Henri IV by the Edict of Nantes. But to Louis XIV, the very existence in his realm of this alien faith seemed an affront to his absolute authority, and for years now the rights and freedom of worship of the Huguenots had been systematically eroded. The trickle of refugees, taking their tales of persecution and hardship to England, to Holland and to the German states, grew to a flood when in that autumn of 1685, while James was still celebrating his victory over Monmouth, the French king finally revoked the Edict.

Large numbers of Huguenots began arriving in England homeless and penniless, with horror stories of imprisonment, torture and the brutality of the *Dragonnades*. James, who was forever preaching the virtues of tolerance, initially made the right noises. He told the Dutch ambassador that Louis's conduct was not even politic, let alone Christian. But to suspicious Protestant subjects, his protests lacked the ring of conviction. It was noticed, for instance, that the *London Gazette*, the only official – and heavily censored – newspaper of the day, 'never in all this time spake one syllable of this wonderfull proceeding in France'. The king also did his best to stop Huguenot refugees coming over to England, delayed for as long as he decently could the collection of funds for them and, once they were settled, forced those who had fled from religious persecution to conform strictly to the rules and rites of the Anglican Church.

He hoped, however, that his subjects would learn one lesson from the fate of the Huguenots: and that was the iniquity of persecuting men for their religion. He himself wanted no forced converts, he told Ronquillo: he only aimed 'at the Roman Catholics being no worse treated than the rest, instead of being deprived of their liberties like traitors'.

To give his subjects an instance of what he had in mind, James had given commissions in his new standing army to some eighty-six Catholics: a very modest proportion of the officer total. Since their employment was actually illegal, he had dispensed them from taking the oaths required by the Test Acts, and he knew he could expect storms when Parliament reassembled. Determined to stand no nonsense, he decided to attack first. When he opened Parliament on 9 November, he told the assembled Peers and Commons not only that he needed funds for the upkeep of his enlarged standing army, since the militia had proved unreliable, but also that he had employed some officers who had not taken the oaths, and had no intention of parting with them.

To his surprise and displeasure, he was met by courteously phrased but uncompromising resistance. In the minds of both Houses, the handful of officers were the thin end of the Catholic wedge, and a standing army the instrument of tyranny. 'In peace there is nothing for an army to subdue but Magna Charta,' was one pointed comment.

In the House of Lords, the Bishop of London, Henry Compton – who had seen active military service in his youth – was particularly outspoken on the subject of these Catholic officers. Their appointment, he declared, was simply the prelude to the eventual transformation of England into a Catholic state. 'The laws of England were like the dikes of Holland, and universal Catholicism like the ocean – if the laws were once broken, inundation would follow.' He spoke for all the bishops, who rose as one man in agreement, and James, who was not to forget Compton's words, angrily prorogued Parliament till February.

But February 1686 came and went, and there was no sign of Parliament's recall. Instead, the long-absent faces of Catholic peers began to be seen at Whitehall: the elderly Marquess of Powis, the seventy-eight-year-old Lord Arundel of Wardour, the crippled seventy-two-year-old Lord Bellasys. All three had been imprisoned for months during the Popish Plot, and their families had led discreetly retiring lives for decades. Now they emerged, blinking, into the glare of Whitehall public life.

Even the most rabid anti-papist could hardly object to these diffident old gentlemen – it was natural, after all, that James would wish to surround himself with fellow-Catholics. And there was still a reassuringly strong Anglican presence at Court: James's old seagoing friend Lord Dartmouth; his brother-in-law Lord Rochester, patron and staunch friend of the Church of England; his other brother-in-law, another pillar of the Anglican establishment, Lord Clarendon; Churchill, Lord Preston, Lord Nottingham, the influential Tory, Edward Seymour.

It was public knowledge, too, that the most experienced of James's Catholic advisers, like the landed Catholic gentry, all urged moderation on him: one step at a time. Cardinal Howard was Protector of England at Rome, and in October 1685 he sent over to London his former secretary Dr John Leyburn as the first vicar-apostolic appointed to England since the time of Charles I. Leyburn was a modest, cautious man in his sixties, with long first-hand experience of English-Catholic problems. Howard's choice of nuncio – Ferdinand, Count d'Adda, Archbishop of Amasia – was a lightweight by contrast, an agreeable young charmer. But both men had been carefully briefed by Howard and Pope Innocent XI, and they did their utmost to impress on James the dangers of trying to do too much too soon. James welcomed them both with open arms – much more publicly than they thought wise – and lodged Leyburn in Whitehall with a pension of £1,000 a year. He showed, however, no inclination to listen to their sober, sensible advice.

Instead, he turned to an old Catholic friend, Father Edward Petre. This fifty-five-year-old priest belonged to one of England's oldest Catholic families, but by the time he inherited his father's baronetcy in 1679 he was a fully fledged Jesuit, trained abroad for the English mission. His superiors noted his 'boldness and address' and he was soon promoted to vice-provincial of the Society. When this leaked out, in the hysteria of the Popish Plot, he was promptly arrested and he languished in prison for three years.

Free again, he was soon drawn into the family circle of James, who admired him as a 'resolute and undertaking man'. He gave advice regarding the education of James's illegitimate sons and, on the accession of James, he was at once summoned to Whitehall: his hour had come. From superintendent of the Royal Chapel he rose to Clerk of the Royal Closet; from humble lodgings he was promoted to the king's splendid former apartments in Whitehall; and from advising the king on his spiritual health, he evolved into an *éminence grise* of growing power and importance. It was no secret that the Jesuit was one of the regulars at the weekly dinner meetings of the 'Catholic Council' over which the king's chief minister, Lord Sunderland, presided.

To the horrified English, Father Petre at Court seemed the living embodiment of the papist menace, especially since this smooth-talking cleric enjoyed the king's complete confidence. 'A cunning dissembler . . . and a hot-headed ignorant churchman,' were among the kinder remarks made about him. Many Catholics shared Protestant suspicions of the Jesuit order, and Father Petre's presence at Whitehall dismayed them. 'Why give this excuse for an outburst to the Protestants,' they lamented, 'cause them to say they're ruled by a Jesuit?'

Even the devout Mary Beatrice disliked him, and later said that she thought his influence on James 'most unfortunate', while James himself – much too late – admitted that the Jesuit had 'a weak and shallow judgement'. It was said of James that he 'was soon determined by those he trusted; but he was obstinate against all other advices'. Unluckily for the nation's Catholics, it was now Father Petre – counselling neither caution nor moderation – whom James trusted implicitly. So much so that as early as September 1685 James was confidently writing to the pope to ask for a bishopric for him. And in February 1686 he dispatched England's first envoy to the Holy See in more than a century to press the Jesuit's claims. Was it possible, he wondered, that Father Petre might be given a dispensation allowing him to fill a vacant see in the Church of England?

James's choice of ambassador was as unfortunate as his mission. Pope Innocent XI was no lover of the Jesuit order, and Roger Palmer, Earl of Castlemaine, was hardly the man to change his mind. Not only was it common knowledge that Castlemaine owed his title to his wife's long-standing and much-publicized liaison with Charles II, but his diplomatic ineptitude, together with James's mule-headed persistence, soon made him the laughing-stock of the Roman *corps diplomatique*. Innocent XI, it was reported, kept a little silver bell on his table which he rang as a signal to visitors that it was time for them to take their leave: '. . . that lord very often scarce began his discourse but the bell rang'. The pope despised this noisy Englishman, who even ventured to contradict him, and to James complained bitterly of his 'vehemence', compelling the king to beg an abject pardon.

Apart from Father Petre, the most influential person at Court was almost equally detested by Catholics and Protestants alike: the cold, saturnine figure of Robert Spencer, Earl of Sunderland. For this re-sourceful career politician who had twice switched his allegiance to save his skin, political success was essential to his very survival, since he spent money like water and gambled fortunes away. From the start he was determined to be indispensable to James – though he had also secretly accepted a handsome pension from Louis XIV – hinting to the gullible king that he was seriously attracted by the Church of Rome, and he set himself the task of carrying out James's most ardent wish – the emancipation of English Catholics.

James had been confident at first that he could browbeat Parliament into repealing the hated Penal and Test Acts. Once this was done, he was certain, there would be a flood of converts among many who only hesitated now because they feared to sacrifice their career chances. But after the resounding negative he had been given by Parliament in November 1685, he changed tactics in 1686 and tried bullying: all office-holders in either House who refused to support his policy were dismissed. It was still highly doubtful whether enough members might have changed their minds, and Parliament was prorogued again till May, and in May again until November, amid growing rumours that it would never meet at all.

In Scotland his tactics were simply high-handed. After two long spells of exile in Scotland, James flattered himself he knew how to manage these tough northern subjects of his: by a display of great firmness. The Scottish Estates were ordered to give relief to his Roman Catholic subjects in Scotland. When to his considerable astonishment they refused, he invoked his dispensing power to have Catholics admitted to office in droves, many becoming members of the Scottish Privy Council, while judges were ordered to treat all laws against Catholics as null and void. Municipal elections, meanwhile, were suspended: in future James would make the most important new appoint-ments to office himself.

Church of England uneasiness was by now growing rapidly: James had given them plenty of reasons. A carefully rigged test case in July 1686 confirmed the king's legal right to dispense certain individuals from the Test Acts; and four Catholic peers had immediately been

sworn into the Privy Council. The same month the hated old Ecclesiastical Commission – a regulatory body for the Church of England –
was revived, and its first act was to suspend Henry Compton, Bishop of
London, who had spoken out against the employment of Catholic
officers, and whose strong antagonism to Catholicism was well-known.
In defiance of orders from James that the Anglican clergy should
refrain from 'disputes', the Dean of St Giles, in a highly controversial
sermon, had referred to Catholics as 'idolaters'. When Compton refused
to suspend him as requested, he was himself suspended.

Events in Ireland did nothing to calm English fears. In December
1685 James's brother-in-law Clarendon was appointed Viceroy of
Ireland and, when he arrived in Dublin, he found that Irish Protestants
were already deeply unhappy about the encouragement now being
given to Catholics. It was the work of James's old Irish friend, the
hotheaded Richard Talbot, Earl of Tyrconnel, who as lord-lieutenant
was soon exceeding his instructions, while James turned a blind eye.
Church preferments were being kept open for Catholics, Catholic
bishops were appearing in public and holding assemblies quite openly;
Catholics were being appointed as justices of the peace, sheriffs and
judges. Most alarming of all, the Irish army was being progressively
stripped of its Protestant officers and men, and was fast being turned
into a much bigger, and Catholic, force.

Clarendon protested in vain: in the New Year of 1687 James relieved him of his office, and at once appointed Tyrconnel in his place.
The other pillar of the Anglican establishment had crashed only days
earlier, when his brother Rochester was dismissed from the treasury.
James had tears in his eyes when he broke the news to his brother-
in-law, after weeks spent vainly trying to convert him. 'I cannot have
a man at the head of my affairs who is not of my opinion,' he told
him.

Despite his failure with Rochester, James went on to try his powers
of persuasion on other leading Protestants. One by one they were
summoned for little chats about their souls, in a procedure nicknamed
'closeting', and asked for their promise that they would vote for the
abolition of the Test and Penal Laws. Closeting was both unpopular
and unproductive. No streams of eager converts resulted. Instead,
several national figures were provoked into outright opposition. The
most sensational of these was Arthur Herbert, a career admiral in the
navy, whose interests had been promoted by James, who could ill
afford such gestures since he was not rich, and whose loose-living and
foul language were so notorious that his resignation on a point of
conscience astonished everyone. Soon afterwards, the distinguished

young Earl of Shrewsbury had the cavalry regiment of which he was colonel taken from him when he proved resistant to closeting.

By the spring of 1687, it was beginning to be obvious even to the king that his new tactic was a resounding flop. His Parliament had dug its toes in, and neither threats, cajolery or bribery were going to change its mind. James now decided to go it alone. On 18 March he wrote casually to William of Orange, announcing a dramatic change of plan:

'I have this day resolved to prorogue the Parliament till the 22 November next and that all my subjects may be at ease and quiet, and mind their trades and private concerns, have resolved to give liberty of conscience to all dissenters whosoever, having been ever against persecuting any for conscience's sake . . .'

A fortnight later, he made his *grand coup* public. In an Edict of Toleration published on 4 April, he suspended the Test Acts and brushed aside the old Penal Laws of Elizabeth's reign under which so many Catholics had suffered for their faith.

In its preamble the Edict seemed impartial: 'there is nothing . . . that we so earnestly desire as to establish our government on such a foundation as may make our subjects happy . . . which we think can be done by no means so effectually as by granting to them the free exercise of their religion.' But James made no secret of his real hope: 'We cannot but heartily wish, as it will be easily believed, that all the people of our dominions were members of the Catholic church.'

Her father's Grand Design filled Anne with horror and consternation. 'By this one may easily guess what one is to hope for henceforward,' she wrote to her sister Mary in May, voicing the outrage and concern of the English, 'since the priests have so much power with the King as to make him do things directly against the laws of the land, and indeed contrary to his own promises.'

In his declaration, James had undertaken 'to protect and maintain our archbishops, bishops and clergy, and all other our subjects of the Church of England', but to the stunned Protestants these words rang hollow. 'It is a melancholy prospect that all we of the Church of England have.'

The moderate Catholics – Arundel, Powis, Belasys – were almost equally dismayed. 'These measures will ruin us all,' they told Ailesbury despairingly. And the Earl of Chesterfield summed up Protestant feelings: 'Though we have now a Prince whose study is his country's glory, whose courage would give him lustre without a throne . . . yet heaven, it seems, hath found a way to make all this more terrible than lovely . . .'

The one consolation for Protestants – and the great chagrin of James

– was that there was no Catholic heir to the Crown. As long as James was king, and able to exercise his dispensing power, the Test Acts could not be enforced against Catholics. But it was four years since the queen's last pregnancy which, like the previous one, had ended in a painful miscarriage; and short of a miracle, she was unlikely to bear him another child. He himself could not expect to live to a very advanced age – he was already fifty-five – and at his death, his Protestant daughter Mary and his son-in-law William would succeed him.

James had no illusions about what would happen then. The first Parliament they summoned would – with their full approval and consent – call for the Test Acts to be enforced, and Catholics would once more become a persecuted minority cut off from the life of the nation.

As every effort to persuade the Prince and Princess of Orange to support his policy of Indulgence had failed, it was imperative for James to have it endorsed by Parliament. And since the present Parliament, with its majority of Tory Anglicans, would never cooperate, only one option was left open to him now: to dissolve Parliament and, with the help of that wily manipulator Sunderland, procure a docile new House of Commons. If this plan was to have any chance of success, it called for some unlikely new allies: the Dissenters, once regarded by James with loathing as rebels.

No effort to achieve this cooperative Parliament was to be spared, and for James the issue was important enough to go campaigning himself. But it was not only politics that took him on the road for a prolonged Royal Progress through England. Haunted by the vision of what might yet be if only he had a son, James also meant to offer up prayers for an heir at a shrine that had always been popular with English Catholics – St Winefride's Well in Flintshire.

The queen was to make a more secular pilgrimage at the same time: to Bath, where she would stay for a few days to take the cure at this famous spa, in the hope that it might give the miracle a helping hand.

Having dissolved Parliament, James left London in August to travel to Winchester, Portsmouth and Southampton. His route took him through Monmouth country, where memories of the Bloody Assizes of two years earlier were still vivid. But James was now particularly affable to his subjects here, going out of his way to reassure Protestants and Dissenters alike. 'You see,' he told them, 'I may have admitted a few Catholics into civil and military posts, but I haven't made any of them MPs: so how can I do anything to upset those of other faiths?'

He joined the queen for a couple of days at Bath, and to the great fury of the local bishop, Thomas Ken, held a Catholic service in the Anglican Abbey, with a 'great healing' as its main feature. James always took the royal tradition of 'Touching for the King's Evil' very seriously, and had transformed it from an Anglican rite into an elaborate Catholic ceremony. 'I had not time to remonstrate,' an unhappy Ken wrote to Archbishop Sancroft, 'and if I had done it, it would have had no effect but only to provoke.'

After Bath, his Progress took James to Gloucester, Worcester, Ludlow, Shrewsbury and Whitchurch, and from there to the miracle-working shrine, where he prayed with great fervour for a son. This highly publicized visit to St Winefride's Well was a fresh source of irritation to his subjects, vexed that their king – who everybody knew was no saint – should make 'such a spectacle of himself in the guise of a superstitious pilgrim'.

The next stop was Chester, where James met Lord Tyrconnel, his deputy in Dublin, to discuss their secret plans for Ireland's future. Barillon later sent Louis an account of these plans. The Revolution Settlement sacred to Irish Protestants was to be set aside, and their property restored to Irish Catholics. 'The overthrow of this Settlement,' he reported, '. . . if it can be carried out without opposition, will result in an entire separation of Ireland from England in the future.'

After Lichfield, Coventry and Banbury, James arrived at Oxford on 13 September to a splendid reception. The streets were decorated with green boughs, and on his way in procession to his lodgings at Christ Church he was cheered by crowds lining the route. But some of his hosts shook in their shoes; the Fellows of Magdalen College had been at loggerheads with His Majesty since the spring, and once again, it was James's Catholicizing policies which had created the problem.

On 24 March that year, Magdalen's president, Dr Henry Clarke, had died. Hardly two weeks later, they received a royal mandate ordering them to elect a certain Anthony Farmer, a Roman Catholic sympathizer, as his successor. This candidate, whose 'piety, loyalty and learning' were vouched for by the king, had never been a Fellow of Magdalen College, and was therefore ineligible according to the college statutes, so it was decided to ignore the king's wishes, and a Dr John Hough was hurriedly elected.

When James insisted on Farmer, the Fellows, all good Anglican divines, did a little research into the suitability of the king's candidate. They were shocked – and perhaps satisfied – to learn that the thirty-year-old Farmer had a colourful string of misdemeanours to his name. He had been expelled from Trinity College, Cambridge, for misbehaving in a dancing class; he had been asked to leave Oxford 'for his troublesome humour and unquiet temper'; he had seduced undergraduates to debauchery and provided a naked woman for their entertainment; he was constantly drunk and, worst of all, 'he declared to some of the Fellows . . . that whatsoever he pretended, he was really a Member of the Church of England, and that he made an interest with some R Cs only to get preferment by their means . . .'

These revelations finished Farmer's candidacy, but James went on to demand that the Fellows elect another crypto-Catholic – the Bishop of Oxford, Samuel Parker – as president in Hough's place. Shortly before James's arrival at Oxford, he learnt that this demand, too, had been rejected, on the grounds that in Dr Hough the college already had a duly-elected president.

The Fellows now braced themselves for the worst, but the king let them sweat it out for two days before he sent for them. 'You have not dealt with me like gentlemen,' he raged. 'You have done very uncivilly to me . . . you have affronted me, know I am your King and I will be obeyed. Is this your Church of England loyalty?' Cowering before him, his audience noted that he had changed colour and was almost choking with anger. 'Go back and show yourselves good members of the Church of England . . . Get you gone, I command you to be gone, go and admit the Bishop of Oxford Head, Principal or what do you call him –' he hesitated until somebody prompted – 'President of the College. Let them that refuse it look to it.' He ended with a threat: 'Go and obey me or you shall feel the weight of your sovereign's displeasure.'

Despite this astonishing outburst, the Fellows continued firmly to maintain that it was not in their power to elect the bishop. And James left Oxford the next day in such a temper that when refreshments were offered him in Bodley's beautiful new library, he sat down to eat without inviting anyone else to join him. Twenty-five of the twenty-eight fellows later refused to make a formal apology and were promptly expelled and incapacitated – thus in effect deprived of their livelihood.

Apart from this painful episode in Oxford, James was convinced that his Royal Progress had been a triumphant success. The *London Gazette* was filled day after day with reports of the 'Dutiful Demonstrations of Loyal Affection that His Majesty has met with in all places where he has been'. The king was particularly impressed by the great number of loyal addresses thanking him for his 'late Gracious Declaration' of Indulgence, though many of these took the chance to remind him of 'repeated Assurances to preserve us in our Liberties, Properties and Establish'd Religion'. And by the autumn he was feeling sufficiently confident to put into operation a simple, foolproof scheme – as he thought – for ensuring a docile electorate.

Up and down the country his lord-lieutenants were instructed to put three questions to every man who had a vote. First, if he were elected to local office or the House of Commons, would he be in favour of 'taking off' the Tests and Penal Laws? Second, would he use his influence to elect candidates committed to this policy? Third, would he support the king's declaration for liberty of conscience by 'living friendly with those of all persuasions, as subjects of the same Prince and good Christians ought to do'?

But once again he had miscalculated, and his 'Three Questions' referendum backfired disastrously. Far from mobilizing public opinion on his side, the exercise gradually made clear to everybody the strength of the opposition. In the view of the Imperial ambassador in London, it 'has done more harm than one can express, seeing chiefly that nearly everywhere a negative reply was given'.

Some of the lord-lieutenants simply refused to put the questions at all. The Dutch envoy, Aernout van Citters, reported to Holland that only six out of seventy gentlemen in Norfolk answered the questions as the king had liked, and about the same proportion in Wales. As John Carswell puts it: 'For several months that autumn messages must have been passing from one country-house to another. Quiet shoots among the stubble-fields, serious evenings after the foxhunt, gradually worked out for groups and clans and interests formulae of evasion or defiance. The King had started a national debate.'

By late autumn, only the king and the more extreme of his advisers were still optimistic about his chances of success. More clearsighted and moderate Catholics were plunged in gloom, and James's plans certainly bristled with difficulties. His new allies, the Dissenters, were proving much less cooperative than he had hoped, as he realized after he replaced the Anglican Lord Mayor of London and the City aldermen with Dissenters. He genially urged the new mayor, a Presbyterian, to use what form of worship he pleased in the Guildhall Chapel, and was disagreeably surprised and disappointed to find, however, that the new mayor and aldermen not only all swore the oaths as a matter of course, but that one of their first acts was to order that 5 November – invariably an occasion for rabid anti-Catholic demonstrations – should be celebrated with all its usual stridency. And far from ordering Presbyterian services to be held in the Guildhall Chapel, the mayor not only ordered Anglican services to continue as before, but quite often attended them himself, looking suitably grave.

None of the king's plans were producing the results he had hoped for, and by autumn 1687 experienced politicians like Sunderland were now becoming frankly pessimistic about his chances. This minister admitted to Bonrepaus, a French naval envoy, sent by Louis in 1686, 'that he was finding things more difficult than he had expected at first, and whatever statements were made in public, the government would be in no hurry to summon parliament'.

Into this atmosphere of doubt and confusion, the first rumours in late October that Mary Beatrice might be pregnant came like a bolt from the blue. Official confirmation of the pregnancy a few weeks later plunged Whitehall – and England – into crisis.

TWO

THE ORANGE FACTOR

In the autumn of 1686 an unusual special envoy from Whitehall arrived in The Hague. It was the well-known Quaker, William Penn, founder in 1680 of a new transatlantic colony, Pennsylvania, and – James hoped – a persuasive ambassador for his policy of religious toleration. Six months earlier, James had sent out circular letters to all justices of the peace, giving Quakers immunity from prosecution under the Penal Laws, and Penn was now among his most enthusiastic admirers. Like James himself, Penn believed strongly that Penal Laws against particular religious sects were not only evil in themselves, but also against any nation's best interests: trade and industry flourished when communities were free to follow their own consciences. Prosperous Holland, where religious persecution had been unknown for decades, was often quoted by James as illustrating this truth, and he could point to France – dramatically impoverished by its eviction of Huguenot talent and ability – as more evidence for his case.

Such arguments, put forward by such a distinguished Dissenter, must surely carry powerful weight with the king's Dutch son-in-law, William of Orange. And William's endorsement of James's policy, together with that of his wife Mary, heiress to the English throne, was now indispensable if it were to have any chance of being ratified by Parliament. If such staunch Protestants could be persuaded to give their public blessing to his policy, much of the opposition in England would crumble.

But if James counted on complete understanding from his Dutch son-in-law and his daughter, he was to be disappointed. William told the Quaker that he was certainly in favour of repealing the harsh Penal Laws, by which Catholics and Dissenters could be heavily fined for not attending Anglican services regularly – laws which had been virtually a dead letter for years. The prince readily consented, he told Penn, 'to a toleration of popery as well as of the Dissenters, provided it were proposed and passed by Parliament'. The Test Acts, however, were another matter. 'He looked on [them] as such a real security, and indeed the only one, where the King was of another religion, that he would join in no counsels with them that intended to repeal those laws.'

James was not easily discouraged. Early in 1687, he sent an official ambassador to the Republic, Ignatius White, Marquis d'Albeville. This Irish Catholic adventurer – according to one Protestant contemporary, 'a most contemptible and ridiculous man' – was to discover if William could not be persuaded to change his mind about the Test Acts. The prince made short work of these delusions, using a practical argument. It was unknown in history, he pointed out, 'that there should exist simultaneously two dominant religions in the same kingdom or state'. He feared that any attempt to bring this about would lead to 'troubles and disorder which would put the Monarchy itself at risk'. He was no believer in religious persecution, but to approve of a dominant Roman Catholic church – which must certainly result from James's policies – was for him out of the question. 'The English people would never swallow that.'

It occurred to d'Albeville that the princess might be more easily persuaded than her husband, and he decided to sound her out separately. To his astonishment he found that, if anything, she was more intractable on the subject than the prince himself. Up to now Mary had avoided a direct clash with her father, but she reacted with unexpected firmness to the envoy's advances, explaining: 'I speak to you, Monsieur, with less reserve and more freedom than to the King my father, because of the respectful deference which I am obliged to have for him and for his feelings.'

His daughter's tough line was deeply resented by James. 'Neither she nor the prince could oppose his unalterable plans without displeasing him,' William was told imperiously. '. . . Their duty was to deserve a continuance of goodwill by an entire submission to his judgement.' When even appeals to family loyalty failed to persuade, James remarked bitterly that although he was the head of the family, the prince had always set himself against him. But even without their approval, he had determined to press ahead, and in April 1687 he had published his first Declaration of Indulgence.

For all his imperious talk, James knew very well that the refusal of William and Mary to concur in his policy might be fatal to its chances of success in Parliament, and he continued to press them in personal letters, through d'Albeville and through the envoy William had sent in exchange, Everard van Weede van Dijkvelt. But the couple remained adamant, and the final negative came from William: 'You ask me to countenance an attack on my own religion. I cannot with a safe conscience do it, no, not for the crown of England, nor for the empire of the world.'

William's rebuff was hard for James to swallow. 'The King of England is more embittered against him than ever before,' wrote Bonrepaus to Versailles, and James showed his displeasure in a curt note: 'As the reasons I asked Dyckveld to put before you have not been able to convince you, obviously no letter of mine will do so, and I shall spare myself the trouble.'

James should have known better than to try to browbeat his son-in-law. William, orphaned at the age of ten, had always made it clear that he had a mind of his own. When he was twelve his great-aunt Elizabeth, the Winter Queen, commented on his intelligence: 'not the wit of a child who is sufficiant, but of a man.' And his grandmother, the Dowager Princess Amalia of Orange, herself a rather formidable lady, was already slightly in awe of him when he was only fourteen. She 'dares scarce herself to speak anything to him that she thinks will displease him', an English diplomat wrote to London. By the time he was a grown man, the impression was universal: 'A young man of the most extraordinary understanding and parts.'

One of his most remarkable traits was an astonishing self-command, consciously acquired under the eye of his first tutor, Sir Constantijn Huygens, who had drilled the lesson into him: 'Who is master of himself, is master of all others.' Equally striking was his reserve. 'The closest man in the world,' was one description of him. The habit had become ingrained in him as a matter of policy at an early age, and by the time he was adult it was as much an effort for him to be communicative – outside a tiny circle of intimates – as it is for many people to be discreet. All his life, William played his cards close to his chest, from force of habit.

At a precociously early age, the pale, asthmatic and strangely self-contained young prince had been conscious that destiny set him apart from other men. And this conviction guided him during his whole life. '*Grand résolution, grand fermeté, grand courage dans des entreprises,*' remarked the Venetian ambassador. As a child he was fascinated by the proud history of his family, starting with the famous William the Silent, born Prince of Nassau-Dillenburg, but at the age of eleven heir to the royal title of Prince of Orange. At his call a century earlier, the Protestant Netherlands had first risen against the rule of Spain, and the terrors of the Spanish Inquisition. And under the leadership of William the Silent's two sons, Maurits and Frederick Hendrick, the Dutch had finally achieved their independence as the United Provinces in 1648.

By that time the Orange–Nassau family had married into every leading European dynasty, among them the Bourbons of France and Sicily, the Stuarts of England and Scotland, and the powerful Medici family. They felt, indeed, thoroughly royal themselves, although Orange was the tiniest of principalities, an island surrounded by French territory, and even though their position of Stadholder – or Governor – of the United Princes was an elected one and not hereditary. Almost inevitably, too, they tended to consider themselves as virtual sovereigns of the Dutch Republic, a very loosely knit federation of seven provinces governed by a Parliament of sorts, the States-General. But the ruling class of Holland, and of rich and powerful Amsterdam in particular, was fundamentally republican. And although they grudgingly accepted the Orange hegemony in times of war and crisis, they wanted to be their own masters in times of peace.

William III of Orange, born on 14 November 1650, eight days after his father died of smallpox, was the first victim of this 'republican' tendency. The Regents of Amsterdam, still smarting from a bitter confrontation with his father, persuaded the other Provinces to hold up indefinitely the election of the baby prince to the title of stad-holder.

Their decision was a slap in the face for his mother Mary Stuart, daughter of England's Charles I and younger sister of Charles and James. In fact, her personal unpopularity may well have prompted it. An arrogant, insensitive woman, she was intensely disliked in Holland; and in her turn, she never bothered to disguise her contempt for the nation of 'petits commerçants' and republicans among whom she was forced to live. Their refusal to give her son the honours she felt were due to him deepened her dislike of the Dutch. And in the 50s she snatched at every chance to escape to the roving court of her two dashing brothers – exiled from Cromwell's England, and always flat broke, but much more fun than the provincial company of The Hague.

As soon as Charles was restored to the English throne in 1660, Mary followed him happily to London, abandoning her ten-year-old son William to the care of his grandmother, Amalia von Solms-Braunfels. He never saw her again: a year later, she died in England of smallpox.

In the first ten years of his life William had seen much of his uncles Charles and James during their trips to The Hague to visit Mary. But under pressure from Cromwell, the States-General put a stop to these visits. And after the Restoration and his mother's death, the young orphan saw no more of his English uncles, although Charles wrote an occasional letter to him. Both he and James had at first taken a kind, avuncular interest in the education and welfare of their little nephew. But for all their warm protestations of affection, they ditched him without hesitation when in 1672 Louis XIV, embarking on a fresh 'rationalization' of his frontiers, sent his armies storming into the Republic. In the hope of rich pickings, Charles and James sided with France, and William, who emerged from this first confrontation with France as the saviour of his country, never completely trusted either of them again.

His mistrust was well-founded. While William was to make it his life's work to resist the expansionist policy of France, and to construct a European alliance to contain Louis's ambitions, his English uncles were content to watch from the sidelines. It was in the hope of committing them to an anti-French policy that the Prince of Orange finally made up his mind in 1677 to a project that had been talked about for many years, a marriage with James's eldest daughter Mary.

Nobody was particularly enthusiastic about this match. Charles agreed to it as a sop to English national feeling, grown restive at James's increasingly open profession of his Catholicism. James, who had dreamt of marrying his daughter to the French dauphin, obeyed the king's wishes as a matter of principle, but with the utmost reluctance. William, who was inclined to look down on Mary as the daughter of his mother's lady-in-waiting, Anne Hyde, hoped that his marriage would at least be the guarantee of a long-lasting Anglo-Dutch alliance against France.

As for the bride herself, a day-dreaming teenage beauty, she was appalled by the prospect of marriage to the solemn, slightly built and decidedly plain cousin she had only once met. When her father broke the news of her fate to her, she wept 'all afternoon and all the following day'.

The King of France was livid. 'You have given your daughter to my mortal enemy,' he wrote to the duke. Through Barillon, his ambassador in London, he warned him that 'he should consider the Prince of Orange the idol of England', and predicted – only too accurately, as it turned out – that 'such a son-in-law would infallibly be his ruin'.

James may have recalled this prediction when in 1679 the House of Commons made the first of several determined efforts to exclude him from the succession, and it became obvious that there was a strong party for his Protestant son-in-law. After a second attempt in 1680, Charles sent James into exile in Scotland for his own safety, and dissolved Parliament.

Against his better judgement, William was persuaded by his English supporters to visit London at this point. He still hoped to talk Charles into summoning a new Parliament, and to enlist him in the anti-French coalition which he was painfully patching together. He came home not merely empty-handed, having failed in both these objectives, but smarting from a public humiliation into the bargain. During his visit, he had twice accepted an invitation to dine in the City as the guest of the Whig Lord Mayor, and each time, Charles had ordered him to appear at Windsor instead, sending last-minute excuses to the City.

The prince had, however, learned one thing of interest. In the view of Charles, that shrewd judge of men, 'whenever the Duke of York should come to reign, he would be so restless and violent that he could not hold it for four years to an end.'

Once Charles had made it plain that William could expect no active support from England, the French moved briskly. Just weeks after the prince's return from London, French armies stormed and took the city of Strasburg on the Rhine and, soon after, moved on to blockade Luxemburg. Even the most pacific Dutch took fright at this, and the Spanish, prodded by William, threatened to suspend Anglo-Spanish trade if Charles refused the assistance he was committed to by an earlier treaty, whereupon Louis XIV gracefully withdrew from Luxemburg – for the time being.

Like Churchill in the 1930s, William's was a lone voice arguing for energetic resistance, while all those around him were voting for appeasement. Many of the Dutch themselves suspected the prince of warmongering for his own personal ends, and refused to believe that Louis's ambitions represented any real threat to their cosy, prosperous existence. The Spanish lacked either the will or the military strength to put up a fight. And Charles II's attitude might be summed up in a phrase: anything for a quiet life. As Churchill found in the 1930s, William thus made himself extremely unpopular with precisely those whose support was essential to him.

He badly needed their backing since at home in the early 1680s, he found himself increasingly isolated politically. Louis XIV employed in the Republic his ablest diplomats, and by Jean-Antoine de Mesmes, Comte d'Avaux, he was spectacularly well served. With the help of bribery or intrigues, d'Avaux saw most of the diplomatic reports that left The Hague – including those of d'Albeville, whose active cooperation he had bought for a pension of 4,000 livres annually. And he played incessantly – and successfully – on the fears and suspicions of the Amsterdammers, in order to undercut William's position. War was disastrous for trade: it was almost as simple as that. A war which involved the Dutch, while leaving their great trade rival England on the sidelines, was the worst option of all. Why not live peacefully with France, who had no designs on Dutch territory?

It was d'Avaux, too, who spearheaded a vicious personal campaign against this tiresome little Dutchman who was putting up such determined opposition to the Sun King's plans. The Frenchman was ordered to pay no court to the prince, and to demand equal honours from the States-General. Meanwhile, William's estates within French territories were either confiscated or subjected to punitive taxes and levies: among them Meurs and Breda, and the domains of Viande and St Vith, swallowed up when the French occupied Chiny.

If the Amstersdammers and Charles II believed that Louis XIV would be content with what he already had, however, they deluded themselves. Given his ambitions for France, Louis could not afford to sit still.

The key to European politics in the 1680s was the ailing, imbecile and impotent Habsburg King of Spain, Carlos II. He might die at any minute. When he did, who would inherit the Spanish Habsburg territories, which still included the Spanish Netherlands, the 'Barriere' between France and the Dutch? Through his Spanish wife Maria Theresa, Louis considered he had a legitimate claim. But so, too, had the Emperor Leopold I, another Habsburg. Louis's chances of a successful bid were small, but the vision of a France encircled by Habsburg territories, all under one powerful hand, was a recurring nightmare at Versailles.

Leopold's territories included Austria and Silesia, Moravia and much of Hungary. But Leopold was also, since 1658, Holy Roman Emperor, elected by seven German princes, and ruling over the patchwork of German states, large and small, known as the empire. Any advance – either of territory or of influence – that Louis made eastwards was therefore necessarily at his expense. And since the early 1680s, Louis had been pushing France's frontiers steadily eastwards towards the Rhine, swallowing up most of what is now Alsace–Lorraine and Franche-Comté, and fortifying the key city of Strasburg on the Rhine.

So when in the spring of 1683 an army of 100,000 Ottoman Turks massed near Belgrade, poised to overrun the empire and perhaps all central Europe in the name of the Prophet, the most Christian King Louis seemed curiously unperturbed. Even when the Turks were at the gates of Vienna, and Pope Innocent XI was calling for a Holy Crusade to halt them, Louis declined to lift a finger. Instead, his armies pounded Luxemburg into submission. The Prince of Orange pleaded in vain that the Dutch should send troops to help defend the fortress. But the Dutch were tired of war, the Spanish treasury was exhausted and, to William's fury, both countries concluded with France the twenty-year

Truce of Ratisbon in June 1684, which allowed Louis to hang on to his territorial gains – including Strasburg and Luxemburg. With one eye on the Turks, the Emperor Leopold signed too. This peace, commented William sourly, would give France the chance of making more conquests 'in peacetime than she did by war'.

The unexpected death of Charles II in February 1685, and the accession of James seemed to their nephew to hold out the hope of a fresh start. The new king had actually called a Parliament, he appeared to be on excellent terms with it, and they had voted him a handsome income for life – thus making him potentially independent of France, as Charles had never been. William – and Protestant Europe – had everything to gain from James's good will. Determined to be conciliatory, the prince at once sent a personal envoy to London, his kinsman Hendrik van Nassau van Ouwerkerk, to deliver his condolences and congratulations. James gave the envoy a cool reception, but the submissive attitude of his nephew surprised and pleased him. William, he learnt, was willing to meet James's demands as far as possible.

One of James's running grievances against the Dutch and his nephew concerned the six English and Scottish regiments traditionally based in the Republic. These had been formed and trained there nearly a century earlier, when Queen Elizabeth came to the help of the Dutch in their War of Independence against Spain. Over the last few years, however, they had become – like the Republic itself – a refuge for English political refugees and malcontents. William now agreed to purge from them those officers known to be disloyal to James. And when James pressed him to moderate his hostility to France, he offered some vaguely phrased assurances.

Four months later, William had a chance to demonstrate his new good will. In 1682 Charles II had reluctantly banished his bastard son, the Duke of Monmouth, after he was suspected of complicity in a plot against the two royal brothers. In 1684 Monmouth had found refuge in Holland. For months he stayed at The Hague with the Prince of Orange and his wife, who found him a lively and agreeable guest, although William warned him that 'if he thought of the crown, he could not be his friend'.

For James, Monmouth's presence in the court of his son-in-law was an affront, and in all his letters of 1684 he had protested angrily to William, with Charles joining in the chorus. The prince ignored these letters, but Charles's death changed his mind. Mary was now Heiress Apparent to the throne, and the presence in his household of Monmouth – a potential rival – could only be embarrassing. But before he sent Monmouth on his travels, he had warned the young man not to undertake any reckless enterprise against the new king. When Monmouth forgot his promises four months later and landed in the west of England with a small army, William at once helped James defeat the young pretender by sending over from Holland three of the English regiments.

He also sent his closest friend and confidant, Hans Willem Bentinck, with fresh assurances of support, and an offer to come over in person 'if [the king] thought this useful for his service . . .' James turned down this suggestion, but it did William no harm at all. As a courtier remarked, there appeared to be now 'a perfect understanding between them . . . the King has declared that he will henceforth look upon him as his successor.'

The good personal relationship was officially sealed when, in August of that year, to William's great relief, James gave signs of adopting an anti-French policy, and the Republic and England renewed their old treaty against France.

Louis XIV was not pleased by this apparent reconciliation between his arch-enemy and the new King of England. Barillon lost no chance of insinuating that 'the submission and respect of the Prince of Orange are not sincere, and that he will continue to behave in his present manner only as long as he is forced to do so by circumstances'. For the time being, these warnings fell on deaf ears. James was a wholehearted patriot, as the indolent Charles had never been, and although he was at first moved by the offer of a 5 million livres subsidy from Louis XIV, he was soon showing welcome signs of a desire to pursue a foreign policy independent of France.

The *entente* between James and William was, however, short-lived. In the late summer of 1685 came the first rift. Its cause was James's decision to recall Henry Sidney, the commander of the six English and Scottish regiments in Holland. After crushing Monmouth's rebellion, James had sent back these well-trained troops, but he seized the chance to vent a personal grudge against their commander.

James had every reason for disliking the handsome forty-five-year-old Sidney. Not only was it rumoured that this nobleman, of whom it was said that he had 'no malice in his heart, but too great a love of pleasure', had been the lover of the king's first wife Anne, but he had been one of the most vocal supporters of Exclusion, and he was a leading member of the new 'Whig' party. It was an additional grievance that the Prince of Orange considered him his closest English friend and adviser, and although William pleaded hard for his favourite hunting and drinking companion to be retained, he was compelled to bow to the king's decision.

But when James proposed the Roman Catholic Lord Carlingford as his successor, and insisted that William should replace some of the regimental officers with Roman Catholics, William dug his heels in: even in the tolerant Dutch Republic, this was contrary to national policy. 'It would hurt me extremely if I gave the commands of these six regiments to a person of that religion,' he wrote anxiously to Bentinck. Furious, James began to consider recalling the regiments altogether.

Long before he actually did so, relations between the king and his nephew plunged to a new low when James deliberately stirred up trouble in the Orange household. Thanks to his spies at The Hague, James had learned of a rift in William and Mary's marriage, and he probably saw this as a useful lever against his uncooperative son-in-law.

For years the prince had been carrying on an extremely discreet affair with one of Mary's ladies-in-waiting, the plain but spirited Elizabeth Villiers. Mary had certainly guessed at it, and was deeply hurt by it; but having spent much of her teens in the Restoration Court of Charles II, she was unlikely to have been very much surprised by the fact; over the years she had come to terms with it.

Her English household, however, were less forgiving, and from her 'mam', Mrs Anne Trelawney and her chaplain Dr Covell in particular, a steady supply of scandalous gossip was relayed to her father in Whitehall, through the English ambassador at the time, Bevil Skelton. In the autumn of 1685, at James's prodding, Mrs Trelawney confronted the princess with news that her husband's adultery was now public knowledge.

Desperately upset, Mary late one night tackled William with her grievance. According to Daniel de Bourdon, a French friend of one of her ladies-in-waiting, William 'heaped reproaches on her to which she only replied with tears'. Then she fled to her bedchamber, to which 'the Prince did not come for several days'.

William was not a man to take lightly such an invasion of his domestic privacy. He soon found out the source of the trouble, and one day intercepted a packet of letters from the 'spies' on its way to Skelton, and Whitehall. 'Your Honour may be astonished at the news, but it is true the Princess' heart is like to break . . .' read the angry William. 'The Prince has infallibly made her his absolute slave . . .' According to Dr Covell, 'the Prince will for ever rule the roast,' when Mary came to the throne. 'I beseech God preserve the King many and many years.'

According to de Bourdon again, William at once sent for his wife, and pointed out to her that some of her English court were out to destroy their marriage 'by making her believe falsehoods'. When she asked if the rumours were true, he assured her 'by all that is most sacred that what has caused you pain was simply a distraction'. Disarmed by these loving assurances, Mary told him to do as he thought fit, and within a few days Dr Covell, Mrs Trelawney and others had been sent packing back to England.

The next step was to get rid of Skelton. In a stiff letter to the Earl of Rochester in London, William told the whole story of the correspondence between Covell and Skelton. 'You can judge well,' he said, 'whether after this I can continue to live on good terms with him.' He asked him to propose Skelton's immediate recall. In the circumstances James found it difficult to refuse – and he could hardly take a high moral stance, since his own long-standing affair with Catherine Sedley was public knowledge. But his deep resentment burst out one day in the hearing of the French ambassador; the prince had shown 'his bad will against him when he is so upset by the knowledge that his minister is informed of what goes on in the house of his daughter and son-in-law'.

In the middle of this family row came tragedy on a grand scale. Two days after Louis XIV revoked the Edict of Nantes on 2 October 1685, French troops occupied William's own principality of Orange, and razed its fortifications. If the revocation of the Edict was strongly resented by the Dutch, many of whose compatriots had settled in France, the second was clearly intended as one more personal affront to the Prince of Orange.

The French commander, the Comte de Tesse, on Louis's personal orders, did not spare the prince's subjects. He imprisoned the pastors, burnt every Protestant Bible that could be found and tried forcibly to convert to Catholicism those inhabitants unable to flee. The prince's resentment was savage and enduring: his struggle against Louis XIV took on a personal dimension. 'I will one day make him feel what it is to have exasperated a Prince of Orange,' he was often heard to say. Together with Mary, he at once asked James to take up the case of Orange at Versailles, and the English ambassador made repeated strong protests. But when Louis replied grandly that he did not acknowledge the sovereignty of Orange as belonging to the prince, James backed down. 'He could do no more in that matter,' he wrote to Mary, 'unless he should declare war upon it.'

The princess, already upset by her father's intervention in the Villiers affair, never forgave him what she felt as a personal slight to her husband, and later complained bitterly that in the case of the principality, 'my father preferred to join with the King of France gainst my husband.'

In the months that followed, the Prince of Orange studied events in England with steadily growing concern – particularly James's appointment of numbers of Catholics to key government posts. In European affairs, William would have been happy to settle for a neutral England. But if his father-in-law persisted in his present policies, at odds with his Parliament and with the vast majority of his subjects, it was more than likely that he would end up in the arms of France. And in the summer of 1686, as it happened, came sinister confirmation of these fears.

The Dutch ambassador to London, Aernout van Citters, got hold of a copy of a document called *A Remonstrance Made to the King by his Council*. It advocated immediate war on Holland, which according to its author had fomented Monmouth's rebellion and still gave shelter to rebels; a close alliance with France – even, if necessary, financial dependence on her; and that Louis XIV should be made arbiter of the English succession, presumably in favour of a Catholic heir.

Other copies of the document had already been procured and sent to Louis XIV by both Barillon and the efficient d'Avaux, who added copies of van Citters's reports on it to the States-General. James finally learned of its existence and summoned van Citters to an audience, in which he denied any knowledge of it in the strongest terms. 'I have had many misfortunes, much adversity in my life, but no one, not even my greatest enemies, would dare accuse me of such infamy,' he said emphatically. And he kept repeating in horror, 'Vassal? Vassal of France?' He was equally outraged by the suggestion that he might set aside his own children's rights to the throne in favour of some chosen Catholic. Van Citters was instructed to assure the States-General of his 'benevolent dispositions' towards them.

To William, the king's protestations rang completely true: James was nothing if not honest. But the very existence of such a document – which if genuine was probably drafted by James's Jesuit advisers and some of the more extreme Catholics, such as Tyrconnel – was disturbing for the Prince and Princess of Orange. Such advisers were certainly capable of pressing for a change in the succession: there were already rumours going round that Princess Anne and her husband, Prince George of Denmark, were ripe for conversion.

Equally dismaying for William was the discovery of such a powerful anti-Dutch party at Whitehall. The *Remonstrance* had specifically warned James against the growth of Dutch 'insolence' if he failed to crush them now: 'The faction of the Prince of Orange would become strong enough to overthrow his prerogative, force him to abandon his valuable projects for Religion, and even transfer the Government to the Prince of Orange as natural successor.'

Although James had assured van Citters of his warm affection and regard for his children, he had shown little evidence of either. William had not forgotten that on James's accession, he had given Mary none of the honours or rich jewels suitable to a king's daughter; that he had refused to give the title of Royal Highness to William, who in consequence would have ranked lower than Prince George of Denmark in any English company; and that Mary had hardly received one penny of a stingy dowry from England, although Anne had had a handsome income settled on her.

If James had ever felt real goodwill towards his son-in-law, William felt it would be unwise to count on it at a time when the king was enlarging and strengthening his navy. And in fact earlier that year the French naval envoy Bonrepaus had reported to his chief, the Marquis de Seignelay: 'The King of England can hardly conceal his hatred for and his jealousy of the Prince of Orange.' Suspicion and hostility were now mutual.

One reason for James's jealous resentment was well-founded: the Republic was becoming a natural focus of political opposition to the Catholic king, and from early in 1686, The Hague saw arriving a steady stream of English refugees. James badgered William and the States-General to have them expelled from the United Provinces: 'so long as those rebellious people are permitted to stay there, they will still have the opportunities of corresponding with the disaffected here and stirring them up to sedition.' The prince and the States-General made soothing noises – but took no action. And the refugees continued to arrive.

One of them was a leading Whig peer, Lord Mordaunt, who urged the prince to act before it was too late, and give the lead for a bloodless revolution which would replace James with William and Mary on the throne. 'He pressed him to undertake the business of England,' wrote another political exile, Bishop Burnet, 'and he represented the matter as so easy, that this appeared too romantical to the Prince to build upon it.'

Many of the refugees – as James rightly suspected – shared Mordaunt's views and, as an act of faith in William, joined the Dutch army in the hope that they might one day help liberate their country from the king's oppressive regime. They fled in such numbers that Lord Sunderland, the Secretary of State, was obliged to give orders 'to stop alle persons endeavouring to join the service of any foreign Prince and state without leave'. It was no secret against which prince and state this order was directed: Lord Dumblane, son of William's old ally Danby, applied for a passport to go overseas, and was told by James, 'with some heat, Provided it be not into Holland, for I will suffer nobody to go thither'. Lord Dumblane protested 'that he had no design of anything but to see a country he had not seen'. Perhaps so, replied the king darkly, but he had relations who had other designs there.

All of these refugees clamoured for action, and some of them warned William that if he hesitated too long it might be too late: with the help of his huge army, James might establish himself as an autocrat, ruling without a Parliament and imposing his will on a defenceless nation: a course of action which would certainly involve close alliance with France. Alternatively, the opposition might take matters into their own hands. William's claims to the throne might then be swept aside, and chaos or even civil war might result in a republican England once more. From the Dutch point of view, this would be the worst of all possible worlds. Under Cromwell, the English had pursued a policy of relentless commercial expansion which led to the crippling Anglo-Dutch war of 1652–4 and nearly brought the Dutch to their knees.

Thus there were compelling reasons why William could not remain a passive spectator of events in England. His reaction to these first advances, however, was one of extreme caution. He committed himself to nothing definite, only assuring Mordaunt that he would follow events in England closely, and arrange his affairs 'so as to be ready to act when it should be necessary'. If the worst came to the worst – 'if the King should go about either to change the established religion or to wrong the Princess in her rights' – he would do what he could.

By the New Year of 1687, this seemed a fair summary of James's intentions. Rochester had fallen and Clarendon was obviously on the way out, with Tyrconnel waiting in the wings. Father Petre was luxuriating in splendid new Whitehall apartments; the Anglican Church was bracing itself for the worst; and Parliament, prorogued four times, seemed unlikely ever to sit again.

But before William could make any concrete plans for the future, he determined to make a last effort to win James's good will. He also needed reliable first-hand information about the situation in England. Everard van Weede van Dijkvelt was the perfect choice as William's special envoy for this important and delicate double mission. A career diplomat of great charm and ability, Dijkvelt had been on several previous embassies to Whitehall and had extensive contacts both at Court and among the opposition. In February 1687 he arrived in London, carefully briefed.

According to his instructions, Dijkvelt was 'to expostulate decently but firmly with the king, upon the methods he was pursuing both at home and abroad; and see if it was possible to bring him to a better understanding with the prince'. He was to take assurances to the Anglicans 'that the prince would ever be firm to the Church of England'. Dissenters, now being warmly wooed by James, were to be promised no less by William – 'full toleration; and . . . a comprehension, if possible, whensoever the crown should devolve on the princess.' Much the most important part of Dijkvelt's mission, however, was undercover: he was to sound out the strength of support for William, 'and to remove the ill impressions that had been given of the prince'.

Dijkvelt stayed in London until the end of May, and although his attempt to change James's mind failed dismally, his secret mission brought a startling harvest. Many of the most prominent men in England, Tories as well as Whigs, not only sent the prince verbal assurances through Dijkvelt of their support, but put it in writing too.

The most significant of these letters brought assurances that William could count on the moral support of Mary's younger sister Anne. She was resolved, he read, 'by the assistance of God, to suffer all extremeties, even to death itself, rather than be brought to change her religion'.

Two eminent Tory politicians were prepared to stick their necks out. Lord Nottingham wrote of 'the universal concurrence of all Protestants in paying the utmost respect and duty to your Highness, for you are the person on whom they found their hopes . . .' Lord Danby had been instrumental in promoting William's marriage to Mary. He went further than Nottingham, suggesting that if he and others might have a personal conference with the prince, 'overtures might be made which would be of use to your service'. The king's disgraced brothers-in-law, Clarendon and Rochester, both wrote too – but in such guarded terms as to give William little satisfaction. He must have turned with relief to the warm enthusiasm with which the young Whig Earl of Shrewsbury addressed him: '. . . though I hope you have a great many servants and friends in this place, yet there is not one more entirely and faithfully so than myself'.

By late summer, events were moving steadily to a crisis. Tyrconnel was driving Protestants out of Ireland; James was doing his best to turn Oxford's wealthiest college into a Catholic preserve; Parliament had been dissolved, and James was planning to replace it with a docile new House packed with his supporters – news that filled William with painful anxiety.

But with the first rumours of Mary Beatrice's pregnancy in the autumn, the situation at once took on an appalling new urgency. From now on, in the prince's mind, the question was no longer if he should actively intervene in English affairs, but when – and how.

THREE

FAMILY FRICTION

One of James's bitterest grievances against William was that for months he had entertained at his Court in The Hague a man whom James considered as one of his greatest enemies, the Scottish Bishop Gilbert Burnet.

Brought up a Scottish Calvinist, Burnet was one of the most gifted and popular preachers of his day, and he was equally fluent on paper. His *History of the Reformation*, an eloquent *apologia* for the Church of England, had earned him a formal vote of thanks from both Houses of Parliament. As chaplain to Charles II, Burnet already had a reputation for directness, not hesitating to lecture even the king and his brother about their sexual vices. Charles shrugged and laughed, but it added to James's resentment of a man he soon had plenty of other reasons to dislike.

Burnet's *History* had provided powerful anti-Catholic ammunition – 'a Church which has all along raised its greatness by public cheats and forgeries' – and he was on friendly terms with 'republicans'. Both crimes were enough to damn him in James's eyes so, at the beginning of the new reign, the bishop had prudently left on an extended tour of Europe. Even abroad, however, his witty and merciless pen pursued James, in tracts on the religious and political situation in England that were widely read and quoted – and had the king writhing from their barbs.

He attacked James at his most vulnerable points: '. . . instead of making himself a terrour to all his Neighbours, he is contented with the humble Glory of being a terrour to his own People . . .' The king should not be surprised at opposition to his plans even from the loyal Church of England: 'It is true, they have generally expressed an un-willingness to part with the two Tests, because they have no mind to trust the keeping of their Throats to those that will cut them.' And he expressed a sentiment with which most Catholics would have agreed, when he wished that the king 'would be content with the Exercise of his own Religion, without Imbroiling his whole Affaires, because Father Petre will have it so . . .'

To add to these offences, Burnet eventually wound up at The Hague, where his experience and his wide-ranging contacts in Court and Church circles made him useful to William, who was soon consulting him regularly on English affairs. A sociable, tolerant, warm-hearted man of the world, Burnet rapidly won the confidence of both William and Mary, and soon he was an intimate of the Orange household, as James's spies were quick to inform him. It was too much for the resentful James. When d'Albeville was despatched to The Hague in January 1687, 'his first Instructions was to get this dangerous Man for ever banish'd from the Presence of both their Highnesses . . .'

William was particularly anxious for his father-in-law's goodwill at this time, so Burnet was ostentatiously dismissed from Court, although the prince continued to consult him in secret. The bishop left The Hague reluctantly. His months spent there had given him a grandstand view of state affairs and he had grown attached to the prince and his wife. For Mary in particular he had nothing but praise. 'She had a modesty, a sweetness and a humility in her that cannot be enough admired . . .' he later wrote glowingly, 'an open and native Sincerity . . . a charming Behaviour . . . and the Sprightliness as well as the Freedom of good humour.' Much impressed by her intelligence, he thought she 'shewed true judgement and a good mind' when he talked to her about the state of the English Court, and explained to this eager listener 'the intrigues of it, ever since the Reformation'.

Burnet was an admirer of the prince, too, but with reservations: clearly even the sociable bishop found him difficult to get along with. 'He had observed the errors of too much talking, more than those of too cold a silence,' was a roundabout way of saying that he was often boorish, a cold fish of a man. Burnet was struck by his passion for hunting – almost the only interest William and James had in common – and by his horror of paperwork, although he was good at putting on 'some appearance of application'. But of one trait in the prince's character Burnet was never in doubt: it was the strong Calvinist faith which had made him a dedicated enemy of Louis and the Protestant champion of Europe. 'The depression of France was the governing passion of his whole life,' was Burnet's considered opinion.

Few people ever came to know William as well as this, and outsiders wondered how the reserved Prince of Orange could put up with the Bishop's familiarity, and his relentless, prying curiosity about other people's business. They were not to know that it was thanks to this busybody that the prince had been able to resolve a question which had silently preoccupied him for years.

As grandson to Charles I, the Prince of Orange had always been confident of his right to the throne of England. Not only was he the only male heir in the direct line, but in his view the two daughters of James, who preceded him, were the offspring of what would have been considered a morganatic marriage in any European court. Anne Hyde had been his mother's lady-in-waiting when the Duke of York met her, and it had been a shotgun wedding, into which the duke had entered reluctantly.

As early as 1674, discussing English affairs over dinner, William had remarked to the company that when the duke should die, 'there would be a dispute if his daughters should precede him when it came to the crown'. Initially, the thought of marrying one of them simply in order to secure his rights never crossed his mind. There had been plans for him for a match with a Danish princess, and even with the widowed Queen of Poland. Only when it became obvious to him that the dubious marriage of the duke was perfectly valid in English eyes and that, as a result, his cousins' claims to the Crown would take precedence over his own, did he make up his mind to marry Mary for the sake of his own country, and the Protestant cause in Europe.

During the long-running dispute over the succession between his Catholic father-in-law and Parliament, the different parties very often looked across the North Sea for a way out. And when in 1679 James's position as heir presumptive was first seriously questioned, Charles II tried to rescue the principle of direct succession by proposing William as 'Protector'. To make this possible, the prince was to be made a member of the Privy Council and given the title Duke of Gloucester, to entitle him to take a seat in the House of Lords. The suggestion collapsed when William pointed out that, as Stadholder of the Dutch Republic, he was unable to swear an oath of allegiance to a foreign sovereign. But he made his thoughts on the matter very obvious to his friend Sidney. 'He is convinced that the Duke will never have the Crown,' Sidney wrote after a fireside talk with William in his Honselaersdijk Palace, 'and I find would be very willing to be put into a way of having it himself.'

In the second Exclusion crisis, in 1681, another idea for the succession was put forward: the Duke of York should be exiled for life, and his daughter Mary made regent. William made his lack of enthusiasm for this proposal very obvious, and after some hasty rethinking, another possible plan emerged: he and his wife should be regents jointly.

Since Charles almost immediately dissolved Parliament to end the whole discussion, no more was heard of either suggestion. But to the Prince of Orange, the question was one of painful importance. When James died, Mary's claim to the throne was higher than his; and in theory she would become queen, and he no more than her consort.

A docile and unassuming wife, Mary had never stopped for a moment to consider what William's exact role would be when she succeeded to the throne. The gulf of reserve between the couple, and his own pride, had made it impossible for her husband to discuss this question with her. Burnet had no such inhibitions about broaching a subject of such burning interest, and – perhaps at William's prompting – he lost no time in sounding her out about it. He was surprised to learn that she 'fancied that whatever accrued to her would likewise accrue to [William] . . . in right of marriage'. Burnet pointed out to her the parallel with Mary Tudor. When she married Philip II of Spain, the Spaniard had no more than a titular kingship in England – 'no acceptable thing to a man'.

The Princess of Orange was astonished, and asked Burnet what she ought to do. His advice was unhesitating: she should promise William to give him 'the real authority as soon as it came into her hands, and endeavour effectually to get it to be legally vested in him during life'. She should think hard before committing herself, Burnet added, but Mary at once said impulsively that 'she would take no time to consider of any thing by which she could express her regard and affection to the Prince'.

William, probably aware that this conversation was taking place, had taken himself off hunting that day. But the next morning Burnet, as self-appointed go-between, reported the whole conversation to him, and he was present when Mary told her husband that 'she did not know the laws of England were so contrary to the laws of God . . . she did not think that the husband was ever to be obedient to the wife: she promised him, he should always bear rule . . .' Falteringly, she added that she would only ask 'that he should obey the command of Husbands love your wives, as she should do that, Wives be obedient to your husbands in all things'.

Burnet witnessed a turning-point in the couple's nine-year-old re-lationship which, as he put it, had been 'a little embroiled' at the time of his arrival in the Orange Court: it was only a year since the Elizabeth Villiers drama. Even before it erupted, the relationship of this oddly-matched couple had never been easy. The adolescent Mary soon fell in love with her solemn and much older husband, readily transferring to him the romantic passion she had formerly lavished on a fantasy lover. But she found it almost impossible to penetrate his deep layers of reserve. On his side, William did his best in the early months of their marriage, but it was soon obvious that he was bored by his warmhearted and charming but very immature bride, supposing that she was not interested in the affairs of state that absorbed so much of his time and energy.

Under Burnet's coaching, however, Mary was developing a strong interest in what was happening at Whitehall, an interest she demonstrated for the first time by venturing to protest to her father in writing, when he suspended Henry Compton, Bishop of London, for refusing to reprimand a clergyman who had preached against 'the King's Religion'. James was not pleased by his daughter's intervention, and his reply to her was a bitter attack on the bishop, 'not without some sharpness of her meddling in such matters'.

Anne, too, had been shocked by the suspension of one of her most trusted advisers in religious matters. She was deeply in awe of her authoritarian father, and lived in constant fear that he would try to convert her. Mary, conscious of her Protestant sister's isolation in a Catholic Court, wrote bracing letters of encouragement: popish wiles must be resisted. Anne's replies were reassuring: 'I hope you don't doubt that I will be firm to my religion whatever happens . . . I must tell you that I abhor the principles of the Church of Rome as much as it is possible for any to do.' She calmed her sister's anxieties with the assertion: 'I do count it a very great blessing that I am of the Church of England, and a great misfortune that the King is not.'

Anne could not discuss her fears with her lethargic husband George. Instead, she confided in her close friend, Sarah Churchill, and her husband John. This able young military commander had begun his career as pageboy to James when Duke of York – a position he owed to his sister Arabella's liaison with James at the time. Under James's patronage, Churchill's advancement had been spectacular, and the couple had reason to be grateful to Mary Beatrice too. Sarah had been one of her ladies-in-waiting, and the young Italian queen had gone out of her way to promote the match, presiding at their marriage, and giving them a handsome – and more than welcome – wedding present of cash. But as a convinced Protestant, it was becoming clear to Churchill that he could expect no further promotion from James, who had passed him over for the French Catholic Feversham when picking the commander of the royal army sent against Monmouth in 1685. James was also beginning to be wary of Churchill influence over his daughter Anne, whose lady-in-waiting Sarah now was, and not without reason: Churchill had been heard to remark that 'if the King was ever prevailed on to alter our religion, [he] would serve him no longer but withdraw from him.'

Churchill was thus a logical choice of go-between for Anne when Dijkvelt arrived in London in February 1687. The Princess of Denmark was eager to talk to him but, knowing that she was constantly watched, she sent Churchill to assure William, through his envoy, that she would be true to her faith. Churchill seized the occasion to make a formal transfer of his own loyalties: '. . . my places and the King's favour I set at naught, in comparison of the being true to my religion.' The prince and princess could depend on him not to betray Anne to her father: 'the Princess of Denmark is safe in the trusting of me.'

Family relations in the York household had not always been so strained. When their father, three years after the death of their mother, married his teen-aged Italian bride, both Mary and Anne, after the initial shock, had grown very fond of their pretty young stepmother, who brought a breath of life and femininity into the home of the widower duke – exactly the 'playmate' he promised his daughters when he introduced her to them. Mary in particular took to her step-mother at once, and clung to her desperately when the time came, in November 1677, to leave England for Holland with a Dutch stranger for husband. And in the first years of Mary's marriage, Mary Beatrice had paid several visits to her daughter-in-law at The Hague, where she bestowed the teasing nickname 'Lemon' on the new Princess of Orange. 'I love her as if she were my own daughter,' she said. William, too, was charmed by the intelligent and forceful Mary Beatrice, who, although she was nine years younger than he, still addressed her artless, chatty letters to 'my sonne the Prince of Orange'. Over the years they kept up an intermittent correspondence, and as her letters show, she appreciated the friendship of this normally taciturn man. 'I am as sensible as I ought to be of your kyndnesse to me,' she wrote after one of her trips to The Hague in 1679. 'You can not shew it me mor then in rejoycing at my coming hether again; for tis the thing in the world I wisht for most.'

When after the accession of James in 1685, William sent her a formal letter of congratulation, Mary Beatrice wrote back reproachfully, 'Pray follow my example and write to me without any ceremony, for it is not to be minded between such friends as we are.' Even two years later, when exchanges between the prince and the king had become distinctly chilly, his relationship with the queen remained – on the surface – one of warm regard.

'The friendship you have showed me on all occasions . . . makes me hope I may have a share of your compassion in the great grief I now lie under,' the queen wrote to him confidingly on the death of her mother in July 1687. But for the Prince of Orange, affairs of state were more important than people. The handsome cavalry officer, his cousin Willem Frederik van Nassau, Heer van Zuylestein, who brought her William's sincere condolences, had an undercover mission. And the pleasant fortnight Zuylestein spent in London ostensibly catching up with old friends – he was half-English himself – was actually employed in gathering intelligence and contacting political allies for the prince. The unsuspecting queen sent William back a warm note of thanks: 'I have desired this bearer to . . . assure you that I do desire above all things the continuance of your friendship, which I cannot but think I do deserve a little . . .'

Not all Mary Beatrice's charm, however, could secure the affection of her younger stepdaughter, Anne. Temperamentally, the lively young queen and the dull princess were poles apart. A certain imperiousness of manner on the queen's part, and on Anne's the natural jealousy of a plain, rather stupid woman for a vivacious and forceful beauty, soon finished even the pretence of friendship between them. And what had begun as the easy affection of two young girls had changed over the years into a mutual – and on Anne's side, intense – dislike. 'She pretends to have a great deal of kindness to me, but I doubt it is not real,' Anne told Mary. The queen, she wrote in another spiteful outpouring, was highly conscious of her position; she was 'of a very proud, haughty humour; and although she pretends to hate all forms and ceremony, yet one sees that those that make their court this way, are very well thought of.'

'One thing I must say of the Queen,' she told Mary in Holland, 'is that she is the most hated in the world of all sorts of people; for everybody believes that she pressed the King to be more violent than he would be of himself . . . one may see by her that she hates all Protestants.' In the same letter Anne assured her sister that she was resolved always to pay the queen 'a great deal of respect', but at Court what was obvious to everybody was her increasing resentment and hostility. 'Seeing that the Catholic religion has a prospect of advancement,' wrote Terriesi, the princess 'affects more than ever, both in public and in private, to show herself hostile to it, and [to be] the most zealous of Protestants, with whom she is gaining the greatest power and credit.'

Sarah Churchill, frustrated in her boundless ambition for the husband she idolized, probably shared this view. It was to her that Anne commented waspishly on a present of 'a watch with her Picture on it sett with diamonds' that Mary Beatrice had given her: 'among friends I think one may say without being vaine that ye Godess might have showered down her fayvours on her poor Vassalls with more liberality.'

Rather to Anne's surprise, James never made the all-out attack on her Protestantism that she always told everyone was imminent. In fact he seems to have respected her religious views, however much he regretted them. During the Yorks' exile in Brussels, Anne had her own private chapel, and her Protestant servants later revealed that James never put any pressure on her to go to mass with him. After his accession, he always had grace said publicly at his dinner-table. Since Anne pointedly looked the other way, he remonstrated with her gently – 'he said it was looking upon them as Turks, and looked disrespectfully to him,' but even then he left her in peace, as she related to Mary, saying that 'he would not torment me about it, but hoped that one day God would open my eyes . . .'

The king's deep religious convictions, however, and his concern for Catholicism in England, made it hard for him to resist an attempt at his eldest daughter's conversion in the winter of 1687–8, when Mary gave him the shadow of an excuse.

She had mentioned to d'Albeville her curiosity to know what had brought about James's conversion – a remark duly reported to James. He at once sat down and wrote her a long letter describing his conversion, which was, in effect, a passionate plea for her understanding, and for a more open mind.

The last thing Mary wanted was to be drawn into religious controversy with her father, and she replied evasively, but another letter from James arrived just before Christmas. This time she shut herself up in her study to compose a lengthy and carefully thought-out reply which she hoped would bring the discussion to an end. James, however, could not lightly give up this faint hope of a convert he yearned for. He wrote again, complimenting her on the forcefulness of her arguments; he begged her to consult a Jesuit priest at The Hague; and he sent her books to read, as well as an account of her mother's conversion, which had already failed to move Anne.

Mary was not impressed by James's arguments, nor by those of the mother she hardly remembered: 'I found her reasons as strange as they were surprising for a woman of whom I had always heard it said she possessed great intelligence.' Laboriously, she composed another long reply, and this time, rather diffidently, she showed it to William, who was surprised, 'not thinking me capable of such a thing'. After a final exchange, her father was obliged to admit defeat, and no more books of religious controversy appeared, to Mary's great relief. 'That was what I hoped.'

The political clashes between her husband and her father, and this more personal difference with James had never marred, however, the warm affection between the princess and her stepmother. And when she heard the news about Mary Beatrice's pregnancy at the end of 1687, Mary's first reaction was one of undivided pleasure. She was not at all upset by the prospect of a little rival for the throne of England. On the contrary, she had grown to love her tranquil, orderly and undemanding life among the Dutch, and she had not the slightest desire to be queen – 'God having given me such a contented mind and no ambition other than that of serving my creator.'

FOUR
THE THREE QUESTIONS

Few pregnancies in history can have provoked more emotion, speculation and intrigue than that of the Queen of England, as Christmas
1687 drew near.

For James it was a clear sign of God's favour, the miracle for which
all Catholics had been waiting. He was positive from the start that it
would be a boy. Anything was now possible. And he discussed his
plans for England's future with manic enthusiasm, brushing aside the
objections of seasoned advisers like Sunderland. His Catholic advisers
shared his obsessive confidence.

For his son-in-law the Prince of Orange, on the other hand, no news
could have been more unwelcome. Events would no longer wait for
him: he would have to make decisions in a hurry, plan for half a dozen
different eventualities. His need for reliable, on-the-spot intelligence
became acute. It was Burnet, once more, who came to the rescue. His
young cousin, James Johnston, was the very man William needed.
Cautious, expert and courageous, the Scotsman had a number of useful
contacts, friends and relations in Whitehall, including the Quaker
William Penn, and one of the queen's doctors. His sister Mrs Bailey
could be particularly useful, since she was a close friend of the Queen's
Woman of the Bedchamber, Margaret Dawson.

Posts to Holland were now being regularly searched, so Johnston set
up an elaborate system of accommodation addresses, between which
would pass apparently innocuous letters on their way to Bentinck. But
when they were soaked in a special solution, more interesting matters
would be revealed. Code names were agreed: the king and queen were
Mr and Mrs Kemp, William, Mr Oughtred, the indispensable Sidney,
Mr Stourton.

Within weeks of the first rumours, Johnston was in London, and
long, detailed accounts of Whitehall politics, rumour and gossip were
travelling back to The Hague to be weighed up and pored over by
Bentinck, Burnet and the prince.

Given Mary Beatrice's long, dismal record of miscarriages, the great question was, of course, whether she was actually pregnant, and if so, how good were her chances of a normal delivery. Johnston's contacts did not fail him. The queen had not had her 'courses' since her return to Windsor towards the end of September, he reported on 16 December. This in itself was not necessarily conclusive – she had gone as long as seventeen weeks between periods in the past without being pregnant. Moreover, she was painfully thin, and her over-active doctors had bled her for some fancied disorder. But now, in the last few days, her breasts had begun to swell. 'Her Majesty begins to believe it, – and carries [it] highly to the Princess.'

Mary Beatrice was not very strong, however, and a fortnight later came the first fright, when she began bleeding for a little while. The Thanksgiving planned for the New Year was put off, and a day or two later, there was a fresh fright, this time much more serious. The bleeding started again, and the overwrought young woman – with such tremendous issues at stake on her pregnancy – had a nervous collapse. 'She cried that she was lost, ruined, wretched for ever . . . she started to tremble right through her body as though she had a fever, which lasted an hour.' Doctors and midwives came running, trying desperately to soothe the poor, distracted woman. Finally, she was given laudanum, and fell into a heavy sleep. 'The King has never looked more defeated.'

This alarm too, subsided; by 4 January the Queen's breasts were 'full and round', and all her ladies now believed her pregnant.

Like James, Sunderland was gambling all his hopes on a royal heir. It was fairly certain that Mary Beatrice would outlive her husband, to become regent to the young Catholic Prince of Wales: in which case, as her established favourite, he might look forward to a position of unprecedented power and wealth.

But both James and Sunderland were obliged to consider what might happen if Mary Beatrice had another miscarriage. It was being said, reported Johnston in December, that 'if ye Greate Belly should any way fail . . . ye Court will pursue much warmer measures, and yt a stricter Alliance being lately made, between us and France – 'tis believed ye Dutch may next summer find ye effects of it . . .'

One of these 'warmer measures' was a device for giving the royal supremacy, together with the Dispensing Power, a legal sanction they had never before enjoyed. A convocation of all the clergy would be called, and the question of the king's supremacy – already determined by judges – would be laid before them. The clergy would be commanded to acknowledge it – there was a precedent for this from the reign of Henry VIII – under pain of losing their livings and personal

estates. 'It must be acknowledged,' Johnston noted, 'that there are
Laws about the Supremacy so unhappily worded, that a kind Judge
will have a fair occasion to shew his zeal for H M's service.'

Nobody could doubt that James would be perfectly willing to carry
out such a scheme, after his vindictive treatment that autumn of the
ejected Magdalen Fellows. Many of them had been made penniless by
their expulsion, and when the king heard that several of the nobility
and gentry intended to present livings to them, he promptly had the
Fellows declared incapacitated.

The convocation scheme delighted James, though Sunderland did
his best to talk him out of it: 'he hoped sober men would be gained
without such extremities.'

Much more worrying for William was James's apparent success in
wooing the Dissenters, his new political allies, with whose help he
hoped to secure a submissive Parliament. William's own views on
the whole subject of toleration had been widely misrepresented in
England. Catholics and Dissenters were told they could expect nothing
from him, while the Church of England were alarmed by rumours that
a Dutch Calvinist was very unlikely to be a staunch defender of the
Anglican establishment. It was even rumoured – and widely believed –
that the prince had turned Catholic and was in favour of repealing the
Tests.

What was needed now was a manifesto for the English public of
William's exact intentions. And, as it happened, the pretext for pub-
lishing just such a document lay conveniently to hand. A former
Scottish Presbyterian refugee, James Stewart, now back in England
and reconciled with James, had been corresponding with another refugee, William Carstares, in the hope of persuading him to approve
James's policy of toleration. Carstares suggested that he approach one
of Holland's most eminent statesmen, the Grand Pensionary Caspar
Fagel, who was known to be a close friend and supporter of the prince.
Stewart was delighted by the idea and, in reply to his approach, he
received a long letter from Fagel. It had been drafted with William's
help, then translated by Burnet into English, and it was also being
prepared for publication in the form of a pamphlet, *Their Highness the
Prince and Princess of Orange's Opinion about a General Liberty of Conscience*.

Johnston saw it in draft form before he left for London in November,
and almost as soon as he arrived, he began pressing for its immediate
publication. 'It must be . . . soon, before the Elections, that the Dissenters may take their Resolutions . . . all Dissenters will look upon
that Letter as a Magna Charta to them.'

By mid-January it was printed, and thousands of copies began flooding into the country, to be distributed nationwide, despite frantic efforts by Whitehall to suppress it – 'they search both Coaches and Carriers'. Its readers learned that the prince and princess were in favour of freedom of religion for Catholics and Dissenters, but they believed that the Test Acts must be maintained to give Anglicans a monopoly of office. The prince had no intention of imposing the Dutch system on the English, whose Parliament must make its own decisions, but he assured them that when Mary came to the throne, there would be no more religious persecution.

Its effect was sensational. Dissenter support for James's policy began crumbling almost immediately – William's promises looked much more substantial. Even prominent members of the Dissenting community warned James that they could no longer guarantee the support of their followers – 'they said that Mr Fagel's Letter . . . take[s] all their people out of their hands.'

Enthusiasm for the *Opinion* was widespread. 'People are in raptures,' the Earl of Devonshire wrote to William, 'to find the sentiments of your Highness and of the Princess in matters of religion, not only so equitable, but so agreeable to the interest, and to the taste of all the nation . . .'

In his frustrated rage, James now made another epic miscalculation. Secret plans to recall the six English and Scottish regiments from Holland had been hatched months earlier between James, Sunderland and Barillon. Louis XIV, delighted by the chance to set James and the Prince of Orange at odds, had agreed to contribute to the cost of maintaining them once back in England. Their recall now, James reckoned, would not only be a humiliating public rebuff for the prince, it would also seriously hamper any warlike plans he might be making against his father-in-law. Within days of the *Opinion*'s publication, James wrote to the States-General demanding that the regiments be repatriated.

The States-General took a leisurely fortnight to consider, 'with the most wise advice of the Prince of Orange', before sending their reply. While they would be happy to give James any help he might need in an emergency, 'with as much readiness, willingness and promptitude', as in 1685, they did not feel under any obligation to return to the king's service troops that had been raised, trained and paid for by the Republic. They eventually conceded that those officers who wished might leave, and a total of around seventy, including four colonels, four majors and nineteen captains actually did so, perhaps tempted by the handsome bounties James was offering. Ordinary soldiers, ruled the States-General, must stay at their posts or be treated as deserters.

James's coup had as dramatic an impact in Holland as Fagel's letter in England. He was overjoyed to learn that shares in the Dutch East India Company plunged 13 per cent immediately. But the Prince of Orange had been trying for months to bring about what his father-in-law now achieved for him almost overnight. Dutch public opinion was at once united in suspicion of hostile Anglo-French intentions – it was rightly assumed that the move had been made in concert with Louis XIV – and in agreement on the urgent need to rearm. Also, in purging the regiments of those officers loyal to himself, James actually did the Prince of Orange a service in the long run.

Anglo-Dutch relations, meanwhile, plunged to a new low, and for some time, elated by the sensation he had produced, James actually seems to have contemplated making war on the odious Dutch. He sent for the stout and choleric Admiral Sir John Berry and told him he would soon have 'business' for him. Sir John 'begged leave to tell him that in case the business was matter of action, he would put no Popish officers in, for he was sure the seamen would knock them on the head'. The king retorted nastily that when he wanted Sir John's advice, he would make him Privy Counsellor, and stormed out of the room.

The cooler counsels of Sunderland prevailed for the time being, and Sunderland himself was still working hard at constructing James's dream Parliament, but in private he was deeply pessimistic about its chances of success. And both James and his advisers were in a state of permanent dither on the subject, 'not three days of one mind about the methods that are to be followed'.

The Three Questions campaign, it was now admitted, had been a mistake, which had 'angered and united the Nation'. Moreover, the number of lord-lieutenants who had proved uncooperative was disturbing. Between August and November no fewer than ten – all leading territorial magnates, of considerable influence – had resigned or been removed, while at the end of the year the purge had been extended downwards, into the ranks of deputy lieutenants, sheriffs and justices of the peace.

In the New Year James's campaign picked up speed: among the peers forfeiting their lord-lieutenancies – a position of honour and standing in their counties – were the Dukes of Newcastle and Norfolk, and the Earls of Bath, Dorset and Oxford. By February, thirteen lord-lieutenants had been replaced by Catholics or Court nominees such as Father Petre, Lord Dover, Lord Preston, Chancellor Jeffreys.

'Not since the Norman Conquest,' as J. H. Plumb has remarked, 'had the Crown developed so sustained an attack on the established political power of the aristocracy and major gentry.' But here, too, there were considerable difficulties. After Fagel's pamphlet, many Dissenters were backing away from the king, and some corporations had to be remodelled over and over again: 'at Reading the Mayor and 24 Aldermen being turned out, 23 of those put in their places, told plainly that they were of the same opinion with their predecessors and they are turned out too.'

By the end of February, Johnston believed that James and his ministers were still determined to press ahead, by whatever means – 'they will have a Parliament *perfas et nefas*' – but William in his calculations had to take into account the possibility that more violent and extreme counsels might be followed, if the packed Parliament was seen not to be feasible. Johnston sent back warning after warning of assassination attempts planned against Burnet and the prince himself, and Sidney, Dorset, Halifax and Shrewsbury had all received anonymous death threats if they did not 'repent'.

But Parliament or no, all speculation about James's future conduct came back in the end to the same point: would the queen's child be carried to full term? If so, would it be a son? And growing numbers of people were asking another question: is the whole business of the queen's pregnancy a Catholic fraud on a grand scale?

These rumours had already started by the New Year, as Clarendon had noted. They were seized on by the gutter press of the United Provinces, and a venomous war of words was soon raging. The satirists sneered at Catholics for believing 'her Majesty to be with child almost before she knew it herself', and jeered viciously at the possibility of 'the King's having male issue of a vigour to live, considering both his Majestie's condition and the Queen's . . .' They warned, finally, that if the papists should try to 'banter a supposititious brat upon the Nation . . . there are many faithfull and waking Eyes that will be ready and industrious to discover the cheat.'

At The Hague, Mary at first refused to take these rumours seriously. She had no reason for such dreadful suspicions of the young stepmother who wrote so guilelessly from Whitehall that she was already very big, ''tho I dont reckon myself gone above twenty weeks'. But the savage chorus continued, and soon a voice that Mary found much harder to ignore was added to it: that of her own sister.

On 14 March Anne voiced the first doubts in a letter: 'Her being so positive that it will be a son, and the principles of that religion being so much that they will stick at nothing, be it never so wicked . . . give some cause to fear there may be foul play intended.'

A week later, Anne's suspicions had hardened. '. . . There having been so many stories and jests made about it, she should, to convince the world, make either me or some of my friends feel her belly; for quite contrary, whenever one talks of her being with child, she looks as if she were afraid one should touch her,' she reported to Holland. 'And whenever I happen to be in the room and the Queen has been undressing, she has always gone into the next room to put on her smock ... nobody will be convinced it is her child except it prove a daughter.'

Anne was so aware of the risks she took putting such thoughts on paper that she began to use code names: James, for instance, was Mansell. 'It is all treason that I have spoke,' she exclaimed in one of her letters, 'Pray burn it!'

These letters put Mary in a dilemma. Despite her friendship with Mary Beatrice, it was impossible to ignore letters which gave her, as she confided to her journal, 'just cause to suspect there had been some trickery'. There was another consideration that, consciously or unconsciously, weighed even more strongly: her husband's claim to the throne. 'The love I have for the Prince brings me to wish for him all that he deserves ... I regret having no more than three crowns to offer him.'

She may have been sceptical of her sister's insinuations of a Catholic plot, but she was willing to be convinced for the sake of William and the Protestant religion. And by the spring of 1688, it seemed that there was no longer any need to rely for evidence on the spiteful speculations of Anne. Grave and senior politicians seemed to be taking the rumours very seriously indeed. On 27 March, Danby wrote to William: 'Many of our ladies say, that the Queen's great belly seems to grow faster than they have observed their own to do.' He hoped that Mary would insist on Anne's being at hand when the time came, to see that 'the midwife discharges her duty with that care which ought to be had in a case of so great concern'.

Of all the English politicians and noblemen who wrote to William, the only one still urging a policy of wait and see by this time was the cautious Halifax. Almost everyone else was agreed that 'the business of England' was coming rapidly to a crisis. The Earl of Devonshire wrote on 13 March to tell him that Parliament was likely to be called around the time of the birth of the queen's child.

'The Catholics incline absolutely that it should be a son; and besides, the army at Hounslow will be in the neighbourhood ... it is certain that we expect great extremities ...'

FIVE

LAMBETH V. WHITEHALL

In the wild Veluwe forests north of Arnhem, William and Mary were building a beautiful new home, the palace of Het Loo. And while they were spending a few days supervising the work in the exceptionally wet spring of 1688, two visitors arrived from England. One was Admiral Edward Russell, a former Navy friend of James who had turned away from him after the execution of his cousin William in the Popish Plot. The other was his colleague Rear-Admiral Arthur Herbert, disgraced by James after his refusal to turn Catholic.

'I will not tell you what they said to me,' William wrote to Bentinck, 'since that is better done by word of mouth.' Bishop Burnet, however, learned full details of the conversation from Russell himself, when he returned to The Hague. Pumped by the inquisitive Burnet, the admiral finally revealed that he had been 'desired by many of great power and interest in England to speak very freely to the Prince and to know positively what might be expected from him'.

William's response was heavily conditional. He was no feckless adventurer, and he would not repeat Monmouth's mistakes. He was prepared to commit himself to the huge and risky enterprise of intervention only 'if he was invited by some men of the best interest and the most valued in the nation . . . to come over and rescue the nation and the religion'. If the English were prepared to commit themselves to this extent, he believed he could be ready by the end of September. The two seamen returned to England with this promise. And if there had been any lingering reluctance among James's opponents to sign an official invitation to William, the king himself removed their final doubts.

Throwing his last remnants of caution to the winds, James had asked the pope in January to divide England into four districts, appointing a vicar-apostolic to each: England's Catholics had been without an episcopacy for over fifty years. Four had been publicly appointed, to be given an allowance of £1,000 a year by the king. The resurrection of a Roman Catholic hierarchy was offensive enough to the Church of England, but there was worse to come.

At the end of March, James's nominee as president of Magdalen, Bishop Parker, had died. Speculation about his successor reached fever point – but even Catholics were stunned when James airily appointed Dr Buonaventura Gifford, one of the new vicars-apostolic, to succeed him. Bishop Leyburn, the first vicar-apostolic, boldly told James he thought this action grievously wronged the Magdalen Fellows, but James brushed his objection aside. Oxford's wealthiest college, 'filling apace with Popish Priests and others of the Roman Communion', seemed destined to become a seminary.

To add insult to injury, the new president was solemnly consecrated Bishop by d'Adda on 22 April, with maximum fanfare and ceremony in the Banqueting Hall.

Five days later, the final blow fell. It had been rumoured for some time that James would once more issue his Declaration of Indulgence, and that it might be even more far-reaching than its predecessor of 1687. Rumour proved well-founded. On 27 April the king did indeed renew his Declaration. He added that he intended to stand by it, and that in future only those who supported it could hope for public employment – a fact now obvious to the dimmest of his subjects. But the publication was swiftly followed by an order-in-council on 4 May: the bishops were to distribute copies of it to their clergy and have it read from every pulpit in the land.

There were perfectly good precedents for such an order. Exactly seventy years earlier, James I had ordered all his clergy to read out from their pulpits his Declaration of Sports – a blast against Puritan Sunday killjoys – in which he laid down that once his subjects had attended divine service, they were not to be 'disturbed, letted or discouraged from . . . dancing . . . archery . . . leaping, vaulting, or any such harmless recreation, nor from having May games, Whitsun ales and morris dancing . . .' And only seven years earlier, Charles II had had his reasons for dissolving Parliament read out in the nation's churches.

But even so, James's initiative caught the Church of England off balance. More than a week went by before its leaders pulled themselves together, and began to consider what action might be taken: and as James had no doubt intended, the order gave them little time for reflection – it was to be read on 20 May.

In addition to the problems of communicating at speed with their brethren up and down the country, there was the further difficulty that many of those brethren would certainly obey James's order. Nathaniel

Crewe, Bishop of Durham, had actively promoted Indulgence throughout his diocese. A handful of other bishops were certain to toe James's line – Thomas Cartwright of Chester, Thomas Sprat of Rochester, Dr Watson of St David's. Others couldn't be counted on to join in formal protest – the Bishops of Hereford, Exeter, Coventry and Lichfield among them. Many of the lesser clergy, too, would be unhappy about disobeying a formal command from the king, however much they disagreed with his policies. Only a very strong lead from above would push them into disobedience.

What was crystal clear was that divisions and disagreement within the Church could be fatal, since they would certainly strengthen James's hand. At all costs, the Church of England must present a united front.

The first hurried consultation was at Lambeth Palace, on Monday 7 May, when Clarendon and the Rector of St Martin-in-the-Fields, Dr Tenison, dined with Sancroft. By Saturday a number of other bishops had reached town and hurried to Lambeth to confer. As well as Clarendon, there was Henry Compton, Turner of Ely, White of Peterborough, and Cartwright and Watson. As long as the two last were present, the discussion was general, and nobody committed themselves. But the minute they left, the company got down to business: '. . . after full deliberation it was resolved not to do it . . . The resolution was, to petition the King in the matter, but first to get as many bishops to town as were within reach.' '. . . The Bishops of Winchester, Norwich, Gloucester, St Asaph, Bath and Wells, Bristol and Chichester should be written to, to come to town.' All these were good 'solid' men.

By Wednesday Lloyd of St Asaph had arrived in London to be Clarendon's guest for these tense days: he and Ely went off to Lambeth, where they found that Compton had been busy – most of the City clergy had decided not to read the Declaration. 'More were for reading than against it,' reported one of William's spies, 'but those who were against it were more active and warm.' By Thursday evening six bishops were gathered at Lambeth with Sancroft to decide on their action. With only two days left to go, Friday morning was spent drafting a petition to be presented to the king: as well as Sancroft and the six bishops, some of the country's most distinguished clergymen – Tillotson, Dean of Canterbury, Tenison and Stillingfleet, Dean of St Paul's, among them – sat in on this council of war. By nightfall it was finished.

Sancroft had been forbidden the Court because of an earlier clash with James, so the other six crossed the river without him to beard the king, but as a sign of his solidarity, the archbishop had copied out the petition in his own hand. None of them can have looked forward very much to the interview, given the explosive nature of the document they carried with them. Their 'humble petition' expressed 'the great averseness they find in themselves to the distributing and publishing in all their churches your Majesty's late declaration for liberty of conscience'. It was not from any want of duty to the king, or 'due tenderness' towards Dissenters (Catholics were not mentioned), but 'because that declaration is founded upon such a dispensing power as hath often been declared illegal in Parliament'. The matter was of 'so great moment and consequence to the whole nation' that they could not 'in prudence, honour or conscience' be parties to it. They therefore 'most humbly and earnestly' begged His Majesty not to insist on its distribution and reading.

James received them graciously: for a wild moment, he may actually have believed that this was yet another Address thanking him for his Declaration. He was soon undeceived. He read it with mounting astonishment, then turned to the six bishops and broke out angrily: 'This is a great surprise . . . I did not expect this from you . . . This is a standard of rebellion!' Trelawney of Bristol, the youngest of them, was devastated by the charge. He fell to his knees and reminded the furious king that he had served him against Monmouth. 'Sir,' chimed in Chichester, 'we have quelled one rebellion and will not raise another.' 'We rebel? We are ready to die at your feet,' echoed Ely dutifully. Bishop Ken interrupted these loyal cries to make a shrewd point: 'Sir, I hope you will give that liberty to us which you allow to all mankind.'

James had a point of his own to make in reply: 'Do you question my dispensing power? Some of you here have printed and preached for it, when it was for your purpose.' 'It was declared against in the first Parliament called by his late Majesty, and by that which was called by your Majesty,' parried Lloyd.

Appeals and threats proved equally useless. Realizing that he was getting nowhere, James dismissed them: 'I will be obeyed in publishing my Declaration,' he insisted.

News of this confrontation would certainly have spread rapidly around Whitehall, and gradually spread through the length and breadth of the land. But Sancroft and his co-conspirators needed maximum publicity, and fast, if their stand was to be influential nationally. Within twenty-four hours, hundreds of copies of their petition had been printed – it seems likely that the energetic Compton, eager for a showdown, was responsible – while news of the strong line taken by the bishops spread like wildfire. 'As to the reading of the Declaration, I believe it will scarce be read,' wrote the Bishop of Carlisle to a friend, 'for I am resolved to concur with my brethren . . . and so, it is believed, will all the rest of the Bishops except a very few.'

He was right. On Sunday 20 May, the Declaration was read in only four or five London churches, and in the week that followed news trickled in from all over England: it had been read in perhaps 200 churches. Predictably, James's loyal stooges, the Bishops of Chester, Durham, Rochester and St David's, had dutifully circulated it to their clergy: but even here, by no means all of them had complied. A few of the clergy arranged diplomatic absences from their parishes – among them, Stillingfleet and Tillotson. One parson actually told his congregation that although he had to read it, they didn't have to listen to it. After a pause – during which his congregation took the hint – he read it to rows of empty benches.

During the days that followed, speculation reached fever pitch: how would the king react? While the bishops collected their forces for the coming crunch, James debated his next step. If he proceeded against the bishops, he not only risked turning them into martyrs: much more important, he would be inviting a highly public display of opposition by the 'loyal' Church of England.

Worse still, leading Dissenters were already making it plain that their sympathies were with the bishops, not the king. If James did nothing, on the other hand, his royal authority would be seriously compromised. His advisers seem to have been divided; Chancellor Jeffreys was frankly unhappy about any suggestion that the erring Seven should be dealt with in the courts. Even Father Petre, it was rumoured, was doubtful about the wisdom of further action. For some days, James hesitated: more than once, he decided to let matters go, with a display of royal graciousness.

But all his instincts pushed him towards confrontation. 'I will make no concessions,' he was fond of saying. 'My father made concessions and he was beheaded.' The Catholic hotheads at Court egged him on. He delayed action till the second Sunday on which the Declaration should have been read. Then as reports came in of nationwide disobedience, he made up his mind. Archbishop Sancroft and the six bishops were summoned to appear before the Privy Council on Friday 8 June – just under two weeks later – 'to answer to such matters of misdemeanours as shall then be objected against them'.

During this time the bishops had not been idle: the petition had been circulated to and signed by another eight bishops, including Compton. Now, on Clarendon's advice, they hired the best lawyers in town, regardless of expense: one man was engaged all night copying documents that might be relevant. A total of £540 was eventually

spent on legal fees. Clarendon raised a vital point in a final meeting
with the bishops on the eve of their arraignment: 'I asked them if they
had well considered what to do, or say, in case they should be required
to find bail for their further appearance (for such a thing was whispered) and I found they had not; whereupon I earnestly pressed them
to go this very evening and advise therein with Sir Robert Sawyer . . .'

The choice was apt: a brilliant lawyer, Sawyer had been attorney-
general since 1681. Six months earlier, however, he had been dismissed because of his well-publicized refusal to uphold the dispensing
power of the Crown. He joined a strong defence team, who between
them commanded a great deal more experience and expertise than the
Crown could muster. How this eminent counsel had advised them
became apparent next day. At half past five in the afternoon the Seven
were summoned in before the king and the Privy Council – including
Father Petre. Chancellor Jeffreys opened the proceedings by showing
Sancroft his petition and asking if it was his? Well briefed, Sancroft
declined to incriminate himself by replying. Chicanery, said James
impatiently. Eventually, on a royal command, they all admitted
signing it. A hurried conference followed, then they learned that they
were to be proceeded against, and must enter into a recognizance that
they would appear. As Sawyer had advised, they declined, quoting
suitable legal precedents. Their refusal took king and Council by
surprise: the previous evening, Sancroft had led them to believe that
they would pay up as suggested.

James was bewildered by this move: 'I offer you this as a favour, and
I would not have you refuse it.' Still the bishops persisted, and James
and his chancellor began to realize the pit that yawned before them.
By this time, too, huge and restive crowds were gathering in Whitehall
to know the outcome. For hours more the king, Jeffreys and Lord
Berkeley attempted to talk the seven out of their decision. Finally, the
serjeant-at-arms came out with a warrant signed by fifteen of the
council to commit them to the Tower. (Father Petre at least had
the self-preserving sense not to sign it.)

The seven bishops emerged into history. To forestall angry demonstrations, they were hustled out into the waiting royal barge to be
taken to the Tower by water, but the crowds streamed down to the
river bank chanting and shouting. 'Some persons ran into the water to
implore a blessing . . . both banks of the Thames were lined with
multitudes, who when too distant to be heard, manifested their feelings
by falling down on their knees,' the States-General learned from their
ambassador, Aernout van Citters.

'. . . Affairs move every day closer to a catastrophe,' the Imperial envoy, Hoffmann, wrote at this time to the emperor, '. . . and although the King seems to know that he is in trouble, he does not in the least give the impression that he has any intention of giving up his project.'

William followed these developments with the keenest interest. He was still waiting for an unequivocal invitation from leading Englishmen, and knew that his friend Henry Sidney was busily canvassing signatures. The arrest of the bishops could only help his cause. Almost immediately came the final incentive to waverers: the long-awaited – and much dreaded – birth of Mary Beatrice's child. And as the Catholics had always predicted, it was a boy.

SIX

'IT IS A BOY'

For the last few weeks, Mary Beatrice had been busy with preparations. She refused to be delivered in the noisy public palace of Whitehall, and as Windsor was too distant for this controversial birth, the queen had chosen to lie in at St James's. She felt a special attachment to this palace, her family home, where all her other babies had been born. Repairs were being carried out, and on Saturday 9 June – in a typical pre-natal bustle – Mary Beatrice kept calling in at the palace to hurry up the workmen. She told them she was determined to sleep that night in her own bedroom, even 'if I lie on the boards'.

She stayed up late playing cards, and it was after eleven when she was carried in her sedan chair to St James's. Her bedchamber was just ready, with its big bed in place, an elaborate piece of furniture decorated with carvings of crowns, ciphers, swags of flowers and fruit, and with thick brocade curtains hanging from its high canopy.

The king and queen were already up the next morning when at eight o'clock she felt the first contractions. A message was sent to the king, who had gone to his dressing-room, while Mary Beatrice's women hastily began making preparations. The baby had not been expected for at least another fortnight, and nothing was ready. When the queen asked for the special pallet bed in which she had planned her delivery, her Woman of the Bedchamber, Mrs Margaret Dawson, had to admit that there had not been time to air the quilts for it. Instead, her own big bed was 'made and warmed with a warming-pan of hot coals of fire, after which the Queen went to bed again'.

By this time the small stuffy room was filling up with the important people who were traditionally expected to witness the birth of the royal child – a crowd of at least twenty people. Among the first on the scene was Lady Sunderland, who together with other Protestant ladies of the Court had been at church on this Trinity Sunday. By the time she arrived, the queen's contractions were coming very close together, and the midwife, Judith Wilkes, told Anne Sunderland that 'she wanted only one thorow pain to bring the Child into the world', but Mary Beatrice, now in agony, couldn't believe it. 'It is impossible, the child lies so high,' she fretted, and she asked her friend to feel it.

The men, reluctant witnesses, were alarmed by her cries. Lord Peterborough, who had always had a weak spot for the Italian bride he had discovered for James in Modena, could hardly bear to listen. 'I confess the compassion I had for her Majesty hearing her Crys made my stay there very uneasie . . . One of the last especially seemed to me so sharp, as it really forced me for a little time to stop my ears . . .' Lord Middleton, James's chief minister, was equally upset: one of the 'several loud shrieks . . . continued so long, that he wondered how any body could hold their breath so long . . .'

The presence of all these men embarrassed Mary Beatrice so much that she asked James, standing at the foot of the bed, if he could not draw the curtains. James refused, and instead, at her request, came closer and bending down covered her face with his periwig.

At a quarter to ten, after a last long cry, 'most part of lords and ladies there,' reported a newsletter, 'saw the midwife bring the child forth from between the clothes and laying it in a linen cloth.' According to one of the ladies present, Mrs Wilkes was about to cut the navel cord when the queen begged her to wait till the afterbirth had come away. Mrs Wilkes attempted to soothe the anxious young woman, who was only too well aware how much doubt and suspicion surrounded the birth of this baby. But she badly needed reassurance and asked, 'Where is the King gone?' He came forward immediately from the other side of the bed to calm her. 'Why do you leave me now?' fretted the queen, giving Mrs Wilkes permission at last to cut the cord.

While the midwife held up the afterbirth, the queen's dresser, Marie de la Baudie, carried the child swathed in linen cloths next door, followed by the king and those members of the Privy Council who were present. They saw 'Mrs Labadie' sit down near the fire, saying, 'It is a boy.' The triumphant father ordered her to open the cloths so that they could see his son with their own eyes – 'very foul' and 'his Forehead blackish'. Before everybody left, the baby was dosed with a concoction of 'three drops of blood of the navel string . . . stirred with a little black cherry water', at the advice of Mary Beatrice's doctor, who said, 'it was good against the fits.'

A special edition of the *London Gazette* announced the news that same evening: 'This day between nine and ten in the morning the Queen was safely delivered of a PRINCE.' A day later, he was christened James Francis Edward, with Charles's widow, the Dowager Queen

Catherine of Braganza as godmother, while the papal nuncio, Count d'Adda, stood in for the godfather, Pope Innocent XI.

By this time the scandal-mongers were already hard at work. Mary Beatrice's choice of St James's was deeply suspicious; obviously the workmen had been busily installing a secret chamber immediately below hers, from which the baby boy was smuggled directly into her bed through a passage hidden under it. Or else it had been brought into the room in the already notorious warming-pan. The supposed Prince of Wales was in reality the child of a miller – which gave him later the nickname James o' the Mill; or else the child of Mrs Francis Smith, who had been specially brought over from Dublin to give birth, and was later murdered in a French convent. The speed with which the queen had given birth, and the fact that the baby was born two weeks prematurely according to the royal doctors' calculations, were equally suspicious.

Most suggestive of all was the fact that hardly a single reliable Protestant witness had been present, or if they were there, they had been crowded into the back of the room where they could not see what was happening. James's eminently Protestant brothers-in-law Clarendon and Rochester ought certainly to have been there. But Clarendon learned the news almost casually from his pageboy when he left church that morning. He hurried to St James's where he found the king shaving. 'The queen had been so quick in her labour,' said the king, 'and he had so much company that he had not time to dress himself until now.' He did not explain why Clarendon and Rochester had not been sent for in time, but suggested that he should go and have a look at the little prince, now asleep in his cradle, 'and a very fine child to look upon'.

The absence of these two leading witnesses was strange enough. It was even more unfortunate that their niece Princess Anne had not been there to see the birth of the boy who made her now only third in line for the throne. It was being said that Anne, who had been unwell, had been encouraged by her father to take the waters at Bath, to get her out of the way.

In fact, everything indicates that the princess's absence was of her own choosing, and she had an excellent pretext. After a miscarriage on 16 April, her recovery was slow and, nine days later, Clarendon recorded that she was 'extremely ill . . . a fit of the colic'. Her doctors were divided about her treatment, some advising her to go to a spa, others objecting that the journey would be too much for her. Finally, at the end of May, Anne decided to go, at the instigation of Sarah Churchill, who knew that the princess's presence at her stepmother's delivery might be embarrassing for the Protestant cause.

Although Anne knew that the baby was due within the next month, and that Mary Beatrice had a history of premature births and short labour, she chose Bath instead of Tunbridge Wells, which was her usual choice and much nearer London. Her decision surprised the Court, and one of the ladies commented: 'I mutch wonder the Princess of Dermock would not complement the Queen and see her safely delivered before she went to the Barrth.' According to some, James would have loved to have Anne around for the sake of the 'Queen's comfort in the advize and assistance of so near a Relation'. But it is questionable whether Anne would have been willing to play this role. During the last months of the queen's pregnancy, her stepdaughter, who had complained to her sister that she was never allowed to touch 'the Queen's great belly', was hardly ever seen at Court. Mary Beatrice remembered later that the same Anne who, at the beginning of her pregnancy had been 'so easy and kind that nothing could equal it', had changed completely once the danger of a miscarriage seemed safely past. She 'appeared seldom in the Queen's bedchamber'.

James, realizing by this time that he had blundered badly in letting his key witness absent herself, tried to save the day. 'Without losing an instant, he has sent Colonel Ogledorp with a letter in his own hand to the Princess of Denmark ...' Hoffmann wrote to Vienna. 'One remarkable thing is that he has instructed him that it was not sufficient just to hand over the letter, but that he must give her *témoignage de visu*.' Once Anne was back in London, on 15 June, he took her by the hand to bring her to Mary Beatrice and her baby, as he had done to others, 'joking that otherwise they wouldn't believe it'.

Both Mary Beatrice and James at this time still found it hard to conceive that anyone could think them capable of fraud on such a grand scale. As James remarked to Ailesbury, 'those vile forgers of iniquity must certainly think that we do not believe in God, to imagine we could be such wicked impostors.' But it was a conversation with Anne that finally opened the queen's eyes. When she remarked to her stepdaughter that 'she wondr'd how such rediculous falsetys could gain the least credit ... the Princess answer'd very coldly. It was not so much to be wonder'd at, since such persons were not present as ought to have been there ...'

Anne had thought it politic not to be present at a birth which deep in her heart she must have known would be above suspicion. She found it hard, however, to justify her absence to her sister Mary, whom her own letters had convinced of an impending fraud. And in a letter dated 18 June, Anne apologized profusely for her omission: 'My dear sister can't imagine the concern and vexation I have been in, that I should be so unfortunate to be out of town when the Queen was brought to bed, for I shall never now be satisfied whether the child be true or false.' It was all a put-up job, Anne suggested: happening only two days after the queen learnt that her stepdaughter was on the way back to London: 'everybody knows by her own reckoning that she should have gone a month longer.' But it was too late now: 'except they do give very plain demonstrations, which is almost impossible now, I shall ever be of the number of unbelievers . . .'

The same day, she added almost as a footnote, the seven bishops had at last left their prison. 'All the time [they] were in the Tower, everybody flocked to see them; and there was great joy at their coming out.' There had hardly been any celebrations at the birth of the Prince of Wales, but it was another matter when after a preliminary hearing in Westminster Hall, the bishops were freed on bail to appear for trial on 29 June, on a charge of seditious libel. Their release from the Tower was the signal for renewed demonstrations since, as it was reported to Sunderland, 'the meaner sort seemed to understand [it] as a discharge, and, though forbid, made bonfires.'

By this time, many of those around James were having cold feet. Jeffreys twice sent assurances of his good will to the bishops through Clarendon. He lamented that the king was being hurried to his destruction by his advisers, and declared that most of the judges were rogues.

At the trial itself, the four 'rogues' of judges may have been cowed from the start by the glittering array of legal talent and experience that the bishops had lined up in their defence. As well as the former attorney-general, Sir Robert Sawyer, the Crown lawyers found themselves confronting the former solicitor-general, Heneage Finch, and the former judge, Sir Cresswell Levinz – both, like Sawyer, dismissed for their opposition to the king's dispensing power – and a former chief justice, Sir Francis Pemberton. (Levinz originally declined this dangerous honour – upon which his attorneys threatened to bring him no more briefs, and he hastily changed his mind.)

Equally daunting were the huge, hostile crowds packing the narrow streets outside, and the ranks of distinguished peers, led by Halifax, in the Hall itself. The appearance of Sunderland was greeted with derisive cries of 'Popish Dog' and the Crown's witnesses were hissed. At any rate, only one of the four judges, the Catholic Sir Richard Alibone, had his heart in the business. And two of them, Holloway and Powell, insisted on focusing discussion on the suspending power itself – the very last thing the Court wanted.

The two argued that the Crown had no case, since the petition was delivered 'with all the humility and decency that could be . . . and they were not men of evil lives or the like . . . it being the right of every subject to petition'. How could such a petition be illegal? 'They apprehend the declaration is illegal,' declared Powell, 'because it is founded upon a dispensing power which the King claims, to dispense with the laws concerning ecclesiastical affairs. Gentlemen, I do not remember in any case in all our law . . . that there is any such power in the King, and the case must turn upon that.'

It took a sleepy jury most of the night to make up their minds, and at noon the verdict of 'not guilty' was delivered. Halifax, jumping to his feet and waving his hat, led the deep roar of applause. 'A greater joy I have not perceived on such an occasion these many years . . .' noted Sir John Reresby, Governor of York and a loyal supporter of James. The streets were so crammed with cheering people 'that it looked like a little rebellion in noise though not in fact . . .' The bishops were carried shoulder-high down to the archbishop's waiting barge, and when Sancroft stepped out at Lambeth Palace, a troop of grenadiers 'made a line from the river to his gate, and kneeling, asked his blessing'.

The news spread rapidly cross-country. At Lichfield cheering mobs prepared to celebrate with a firework display. When the magistrates sent to stop them, the crowds beat up their messengers.

James was inspecting his armies camped at Hounslow when the news arrived. He was in Lord Feversham's tent when cheering suddenly broke out among the thousands of soldiers, and he sent Feversham to enquire what it was all about. His general returned: 'It was nothing but the joy of the soldiers for the discharge of the Bishops.' 'Nothing?' cried James. 'You call that nothing? But so much the worse for them.' Obviously upset, he left for London, where he immediately issued a proclamation banning assemblies in public.

It was ignored. While happy crowds celebrated with forbidden bonfires – even in front of his own palace, where they burnt an effigy of the pope – he was realizing too late that the trial had been an irretrievable error. The errant Judges Powell and Holloway were dismissed the following day, but the damage was done. 'The King's power to dispense with the laws was extremely arraigned, and the King's council so much outdone, that it was wished at Court that the thing had never been begun,' recorded Reresby.

SEVEN

THE ENGLISH INVITATION

Jubilant crowds were already celebrating the acquittal of the bishops when Admiral Herbert slipped out of London disguised, according to rumour, as an ordinary seaman, and crossed the North Sea to Holland. The document he carried with him sealed James's fate: it was the formal invitation to intervene on which William had insisted, the English commitment to the invasion he was now actively planning. And it was signed, as promised, by a number of England's most distinguished public figures – although only by numbers, in a prearranged code.

The time had come, they told him. If he delayed much longer, the king might have a Parliament packed full of supporters, and an army officered by reliable Catholics. If these failed James, 'other measures will be put in execution by more violent means': in other words, he would call in troops from Ireland or France. Discontent was at such a pitch that 'your Highness may be assured there are nineteen parts of twenty of the people throughout the kingdom, who are desirous of change, and who, we believe, would willingly contribute to it'. This was true, too, of 'much the greatest part of the nobility and gentry'.

The seven who signed it made a solemn undertaking: 'We who subscribe this will not fail to attend your Highness upon your landing and to do all that lies in our power to prepare others to be in . . . readiness.' They were confident the nation would rally to the prince. No more time must be lost: it was now up to him.

The seven signatures were certainly impressive enough: the elderly William Cavendish, Earl of Devonshire, Bishop Compton and the Earl of Danby, as well as William's co-conspirators Sidney, Shrewsbury, Lumley and Admiral Russell. But one name the Prince of Orange had counted on was missing: that of the leading Tory politician, Lord Nottingham. '. . . He was gone very far,' reported Sidney in an accompanying letter, 'but now his heart fails him, and he will go no further; he saith 'tis scruples of conscience, but we all conclude 'tis another passion . . .'

Halifax had not signed, either. He had flirted with the idea of joining the conspiracy for some days, but was now firmly back on the fence. If the bishops had been sent back to the Tower, instead of being acquitted in triumph, or if James had announced other, more drastic plans for dealing with them, he might have been persuaded to join the plotters. But their acquittal had removed the last incentive to action for this supremely cautious politician. William at once gave orders that he should be told nothing about the expedition.

The birth of the Prince of Wales had brought to an instant crisis the plans and preparations of the men in London who were secretly plotting James's overthrow. The faithful Sidney, together with Shrewsbury, Lumley and William's agent Johnston, had all worn themselves out discreetly canvassing opinions, collecting information, and sounding out possible signatories for the vital letter.

But the actual situation, as it was reported to William from week to week, and on the basis of which he would have to make his final plans, was far from clear-cut.

The burning question was whether the royal baby was legitimate or not. To William, who had seen Johnston's reports over the months of her pregnancy, there could be no question that Mary Beatrice had indeed been pregnant, and had therefore given birth to a child. But Johnston's first reports in the week after the birth raised more questions than they resolved. If James and Mary Beatrice had in fact wanted to convince their subjects that the birth was a fraud, they could hardly have set about it more efficiently, as Johnston pointed out: 'The generality of people conclude all is a trick; because, say they, the reckoning is changed, the Princess sent away, none of the Clarendon family nor the Dutch Ambassador sent for, the suddenness of the thing, the time of Sermon, the confidence of the Priests, the hurry &c . . .' The convincing argument in favour of the baby's legitimacy, indeed, was that he had been dangerously ill and was still poorly – just what might have been expected of Mary Beatrice's baby, on past form. And even this didn't convince everybody: 'a trick too, to make people believe it is the K and Qs'.

Johnston's sister, Mrs Bailey, was a friend and confidante of the queen's Woman of the Bedchamber, Margaret Dawson: as one of the few Protestants present, she was a key witness. But Mrs Dawson was also solidly loyal to the queen, and even if she had her suspicions, was very reluctant to commit herself one way or the other. She was adamant on one fact: that the queen had given birth to a baby, in her bedroom, in front of a crowd of witnesses. When pressed, she insisted that even if there had been any trickery, Mary Beatrice was certainly not a party to it: '... the Queen would not be brought to consent to any such thing, having ... told in great confidence, that if ever she did any such thing, which she was resolved never to think on, she was sure she ... should never have a quiet moment in her own mind ...'

Johnston's own theory was that a substitute child had been ready in the next room, in case the queen's baby was either a daughter or – as had been widely predicted – stillborn; that when the newborn baby failed at first to cry – on which point everyone agreed – the midwife, who was also in the plot, assumed it was dead, and rushed it into the next room, swaddled up so that nobody could see it; that it was then found to be alive after all, and so they kept it.

William's friends in Whitehall urged him not to commit himself publicly one way or the other as yet by sending to congratulate James and Mary Beatrice: Sidney wrote specially on 18 June instructing him to wait.

But William decided otherwise. His most burning need at this moment was for reliable, first-hand information about affairs in England, and what exactly he could expect in the way of support. The posts to Holland were being carefully searched, the ports were watched, and the strain was telling on the faithful Sidney: he had been out of action for days with a fever and racking headaches.

The birth of Mary Beatrice's son offered William a chance which he coolly exploited. Once more his handsome, half-English cousin Count Zuylestein was despatched on a personal mission to James, this time bearing letters of congratulation from William and Mary.

Incredibly, the count was allowed to remain in England for over a month, coordinating planning, assessing the political situation, and studying James's own military and naval preparations. The king actually took him to see the army in its summer camp at Hounslow – 'When Mr Zulisten goes back he will give you an account of them,' he wrote to William. He would have been stunned to hear the Dutchman's report on the Association of Protestant Officers, newly formed about this time at Hounslow, among the crack cavalry and footguards regiments stationed in or near London. Its leaders had been approached by Sidney months earlier, and they included three of James's most brilliant officers: John Churchill, Colonel Charles Trelawney – brother of the Bishop of Bristol, one of the Seven – and the hard-bitten veteran, Percy Kirke. The three were friends who had campaigned together in Tangier, and in the Franco-Dutch war of 1672–6. They were also founder-members of the defiantly-named Treason Club, which met from time to time at the Rose Tavern in Covent Garden. And among the younger members who were eager recruits of the Association was

Thomas Langston, Lieutenant-Colonel of Princess Anne's Regiment of Cavalry.

James had only himself to thank for the treachery of these officers. As long as he was king, their career prospects were dismal, except as mercenaries in a foreign army. The previous winter, James had seriously contemplated requiring all his serving soldiers to sign an Address to him concurring in the abolition of the Test Acts and Penal Laws – a move which sent several of his best officers straight to Sidney, to find out what the Prince of Orange had in mind. And through the spring and summer there had been rumours that they might be replaced by reliable Irish papists, or even Frenchmen.

By the time Zuylestein returned to Holland, these officers had already concerted detailed plans with Sidney, and Churchill sent William a written assurance of support: 'Mr Sidney will let you know how I intend to behave myself; I think it is what I owe to God and my country.'

The army conspirators had also made contact with disaffected officers in the navy, among them Churchill's younger brother, and Captains George Byng and Matthew Aylmer – and James gave an added spur to disloyalty when he appointed as admiral Sir Roger Strickland, a Roman Catholic, who was unwise enough to have mass publicly celebrated on board the flagship. (James had to go down in person to quell the mutiny that resulted.)

William was also, of course, in touch with the bishops – 'he was much concerned in their behalf,' he had told them through Compton. And the soldier-bishop wrote back at the end of July that 'both they that suffered, and the rest who concurred with them, are so well satisfied of the justness of their cause, that they will lay down their lives, before they will in the least depart from it.'

There are, for obvious reasons, no written records of the secret meetings at which England's future was settled. But according to strong oral tradition, a favourite rendezvous was Lady Place at Hurley, near Maidenhead. This beautiful Elizabethan mansion, built on the site of a pre-Reformation monastery, was the home of one of William's most ardent followers – John Lord Lovelace. Immensely wealthy, ultra-Whig and an addict of high life and the gaming tables, Lovelace had several times been arrested for political offences: he had recently been called before the Privy Council when he refused to acknowledge the validity of a warrant signed by a Roman Catholic justice of the peace. Well outside London, but within easy travelling distance, Hurley was well-sited for such plottings – and some years later, Lovelace pointed out to William the echoing vault underneath the house's splendidly ornate saloon, in which the conspirators had gathered.

Reports from William's intelligence agent in Scotland, William Carstares, were also encouraging: '. . . the body of the Nobility, Gentry and Commons of the South and West parts of Scotland is zealous for the interest of the Protestant succession . . .' he wrote. The birth of the prince had been received with scepticism, and orders to light bonfires in celebration were widely ignored – several servant-maids had actually refused to carry wood to make the bonfires. 'There was no reason for such joy,' they told their masters tartly.

As the long summer wore on, the conspirators' sense of urgency grew, together with their confidence. 'You never had more friends in England than now,' reported Shrewsbury. Johnston had earlier talked to two leading Whigs, Richard Hampden and Sir Thomas Lee. Both had stressed the need for immediate action. 'After three months it will be in vain to expect any opportunity at all,' had been Hampden's verdict. 'The Nation shall have acquiesced to the Young Prince's Right; a Parliament forced, a Regency established, the Revenue augmented, the Army and Fleet modelled and encreased, and the Spirit of the Nation is like a tyde, which must have an Ebb.' Hampden voiced another objection to an over-long delay – which haunted William as much as any of the conspirators: 'he does not think that the advantage of consulting long here is sufficient to balance the danger of discovery.' Lee had been just as emphatic: 'He said the King in two years' time would have done his business; and he was confident that the Prince had only this summer for it.'

Against these, a few weeks later, the prince could weigh the verdicts of Halifax and Nottingham, whose opinions he had asked: 'I still remain persuaded that there is no effectual progress towards the great design . . .' was Halifax's predictable reply. Nottingham was just as damping: 'I cannot apprehend . . . such ill consequences to our religion, or the just interests of your Highness, that a little time will not effectually remedy, nor can I imagine that the Papists are likely to make any further considerable progress . . .'

But by this time William's plans were far advanced. And all his reports from Whitehall were convincing him that his decision had been the right one.

The birth of the Prince of Wales had filled James with happy confidence again, echoed by the more extreme of his Catholic advisers. 'The Priests are mighty indiscreet, asking people what will become of their Religion now.' Sunderland, more realistic, had been urging James to soft-pedal for some weeks now. He had been opposed to bringing the bishops to trial, suggesting that the birth of the Prince of Wales might be a happy occasion for a royal pardon. James rejected this advice and, in a dramatic bid to recover his waning influence, Sunderland finally turned Catholic at the end of June. He 'went to the Chappel door, and knock'd, with a Candle in his hand; – One within asking his business, he answered, that he came to join with the true Church and to confess his Sins, and be absolved . . .' James and Mary Beatrice were impressed and touched by his newfound faith, but nobody else was, and for once Catholics and Protestants could agree: '. . . all parties do him the Justice to own that he has not changed upon a principle of Religion.'

But it was becoming increasingly difficult to reason with the exalted James. And even the conversion of his first minister could not win James round to more moderate policies. At a Privy Council meeting on 6 July, Sunderland urged James to abandon the idea of getting the Test Acts repealed, accept that Catholics must for the time being continue to be excluded from public life, and settle for more modest advances, together with the repeal of the Penal Laws. No concessions, replied James firmly, adding, as usual: Look what happened to Charles I. Nor was Mary Beatrice ready to be persuaded; she was now firmly under the influence of the hotheaded Scottish convert, the Earl of Melfort.

Instead, the campaign to pack Parliament which had been quietly making progress all summer was stepped up; thirty-two new charters were issued, royal agents were sent out all over the country on a propaganda mission, and a first list of over a hundred royal candidates was approved.

Back in Whitehall, meanwhile, James was happily planning a colossal fireworks display in honour of the new Catholic Prince of Wales. Since Easter, it was reported, 300 men had toiled on this expensive thanksgiving, and the two diarists John Evelyn and Samuel Pepys were among the thousands of spectators watching as £25,000-worth of fireworks went up in smoke.

According to a contemporary reporter, it was a most elaborate affair, devised by Sir Martin Backman, the king's engineer at the Tower. Before the palace at Whitehall, several large lighters were moored on the Thames, covered with scaffolding on which were erected 'many different figures'. Pyramids, 'wreathed with Fireworks from bottom to the top, and at the Main-top Pennants with the Arms of England'; a Bacchus 'bigger than life . . . astride on a large Tun; the figure of a Woman . . . representing Plenty and Peace . . . wrought all in fireworks, wreaths Cornucopia's &c'. 'There were thousands of Rockets flying up in the Ayre a prodigious height', and 'other Combustible Compositions'. The show began at nine at night with a bursting sun, 'the Imperial Crown, the Cypher of the King and Queen's Names', and it lasted an hour, with the great guns of the Tower crashing out as it ended.

James's ambassadors abroad were also encouraged to celebrate the happy occasion in lavish style. Sir Bevil Skelton sent in a bill from his embassy in Paris for £917 2s. spent on 'public rejoicing . . .' The English agent in Rome, Sir John Lytcott, sent in a more modest bill. For a mere £450 he had hung his own palace with red damask, had the entire neighbourhood lit by torches and feasted crowds at the Trinitā dei Monti on a huge roast ox and a fountain spouting wine.

The most impressive celebrations were those laid on at Rome by the English cardinal, Thomas Howard of Norfolk. He assembled no fewer than eighteen cardinals to sing a *Te Deum* in the Church of St Thomas, while the Romans were feasted in the piazza before his palace. A reporter of the celebrations was almost lost for words to describe the splendours: '. . . a great fountain of most noble architecture, painted like marble . . . covered with gold at the corners and edges, on the top thereof the arms of his Majesty of Great Britain' poured out wine non-stop for three days and three nights, 'for the benefit of the public'. On a mound of earth, they roasted a whole ox, turned on its giant spit by six of the cardinal's footmen. It was stuffed with 'young pigs and several sorts of fowls that, from diverse part of the ox seemed, though dead, as if they would fly . . .' and the crowds fought and jostled for a share. The cardinal's palace itself blazed with lights, and was decorated with portraits of the king, the queen and the new Prince of Wales, dominated by one of Pope Innocent XI.

At The Hague, d'Albeville found much less enthusiasm among the Dutch. They looked on laughing when part of the huge triumphal arch erected in front of his house collapsed, sending the royal baby crashing into the street, still seated on its globe and clutching a sceptre and olive branch. The party given by the English consul at Amsterdam, Mr Pettit, fared worse still: it was raided by a furious mob, attracted by the bonfire, and his guests had to run for their lives.

At the Orange Court, there were no celebrations at all. William and Mary had received the news of the birth of the little prince on 12 June. Against the advice of her chaplain, Dr Stanley, Mary at once ordered prayers to be said in her chapel for her half-brother, and both she and William wrote personal letters of congratulation to James and Mary Beatrice for the Prince's cousin Zuylestein to take to London. These gestures were not appreciated by William's supporters in England, and in their letter of invitation, the seven signatories reproached him that his 'compliment upon the birth of the child (which not one in a thousand here believes to be the Queen's) hath done you some injury'. The myth of the warming-pan baby was already essential to the case for revolution: 'the false imposing' of the child, they told him, was 'one of the chief causes upon which the declaration of your entering the kingdom in a hostile manner must be founded'.

Their insistence on this point put the prince in a dilemma. Years later, Ailesbury learned from a most reliable source that he never doubted the child's legitimacy, but as Johnston's reports told him, 'be it a true child or not, the people will never believe it.' However reluctantly, 'out of policy he was obliged to give way to the current of those times,' and prayers in the chapel were stopped.

It seems unlikely that Mary knew of Johnston's account. And from William's point of view, the stronger her suspicions were the better, since her backing for the expedition was essential to his plans. But Mary's doubts were being fanned by letters from Anne, which, as she says in her *Memoires*, made it 'impossible not to have strong suspicions, which upset me very much'. She was eager to know more about the circumstances surrounding the birth, but the next letter from Anne, written on 9 July, brought news instead that the Prince of Wales's life was at risk. 'If he had been as bad as some people say,' wrote Anne, 'I believe it will not be long before he is an Angel in heaven.'

Anxieties for the health of the baby had begun soon after his birth, when the zealous royal physicians had dosed him with one of their powerful concoctions, and then 'by mistake or carelessness, they repeated the dose, which made him so ill, that everyone thought he was dying.' By Monday afternoon he was wheezing alarmingly, and at eleven at night, according to Johnston, 'it grew ill, and was better and worse till 3 when it was for some time dead black and blue. The King fell down on his knees and cried all night.' The resilient baby survived, but another experiment by the doctors again almost killed him. Convinced that so many of the queen's babies had died in convulsions because they had been wet-nursed, the doctors prescribed a regime of boiled milk and breadcrumbs. To this they added, as the papal nuncio reported, a 'water gruell ... composed of barley flour, water and sugar, to which a few currants are sometimes added'. On this unsuitable diet, the baby prince was seriously ill with diarrhoea which lasted several days. Mary Beatrice who, according to Hofmann, '*pleurait abondamment*', had always argued that the child should be breast-fed and finally won the battle. Frances Smith, a brickmaker's wife, was found 'near the house whose milk was just the age of the Prince ... that night the child took the breast', and there were no further alarms.

Meanwhile, d'Albeville had made a strong protest about the public display of indifference at the Orange Court. Nobody had been present at his celebrations and, worse still, no prayers were being said. Mary managed to extricate herself with an evasive answer to the agitated ambassador, but she was firmly convinced that something was wrong, and it was only with great reluctance that in early August she agreed, at the prince's insistence, to have prayers started again. 'All people here wonder why you pray no more for ye Prince of Wales,' Johnston had warned from London on 3 August. 'Mr Kemp [their code name for the king] sais you act as if you had believed him to be the Queens son at first, and now doubt of it. Wise people here . . . say that if you were to come over, as foolish talkes go, this is to give the allarm; and if you are not to come over, *c'est montrer les dents sans mordre*. Before the news of this all was calm . . .'

Once more, prayers for the Prince of Wales were said in Mary's chapel, but this in turn produced an outcry among Wiliam's English supporters at The Hague. 'Dr Burnett, the Rebels, and all the discontented men are mad, for that the Prince of Wales is pray'd for againe,' James learnt from d'Albeville. A distracted William finally ordered a compromise which he hoped would keep everybody happy. In the princess's chapel prayers were henceforth said for 'the King, Queen, Mary, Queen Dowager Catherine, the Prince and her Royal Highness'. Nobody was fooled: 'This was always the form of the prayer before, meaning the Prince of Orange,' explained d'Albeville; 'now they may say they mean the Prince of Wales, but here in these countreys, and especially at Court, when they say the Prince, they mean the Prince of Orange.'

'I have to admit that that was very much contrary to my feelings, to be guilty of such double-dealing with God,' Mary wrote in her private journal. She still found it hard to believe that her father 'could be guilty of so horrible a crime', and in her anguish of mind, she turned to her sister in London, asking her to do some detective work.

Anne had made plans to go to Tunbridge Wells in mid-July, 'tired of putting on a face of joy when one's heart has more cause to ache; and the Papists are all so very insolent that it is insupportable living with them'. But before she left, she received a lengthy questionnaire from Mary. Very much annoyed that her sister had not been on the spot to provide the clinching evidence, Mary now wanted detailed answers to eighteen questions. Among other things, she wanted to know: 'Did any woman, besides the confidents, see the Queen's face when she was in labour? . . . If no woman was called in to hold the Queen? . . . How long did the labour last? . . . Is the Queen fond of it?'

Much upset by her sister's anger, Anne lost no time in summoning one witness she felt could be relied upon to be both forthcoming and discreet – the Protestant Margaret Dawson, already a useful source of information to Johnston – and made ready to cross-examine her. The conversation that followed was disconcerting. Anne began, as Mrs Dawson later remembered, by saying that she had heard 'strange reports concerning the birth of her brother the Prince of Wales'. She now wanted to know 'all the circumstances of it'. 'Madam, do you doubt it?' asked Mrs Dawson in astonishment. Anne, 'putting her hands together and lifting them up', hastily replied, 'Not in the least.' Bristling with loyal indignation, Mrs Dawson told her every detail of the queen's confinement: the labour had started at eight; the king had summoned the Privy Council, who arrived well before the birth; only the queen's ladies were called; it was the longest labour she had ever had; and immediately after the child was born, the king had made a point of asking his Council to follow him into the next room and see it for themselves.

Unasked, Mrs Dawson volunteered other information. It was said that all the Catholics were certain it would be a boy, but the queen herself had not cared one way or the other: 'She would compound for a little girl with all her heart,' she had often told her ladies. And Margaret Dawson wound up her testimony with a warm tribute to her mistress: '. . . of a most gentle milde temper and soe good to her women servants, that it is inexpressible.'

It was not in the least what Anne wanted to hear, and she gave a very selective account of what she had learned in her long letter to Mary the following day. She never mentioned Mrs Dawson's assurance that, in contrast to what she herself had reported, the Queen had 'exposed her great belly every day to all the ladys that had the privillidge of the dressing Room (which was a great number) . . .' Nor did she report that Mrs Dawson also denied statements that the Protestant servants had not been allowed near the queen, as she herself had waited on her every day, apart from two when she was off sick.

Making the best of what she now knew to be a very weak case, Anne could only add that she herself had never heard of anybody feeling the child stir before birth, not even Mrs Dawson, and that she had seen no sign of milk on the queen's smock. To the question whether the queen loved her child, Anne could quote one incident: 'I dined there the other day, when it was said it had been very ill of a looseness . . . yet when she came from prayers she went to dinner without seeing it . . .' Lamely, Anne concluded: 'One doesn't know what to think, for methinks it is wonderful if it is no cheat, that they never took no pains to convince me of it.'

The answers were unsatisfactory, but together with other reports Mary received from England, and Zuylestein's account of general suspicions, they were enough to convince her that the wicked papists had talked her father into this hideous crime. But it was still painful to read her father's reproaches, and in answer to one of his letters on 17 August, asking about prayers for the prince, she skirted around the truth: 'M. d'Albeville can assure you I never told him it was forbid, so that they wear only conjecture made upon its being sometimes neglected . . .' Switching abruptly to a more neutral subject, she concluded: 'this excessive hot weather continues longer than I ever knew it . . . I shall still be your Majesty's most obedient daughter . . .'

EIGHT

MARY'S DILEMMA

'The first moment that I have taken a pen in my hand since I was brought to bed is this, to write to my dear Lemon . . .'

It was cruelly difficult for Mary to respond to this charming little note that her stepmother wrote to her on 6 July, and to keep up a show of their once-close and affectionate relationship. Another letter, a week later, showed that the queen was still ignorant of Mary's dreadful suspicions: 'I did not hope two months ago to have had all well by this time . . .'

But at the end of July, hurt and astonished by the chilly little notes she received in reply, she reproached Mary for the first time: '. . . since I have been brought to bed, you have never once in your Letters to me taken the least notice of my son, no more than if he had never been born.'

Even then the truth did not dawn on her. Unable to imagine that her favourite stepdaughter might have joined the unbelievers, she was driven to conclude that Mary was jealous of this child who had displaced her as heir to the throne. 'By the way you speak of my son, and the formal name you call him by, I am further confirmed in the thoughts I had before that you have for him the last indifference . . .' James had had the same impression. 'The King has often told me, with a great deal of trouble, that as often as he had mentioned his son in his letters to you, you never once answered any thing concerning him.'

At the top of this letter, Mary scribbled a note: 'Answered, that all the King's children shall ever find as much affection and kindness from me as can be expected from children of the same Father.' This coldly evasive answer ought to have been a warning to her stepmother. Mary knew by now that within the next few weeks her husband would be landing in England at the head of a mighty army.

William's acceptance of the invitation from England had been a severe shock to his wife. 'I found it almost unbearable to think of the enterprise on which the Prince was engaged, although at the same time

I could not think he was wrong to undertake it,' wrote Mary in her *Memoires*. All the reports from England had by now convinced her that her bigoted father – abetted by his Jesuit advisers – was endangering the peace of his country, and threatening the very existence of the Church of England.

It was a terrible division of loyalties for her. She loved both her father and her husband, and the thought of one leading an army against the other was deeply distressing. But weighing heavily in the balance against James was her strong loyalty and sense of personal responsibility towards the Church of England. Bishop Compton could take much of the credit for this – which was, indeed, the chief reason why James hated him so much. As Dean of the Chapel Royal in the mid-1670s, he had appealed to Charles II over James's head to insist on confirming James's daughters, the young Princess Mary and her sister Anne. Ever since, he had taken her under his pastoral wing, and his concern for her religious convictions followed her to The Hague, from where her chaplains sent him regular reports. These made heartening reading. 'I think I may give your Lordship the assurance of her R Highnesse being a very dutiful Daughter (as she may in time be as kind a Mother) of our Church of England,' reported John Covel in August 1685. His successor, William Stanley, was enthusiastic. 'The Princess is extremely constant and regular in her public devotions,' he wrote back to Compton in January 1686.

It was probably Compton's influence, too, that had developed in her a deep dislike of Roman Catholicism, which surprised the more tolerant Burnet by its intensity: she was 'much animated against popery'. Ever since he was appointed Bishop of London in the reign of Charles II, Compton had been a zealous foe of Catholics: he had urged that they should be banished from Court, secured the suppression of papist literature, encouraged the publication of Protestant propaganda, and himself translated two of the most offensive pieces of anti-Catholic literature into English and had them printed. At regular conferences for his clergy, he encouraged them to preach against Catholic beliefs such as the intercession of the saints. And he had denounced the Florentine resident and the Portuguese ambassador to the Privy Council for abusing diplomatic privilege by allowing London Catholics to attend mass in their chapels.

Guided by Compton's example, Mary began to take her role as future patron of the Church of England more and more seriously. When the bishop was suspended by James in 1686, she followed the proceedings of the commission with great concern, and often asked for news. She even went so far as to write to James herself, Compton was gratified to learn from Stanley, 'making as far as she can your cause her own'.

As the months went by and the threat to the Church of England became more obvious, her concern grew. 'The Princess is pleased often to send for me to inform her of the affairs of England ... both in church & state,' Stanley told Compton in the spring of 1687. When the Magdalen Fellows were turned out of their college after James's visit to Oxford and left destitute, Mary boldly and publicly contributed £200 to the fund set up for their relief – although James had made it known that he would consider such almsgiving tantamount to treason.

And at about this time, she wrote a very direct note to Sancroft which practically invited him to declare his opposition to her father. 'Dr Stanly can assure you that I take more interest in what concerns the Church of England than myself, and that one of the greatest satisfactions I can have, is to hear how that all the clergy show themselves as firm to their religion, as they have always been to their King ...' Sancroft drafted an eloquent reply, but on reflection decided not to send it. (A year later he told Stanley he was glad he hadn't – 'if I had written to her, they would have said that I had sent to invite them over.')

Sharing the most extreme views of the day on the perfidy of Roman Catholics, it was natural for Mary to believe that her father had fallen wholly under the spell of the Jesuits with whom he had surrounded himself. At Easter 1687 James had actually exchanged his usual confessor, a discreet Capuchin, for the Jesuit Father Warner, former rector of the Society's French college at St Omer. And Mary certainly saw the copy Dijkvelt brought back to The Hague, of a letter supposedly written by the Jesuits at Liège to those of Fribourg. It related how James had become an affiliate of the Society, had shown an infinite joy on this occasion, had promised to make the interests of his adopted Society as dear to him as his own and counted on them for missionaries to convert his kingdom. The letter went on to report a most suggestive conversation. When a zealous Catholic lamented that both heirs to the throne were heretics, James had exclaimed piously: 'God knows well how to raise up an heir exempt from heresy.' Dijkvelt confronted him with a copy of the letter – he read it, hung on to it and never mentioned it again.

The steady barrage of Protestant propaganda against her father's integrity and sense of honour finally wore Mary down. D'Albeville told James in April 1688: 'I find that notwithstanding those great assurances you Matie has been pleas'd to give their R.H^{ss} of the succession in the true line, yett the Prince, measuring your Maties conscience by his own, has possess'd her R.H^{ss} that there is no relying on it, and that the Jesuits and priests will at long running prevaile with you, to act against your Maties present assurances . . .'

Were there any lengths to which this infatuated convert would not go? Mary was among those who doubted it. And in the circumstances, William's expedition took on in her eyes the aspect of a holy crusade, deeply painful to her but unavoidable. 'There is no other way to save the Church and the State than that my husband should go to dethrone [my father] by force . . .' An unshakeable faith that William was doing the right thing kept her going. 'This is the thought that sustains me, but I can only speak of it all freely to the Prince, who has seen my tears and pities me.'

Unlike Mary, William had no time to sit at home and brood. Dealing with suspicious Dutch politicians and burghers, haggling over terms and troops with petty German princelings and coping with the logistics of transporting an army of 15,000 men from Holland to England at a doubtful season of the year – all these things kept him in a fever of activity throughout the summer and early autumn. Without the indefatigable Bentinck at his right hand – loyal, resourceful, a brilliant diplomat – he might have been tempted more than once to give up.

William's worst nightmare was of a French onslaught against the defenceless Republic while he was crossing the North Sea with most of Holland's troops. For months now, with Bentinck's help, he had been steadily working to draw the German princes into the anti-French coalition he was building, and secure enough allies for the Dutch to deter Louis from an attack. Much the most important and powerful of these was the young Frederick, Elector of Brandenburg, who had succeeded to the title when his father, the crusty old pro-French Frederick William of Brandenburg, died in 1686. Frederick was not only heir to William's huge estates and personal fortune, but was also an admirer of the prince. William had courted him, lavishly entertained him and his wife at The Hague, and finally won him round. At Minden in September Frederick undertook to secure Holland's defences on her Rhine frontier, as well as furnishing troops for the expedition. When the two men parted Frederick said frankly that he longed to see William on the throne of England, for the good of all Protestant Europe.

Other princes, electors, dukes and ministers had hesitated. It was Louis who made up their minds for them. In June, a week before the birth of the Prince of Wales, the Archbishop-Elector of Cologne died and the French king pushed forward his candidate: Cardinal Wilhelm von Furstenberg, Bishop of Strasburg. On 10 June d'Avaux formally

warned the States-General not to intervene against the election of his
candidate. On 19 July the Bishop of Strasburg was duly elected –
though without the necessary two-thirds majority – and he took his
seat without waiting for the approval of the pope. French interest was
now solidly established in this key town on the Rhine.

The reaction was immediate. The emperor and the Elector of
Brandenburg, who had put forward their own candidate for the coveted
seat, Josef Clemens of Bavaria, were alarmed by Louis's tactics, and
promised William their support. Saxony, Hanover, Zell and Hesse-
Cassell soon followed suit and, after William's meeting with the Elector
Frederick III of Brandenburg at the beginning of September, d'Avaux
reported to Versailles: 'The Elector of Brandenburg will furnish 12,000
men; . . . the Elector of Saxony 6,000, the Dukes of Zell and Wolfen-
buttel 4,000, Hesse–Cassel 3,000 . . . The Prince had paid out money
for these troops, and engaged them for a stated length of time.'

D'Avaux was immediately asked to question the Prince of Orange
about these warlike preparations. 'The King his Master, who up to
now had no greater concern than to maintain the tranquillity and
peace of Christendom was surprised to learn that I had raised such a
considerable army,' William wrote drily to one of his allies, Frederick
Carl, Duke of Württemburg. The prince had affected surprise that the
envoy should be in the least interested. He failed to understand, he told
d'Avaux, why the King of France should be so alarmed by 'this small
levy which consisted of no more than 6 or 700 horse'.

Another important and perhaps even trickier task was to convince
the cautious Dutch that the expedition against England was indispensable if they were to protect themselves against French aggression.
The Dutch had always been suspicious of their stadholder's close ties
with neighbouring England, against whom they had fought three wars
within living memory, and with whom they had had endless conflicts
over matters ranging from North Sea fishing-rights to trading and
settlement claims in the Spice Islands and the East Indies. William's
own Stuart mother, the sister of Charles and James, had been intensely
unpopular, and when the prince married another Stuart princess, they
feared the worst. Mary soon conquered the stolid Dutch with her
charm and easy grace, but the old misgivings about her family and the
English still lingered.

Moreover, the Regents of Amsterdam were merchants first and last,
and hence strongly averse to war. The relationship between the Dutch
capital and the Orange family had never been easy, and for much of
the time their interests were in opposition. The Orange family thought
the Amsterdammers obsessed by their commercial concerns, while these

proud regents in turn were inclined to think that the Orange family was motivated solely by personal ambition.

According to European convention, William, as Prince of Orange, was entitled to use the Dutch army and navy for personal reasons without committing the Republic to war. But he was obliged first to ask the States-General for their permission. And since any discussion of the subject was bound to leak out, he decided to defer asking this until the last possible moment, to avoid prejudicing his chances. The earliest preparations – which began before the end of 1687, when the news of England became increasingly disturbing – were thus made in the greatest secrecy.

After consultation with Grand-Pensionary Caspar Fagel, the Prince invited the three Burgomasters of Amsterdam, Joannes Hudde, Kornelis Geelvink and Nicolaas Witsen, together with the Secretary of the Admiralty of Amsterdam, to a conference at The Hague. There was certainly no discussion of an invasion of England, but the prince only had to mention France to convince the Amsterdammers that action was needed. Quite apart from Louis's threatened aggression at the Dutch borders, the French king had struck at the Republic in the interest closest to its heart: commerce.

A trade war had started that autumn when Louis gave orders to stop the import into France of Dutch herrings. In vain did d'Avaux point out to Versailles that 60,000 Dutchmen depended on the herring industry for a living: an unperturbed Louis went on to prohibit the import of linen and woollen cloth.

The Dutch retaliated by banning imports of French wines, brandy and sugar. But the three Burgomasters and the admiralty secretary knew that stronger measures were needed to safeguard Dutch trading interests. They broke with tradition by summoning representatives of all the Dutch admiralties to The Hague, where the prince invited them to consider what steps should be taken 'to protect trade and seafaring' in the year ahead.

Any measures decided would not need rubber-stamping by the States-General, since the prince, as Admiral-General of the Navy, had the right to decide on the strength of the fleet, in consultation with the admiralties. Even more fortunately, money was not an immediate problem. Thanks to a statute passed earlier in the year, with the stadholder's active support, the admiralties were now authorized to raise the duties on imports and exports. It was thus possible for plans to augment the Dutch navy to be agreed and put in hand in such secrecy that even state papers made hardly any mention of the fact.

A grim and freezing winter held up work in the dockyards, and

although the admirals decided in March 1688 to take all the Dutch
men-of-war – a total of forty-three ships – out of mothballs, it was May
before the whole fleet was ready. By that time the Prince had received
permission to engage 9,000 seamen for a naval force so equipped that
the men could also be used ashore.

So far, it had been straightforward. But once William received a
definite invitation from England, he was immediately faced with another problem: how to talk the Burgomasters of Amsterdam, and
Admiralty-Secretary de Wildt, into agreeing the invasion. After discussions with Fagel, the prince decided that they must be informed of
his real intentions. Events in England, he told them, compelled him to
intervene. The Amsterdammers, Witsen in particular, immediately
objected and began making difficulties. Even with the help of his ablest
diplomat, Dijkvelt, Witsen could not be persuaded to cooperate. And
the headaches this 'grosse ville' gave him became a recurring theme of
the prince's letters to Bentinck: 'I'm desperately afraid of the timidity
of some of the Amsterdam people and the ill-will of others . . . the way
the burgomasters spoke to M. Dijkvelt fills me with dread: if everything
isn't ready soon, all is lost . . .'

At that time Witsen, his colleagues and Fagel were still the only men
who knew of William's plans for a descent on England. The vast
majority of the Dutch were still convinced that the feverish preparations
going on in their country's dockyards were intended for a new war
with France. And to foreign observers like the Polish envoy Moreau,
William's notorious resentment of his high-handed treatment by
France made this highly probable: '. . . the Prince of Orange is the
most ardent and passionate of them all . . . to take his revenge for the
ill-treatment he claims to have suffered at the hands of France . . .'

William did nothing to correct this impression. The trade war
which had started in the autumn of 1687 was by this time beginning to
bite, with Dutch–French trade only 25 per cent of what it had been a
year earlier – lower even than it had been during the 1672 war. And in
the United Provinces, anti-French feeling was running higher than at
any time since the Revocation of the Edict of Nantes.

The French king – always 'helpful' to William – that summer
provided him with an even better pretext for stepping up Dutch
military preparations. It was the work of Bevil Skelton, former British
Ambassador to The Hague, and now James's unfortunate choice of
envoy to Paris. He suggested to Louis XIV that since the warlike
activities of the Dutch were clearly designed against France's ally England, it might help matters if the French made it clear that they would
not stand idly by and watch.

Louis was pleased by this idea for reasons of his own, and on 29 August d'Avaux formally presented a Memorial from his master to the startled States-General. If an attack was made on England, he warned them in the most solemn terms, the French would regard it as an act of aggression directed against themselves. To the startled Dutch, it now seemed obvious that James's expansion of the English fleet and the massive French build-up of troops were directed against their country: it was going to be 1672 all over again. William was thus provided with exactly the justification he needed for his next move.

The admiralties' incomes from the increased duties had still not been enough to cover the high cost of equipping the army and navy; the cost of fitting out the navy alone came to Dfl. 2,288,464. In order to raise extra money, William resorted to a stratagem. He warned the states that the Dutch defences on the Rhine and in the IJssel region were so dilapidated as to be almost useless, and asked for an immediate loan of five tons of gold, valued at four million guilders, for their repair.

The states approved the loan and, with the help of some wealthy French Huguenots, as Moreau reported, the money was raised within fifteen days. What Moreau did not know was that William had summoned Witsen to The Hague again, told him that delay could only strengthen James's position, and that the money was just sufficient to cover the cost of the expedition he intended to lead.

Witsen still hesitated to commit himself to these plans, but in the end the prince succeeded in extracting a half-hearted and heavily conditional promise of support from the burgomaster. 'Though they would not advise the Prince to the enterprise, they would, if it were undertaken without their participation, endeavour to obtain for him such support as might be consistent with their duty.'

It was not from any conviction that William was justified in his claims, or out of personal regard for the prince that Witsen was prepared to go even this far. He continued to regard the entire enterprise as yet another Orange bid for family aggrandizement. And when the prince tried to make clear to him that he personally expected nothing but labour at the end of the day, Witsen told him with typical Dutch bluntness that he did not believe him: 'considering the proximity of the Princess to the crown, he thought some richer reward than labour might be in store for him.'

But his guarded approval was enough to allow William to press on with his preparations, in an atmosphere increasingly darkened by the threat of war: '. . . it will take very little to set ablaze in all Europe a cruel and bloody war,' wrote Moreau to Warsaw at this time.

Moreau's reports were filled with details of the army manoeuvres near Nijmegen: 'troops of 20,000 Infantry with all the Horses and Dragoons'. But while the soldiers were paraded in the east of the Netherlands, a huge fleet of warships and transports – 'more than 60 vessels' – was also being assembled in Dutch ports. And later that summer Moreau reported a growing belief that the Dutch preparations were intended not against France but against England.

'Soon there will appear a manifest under the name of Madame the Princess of Orange in which she shall try to prove that she has every right to watch over matters of religion in England.' According to Moreau, it was her intention to form a council 'which would ensure that the infant Prince of Wales was brought up as a Protestant.'

Three weeks later, at the end of September, it was common knowledge: 'The Dutch people make no bones of saying that [the fleet] is aimed for England.'

NINE

THE HAWKS OF VERSAILLES

In the tense, jittery summer of 1688, European politics became a grand guessing game. The doubtful election of Louis' protégé, Wilhelm of Fürstenberg, as the new archbishop-elector of Cologne had plunged Europe into war-fever, since it not only infuriated the emperor, who had put his own candidate forward, but also the pope.

If Innocent XI refused to ratify his election, Louis had grimly warned, he could not answer for the peace of Europe. To emphasize this threat, most of the French fleet had already been shifted round into the Mediterranean.

Pope Innocent XI was an ex-soldier, tough and authoritarian, not at all the man to be impressed by this sabre-rattling – certainly not by Louis XIV, who was bent on asserting his own authority over the Church in France at the expense of papal supremacy. Moreover, the pope was still seething with resentment at the outrageous behaviour of Louis' ambassador to Rome some months earlier. The French envoy had entered Rome at the head of a large troop of armed men, to assert a right that every other ambassador had willingly renounced, the right to shelter fugitives from Roman justice in the embassy 'quarter'. He was publicly excommunicated by the pope, to whom the Most Christian King was beginning to seem almost another Henry VIII, ready to take his country out of the true fold.

It was thus highly unlikely that Innocent would ratify the election of Wilhelm of Fürstenberg to oblige Louis XIV. But if, as seemed likely, he opted instead for Leopold's candidate, Josef Clemens of Bavaria, how would Louis react?

Since the French had been stepping up their military preparations all summer, it was obvious that their armies would soon be on the move. But where? And against whom? The United Provinces? The Rhineland princelings who challenged Louis's mid-Europe supremacy? The Austrian Empire? Would the Turks be able to hold out in Belgrade, where they were now being besieged by a Christian army under Leopold's son-in-law Max Emmanuel? If Belgrade fell, would the Turks make peace with the Emperor? And if they did, what would Leopold's next move be? Considerations like these were to the forefront as William made his plans.

James's England was another riddle which gave diplomats head-aches. After the affair of the bishops and the rumours of a bogus royal baby, was civil war a genuine threat? Would James really call a Par-liament, as he still planned? And if so, would he get the pliable, acquiescent House he imagined, full of grateful Dissenters, and prepared to vote away the Tests and the Penal Laws as its first act? And if it did, how would the English react?

The designs of the United Provinces in general, and William of Orange in particular, were even more of a riddle. It was no secret that the Dutch had been feverishly strengthening their fleet, and raising huge musters of men all summer. But then with the French armies massing on the Rhine, what else was to be expected? And if William's plans were indeed directed against his father-in-law and England, as it was being rumoured, why would he be having endless discussions with the German princes, who, surely, had problems enough of their own?

To James in Whitehall, it seemed wildly unlikely that the Dutch army and navy could be designed for the invasion of England. The most likely scenario, to his mind, was that Louis planned a blow directly at the empire: and the endless consultations between William and the German princes that had been going on since the spring suggested that the Dutch thought so too. French behaviour towards the Dutch had been provoca-tive, to put it mildly, if they were not planning to go to war with them.

With a major war about to engulf central Europe, surely the Dutch would be lunatics if they allowed their stadholder-prince to strip the nation's defences, and remove himself, together with their army and navy, in pursuit of what seemed almost a family affair?

Straight almost to the point of naïveté himself, James found it im-possible to follow the subtle shifts of William's *realpolitik*. He clung to the ingenuous belief that if nothing else deterred his dangerous son-in-law, surely family ties might?

Above all, he could not bring himself to suspect that Mary, too, could be plotting against him. He was reassured by the little notes which still arrived from her regularly – she never missed a single post, although she sidestepped references to her new half-brother. Occasion-ally she fed him snippets of disinformation: the prince had just left for military maneouvres at Minden, she told him. 'The Prince of Orange had too much to alarm him on the banks of the Rhine and the Meuse to bother about the Thames,' James quite naturally concluded.

As for affairs in England, there were moments that summer when

James must have begun to think that success was within his reach. His campaign to produce a docile House of Commons was getting into top gear. As the summer wore on, more charters were recalled, more 'right' candidates approached and secured, more Tory or Anglican justices of the peace sacked and replaced by 'fanatics' who often lacked every other qualification. '. . . Now all honest men and friends to the church are dis-countenanced,' commented Clarendon bitterly at the end of August.

Sunderland had his doubts, but given James's mood, probably felt it politic to join the chorus of optimism. During a grand dinner party that he gave about this time, he declared boldly 'that they were now sure of their game'. It would be an easy matter, he said, to have a House of Commons to their minds, and there was nothing else that could resist them. The elderly Earl of Bradford asked if the Court was equally confident that the House of Lords would give the king their votes: he believed, he said, that they might run into unexpected op-position there. Lord Sunderland turned to Lord Churchill, sitting next to him, and in his shrill voice cried, 'O silly! why, your troop of guards shall be called to the house of lords . . .'

It was beginning to look as if the Whigs who had warned William that time was on James's side might be right. By August, indeed, the national furore over the bishops had died down; the whispering campaign against the Prince of Wales was fast losing its momentum, and the extremist Catholics at Court were cock-a-hoop. And by the last week in August, writs for a new Parliament to meet at the end of November were ordered, to be sent out three weeks later. All Jeffreys hoped for, he told Clarendon, was that 'the King would be moderate when the Parliament met'.

Sunderland made a desperate bid around this time to add Halifax – a powerful voice for sanity – to the king's advisers, 'to have helped me resist the violence of those in power; but he despaired of doing any good and would not engage'.

James might have been more alarmed if he had seen d'Albeville's dispatches from The Hague with their reports of the military and naval build-up in Holland. But months earlier Sunderland had arranged that these came directly to him. Not until the British envoy arrived in London in person on 14 August and had an audience with the king did James learn for the first time how extensive and how far advanced these preparations were. Even then, d'Albeville was allowed to remain in London enjoying a well-earned leave instead of being posted straight back to The Hague. But his reports, together with that curious business of the on-off prayers for the Prince of Wales at the Orange Court, finally prodded James into action.

In response to intensive Dutch naval rearmament that spring, the British naval dockyards had already been unusually busy. In June a squadron of twenty ships under Admiral Strickland had been sent to the Downs – a very reasonable precaution – with orders to cruise in the North Sea and report any suspicious movements of foreign warships. But at the beginning of August Mr Secretary Pepys sent word to Strickland that no greater force would be needed at sea that year. D'Albeville's mid-August revelations were a breath of cold reality – and James reacted with creditable speed. All leave for the navy was stopped, one of the royal yachts was dispatched to Holland to report on the movements of the Dutch fleet and two warships already available were immediately added to Strickland's squadron. At the admiralty, meanwhile, Pepys, acting on the king's personal orders, was doing his utmost to infuse his own sense of urgency into the Navy Board. The crews of Strickland's ships were to be brought up to their wartime complement, six fire-ships were to be prepared, one third-rate and six fourth-rate warships were to be sent to sea, together with six scouting boats, while another seven third-rates were to be rigged and made ready, 'all to be dispatched as for Life & Death'.

Nor were military preparations neglected. On 23 and 24 August all leave was stopped for the army; deputy lieutenants and governors of garrisons were ordered to their posts; and orders were issued that troops and companies should be brought up to full strength. Inland garrisons were stripped of troops so that the coastal defences could be manned. And the Scots Guards marching north from their summer camp at Hounslow were stopped at Hull so that they could reinforce this strategic east coast port.

'We heare that his Majesty is in much forwardness in his navall preparations,' a newsletter reported at the end of August, while another boasted: 'His Majesty had commanded such care to be taken that we shall be in such a condition as not to fear any insult.'

As late as the end of August, the nation was still on full alert. 'The Court was in some trouble and the King out of humour (though he was always of so even a temper that it was hard to discover it) at the news of the Dutch having set out a great fleet as designed against us . . .' Reresby noted, when he took his wife and daughter to Windsor Castle on 25 August. But a day or two later, the sense of urgency was already fading.

It was known at Whitehall by this time that Louis's armies were mobilizing on the lower Rhine. And on 25 August, Bonrepaus arrived at Whitehall from the Court of Versailles, to offer a naval treaty between France and England. He was coolly received. Louis's extraordinary defiance of papal authority – he had actually been ex-communicated – had outraged and alienated the pious James. And both he and Sunderland were by this time almost as suspicious of Louis's good faith as they were of William. Offers by the French king in June to lend James twenty warships – an offer repeated in July – had been turned down as unnecessary. Was it possible that he was attempting to intimidate the Dutch by suggesting the existence of a secret Anglo–French treaty? Was James being set up?

'The sending of Bonrepaus at this nice Juncture, was the most un-friendly Turn that his brother of France cou'd have done him,' declared James irritably to the Spanish ambassador, Ronquillo: 'he wish'd it had been in his Power to send him back the next Day after his Arrival; but since in Decency he cou'd not do that, he would . . . give him but small Encouragement to stay.' James added meaningfully that 'he had much rather entertain a good Correspondence with *Holland*, than be thought to have a strict Alliance with France.'

News of d'Avaux's Memorial to the States-General a few days later confirmed their worst suspicions: in it Louis had referred to 'the bonds of Friendship and Alliance between [himself] and the King of Great Britain'. Sunderland and James were appalled by this *démarche*, which took them completely by surprise. When the States' envoy van Citters expressed Dutch anger at this evidence of close ties between the two monarchs, James strongly denied that any such ties existed. 'I don't need a protector, and I have no desire to be treated like the Cardinal of Fürstenberg!' he burst out in a fury.

The wretched Skelton, whose bright idea the famous Memorial had been, was recalled to London in disgrace and thrown into the Tower. And in a desperate fence-mending operation, James had sent off by express instructions to d'Albeville: he was to declare to the States-General not only that no Treaty between James and Louis existed, but that the English king was ready to enter into a strict alliance with them, even to the point of declaring war on France if necessary. (Hedging his bet, Sunderland showed a copy of the dispatch to Barillon: he hoped the Sun King would forgive James's overture to Holland. His Majesty was a drowning man clutching at straws, and this was simply a ruse to delay or put off the Prince of Orange's departure.)

As usual, James ensured for himself the worst of both worlds. Louis was deeply affronted by his reaction, while the Dutch didn't believe a word of the English denials. Van Citters, however, assured James that the naval and military preparations going ahead in his country had nothing to do with England. These assurances were believed. The Dutch envoy was soon able to report to The Hague: 'Although the general fright has subsided somewhat on my arrival, yet the King's uneasiness remains.' Sunderland, however, was still a victim of his own delusions: 'As to the noise of the preparations made by our neighbour,' the minister wrote to Tyrconnel in Ireland, 'the King is very well assured that whatever the design may be, it is not against him.' Barillon noticed that under Sunderland's influence, it had now become 'fashionable at court to laugh at everyone who believes that the Prince of Orange intends to make a descent on England'. Bonrepaus himself probably contributed to the general unconcern. He had been told by his chief, Seignelay, that because of a shortage of troops and sailors, the Prince of Orange 'would not attempt anything this year'.

Despite James's fury and resentment of French behaviour, however, he had no desire to offend the powerful King of France, so when Bonrepaus returned to Versailles he carried the draft of a secret naval treaty between the two countries – but it had blanks where the number of ships still had to be filled in. The Frenchman took back to France a very poor opinion of James's Roman Catholic advisers: 'a contemptible lot on account of their lack of capability, and by their almost total ignorance of political matters; however all together they carry the King of England with them.'

Meanwhile, the succession of little notes from James to 'my sonne-in-law' continued as if nothing had happened. On 31 August, the day after d'Avaux's Memorial to the States-General, James wrote imperturbably from Windor: 'this place of itself affords little news,' adding a wry query – 'What news from your side of the water?'

This particular letter followed an obliging one from William, according to Lady Rutland, lady-in-waiting to the queen. In it the prince coolly assured his father-in-law that 'the States-General hath not the least thought of being the aggressors at this juncture and would only act defensively.' This was a half-truth: not only was William still hard at work trying to get wholehearted Dutch support, but if an attempt against England were to be made, it would be in his own name, not that of the States-General.

Barillon, who by early September was convinced, like Louis himself, that William's preparations were designed against England, found the King's blinkered optimism breathtaking. He had ventured to suggest to James that he should send to Ireland for loyal Catholic troops for the country's defence: this suggestion had been promptly countered by Sunderland: '. . . they would alarm England . . . Ireland ought not to be left defenceless . . .' It was Sunderland, increasingly jumpy but still gambling on the success of the Grand Design, who was responsible for James's unruffled calm; 'they neither of them believe that the Prince of Orange has any design to make a descent on England, and they imagine if he does, no man who has any property will declare for him.'

Louis XIV by this time had his own problems. Early in September Belgrade had finally fallen, putting a full stop to Turkish adventures in Eastern Europe. They would have to make peace with the emperor, and from now on Leopold and the German princes could be counted on for a much more aggressive stance on the Rhine. For the first time in years, the balance of power in Europe was tilting decisively against France.

But Louis was now committed to a hawklike policy. His objectives were threefold. He was determined to maintain French influence on the upper Rhine by imposing his candidate, Cardinal Fürstenberg, as Elector of Cologne. He wanted to secure for his sister-in-law, the garrulous Liselotte, those Palatinate territories on France's eastern frontiers, to which he had already laid claim on her behalf. And most urgent of all, he was determined to seize control of Philippsburg. The 1684 Truce of Ratisbon had left this key city in the hands of Leopold, who had promptly fortified it to the hilt. But Philippsburg straddled the Rhine at a crucial point: through this 'gate' German and imperial forces could be sent surging westwards into French territory at any moment. Louis's most trusted military advisers were adamant that the 'gate' should be closed. The usual French tactics of threat, bullying and bluster, allied to a strong show of force, would probably gain all three objectives: they might even encourage the Turks to go on fighting.

The Dutch were, so to speak, the joker in the pack. Louis was perfectly well informed of William's plans to invade England: he had had d'Avaux's detailed and reliable reports of the prince's preparations since mid-August. And although Louis had no notion of actually going to war on behalf of his luckless fellow-monarch, he hoped that the Memorial presented by d'Avaux might at least give the Prince of Orange pause.

But what William planned and what the States-General might agree to, Louis must have reasoned, were not necessarily the same. It was still possible that once France made the first aggressive move, the States-General might be persuaded to join the alliance against her. As an added bonus, the French Memorial might also drive a wedge between William and the States-General, cloud the issue and delay any Dutch action indefinitely. These tiresome, heretic butter-and-fish merchants must be told in no uncertain terms what their fate would be if they did so. Meanwhile, d'Avaux was instructed to ram home the message by delivering a second memorial to the States-General, in which Louis warned that any Dutch interference in the *affaire* Fürstenberg would mean war. To put teeth into these threats, Louis gave orders that all Dutch ships in French ports should be seized and their crews forcibly converted to Catholicism.

Louis made three serious miscalculations. Firstly, he overplayed his hand against the Dutch, although d'Avaux had expressly warned him that such tactics were more likely to alienate than intimidate them. Secondly, he overestimated the strength of James's position. The English king had a large and well-trained army (thanks to a little help from Louis), and an adequate navy. Even if he did succeed in landing, William might be eliminated as a factor to be reckoned with altogether, while England might be plunged into years of confusion or even civil war. Neither Louis nor d'Avaux, however, realized just how vulnerable James was, for the one secret which d'Avaux never succeeded in discovering was the extent of the English conspiracy – or even its existence. The third of Louis's miscalculations was the most disastrous of all: it was his consistent undervaluation of '*le petit sieur de Breda*', William of Orange – of his resourcefulness, of his diplomacy, of the ardent Calvinist faith that drove him, of his sheer guts. Frankly, Louis didn't believe William capable of such an undertaking.

All the same, Louis considered that James ought to be put on his guard against his son-in-law, since the English intelligence services at The Hague were so ludicrously incompetent. Through Barillon, the French king twice sent explicit warnings to James, on 6 September and again seven days later, but having done so, he turned his attention back to central Europe. On 14/24 September he published a pompous manifesto in which he demanded that the fortifications of Philippsburg should be razed until the Truce of Ratisbon had been converted into a binding treaty; staked Liselotte's claim to the Palatinate territories, and insisted that Fürstenberg, elected in July, should be confirmed as Elector of Cologne.

Louis still believed that the States-General might be preparing to join the lists against him, but a dispatch from d'Avaux arriving on 17 September left no more room for doubt about William's plans: 'there is nothing to be done but wait and see,' Louis dictated with a shrug on the minutes of this correspondence. To Barillon he sent unctuous expressions of regret: he wished his ports were full of ships to come to James's rescue. 'Let me know what the King of England may think I can do to be useful to him,' he wrote.

Oblivious of the storm-clouds massing over his head, the King of England continued to act as though everything was going according to his plans. The machinery for the carefully manipulated elections had been getting into top gear. A preliminary list of over a hundred approved royal candidates had been drawn up, writs were ready to be sent out, and when the first reports came in from the electoral agents who had been sent out in the summer, they were encouraging.

When the Presbyterian Lord Mayor of London died, James displayed his usual insensitivity to public opinion by replacing him with – an Anabaptist. And a near-mutiny at Portsmouth was met by a characteristic but ill-timed display of royal toughness. James's bastard son, the Duke of Berwick, had forty surplus Irish soldiers to dispose of, and solved the problem by distributing them round various companies of his regiment at Portsmouth. The lieutenant-colonel and five captains refused point-blank to accept them on the grounds that they were 'foreigners'. Berwick was obliged to court-martial the six, but he did his best to smooth matters over. When the officers refused to climb down, however, James determined to make an example of them. They were brought to London, disarmed, thrown into prison and, on 10 September, at a special council of war, they were formally stripped of their rank. This exemplary treatment turned the six into national martyr-heroes overnight – just like the Seven Bishops. Other lieutenants and ensigns of companies followed their example, a slow trickle of desertions began, and portraits of the six were displayed and sold everywhere in London.

On the very day the officers received their sentence, an unconcerned James assured Barillon that even if William did invade, there was no chance he would succeed. The troops would do their duty: it would be Monmouth all over again.

Days later, the scales finally fell from James's eyes. On 18 September dispatches from d'Albeville brought urgent and detailed news of mass mobilizations, troop movements, loading of ships. Two days later James was summoned back from a tour of the royal dockyards in the Medway to read another warning from his envoy. Louis's Manifesto had already made it clear that no help could be expected from the French. And by 24 September another express – giving chapter and verse – left no more room for doubt: 2,000 men were already shipped, another 7,000 were on their way to Dutch ports for embarkation.

Going to the king's levee the same day, Clarendon was told by him that 'the Dutch were now coming to invade England in good earnest.' Clarendon ventured to ask if James really believed it, to which he replied with warmth, 'Do I see you, my lord?'

TEN

THE DUTCH INVOLVEMENT

All uncertainty about the intentions of Louis XIV ended on 17/27 September. The French armies under the nominal command of the dauphin, 70,000 strong, were launched against the Rhine, marched into the Palatinate and laid siege to Philippsburg. 'Never had news more rejoiced the Prince of Orange,' commented a bitter d'Avaux, whose warnings of the prince's invasion plans had so often fallen on deaf ears at Versailles, 'for he feared they would come into Flanders or from the side of Cologne.' William's calculated gamble had come off.

Philippsburg was over 200 miles from the Republic's frontiers. But on 11/21 September, a sizeable detachment of the French army had already marched into Bonn, only sixty miles from the 'Barriere' fortress of Maastricht on the Meuse, and the French assault on Philippsburg was planned in the utmost secrecy: until the army was well under way, many even of the French command were unsure of its destination.

Thus for the last fortnight of September Europe, including the United Provinces, held its breath, waiting to see which way the French would move. D'Avaux's Memorial, in the circumstances, burst like a bombshell, and the Prince of Orange coolly capitalized at once on the general alarm it raised. On 28 September Fagel announced to the States that in view of the current crisis, their stadholder had taken the initiative of concluding an agreement with Brandenburg and other German states to hire 13,000 soldiers from them. The States approved without a murmur.

Listening in a state of shock, they heard that since 'the fire was burning so close to the frontiers of this state, and that religion, freedom, shipping, trade and the general welfare of the country was in such danger', their delegates had agreed that 'the current conjunction in time and affairs demanded that the State should put itself in a posture of defence in order to resist all insults.' As their stadholder suggested, they had decided to take these troops into the service of the state, and also 'to recruit and strengthen the ordinary militia, foot as well as horse'.

The States' assembly asked for time to think it all over, but four days later they came back with William's proposals automatically approved by their local councils, to advise that they should now be referred to the States-General. Here in turn William won their agreement: they even accepted proposals that a further 10,000 men should be recruited and, a little later, that another 6,000 soldiers should be hired from the King of Sweden.

This point gained, the stadholder had another shock in store for the States' delegates: it was time for them to learn his true intentions. Once more William asked Fagel to be his spokesman. The grand pensionary was by now almost a dying man, but he left his sickbed to address the States in a speech of passionate eloquence.

King James had always considered the Dutch as his enemies, Fagel pointed out. He had blamed them for his problems with his Parliament, he had protested over and over again at the presence of English refugees in Holland, he had shown his ill will by recalling the English and Scottish regiments, and he had now clearly entered into a close alliance with the arch-enemy, France. It was no secret that he kept up an enormous army; that since early in the year he had been feverishly strengthening his navy; and that the French naval envoy Bonrepaus had recently spent days in conference in London.

Perhaps England presented no immediate threat to the Dutch, since James had acute domestic problems, but this state of affairs could not be counted on to last for ever. He might carry the day or he might go to the wall: either event would be disastrous for the Republic. Under a successful autocrat, England would ally herself with France against them. And if James lost, and England became a commonwealth once more, there was no need to spell out the consequences. To avert such dangers, there was only one solution: the Protestants of England must be given immediate assistance.

On the stadholder's behalf, Fagel frankly admitted that the Prince and Princess of Orange had a special interest – which coincided with that of the states. They did not wish to lose the throne of England, and this would certainly happen if they did not intervene. Once the papists got the upper hand, the prince and princess, as Protestants, would be excluded from the succession, and if on the other hand the Protestants triumphed, they would never forgive the prince for standing idly by without lifting a finger to help them. For these reasons, His Highness had decided 'with God's blessing to come to the assistance of the English nation, for the maintenance of the Protestant Religion and her freedom and rights'.

The prince had no intention of dethroning James, Fagel stressed in conclusion, 'only of ensuring that by calling a free Parliament . . . the reformed religion might be secure and out of danger'. His one wish was to restore good relations between king and nation, so that England 'could be of service again to her Friends and Allies, and in particular to this state'.

For three interminable days the States of Holland wrangled over the prince's request for help in his momentous enterprise, but at last on 9 October they gave their approval, and on 10 October the States-General followed suit. Now that they were committed, they threw themselves into the conspiracy with enthusiasm. D'Albeville was solemnly assured that the huge forces raised were not meant for an attack on England, although they added that 'they saw with great sadness the unrest, caused by the irregular conduct of some towards not only the reformed religion, but also the freedom and security of the nation.' Their most fervent wish was that this unrest should be calmed by settling the people's grievances.

There was European public opinion to be taken into account, too, particularly that of the Empire and Spain. The Emperor Leopold and the Spanish king might not sympathize with James's policies, or his relationship with France, but they were, after all, Catholic rulers themselves, and they could hardly be expected to look with favour on the overthrow of a fellow-Catholic monarch. In a conversation with Fagel, the Imperial envoy Kramprich insisted that his master could never side with those who wished to dethrone a legitimate king. 'His Highness,' soothed Fagel, 'has no intention of attempting anything against his Britannic Majesty. Apart from the fact that James II is King, he is also uncle and father-in-law to the Prince.'

William wrote in person to the emperor along the same lines as his assurances to the States-General: '. . . the misunderstandings which have subsisted for some time between the King of Great Britain and his subjects are come to so great extremities that, being upon the point of breaking out into a formal rupture, they have obliged me to pass the sea . . .' He had had 'lively and reiterated instances' from English leaders, 'as well ecclesiastical as secular'. To protect himself from those evil counsellors who were responsible for such a sorry state of affairs, he proposed to take 'some troops of infantry and cavalry'. But no matter what rumours were being spread, he assured the emperor that he intended no harm either to the king or his rightful heirs, 'still less to make an attempt upon the crown'. If all went well, finally, William made a solemn promise: 'I will employ all my credit to provide, that the Roman Catholics of that country may enjoy liberty of conscience, and be put out of fear of being persecuted on account of their religion . . .'

It is unlikely that the emperor believed all William's pious dis-
claimers of personal ambition. But the prince's chef de cabinet, Simon
van Pettekum, put it in a nutshell: 'Would it not be very advantageous,'
he asked Kramprich, 'for the Emperor to have a King of England
completely in agreement with the House of Austria about France?'
'Yes, no doubt,' replied the Imperial envoy cautiously, 'but the Emperor would not wish the price of so great an advantage to be such a
black action as that of a prince dethroning his uncle and his father-in-
law.' 'Oh really,' said Pettekum bluntly, 'what does it matter to the
Emperor if the King of England is called James or William?'

The governor of the Spanish Netherlands was much more easily
persuaded. He not only approved the expedition, but actually begged
to be allowed to go along too. And the Spanish envoy at The Hague
went further still: he had prayers for the prince's success said in his
chapel, and just before the expedition sailed he gave a tremendous
dinner for the leading members of the States-General. Raising his glass
he promised a toast: 'To the Prince of Orange! As King of England
may he enter Paris a year from now, at the head of 100,000 men.' In
Europe and the Republic at least the Prince of Orange had disposed of
the last obstacle to his plans. The next was miles of stormy North Sea.

To lead this venture without parallel in modern history, the prince
had chosen Arthur Herbert, not only because he was an outstanding
naval commander – bolder and much more decisive than Dartmouth
– but mainly because he was an Englishman. It had been William's
deliberate policy from the outset to involve the English themselves up
to the hilt in his enterprise.

Early in September, however, Herbert's appointment had hit a
ludicrous snag. The English Admiral Dartmouth – 'hearing you said
very reflecting things on him' – challenged his rival to a duel. Anxious
'to bee at his owne disposal and liberty to meet Ld. Dartmouth, if he
should call upon him', Herbert hesitated to accept the prince's commission. Fortunately for the Protestant cause, this call never came.
Herbert was free to join the prince, who advised him to pocket the
challenge with the promise that 'he should meet Lord Dartmouth at
Sea'.

A much more thorny task for William was to get Herbert's appointment approved by the Dutch commanders. The obvious choice as
commander of the fleet was Holland's greatest living admiral, Cornelis
Tromp. But ever since a blazing row five years earlier about the appointment of officers and financial matters, he and the prince had hardly
been on speaking terms.

Up to now, accordingly, work on the Dutch navy had been overseen by the proud Zeelander, Lieutenant-Admiral Cornelis Evertsen, seconded by the Hollander Vice-Admiral P. van Almonde. It took all the prince's considerable diplomatic talents to persuade them to stand aside for an Englishman. On the day that the States of Holland finally approved his English enterprise, the prince called both the Dutch admirals to The Hague. Up to then, both men had been kept in the dark about William's plans, but the urgent expansion of the Dutch fleet, now far larger than its normal peacetime size, had aroused their suspicions. The prince told them frankly what his plans were, and explained why he intended to appoint an English commander for this expedition. As a sop to their professional pride, he assured them that Herbert would only take over command once the fleet had sailed, and that all command decisions would be taken after joint consultation. Greatly to his relief, Evertsen and van Almonde accepted his decision without protest, and on 6 October Herbert swore an oath of allegiance to the Prince of Orange.

Herbert was only one of hundreds of Englishmen involved in this enterprise against James II. The six English and Scottish regiments – thinned out at the start of the year by James's summons – were now back up to full strength, thanks to a steady influx of English soldier refugees, from Northern Ireland as well as England. They were ear-marked for the vanguard of the invading army – and the Dutch men-of-war had hundreds of British sailors among their crews. The choice of commander for the invading army, under William himself, had been solved weeks earlier, thanks to an inspired suggestion from Sidney. It was the Protestant Marshal Schomberg, who had been one of France's most brilliant generals until the Sun King's own policies compelled him reluctantly to exile the marshal. Schomberg was 'extremely beloved' in England, as Sidney pointed out, and his appointment would give weight and respectability to the enterprise. After much haggling over salary, the veteran marshal had agreed to be enlisted, and he arrived in Holland in September.

Sidney himself was already with William, after making a complicated and roundabout trip to evade detection. As Bentinck wrote to William at the end of August: 'Having been for a long time at sea, he has passed through Flanders, and as he had said he was going to Aix, he has come here to Appeldoorn incognito.' Sidney brought a valuable boost to morale with his news of the English army conspirators. But his de-parture from London removed a close link between William and the English end of the enterprise; and William's need for detailed intel-ligence on James's military preparations was more rather than less urgent now. So Bentinck proposed that a former secretary of his, the capable Jacob van Leeuwen, should be sent over to London. Cover was easy: he went as secretary to Van Citters, who left for London the day after d'Avaux's Memorial was presented.

Van Leeuwen found the English conspirators, deprived of Sidney's cheerful and optimistic presence, desperate for news and in a state of pardonable jitters. At a meeting at Danby's house, he learnt that some of them expected to be arrested for treason from one day to the next, and they begged him to return to Holland as soon as they had told him what they could. He pointed out that he had a solid cover, but they still insisted that he should leave at once – 'otherwise I should expose not only the Lords and myself, but your Highness' designs as well, to great danger.'

In the end, they reluctantly decided he should stay, and Russell crossed to Holland instead, accompanied – in a hired fishing boat – by the Earl of Shrewsbury. The young man brought a more concrete token of English solidarity: £3,000 in cash, raised on his estates.

Their arrival was just the tonic William needed. Stress always affected him physically, and during that long summer with its slogging hard work and succession of crises, he had been in poor health, suffering from attacks of asthma which lowered his spirits. The loss of nerve and the pessimism of his future English hosts did nothing to reassure him, and when he received a letter from a suddenly timorous Danby, in which the older man advised him to put off the whole expedition to the following spring, he admitted gloomily to Bentinck: '*Il ne me mest pas en peu de peine . . .*'

Not surprisingly, there were moments when even William's courage failed him, though he would only admit as much to Bentinck and Fagel. For instance, when it became obvious that the operation couldn't be kept secret in England much longer, he wrote desperately, 'I am in the utmost uncertainty and anxiety . . . I must admit that it all gives me horrible doubts, and that more than ever, I need the Divine direction.'

But there was little time to indulge these qualms. Shrewsbury had also brought Danby's draft of what was to become William's Declaration, and he didn't care for it at all. 'I put myself completely at the mercy of a Parliament,' he wrote to Bentinck, 'and though I fear that this cannot be otherwise, to hand over one's fate to them is not without hazard.' Together with Fagel and Dijkvelt, Bentinck sat down to re-draft the manifesto, and the first version was ready on 10 October. At the prince's express request, it was shown to at least one refugee, the Scottish Earl of Melville, 'in order to know his sentiments', and Burnet gave it a final polish. This extra secret weapon – a personal appeal to the English nation from the Prince of Orange – was to be printed by the hundred thousand, taken to England and distributed nationwide just before the prince landed.

The Declaration was only one of William's many worries. Far more time-consuming was the invasion flotilla, and hours were spent going over plans with Herbert. The prince had promised the Englishman that 'he should meet Lord Dartmouth at Sea'. But a naval battle was the very last thing William wished for. 'If an accident should happen, everything would be lost,' he told Bentinck. 'It is therefore necessary that you make Mr Herbert understand that as far as possible he must avoid a battle.'

Dutchmen killing Englishmen and sinking English ships would be bad enough, but Englishmen killing Englishmen would be a hundred times worse, threatening the entire enterprise with disaster, and perhaps precipitating the civil war William wanted to avoid at all costs. An almost equally important consideration was the need to preserve the English fleet intact: it would be needed against France before very long.

In his official instructions to Herbert on 6 October, when all the soldiers had been embarked, the prince therefore stressed again that the admiral was not to seek out the English navy. He had already received reports that Dartmouth's sailors had no enthusiasm for a fight with the Protestant fleet anyway, and Herbert had instructions to salute the English fleet if it was sighted. Then he was to send across a yacht with 1,500 copies of the Prince's Declaration in order to 'make known to the commander of the forementioned fleet, the captains and the common people . . . the reason of his coming'.

He was also to distribute a manifesto William had composed especially for the English sailors. Probably drafted by Russell, it assured these 'Gentlemen and friends' that the prince had 'no other designe in this expedition but for the good of England and the preservation of the Protestant religion, the total ruine of which in these kingdomes is as much designed as it is already accomplisht in France'. He appealed to them, hoping 'God will put it into your hearts at this time to redeme yourselves, your religion and your country from those misrios which in all human appraiance can only be done by giving me your present assistance.' It was signed, 'your truely welwishing and affectionnate friend, G. Prince d'Orange'. Should the English accept the prince's invitation, Herbert was to lower the Dutch colours, raise first the king's standard and then the prince's colours, and the two fleets would sail peacefully together up river to London, to demand that a free Parliament be summoned.

William's desire to avoid a battle was understandable on any count. He had a strong fleet of forty-three men-of-war, four light frigates and ten fire-ships, as well as seven light yachts which acted as the fleet's messengers. But the task of this navy was not to defeat James's fleet, damaging William's popularity in England and losing the support of the Dutch, but to protect the enormous and highly vulnerable fleet of slow-moving transports. This consisted of over 400 flyboats needed for over 15,000 soldiers: eighteen battalions of infantry, each of 600 men, and 4,092 cavalry; 4,000 horses and the huge stocks of ammunition and provisions which had been piling up in Dutch warehouses since July. There were arms for 20,000 men, 300 tons of hay, pontoons made of tin, waggons, corn, flour, biscuits, medicaments and hospital stores, bridges to embark the cavalry, four tons of tobacco, 10,000 pairs of boots, fifty hogsheads of brandy at F. 50 each, 1,600 hogsheads of beer (a total of 2,400 barrels) and 6,000 guilders' worth of a Dutch speciality, salted herring. There had to be three months' pay for the troops, and of course a die for coining money – put on it the '*effigie de la Princesse et moy*', William told Bentinck – and, finally, a printing-press: the prince thoroughly understood the value of propaganda.

As had been agreed, Herbert worked closely with the two Dutch admirals, Cornelis Evertsen and Philip van Almonde – each commanded a squadron – and the three were satisfied with the plans ready in case of a possible confrontation with the English fleet. Herbert was less sure about the effects of an encounter with the French, and he proposed that every man-of-war should be equipped with 'an extraordinary allowance of ammunition, of spare cordage, of spare convas, of spare sayles, of masts, planck deall boards ... and finally with all things, requisitt to refitt the fleet after an engagement without being obliged to return home'. The penny-pinching English Navy Board would have gasped with horror at such extravagance, but William agreed at once.

From past experience, Herbert was also thoughtful for the men's comfort. In their crowded transports they might be at anchor or at sea for weeks on end, and he insisted on ships that were good sailers, but also 'capable of receiving ayre, the more the better'. For the horses he suggested 'smacken' or galliots: they would save time at the end of the voyage because the horses could be disembarked directly, without having to be shifted to smaller boats.

The main problem was, where to land this enormous army? In a *Memoire* written early in October, Herbert acknowledged that it was difficult to decide about the 'place of the mayne desent', and William himself had not as yet made a final decision about the choice of landing-place. At the beginning of the year, he had scribbled on a sheet of notes headed, '*Prevention necessaire pour le dessin de Luilliet 1688*', the questions,

'Where to land? To several places or one? Should we at the same time make a descent on Scotland?' He had finally made up his mind to 'act according to occurences'. To keep his options open, the Dutch fleet carried a large number of English pilots familiar with various stretches of the English coastlines. Bentinck composed a list of possible 'places judged capable in England, starting in the north and ending in the west'. The list was impressively long, with a total of twenty-five possibilities: from Tynemouth to Stockton, Hull, Yarmouth and Harwich in the north, and Margate and Newhaven, to Portsmouth, Southampton and Torbay in the west.

According to Burnet, the Prince of Orange gave preference to a landing in the north, after which the fleet would go southward 'to lie in the channel', but Herbert made the obvious sailor's point before their departure: 'after all it is by the winds that in a great measure the desent must be governed.' He had his own ideas, however, and he made no secret of his aversion to a landing in the north – 'a very dangereux coast . . . especially soe late in the year, an ill and deep country to march in after raynes, no manner of harbour to shelter considerable ships,' and the men-of-war would be 'quite out of the way to hinder succours from France and Ireland'. The few advantages of landing in the north were a large population 'very much disaffected to the present government' and that it was 'well furnished with all necessary provisions and horses'.

The west, on the other hand, argued Herbert, had nothing but advantages. The single drawback was the distance, 'in which the horses may suffer', 'and a fayre winde takes even that off too'. For the rest it was a 'populeux cuntry', also disaffected to the government, 'well stored with all manner of provisions and horses for the cariadge and dragoons, many convenient places for a dessent and many convenient roades and harbours for securing the fleet'. If the French came to James's rescue, finally, Herbert and his fleet would be on the spot to deal with them.

Even at the end of October, a final decision had still not been made. In the sailing instructions William issued to Admiral Herbert on 27 October, Article 5 instructed the Englishman that after the troops were disembarked, he should 'saile to Scotland, and there try to make similar diversions'. But no point of disembarkation was named.

Three days earlier, huge stacks of the final version of William's Declaration for the English were printed and ready. It amounted to a comprehensive catalogue of James's crimes. But James himself was hardly mentioned: the villains were 'those Evill Councellors' who now had 'the chieffe Credit with the King'. It was they who were responsible for 'Arbitrary Government', the appointment of Catholics to civil and military offices, and the rigging of the test case which confirmed the king's dispensing power – 'as if it were in the power of twelve judges, to offer up the Lawes, Rights and Liberties, of the whole National, to the King'.

'Those Evill Counsellors' were also responsible for 'the deplorable State to which the Protestant Religion is reduced', a wholesale attack on the nation's civil liberties, the suspension of the Bishop of London, the illegal ejection of the Magdalen Fellows; the building of Catholic churches and chapels, and the opening of Jesuit colleges. The prince and his 'Dearest and most Entirely Beloved Consort' had expressed their great regret to James at these proceedings, but his wicked advisers 'have put such ill constructions on these our good Intentions, that they have endeavoured to alienate the King more and more from us: as if we had designed, to Disturb the quiet and Happiness of the Kingdome'.

No doubt to the fury of his English supporters, William refused to commit himself to a forthright statement that the Prince of Wales was an impostor: instead he stressed that despite 'so many just and Visible grounds of Suspicion . . . there was not anything done to Satisfy them, or put an end to their Doubts'.

The Declaration concluded with a disclaimer of any other design 'but to have a true and lawful Parliament assembled, as soon as is possible', and an invitation to all the nation to rally to this army of liberation.

The strong western winds that had forced the prince to delay his departure had given James the chance to make a number of con- cessions, so on 24 October William added a few extra paragraphs, pointing out 'how little weight there is to be laid, on all Promises and Engagements that can be now made . . . for they lay doune nothing which they may not take up at Pleasure . . .' The safety of England still lay in the 'free Assembly of the Nation, in a Lawful Parliament', which William guaranteed.

Three days later the winds – just as anxiously watched by William as by James – veered to the east, and on Tuesday, 27 October it was time for William to take his leave of the States-General. At eleven o'clock that morning the stadholder entered the States-General's headquarters in The Hague – the beautiful Binnenhof Palace where the provincial deputies waited to hear him in the medieval Knights' Hall. They listened in silence as the prince, deeply moved, told them: 'I have always served you faithfully, and kept the welfare of this state constantly before me.' It was not necessary to go again into his reasons for leaving his country now, but he hoped that 'if it pleased God to allow to happen to him what happens to many people', and he were to die, they would take his wife Mary under their protection. With tears running down his cheeks, he added: 'She could nowhere find a better place to shelter than under the wings of this state.'

The princess herself had spent the last few weeks with her husband in The Hague, trying hard to keep up a front of cheerful confidence. On 21 October William's Dutch secretary, Constantijn Huygens, saw her playing cards with her ladies. D'Albeville came to see her later on, after the prince had twice refused to speak to him that day, 'but she looked very cool at him after which he at once left'.

It was the ambassador who was now *persona non grata* at the Orange Court, while the man who at James's insistence the prince had banished from it at the beginning of the year, Gilbert Burnet, was back bustling importantly about and in the thick of affairs. The bishop was specially concerned about Mary. Any hint that her support for the enterprise was less than wholehearted could be disastrous. But quite naturally the realization that her father and her husband might soon be confronting each other on a battlefield sometimes overwhelmed her. It did not escape Burnet's notice that a few days before their departure, 'she seemed to have a great load on her spirits'. Bluntly, he reminded her that she had a vital role to play. He knew, he told her, that she was strongly convinced of the righteousness of her husband's actions; and he urged her to remain so, stressing that 'if there should happen to be at any time any disjointing between the Prince and her, that would ruin all.' Mary, 'very solemn and serious', assured him: 'I needed fear no such thing.'

With so little time left before the start of this perilous and unprecedented venture, the thoughts of the prince were often preoccupied with death, and on 25 October he signed his last will and testament. To the faithful and indispensable Bentinck, he bequeathed the town of Leerdam, which would give him the title of count, together with an estate at Isselstein, while for his loyal supporter Fagel there was a legacy of 100,000 guilders and William's country estate 'De Kruidberg' near Haarlem. On the cover of this will, William wrote: 'To be opened after my death.'

Later the same day, he again faced the possibility that he might be killed in action, this time in terms of Mary's future, and summoned her to his study. 'He said to me that in case it pleased God, that I should never see him again (words that pierced my heart and caused me such a pang, that at the hour I write it has scarcely worn off) if that happened, he said, it will be necessary to marry again.' Mary listened, stunned. 'If the first words struck me so cruelly, this last surprised and shocked me and reduced me to a state as if my heart was broken.'

Recording the conversation a few days later in her journal, she could remember his exact words. 'There is no need, he continued, for me to tell you that it must not be a Papist. He himself could not utter these words without shedding tears, and throughout this conversation he showed me all the tenderness I could wish.' It was only the concern he had for the Protestant religion that made him speak like that, he told her, and she could hardly remember what she answered. 'The grief I felt made my answers confused, but I assured him that I had never loved any one but him and would not know how to love any one else. And apart from that, having been married so many years without it having pleased God to bless me with a child, I believed that sufficient to prevent me ever thinking of what he proposed. I told him that I begged God not to let me survive him; if however I should do so, since it had not pleased God to give me a child by him, I would not wish to have one by an angel.'

At the end of this long and emotional conversation, Mary asked his pardon for all her shortcomings. 'He responded with such tenderness that if it had been possible, that would have increased my love for him even more.'

After his farewell to the States-General, William took Mary off with him for a last hour or two together at their palace, Honselaersdijck. After dinner she drove with him as far as the river, where he took a boat for the port of Den Brielle and the waiting fleet. Numbed with grief, Mary sat motionless in the coach while his boat sailed away, 'unable to tell the coachmen to go as long as I could still see the Prince'. At last she returned to The Hague, where she wrote down in her journal her fear that she might have seen the prince for the last time. 'This thought is very dreadful and for some time robbed me of my senses.'

ELEVEN

Vain Concessions

Many of the English shared James's belief that a seaborne invasion planned for the autumn was the enterprise of a lunatic. The North Sea was a treacherous ally at the best of times, but in autumn and winter, it could be very stormy. 'To me it seems incredible that soe late in the year any wise people should think of an invasion,' Peregrine Bertie wrote from Court to his brother-in-law, Danby. Like everybody else, he soon had no choice but to believe it. Every mail from Holland now brought detailed accounts of troop movements and embarkation. 'Fresh expresses doe confirm the design of the Dutch to be upon England,' reported the chronicler Narcissus Luttrell in his gossipy journal on 28 September, 'that they have 16,000 men on board, besides sea men . . .' And the master of a ship from Guernsey, Peter Valet, told friends in London how in Rotterdam he had been ordered away from the quayside to make room for 'several great vessels that loaded horses, hay and oats, working all days alike for expedition'. He watched while twenty-three hoys filled up with troops – and he was struck by the fact that most of them were English.

In Whitehall, James struggled to come to grips with reality. He found himself torn between two parties. On the one hand his Catholic advisers – those 'Evill Councellors' in the shape of Petre, Melfort and the queen – urged him to stand firm. But the other party, urging a climb-down, was now headed by Sunderland. And Sunderland was in a funk. He had gambled everything on James's success and triumph for the Catholic cause. Now his stake had melted away, and at this moment of crisis, he appeared to have lost his nerve completely. Only days earlier he had confidently assured Tyrconnel in Ireland that everything was going according to plan: 'All the Dissenters are satisfied, and the Church of England's principles will keep them loyall, though they may be indiscreet. In short, I believe there never was in England less thought of rebellion . . .' Almost from one day to the next, he plunged into total pessimism. The king's only hope, he told d'Adda, lay in total surrender to Anglican demands.

From force of habit James at first heeded his panic-stricken prompting. In a Declaration published on Friday, 21 September he announced an about-face: he was still bent on 'an Universal Liberty of Conscience for all Our Subjects', but he was now 'willing the Roman Catholicks should remain incapable to be Members of the House of Commons', and he was resolved 'Inviolably to preserve the Church of England'. The next day or two saw further concessions. The Catholic Admiral Strickland was replaced by his old friend, the solidly Anglican Lord Dartmouth. The peers and bishops were to be consulted in the present crisis; 'he would set all things upon the foot they were at his coming to the crown'; the writs already sent out for the November Parliament were recalled; and all the 'old honest aldermen' who had been turned out of the City were to be restored. To the Bishop of Winchester, who saw him the following day, the king graciously said that he was now resolved to support the Church of England, and that the world should see, he would not lay aside his old friends.

'And now, my lord,' he told Clarendon, 'I shall see what the Church of England men will do.' A consultation with Archbishop Sancroft and some of the leading bishops was set up for the following Friday. The first to arrive in town was Francis Turner, Bishop of Ely, who had been one of the seven heroes three months earlier. Desperately anxious to know how the meeting was likely to go, James summoned him to a private meeting on Thursday evening.

In the interval, his stunned Catholic advisers had rallied. Now they counter-attacked. Were such sweeping concessions necessary? Was the king sure that the bishops would deliver even if he did as they asked? He had a strong navy and a large well-drilled army, so why behave as if all was already lost? And the final compelling argument: God Almighty was on his side. Between them they managed to infuse new heart into the dejected king. The Bishop of Ely, reluctantly responding to his summons, was bewildered to find himself making polite conversation – they 'discoursed only of generals'.

Clarendon asked Jeffreys the meaning of this astonishing volte-face. The chancellor replied grimly that 'all was nought; some rogues had changed the King's mind; that he would yield in nothing to the Bishops; that the Virgin Mary was to do it all' – all of which was relayed to the bishops by Clarendon's brother Rochester.

The audience with the rest of the bishops on Friday morning – Sancroft was ill and not among them – was just as indefinite. The king was very gracious, said that it was not the moment to go into details but 'that they should every day find more and more effects of his Majesty's kindness': he had, for instance, given orders that Compton was to be restored to the See of London. The bishops left, deeply suspicious. Turner wrote at once to Sancroft, who was to see James the next morning, urging him to take a tough line.

With his usual genius for putting his foot in it, James had meanwhile published a general pardon for their crimes to all his subjects except those who had committed 'Treasons . . . beyond the seas', forgery, murder, robbery, rape, buggery or tax fraud. The wits commented that apart from the English nation, the king pardoned all his enemies. What the bishops at once noticed was that 'all the clergy were excepted out of it, as bodies polite and corporal'.

In a brief and chilly audience, Sancroft pointed this out to the king: just a mistake, not what he meant at all, replied James airily. In the circumstances the bishops determined to put the screws on. Promises were no longer enough. What they wanted was action. The string of demands they laid before him on 3 October was comprehensive and humiliating. They ended by requiring that he should listen to the arguments of their divines: with God's grace he might return to the communion of the Church of England. When he asked them to compose some prayers suitable for this time of invasion, the collect they produced, a couple of days later, was hardly what he had had in mind. 'Preserve that holy Religion we profess, together with our Laws and ancient Government,' it ran, 'and unite us all in . . . one and the same Holy Worship and Communion.'

Over the next few days James reluctantly conceded some of the bishops' points: the Magdalen Fellows were reinstated, the Ecclesiastical Commission wound up, the ancient charters restored. If he hoped in this way to win back his 'old friends', he was to be cruelly undeceived. Summoning Sancroft to a private audience on 16 October, James told of certain intelligence that the Prince of Orange was on his way. It would be very much for his service if he and the bishops would meet and draft an abhorrence of this attempt. Sancroft stalled, hesitated and finally said he saw no need for such a declaration – 'I could never believe, nor do I yet, that the Prince hath such a design.'

James made one more bid for the bishops' support, when a copy of William's Declaration finally came to his hands. He could hardly believe even now that any of them could have actually invited the prince. Compton was questioned first: had he signed any invitation? 'I am confident that the rest of the Bishops would as readily answer in the negative as myself,' he replied equivocally. The trusting James put the same question to the others and was reassured by their denials. Then he came to the point. Would the bishops make a public statement that they had never invited the prince – and perhaps express their dislike of his design at the same time? 'It will be very much for my service,' he added anxiously. They kept the king in suspense for four days while they hurriedly conferred. Then they gave him their answer: it was no. They had burned their fingers meddling in politics in June, and been viciously slandered as a result. They refused to be drawn now. But they would be quite happy for the king to publish an account of this conversation. When the king continued desperately to beg for their help, they told him implacably that they could serve him best in a Parliament.

'I will urge you no further,' said James, gathering the rags of his dignity round him. 'If you will not assist me as I desire, I must stand upon my own legs, and trust to myself and my own arms.'

This trust, he believed, was well-founded. His new naval commandant, the forty-year-old George Legge, Earl of Dartmouth, was a man in whom he had every confidence. Dartmouth was not the most dashing or enterprising of commanders, but he had had experience of naval warfare in the North Sea, having fought in the two most recent wars against the Dutch. Much more to the point, he was a close friend whose loyalty had never been in doubt since the days when James was still Duke of York and Dartmouth his trusted Gentleman of the Bedchamber. In one of Dartmouth's first letters from his flagship, the *Resolution*, he wrote: 'I am very sensible of the great trust your Majesty is pleased to put in my conduct of this fleet, which to the best of my understanding shall be faithfully performed for your service.'

Throughout September and October, the work of bringing the fleet up to fighting strength went on energetically, directed by a stream of memoranda from the indefatigable Pepys. Chatham and Portsmouth had been put on special alert and arms issued to the workmen there. And to confuse a hostile fleet, the navigation lights at Harwich and the buoys in the Thames were to be moved. When it was learned that the Dutch were short of shipping, an embargo was laid on vessels in all eastern ports and the Thames.

By the end of October, the fleet numbered thirty-seven men-of-war and eleven fire-ships. How far the men could be relied on was another matter. In a letter to Dartmouth, Pepys complained bitterly about the officers, who would turn up at Court 'complaining that their ships are not ready while nothing is wanting towards their readiness but their own attendance on board'. There were the usual manning problems, and despite feverish activity by the press-gangs, the harvest was poor. 'The *Kitchen* yacht came this morning with a parcel of very sorry men which he must keep till he can get better,' Dartmouth heard.

Other important questions were endlessly discussed in letters between Dartmouth and the former High Admiral James, who prided himself on his naval expertise and liked to see himself as a Sailor-King. Where, for instance, was the best station for the fleet, given that the Dutch might make either for a landing in the north, or head for the Channel and a landing in the west? Which of these two options was the Prince of Orange most likely to settle for? Should Dartmouth try to cross to Holland and 'give the Dutch a fright'? The question of the best anchorage became academic and remained so for days, while easterly winds kept Dartmouth and the fleet pinned down in the mouth of the Thames with its treacherous shoals. On 17 October Dartmouth wrote to the king: 'upon the first snatch of winde and faire weather . . . we should fall down to the Gunfleet . . . There we shall be ready to cover Harwich as well as the river Thames.' But the weather conditions filled him with gloom: a move to the Gunfleet would only be possible if he was 'able to go to sea if occasion be, or we can but come up againe at worst'.

James reckoned that the Dutch would send some of their best men-of-war as a diversionary tactic, 'to look you out to engage you, whilst they send their forces to land somewhere else.' At first he had half expected them at Chatham, to repeat their brilliant coup of 1667 when they had sailed up the Medway, stormed the naval dockyards and burnt the *Royal Charles* at its anchor. But according to the latest and most reliable intelligence, the landing was planned for the north.

Dartmouth's letters were reassuring. On 24 October he wrote complacently – in words he was later to regret – 'Sirs, we are now at sea before the Dutch after all their boasting . . . I wonder to hear by so many letters of the frights that are ashore, though I thank God they have no effect upon us here . . . Your statesmen may take a nap, and recover, the women sleep in their beds, and the cattle, I think, need not be drove from the shore . . .'

Both he and James knew, however, that the wind would be the deciding factor in the end, just as it had been six centuries earlier for England's last successful invader, William the Conqueror. The same east wind that William needed to make the crossing to England could pin Dartmouth down, helpless, among the shoals of the Thames mouth – the 'Protestant wind' celebrated in the refrain of *Lilliburlero*, the catchy little song which became ominously popular around this time. To tell him if the wind was Protestant or a good Catholic gale, James had an enormous weathercock mounted on the roof of the Banqueting Hall, where he could see it from his apartments.

If the wind turned Protestant, however, and his navy let him down,

James would have to depend on his army. Thanks to Parliament's generosity at the time of the Monmouth rebellion, he had been able to build it up to a well-trained standing army of some 21,000 men. But many of these had already been detached for garrison duty, leaving a number quite inadequate to put into the field against the army of tough professional men William was likely to bring. So at the end of September orders were issued for ten men to be added to every troop and company in the army, and for several new regiments of foot and horse to be raised. The Scottish standing army was ordered into England; troops from Ireland were summoned, and they began landing at Chester or Liverpool early in October and were sent south.

But the paper strength of this enlarged army was deceptive. The newly raised men were raw recruits, not much use in action, while as for the Irish, they were likely if anything to send the common people straight to the arms of William – inspiring as they did the sort of dismay and even terror that the Danes must have done in the tenth century. Hardly had the 2,000 Irish troops James had asked for landed at Chester when complaints about their lawless ways began flooding in. At Portsmouth, where most of them were based, 'the rude Irish . . . have caused many families to leave that place, having committed many robberies,' reported a newsletter of 11 October. In another incident, 'some Irish men breaking open an alehouse for drink were reprimanded by some English officers, for which they set upon the English, beat and abused them . . . in which quarrel its said four or five were killed.'

If the king had cherished his army, however, he had completely neglected the militia, which he regarded at best as useless, and at worst as dangerous and disaffected. The militia was the responsibility of the lord-lieutenants and their deputies: many of these great noblemen and landed gentry had been swept out of office in James's many purges, to be replaced by men with hardly any local status and no experience in such matters. Those who had not, like the Dukes of Norfolk and Beaufort, the Earls of Digby and Bath, had little good will for their Catholic king, and no enthusiasm for the task. As a result, the militia was ill-organized or non-existent all over the country: '. . . no part of it [the Kent militia] having been mustered,' wrote Lord Teynham from Kent, 'I presume both horse and foot are in the same ill condition with most of the counties . . .'

It was an alarming state of affairs since if William managed to evade Dartmouth and land somewhere out of the immediate reach of James's armies, the nation's first line of defence would be the local militia. So Sunderland wrote hurriedly to the lord-lieutenants all over England, urging them to action. The response was dismaying. 'Being informed that musters are not pleasing to your majesty, they have met but once since your coronation,' smugly replied the Earl of Lindsey from Lincolnshire. The Earl of Bristol informed Sunderland that 'the Militia having beene for some time laid aside, the people charged are unprovided of Armes & Coates . . . the souldiers must all be new listed and sworne, and . . . it will take up two or three months to make a new regulation . . .'

To add to these problems. James was running out of money. The naval preparations in particular had eaten heavily into his reserves, and the City was unhelpful. In desperation he swallowed his pride and turned to Louis XIV. The French king at once dispatched 300,000 livres to Barillon – but with strict instructions not to part with a penny of it unless James looked like being a winner. If he showed any signs of coming to an agreement with William, or if defeat seemed imminent, Barillon was to pretend that there were problems of exchange, etc. and hang on to the cash, all the while assuring James that Louis 'would continue to give him effective tokens of his friendship'.

The most important question of all for James, however, was what could he expect of his people? On their reaction everything depended. He had appealed to their patriotism and national pride in a proclamation of 28 September, telling them that he counted on their 'True and Ancient Courage, Faith and Allegiance'. But could he? The Imperial envoy certainly didn't think so. 'The King of England,' he reported to Vienna, 'has against him all the clergy, all the nobility, all the people, and all the army and navy, with few exceptions.'

By mid-October it was dawning even on James that he had given his people plenty of reasons for mistrusting him. At least one misunderstanding, however, could perhaps be removed. On 22 October 'The King, hearing that the Prince's being borne made so much noise, called an extraordinary council,' wrote Reresby, to which 'all the nobility, bishops, foreign ministers too were summoned, that were in London . . . where the queen dowager, several lords, ladies and the King's and Queen's servants, to above a number of forty, both Papist and Protestant gave pregnant evidence of the true birth of the Prince.'

It was an occasion without precedent, and the king admitted as much, '. . . but unusual diseases demand unusual remedies,' he told a hushed audience. 'The intrigues of my enemies have so much poisoned the minds of my subjects that I am forced to believe that many of them think the son God had given me is not mine at all . . .' He decided to call this council now, he told them, because he believed an invasion was imminent, and he wanted to put his subjects' minds at rest before his departure to the army.

One after another those who had been close to the queen, or actually present at the birth, told their story. Every one of them was adamant in their conviction that the prince was no fraud, and many of them spoke of the queen's cries of pain during her labour, particularly her last. Peterborough, who had put his fingers in his ears, told how he had 'perceived a sudden satisfaction in the faces of the Assistants', when this last cry died away. Anne, Countess of Sunderland, confirmed that at the insistence of the queen she had felt the baby in her stomach. And Lord Middleton said he had seen how the midwife, kneeling at the bedside, had had her arms under the bedclothes from which they reappeared holding the baby. No gynaecological detail was spared the audience. Finally Margaret Dawson, most forthright of all the wit-nesses, told the gathering emphatically: 'I did see the Queen carry her great belly in to that bed, I am sure there was no child in the bed but what the Queen carried into it in her belly . . . I did also see fire in that faimose warming pan so much talked on and I did feel the heat of it . . .'

Two people were absent: Mary Beatrice and Princess Anne. The king, very eager to prove his point, asked the council if they wanted him to call the queen, but they declined to subject her to this embarrassing ordeal, considering that enough witnesses had been called to prove the child was his.

As for Princess Anne, who had stayed away from court for two months, only returning on 17 September, she had excused herself on the grounds that she was pregnant – a fiction she first gave out a fortnight earlier. Since her return she had kept to her own apartments, and although Clarendon had often urged her to speak to the king and persuade him to put himself in the hands of his 'old friends', she had resolutely refused to intervene. Ten days after the sensational council meeting, a delegation waited on her to show her the authenticated documents. She refused to look at them, remarking mockingly, 'My Lords, this was unnecessary. I have so much duty for the King that his word has more weight with me than all this evidence.'

Clarendon called to see her the morning after the council meeting. He found her surrounded by her ladies at her toilette, all making ribald jokes about the evidence. She told the shocked Clarendon that she 'made herself very merry with the whole affair'.

James as yet had no suspicions of her perfidy. But it was slowly becoming clear to him that he could no longer count on his eldest daughter's loyal devotion. D'Albeville's dispatches from The Hague made traumatic reading for him. The mockery of prayers for 'the Prince' had finally ceased at the end of September, and James's own

envoy had become a figure of fun at the Orange court where, reluctantly, on the king's express orders, he still made a regular appearance.
He had to watch Burnet, 'mighty active and stirring' – 'as future Archbishop of York, that being kept vacant for him by God's blessing'. He
had to hear 'his Majties present actions and concessions ridiculed
openly . . .' And he found it 'no little mortification to appear when one
is received coldly by her R H, no man or woman daring to speak to me
but very disaffected men, Traytors, or such as glory to be going to
dethrone his Majtie'.

The embarrassed little notes from Mary continued to arrive regularly
until mid-October. Then on 15 October the post failed to bring one –
'the first time,' James told Clarendon, 'he had missed hearing from her
of a great while.'

Mary might have found it hard to write to him at a time when her
husband was drafting the last orders for the invasion. She must certainly
have found it impossible to reply to the bewildered note Mary Beatrice
had sent on 29 September: 'I am much put to it what to say, at a time
when nothing is talked of here but the Prince of Oranges coming over
with an army . . . I never did believe it till now very lately, that I have
no possibility left of doubting it. The second part of this news I will
never believe, that you are to come over with him: for I know you to be
too good, that I don't believe you could have such a thought against
the worst of fathers, much less perform it against the best, that has
always been kind to you, and I believe has loved you better than all
the rest of his children . . .'

William III: stern, purposeful soldier-hero of the 1688 Revolution, and of many a European battlefield, as the city in flames in the background suggests.

Queen Mary II in regal splendour, with her glittering crown displayed on a table at her side.

Official portrait of James II, painted in full armour, with an anchor to remind us that he had been England's High Admiral as well.

Left: Louis XIV, scourge of the French Protestant Huguenots, whose temples are seen in the background, being destroyed on his orders.

Below: Anne, sister to Mary II, who became queen after the death of William in 1702: an early supporter of William, she changed her mind, and quarrelled violently with him and with her sister Mary.

Left: Mary Beatrice of Modena, the Italian-born wife of James II. Ringletted charm and regal bearing – but she is painfully thin by contrast with her well-rounded step-daughter Mary, and she looks oddly ill at ease.

Above: James II takes a tough line with his bishops as they urge him to call a free Parliament. A portrait of the pope looks on approvingly.

Below: James flees Whitehall by boat on the night of 22 December 1688, taking with him the Great Seal.

Henry Compton, Bishop of London, disgraced by James II for his anti-Catholic views, a ringleader of the 1688 conspiracy.

The Scottish clergyman Dr Gilbert Burnet, William's trusted adviser on English affairs, and an expert on public relations.

John Churchill, James's brilliant and trusted commander, who defected to William.

Hans Wilhem Bentinck, lifelong friend, trusted adviser and right hand to William.

Above: William at Brixham after the landing. The prince's standard is seen floating over the wretched little hut where he spent his first night.

Left: The baby boy born to James and Mary Beatrice was often rumoured to be her son by Father Petre, James's unpopular Jesuit adviser. In this, one of scores of scurrilous political cartoons, he is shown fondling Mary Beatrice while she rocks the baby.

TWELVE

THE PROTESTANT WIND

The wicked Jesuits, it was rumoured, had promised James II that 'the westerly wind should continue until Christmas', and right up to the end of October, it looked as if they might be right. Throughout the month, the Dutch coast was hammered by storms, often of exceptional violence. On the night of 9 October the 'winds were so very high and the Air so tempestuous and stormy, shaking the very houses and People in their Beds . . . that many judged it to be a Earthquake'. Aboard the *Golden Sun*, John Whittle, one of the many Protestant clergymen who had joined the prince's enterprise, reported the next day in his diary: 'The whole fleet was in great peril.' And alarming reports were soon circulating: '. . . the Anchors and Cables of the Men of War were broken by the storm, as if they had been a needleful of thread, so that all the ships were driven here and there and some to one shore and some to another Coast, and as yet they were not heard of . . .'

The reality was not nearly so bad, but when the storm showed no signs of dying down the prince felt it wisest to order the whole fleet, now riding before the coast, back to Den Brielle to assess the damage. It was the first setback, and as William's army commander, Waldeck, remarked to the prince's dyspeptic little secretary, Constantijn Huygens: 'we are taking part in a great and glorious enterprise, but we still have plenty of thorns to get through before we can succeed.' Burnet seized the chance to give Herbert – sailing on the *Leyden* and rumoured lost – a heavy-handed tease about his vices: 'As bad a man as you are, a man cannot hold being extreamly concerned for you . . .' He added waggishly, '. . . after all [which], I hope you feel sometimes somewhat within telling you that perhaps your own leud life had contributed more to stop your voyage than either Albeville's masses or his prayers.'

Exaggerated accounts of the storms reached London, too: 'the first tempest disabled several of the best ships three weeks ago,' one correspondent reported on 28 October, adding: 'Some tell us of the Prince of Orange's being sick and that the bloody flux reigns in their fleet.'

This was certainly wishful thinking and, as it happened, it was on that very day that the prayers and the general fast, which had been decreed throughout the whole Republic – even the Jews joined in, Mary heard – were at last rewarded. The wind veered round to the east, and the prince, now in an excellent humour, gave orders to make ready for departure. With his personal staff he went on board the newly built frigate *Den Brielle* under Captain Johan van der Esch. 'But so many things were to be done it was not possible we could be making sail,' reported Whittle. Finally, by Saturday, 30 October, the fleet was ready to weigh anchor.

The port of Den Brielle was crowded, and all along the coast the beaches were thick with people who wanted to say goodbye to their popular stadholder. 'The top of the Brill Church and Steeple was extream'ly throng'd and the beam . . . made on purpose to view ships was almost broken down with the great crowd upon it.'

The armada they gaped at certainly presented an extraordinary spectacle. The Chevalier de Moustaquet, one of the many French Huguenots who had joined the prince's expedition, was awestruck at the sight of it: 'We admired the beauty of this fleet which, floating with full sails on a splendid day, seemed to stretch as far as the coast of England,' he wrote in his diary. 'We were spellbound at this sight.'

Like everybody else, the effusive Whittle was completely carried away. 'When the spectators perceived that the Fleet was under sail, they could not longer refrain their Eyes from weeping, nor their Cheeks from running down with affectionate tears . . . Thus was our Great Prince crossing the proud waves with all his Fleet round him, enjoying a very favourable wind for England.'

But once more it seemed that James's Jesuits might be right. Hardly had the whole slow-moving fleet emerged from the Maas, and the watching pinnace fired its four guns in a pre-arranged signal that the manoeuvre was complete, when the treacherous winds once more veered round to the west. D'Albeville, who had been watching the departure of the fleet, sent a message to London that 'this may do them some damage'. It was an understatement: the storms that got up that night scattered the fleet in all directions. Mary wrote a few days later: 'Although [the storm] lasted only a few hours, the fleet was completely dispersed . . . the wind . . . blew with such force that in order to save the transports, they were obliged to return to port.'

Those on board the transports had spent a frightful night. 'The men of war were better able to live than the rest,' Whittle noticed, 'for they did not shake themselves half so terrible as the Merchantmen and Pinks, but especially the poor Flyboats.' Moustaquet would have agreed wholeheartedly: on board one of the luckless transports, he had been convinced that they were going under. 'It was horrible to hear the waves breaking against our ship and sweeping over it: the water came in by the scuttles and everything rolled about.' The cables lashing down some barrels of salt on board his ship parted, and soon everybody was covered in salt.

The barrels tossing about, like the carriages, 'which will rowl from side to side, if they break their Stays', were just one of the dangers. 'For there were sundry circumstances which add to the peril of the Storm,' some sailors darkly told Whittle. 'The darkness of the night . . . our pipes of water, barrels of Powder and Ball, and the vast number of Ships together, which was worst of all . . .'

Everybody in the fleet longed for dawn. Huygens, on board the *Den Brielle*, was sick enough himself, and noticed that even the sailors were suffering. On Whittle's ship the soldiers 'vomitted continually after a dreadful rate; you could hear the men groan after a pitiful manner'. Now and then, though, 'a dram of the Brandy bottle' cheered them up a little. There was a moment of panic when in the pitch-dark hold, where no candles were allowed because of the gunpowder stored there, a soldier panicked and shouted, 'I am sure I can feel the hole where the Sea comes in at.' It turned out to be some beer and water from staved casks sloshing about.

Daylight broke at last to reveal a sorry sight. 'Many ships had their Sails blown off; others had their Masts broken . . . some had their Mains broken . . .' But at least it was still possible for the fleet to limp back to land, where the Prince had chosen Hellevoetsluys with its small level dock as his new headquarters. Mary, who had been so worried during the storm that, as she wrote, 'the only thing I can say that I felt it very hard and disagreable to love someone so much,' received at once a reassuring letter from him, but in another letter on 2 November to Fagel, the prince admitted his dreadful misgivings: only half of his transports were safely back in port, and the continuing storm was endangering the warships still out at sea. 'We can only hope that God will bring them safely back.'

It was hard to remain optimistic, and even the normally positive Burnet came close to despair. 'There were few among us that did not conclude . . . that the whole design was lost,' wrote the Scotsman later. It seemed predestined that they should never set foot on English soil, he remarked gloomily to the prince, who at the time declined to comment and was, anyhow, so deeply committed that he would not even for a moment consider giving up. Huygens found him 'very melancholic', but doing his utmost to conceal the fact. In a letter to

Waldeck, William noted matter-of-factly, 'the worst loss is the time and the horses.'

The fate of the horses had been pitiful: of the 4,000 embarked, about 500 had perished and, according to some reports, as many as 1,000. Because they had been stabled with their heads against the sides of the ships, most of these had their skulls smashed in, while others had suffocated when the hatches had been battened down to stop the water coming in. Van Almonde's flagship *Provincie van Utrecht* was so heavily damaged that he had to shift his flag into the *Maagd van Dordrecht*. But in the end, the first estimates of the damage turned out to have been unduly pessimistic. The States of Holland and West Friesland, in session at The Hague, had sent out orders for every available pilot to cruise the seas between Holland and England, rounding up stragglers and guiding them back to port. And, finally, 'they all returned in good form without any other losses than the horses,' Mary heard. She had settled down quietly now, having prayers said twice daily for her husband's enterprise, and waiting impatiently for his letters. He had promised her not to sail again without seeing her, and she was terrified that the wind would change before he had summoned her. Her worries made it impossible to concentrate '*à la meditation et àla prière*', she had sleepless nights, and when she had trouble with her kidneys, her doctor prescribed a bleeding. The appearance of d'Albeville at Court did not help.

The ambassador had told her secretary d'Allonne that he wanted to see her because he had something to give her from the king. Mary consulted Dijkvelt, then sent her secretary to d'Albeville with a message that because of the prince's departure, she was not receiving anybody. If he had something to tell her, he should put it in writing. 'He sent me a document that His Majesty had ordered to be printed concerning the pretended Prince of Wales.' She read it and sent back a message to d'Albeville: 'I'm not suprised that the King should take the trouble to try and satisfy the doubts of his subjects,' she told him, adding that she herself was no competent judge of a question which must be left to Parliament to settle.

Repairs to so many battered ships in the naval dockyards of Hellevoetsluys took ages, much longer than anyone had expected, while continuing storms made departure out of the question in any case. The little dockyard town was so jammed with people that it was hard to find a bed, and provisions were running low. Whittle was horrified by the prices some of the greedy local tradesmen were charging this huge army of foreigners for food: so much that many people were forced to travel inland and buy directly from the farmers. Still the storms showed no sign of letting up, and even some of the lords began to run out of ready cash, and grumble at the prices being asked. They told the prince, who at once informed the States – 'Therefore a positive Order came forth to print what we must pay, and no more,' Whittle wrote with relief. 'So much a pound for Cheese, Butter, Beef . . . So many eggs for a Styver, and so much to sit by the Fire, Eighteen Styvers for one Night, having a fresh pair of Sheets and lodging there no more.'

William had by now recovered from the setback caused by the storm, and when Moustaquet came to ask if he could travel on another ship, he was struck by the prince's calm cheerfulness. 'I could only admire the steadiness and composure of our hero in such trying circumstances,' he wrote. Whittle was just as impressed. Someone told him that the prince was going around trying to encourage his men, saying, 'For my own part, I am not in the least doubtful but that we shall do very well. I know God is a righteous God.'

At last the gales died down and the wind once more showed signs of changing. With the help of Admiralty-Secretary Hiob de Wildt, who rushed to Hellevoetsluys, the prince had been able to convince the fishermen of Scheveningen to lend him sixty smacks as extra transport, while the farmers around the naval port had sold him enough horses to make good his losses. Once again the fleet was ready for departure. William hastily summoned Mary for a final goodbye, and on 10 November Whittle was present when 'Her Royal Highness cam in her Yacht unto the Brill, where his Highness met her, with many English, Dutch and French Nobles, Knights and gentlemen.' They dined together at Den Brielle where, Mary wrote, 'the Prince had the goodness to come just for a couple of hours, his presence being very much needed at Hellevoetsluys.' The road between the two ports, only a few miles apart, was very bad and the prince had difficulty getting through. For both of them, this parting was even more painful than the first. 'When he left me, it was as if my heart had been torn out. I could not even shed as many tears as the first time.'

Mary stayed without moving in the room where her husband had left her praying: 'All I could do was recommend him to God.' After an hour and a half, she had pulled herself together a little. At last she opened the door of the room and, having found out that there was a sermon in town, 'I went there as to the place that suited me best in my situation.'

The next day, Thursday, 11 November, at four in the afternoon, William's fleet put out to sea from Hellevoetsluys. Mary, who had spent the night at Den Brielle, climbed the 315 steps of the church tower, from which, twelve days earlier, a huge crowd had watched the first departure. This time she was alone with her ladies-in-waiting and she could just glimpse the masts of the ships. An hour later, they were all out of sight. She returned by barge to The Hague, a three-hour journey interrupted by a warm welcome at Maeslandsluys, 'where the Prince is particularly loved by the people', and settled down to wait for news. It came the next day. The wind was fair, the weather excellent, and the fleet was sailing for England with 'ardent hopes for their lucky success'.

Reports of the disaster that had struck the Dutch fleet at its first sortie delighted James II. Accounts reaching London had been deliberately exaggerated 'to lull a great Man asleep', since the Dutch States 'or someone employed by them order'd that the Harlem and Amsterdam Courantiers should make a dismal story of it by representing to the World that the Prince returned with his Fleet miserably shattered and torn, having lost nine Men of War and diverse others of less Concern; 1000 Horses ruin'd . . . the loss of Dr Burnet and the chief ministers under the Prince . . .'

It was the best news the king could have wished for, and a Frenchman in Whitehall was present at dinner when James said, laughing, to Barillon, 'At last the wind has declared itself Popish,' and then, lowering his voice and 'resuming his serious air', he added: 'You know that for these three days I have caused the Holy Sacrament to be carried in procession.'

His complacency was shortlived. A much more reliable report from d'Albeville in The Hague, dated 2 November, spoke only of 'the returne of the fleet in some disorder . . . occasioned by a crewell storm'. He had heard that the prince stayed on board, fearing a mutiny, and that he intended to set sail again 'this day or tomorrow'. He believed, however, that the damage might be serious enough to stop the armada sailing for at least a week.

James relayed this information to Dartmouth, by now arrived at the Gunfleet – 'What damage they received by the storme of Saturday night last I do not yett know' – but he warned him to remain alert: 'You can best judge by the winds which have been since what they can do and by that, how to governe yourself.' He still found it hard to take his peril seriously: 'if what is sayd of their coming out with so small a quantity of victuals and water be true "tis next to a madness.'

Dartmouth agreed, joking that the prince's enterprise to him looked 'more like the advice of land men or at least men of desperate fortune than men that knew how to accomplish what they have undertaken . . .' He had heard that the prince had given orders to try and persuade him and his men to join him, 'but pray sir, be assured I will suffer no language to be spoke to them but out of your guns . . .'

It is questionable whether Dartmouth could have put these brave words into action. The formal invitation to William had stressed the navy's disaffection, and Huygens had been told by a skipper who sailed through the English fleet that he had met and talked to the sailors from two of the ships. 'They had summoned their captains and told them that they would never fight the Dutch fleet.' And they had drunk the Prince of Orange's health.

Much the same mood was noticed on the English mainland. Newsletters in October often alluded to this remarkable unconcern: 'Its to be wondered that the people are no more affected with the danger; their countenances making but little shew of the dark apprehension they should have of the expedition.' Reresby noted in Yorkshire that 'neither the gentry nor common people seemed very much afraid or concerned of it, saying, "The Prince comes only to maintain the Protestant Religion – he will do England no harm."'

In some circles it was even believed that stories of a Dutch invasion were a last ploy devised by James – 'to raise a greater army and to call the French and the Irish in upon them,' Francis Viscount Radcliffe wrote from London to his father the Earl of Derwentwater. As the Imperial ambassador had predicted, James's last-minute concessions had convinced nobody: 'they answer that this may be only to blind them till he has made himself strong enough to take all from them at once.'

Six days later, on Friday, 12 November (2 November, O.S.), the Dutch armada was sailing proudly in the direction of England's northeast coastline, with the prince on the *Den Brielle* in the vanguard, Evertsen's squadron on the right, van Almonde on the left, and Herbert in the rear. It looked as if the invasion was heading in the direction so often predicted, somewhere near Hull, Newcastle or Burlington Bay. So sure was everybody that the invasion would be in the north that the French Minister of Marine, Seignelay, was writing confidently to Barillon on 11 November (October 31, O.S.): 'there is no doubt that the design of the Prince is to go to the North of England or to Scotland – all our advice confirms that the descent will be at Burlington Bay in the province of York.'

Up to the moment of the fleet's departure, d'Albeville's reports were also pointing to Hull in particular as William's first choice. One of his arguments was that, of the twenty English pilots who had been enlisted, the man from Hull was the best-paid: 'they give [him] a reward of 6oL sterling for his conduct'. Hull was not going to be taken by surprise.

Lord Middleton, the new secretary of state, sent a warning to its magistrates on 3 November who immediately looked at their provisions and discovered that there was 'a considerable proportion of corne, Butter, Cheese, Liquors among other necessaries sufficient for a longe siege'. When it became known that the Dutch fleet was on its way, orders were given to sling chains across the river mouth, and to open the sluices 'to flood the country for three miles to prevent the Dutch from coming here'.

William did nothing to dispel this belief. The success of his invasion depended to a great extent on support in the north of England, where three of those who had signed the invitation – Danby, Lumley and Devonshire – were actively planning risings; their enthusiasm might be damped by news that William was heading for the south or south-west.

Another consideration was the movement of James's armies. It suited the prince to keep James believing for as long as possible that the landing would be in the north of England, and the stratagem worked. According to one of d'Albeville's informers, Zuylestein having been to 'some creek or place upon the coast of England, where he was to meet somebody', got back to the fleet with the news that James had sent troops off in the direction of Hull. A newsletter of 11 November confirmed this: 'a regiment of fusiliers marched for the north this morning.'

Even in the Dutch fleet, many believed that it was the prince's intention to land in the north if possible, but the captains at least knew better by now. Just before their departure, Herbert, Evertsen, Bentinck and Russell had held a council of war on Herbert's flagship to draw up final instructions. The prince himself was at that moment at the rear waiting for the last of the slow-moving transports to clear the mouth of the Meuse, but the four had sufficient authority to plan tactics. They decided that the whole fleet should sail north-east to the Hoofden, the southern stretch of the North Sea, and then, turning to the south, 'sail along the English coast as near as possible if the wind is north . . . and then to sail into Cowes or the river at Southampton in order to land there where these warships can advance'. Poole was another possibility but of this 'convenient place we hardly spoke for lack of pilots who know the place'; and Exmouth was also considered, 'where we can advance with alle the transport ships as far as Topsom [Topsham, near Exeter] and lie with five hundred ships at the same time to disembark on land without the enemy fleet being able to follow us as there is not enough water for that'.

In the end, however – it had always been acknowledged – a final decision would have to depend on the wind. Should it change, but only then, 'we are to follow a course to the north as is reported in the rendezvous note'. This memorandum, written by Bentinck in his own hand, makes it plain that Herbert's arguments had carried the day, and that the prince and his staff had now opted for the south or south-west. But for the moment they sailed slowly north-east, Bentinck explaining to the prince that it was impossible to change course before morning since nobody 'dared to approach the Hoofden by night with such a numerous fleet'.

During the night of 12-13 November, they rode quietly at sea with slackened sails, 'in the same posture, not making two leagues a watch'. It was not an agreeable wait. Whittle complained: 'The vessels having no sail, would throw themselves from side to side, and all the people in them, after a sad sort.'

In the middle of the night, there was a sudden alarm: 'An advice boat brought us an Account that the English Fleet, consisting of 33 sail, lay to the Westward of ours,' Burnet remembered. The prince's ship fired a gun as a general alert, 'which caused great Consternation in the whole fleet', and convinced everybody that all was lost, but other patrol ships brought news that it was Herbert with some of the Dutch fleet which had been driven apart, 'upon whose arrival, great rejoycing was among us all, and a Signal of Joy was given for it by the Prince'.

Early that morning another council of war was held, this time with the prince presiding, and orders were finally given that the fleet should change course and sail south-west in the direction of the Channel. The Protestant east wind was now blowing in the prince's favour and, as he and Herbert had calculated, the same easterly wind kept the English fleet cooped up in the Gunfleet, unable to stir. Thus Dartmouth and his fleet were helpless spectators when on Saturday at daybreak the Dutch armada sailed past.

Dartmouth, who two days earlier had boasted that it would be 'impossible for us to miss such a fleet', now had to report to the king: 'we saw thirteen saile about three leagues to windward of us.' According to one report, some of the Dutch ships sailed so close to the English fleet that they were 'à une portée de canon'. They veered off hastily but were chased by three English 'friggattes'. One Dutch flyboat with four companies of infantry – 200 men – aboard, lost its rudder when it ran aground on a sandbank and was captured, but the others, despite a few shots fired at them, were able to rejoin the Dutch fleet.

A little later, at eight o'clock, when 'the Sun-beams had dissipated the Mist and dispers'd the Fogg', the coast of England came in sight. 'The wind continued very favourably, and withal blowing a good

Fresh Gale,' the fleet entered Dover Straits at midday in bright sun-
shine. With any threat from the English fleet now safely behind them,
the close defensive formation of the armada could be abandoned, and
the prince gave orders for the fleet to spread into a new and more
impressive formation. '. . . From Dover to Callis, twenty five deep; the
Flanks and rear were guarded by our Men of War,' reported Burnet.
And as they sailed through the narrow Straits of Dover, 'the Trumpets
and Drums [were] playing various Tunes to rejoyce our Hearts'. It
was, he said lyrically, a sight that 'would have ravish'd the most curious
Eyes of Europe'.

His colleague Whittle was just as enthusiastic about the spectacle
organized by the prince, who had ordered that his personal standard
should be run up, 'whereupon the Men of War set out their colours
and so did every Vessel in the Fleet. The whole fleet was resolv'd to
make a Bravado: so each vessel kept a due distance from the other and
bespangled the whole Channel with beautiful Ships and Colours flying.'
Some of the men-of-war approached the English coasts, others neared
the French coast and fired a few shots. Altogether, it was 'a sight
worthy of the greatest Monarch to behold'.

If William had wanted to impress the English and the French, he
certainly succeeded. 'The people both at Dover and Calis . . . were
amaz'd at such a glorious sight,' wrote Whittle, and other eye-witnesses
confirmed this. One reported in awe that the first ships were in sight of
Dover at ten in the morning, but there were so many of them it was
five in the afternoon before the last of them had rounded the straits. A
Mr Bastick told a friend, in amazement: 'They are about halfe Seas
over, and are soe thick there is noe telling of them, but "tis judged
above three hundred saile.' With a good following wind, the armada
reached Dungeness at nightfall, but the prince was determined to push
on and 'commanded us to follow the Signal by Lights he had hung out
to us'.

When the sun came up next morning, the fleet was nearing the Isle
of Wight where its governor, Sir Robert Holmes, was already anxiously
wondering if the Dutch would land. He had sent no fewer than three
warnings to London in October of 'the ill condition of this island', but
to no avail. No troops arrived, and in the end he had to call up 400
men of the local militia.

On this day, though, there was no cause for concern. It was not only
the Lord's Day, it was also William's thirty-eighth birthday, and the
eleventh anniversary of his wedding to Mary. Instead of sailing on or
landing, he decided to 'observe the duty of the day', reported Whittle.
So the fleet slackened sail, 'all were driven of the Waves. Prayers and

Sermon being done, he went to Dinner with some Nobles attending him.'

Over dinner, early that afternoon, they discussed where to land. They had already sent scouts to the Isle of Wight, where Sir Robert was now confronted by a mutinous militia, who were for surrendering the island 'without striking one stroke for it'; but there were no tactical advantages to be gained by landing on the island, so at four o'clock in the afternoon, the prince gave orders to sail on.

Far behind him, Dartmouth had of course understood that there was to be no invasion in the north, and Pepys confirmed 'the appearance of the Dutch fleet [near Dover] and its being gone westward'. Hours too late, the English fleet finally cleared the Gunfleet to follow the Dutch down the Channel as far as Beachy Head. But although Dartmouth's orders had been explicit – 'by all Hostile means to burn, take and otherwise destroy and disable' the Prince's expedition – he stopped there and decided to 'jog easily' while waiting for further orders from James. The pause allowed William, with his much more slowly moving fleet, to sail on undisturbed along the south coast. After his triumphant display in the Channel, the prince no longer bothered to conceal the position of his fleet and that night, after his ship lit up its three lanterns, every other ship followed suit.

'It was no ordinary sight,' Whittle thought, 'for to behold the Seas all cover'd with Lights, the Lanthorns appearing at a distance like unto so many Stars in the Water, dancing to and fro, here and there . . . but above all, the Cabin of that Vessel wherein the Prince was having so many Wax Lights burning within it, glittered most gloriously and (at a certain distance) being well gilt and varnished, it seem'd a Paradise for pleasure and delight.'

The night was so beautiful that many soldiers and sailors escaped from their cramped quarters to go on deck and admire the sight: 'the Stars in the Firmament, and our Stars, the three Lanthorns on the Stern, shining with Wax Lights dazzled our eyes.' The wind was strong and 'blowed very fresh, which caused our Whole Fleet to plow the curling Waves . . . with very good speed and pleasure'. But later that night the skies clouded over. When day broke and the coast of Devon became visible, it was a wet and unpleasant day.

The prince had originally planned to land at Exmouth, but Russell told Herbert that the pilot, 'Mr Gilbert', had advised against it, 'posetive that with this wind the see is too great for the fleat'. He considered it better to go on to 'Dartmouth and torr bay'.

Thomas Bowyer, the Collector of Customs in Dartmouth, could not believe his eyes when 'the morning being very hazy, foggie and full of raine, [it] cleared up about 9 o'clock at which time appeared the Dutch fleet.' Like a good customs officer, he at once started counting: 'about four hundred or 500 sail as neare as we can guess . . .' He did not know that the day before, the prince had planned to send Edward Russell on ahead to the naval base of Dartmouth, with two frigates and three flyboats full of infantry, and orders to capture the two forts on either side of the harbour. Thanks to the heavy mist, and a pilot's error, the main fleet had overshot the harbour, and the infantry raid was cancelled.

'The Capital ships are off of Torbay,' reported a relieved Bowyer later that morning. Whittle knew by now that a landing was imminent, and followed the last phase of the crossing even more attentively than usual. 'Here we were moving for a while very slowly by the shore and could see all the Rocks thereabout very plain,' he wrote. The steep cliffs and the rocks made the coast 'not very commodious for Men and Horses'.

It was not until Tor Bay was reached that a landing seemed possible, but the easterly wind was still strong and it looked as if this bay too would be overshot. The situation was perilous. The next port was Plymouth, heavily guarded by troops under the command of Lord Bath, and a gloomy Russell told Burnet, 'You may go to prayers, Doctor. All is over.' But once again the Protestant wind came to the rescue of the prince. Having blown steadily from the east for four days, it suddenly turned south-west.

It drove Dartmouth, still waiting for his instructions at Beachy Head, to the north, where he had to find shelter in the Downs – making him, as he wrote to the king, 'the most unfortunate man liveing'. But for the Prince of Orange it was what he needed. He gave orders to run up his personal standard, with the white flag above it, 'signifying his most gracious offer of Peace', and the red flag underneath, 'signifying War unto all such as did oppose his just Designs'. The sun by now had recovered its strength, the fog was dissipating and it had turned into a pleasant day.

The south-westerly wind, which James's Jesuit advisers had promised him would blow till Christmas, was now the answer to Protestant prayers – 'the only wind that could blow to bring us safe into the Bay.'

THIRTEEN

'THE PRINCE THAT'S COME'

'It's a wretched little place,' was Huygen's first impression of Brixham. 'Just a few ugly houses, made of the same stone as the whole coast and countryside, roofed in slate. It lies against a mountain, at the foot of which the houses are stuck in short rows.' The inhabitants of this Devon fishing village had woken up to an astonishing sight that morning: the enormous invasion fleet entering their bay.

The Prince of Orange could hardly have picked a more appropriate day for his landing: according to the Continental calendar it was 15 November, but in England, where the old-style calendar was still used, it was Guy Fawkes Day, 5 November, the day on which the English traditionally celebrated their deliverance from popish tyranny. Huge banners waving from the ships spelt out the same message: '*Pro libertate et religione.*'

All the ships had hoisted their colours: red for the English and Scottish regiments commanded by Major-General Hugh Mackay, white for the Prince of Orange's Guards and the Brandenburgers under Count Henrijk von Solms-Braunfels and the blue flag for the Dutch and French, commanded by Count Walraad van Nassau-Saarbruck. No one could doubt it any longer: the Dutch fleet, 'so much talked of in the nation and so long expected by most people', had arrived.

Whittle, enthusiastic as usual, climbed to the highest spot of his ship and, hoping to remove the last trace of doubt, gestured to the crowd with his Bible, 'making many flourishes with it unto the people whose Eyes were fixed on him'. As loud as he could, he shouted: 'For the Protestant Religion', adding, 'It's the Prince of Orange that's come, a zealous Defender of that Faith which is truly Ancient, Catholic and Apostolical.'

The prince and his staff had changed from the *Den Brielle* to the smaller *Princess Mary*, which now entered the bay escorted by four men-of-war. A swarm of merchant ships, pinks and flyboats surrounded it, while on board a last conference was held. It was decided to send von Solms to find out the general mood, but it was already very obvious that the people were friendly. When he returned to confirm this, the *Princess Mary* sailed very slowly in towards land, with the guns of the fleet saluting.

It was low tide, and to reach the small quay the prince had to transfer to a rowing-boat, but even that soon grounded in the mud. William stood up and, in answer to excited questions asking what his business was, he called back with a strong foreign accent: 'Mine goot people, mine goot people, I am only come for your goots, for all your goots.' According to Brixham tradition a wag in the crowd inevitably shouted, 'Yes, and for our chattels too,' but he was an exception. Most people told the prince that he was welcome. 'If that's so,' he replied, 'come and carry me ashore.' Without more ado a sturdy fisherman called Peter Varwell waded out and carried his future king – 'a little and delicate man of light weight', he remembered later – triumphantly to the steps of the quay.

The prince's arrival in Brixham gave rise to a number of legends, one of which says that Peter Varwell was so taken by the prince that he followed him on his donkey to Exeter. The prince, delighted, asked him to come to London, where he promised to make him a great man. When Varwell went to London, however, he promptly fell into the hands of a gang of thieves, who robbed him of the special pass William had given him, so that they received the reward. In a happier version, Varwell succeeded in reaching the prince, who gave him £100, with which he built himself a bigger house.

Some of the crowd couldn't wait and, according to an anonymous Dutch war-reporter, walked into the water to kiss William's hands and, 'showing other signs of joy, [shouting] Godt blesjou, Godt blesjou'.

The prince did not waste his time. With the veteran Marshal Armand-Frédéric von Schomberg who, as commander of the army, now after the landing replaced Herbert as the prince's right hand, and with the other commanders he climbed the hill to view the surrounding terrain and pick a suitable site to make camp. Once again the prince had decided to put on a show for the English, and Whittle loved it: 'the Colours flying and flourishing before his Highness; the Trumpets sounding, the Hoitboys played, the Drums beat, and the Lords, Knights, Gentlemen and Guards, shouted and sundry Huzzas did now echo in the Fleet, from off the Hill, in so much that our very Hearts below on the Water, were even ravished for Joy . . .'

From the crest at Furzeham, 170 feet above sea level, the prince was able to look down on the masses of soldiers marching up the hill, and the frenzied activity at the quayside, where men and equipment were being unloaded at top speed. Before him also was his fleet anchored in a bay whose water was so calm that 'it seemed like a huge pond'. In the distance, hovering protectively at the mouth of the bay, Herbert's squadron was just visible. At the prince's instruction the admiral had taken up this position to intercept Dartmouth if he should finally appear.

His reconnaissance complete, the prince returned to the quayside. For once, everything seemed to be going exactly as he had planned and Burnet noticed that he looked 'cheerfuller than ordinary'. The prince greeted him with a rare joke: 'Well, Doctor, what do you think of predestination now?' But Burnet, who had completely forgotten his own gloomy remark of a few days earlier, replied sententiously that he would never forget 'that providence of God which had appeared so signally on this occasion'. It would therefore be appropriate to hold here and now a small service of thanksgiving, and the prince agreed. To Burnet's annoyance, however, he asked another Scot, William Carstares, to lead the service. For a few minutes all work stopped while the prince and his men sang the 118th Psalm in the half-dozen languages of this multi-national army. 'This is the day which the Lord hath made,' they recited with special fervour. 'Let us be glad and rejoice therein.'

Then it was back to work and Whittle followed it all with fascination. 'The people were like Bees swarming all over the Bay . . . The Officers and Soldiers crowded the Boats extreamly, many being ready to sink under the Weight . . .' Some of the men were so eager to set foot on land again that they jumped out of the boats and waded or swam ashore.

The day closed with a golden sunset, but even after dark the unloading went on by the light of flares, and at last, at three o'clock in the morning, the men and the stores that were needed had all been landed. The horses had to wait till daylight, and the heavy baggage, most of the ammunition and the artillery, were sent on by sea to Topsham to catch up with them at Exeter – miles away.

That first night on English soil was bitterly cold. It had rained heavily for the last few weeks and the ground was soaking, but stars twinkled out of a clear sky over the tents where the sentries stood guard. Until late in the evening soldiers were still toiling up the hill, the slopes of which were dotted with hundreds of camp-fires. Some of the men cooked their rations from their 'snap-sacks', others went foraging in nearby farms or in the village itself. One small band of soldiers were particularly lucky. They knocked on the door of a certain Lady Carew, a Roman Catholic, whose priest, at the sight of the Dutch fleet, had concluded it was the French coming to James's rescue. He had summoned the whole household to sing a Te Deum, after which they were going to share a celebratory dinner. For Lady Carew and her priest the sudden arrival of the Dutch soldiers at her door was a bitter disappointment – but the guests certainly appreciated the feast.

Down in Brixham the local alehouse, the Buller's Arms, did a roaring trade until the supply of ale ran out – 'a very happy time for the Landlord, who strutted about as if indeed he had been a Lord himself, because he was honoured with Lord's company,' Whittle thought. Moustaquet felt instantly at home. Coming from Normandy he was delighted to discover and try the powerful local 'scrumpy', or cider, and it tasted excellent with the fat goose he and some friends had been able to scrounge. Over at the 'Crouned Rose Tavern', Huygens was less happy. The fricassee of mutton which they served him there was tough. However, he had a bed.

Indeed, he was better off than the prince, who had to make do with a mattress on the floor in Peter Varwell's little house in Middle Street. The only sign that an important guest was staying there was the prince's standard fluttering over the roof. William, after years of campaigning, was used to roughing it, and at least he kept dry, unlike most of his soldiers.

The clear starlit night turned into an extremely wet morning. The rain was teeming down, but the disembarkation had to go on. It was the turn of the 4,000 horses, and the prince feared it would take days before they would all be on land. But the local fishermen came to help and showed him a spot half a mile away where the coast shelved so steeply that the ships could be brought in almost to the shore, so that the horses had only a twenty-yard swim. 'There was a dead calm that morning and in three hours' time all our horses were landen,' Burnet reported.

The villagers were amazed by the efficiency and speed with which the horses, fully harnessed, were led stumbling, one by one, onto the beach. The small crowd from the day before had grown as people from all over the region came swarming in to look at the prince and his soldiers. Huygens was not very impressed by them – 'never seen such dirty people' – but others were less sniffy and appreciated the gifts some brought, apples and jugs of cider. The prince seized the chance and gave orders for the distribution of some of the thousands of copies of his Declaration, which he had brought from Holland. A local historian tells how one girl had helped with the distribution with such enthusiasm that not one was left for herself as a souvenir. Instead, the family treasured for generations the velvet purse and the golden chain which the girl had been wearing when she shook the hand of the Prince of Orange.

Having landed unexpectedly in Brixham, none of the people who had invited the prince to come over were there, and he knew that he had to wait till he reached his first big city, Exeter, before they would join him. But the start seemed promising. The only gentleman of substance around Brixham, a Mr Nicholas Roope, came to William to offer his allegiance. Mr Roope would later claim to have been 'the first that came to the Prince'. He was rewarded when William in January 1689 signed the warrant that made Roope governor of Dartmouth Castle, an appointment he confirmed when he was king.

Roope reached the prince just in time. The horses were now all safely disembarked and it was time to leave the coast. Before the departure, the prince held a review of his 15,000 men, regiment by regiment, had a last meal in the village and gave the signal to march. Slowly the enormous army train began to move, with William – as was to become his habit – riding in the middle line, together with Schomberg, Solms, Nassau, Bentinck and Shrewsbury.

But one man was left behind, seriously ill. When he died, a fortnight later, they buried him simply in the graveyard next to St Mary's Church in High Brixham. The burial records state: '21 November, a foreigner belonging to the Prenze of Orange.' In another book, containing an account of those buried in wool – in accordance with a law passed to encourage the wool trade – the entry reads: 'November 21. *a Dutchman cujus nomen ignotum*.' This Unknown Soldier was to be one of the rare casualties of William's invasion.

Huygens, whose horses had not yet been unloaded, left a few hours after the prince, and immediately lost his way in the labyrinth of narrow, muddy Devon roads. When it was getting dark he met up with some infantry men and blundered about the countryside with them till half-past seven, unable to locate the prince, who was supposed to be at Kingskerswell. At last he found a friendly soul who offered him shelter in his small tent from the rain still pelting down.

It's not surprising that Huygens was unable to find his master: just where William spent his second night on English soil is a mystery. Some sources mention an old posting-house, 'the Crown and Anchor . . . a commodious inn with . . . stabling for a large number of horses', while Whittle mentions 'a certain Gentleman's House about two miles off', which might have been in Yalberton. Another mystery is what William did the third day. It is said that he went to Longcombe where, in another farmhouse, he had his first meeting with the local gentry, who promised him that they would join him in Exeter. Both farmhouses are still in existence. The one at Yalberton is called King William's

Cottage; the one at Longcombe, where William is supposed to have had his first 'parliament', still bears the name Parliament House. Tradition says that the prince had a meeting here with the Tory leader Sir Edward Seymour, who lived in nearby Berry Pomeroy, but any documentation about these visits must have been destroyed. The people in Devon, as Huygens would discover, had not forgotten the bloody aftermath of the Monmouth rebellion only three years ago.

For the thousands of soldiers, the march had got under way in earnest the day before, Tuesday. The last had left Brixham, and the now empty transport ships were at sea waiting for orders, while those whose cargoes were not needed before Exeter were sailing up the bay towards Exmouth. A number of the horses had been injured during the crossing and disembarkation, and although most of the 400 lost in the first storm had been replaced, they were almost all in poor shape, unsteady on their legs, and remained so for two or three days. To spare them till they were fit again, '. . . every Souldier was commanded by their officers to carry some thing or other besides his own Arms and Snap-sack'. Nobody was very happy about this, and many of the men, in little better shape than the horses, stumbled and fell, 'because of the dissiness in their Heads, after they had been so long toss'd at Sea'.

Progress was slow; it was raining again, the march lasted till late in the evening and the going was rough. 'The Lanes hereabouts were very narrow and not used to Wagons, Carts and Coaches,' Whittle noticed, 'and therefore extream rough and stony.' The Dutch soldiers, used to better roads at home, grumbled to the chaplain that they 'wished themselves back in their own country'. Huygens joined the chorus of complaint: 'the roads were amazingly bad, all made of stone and strewn with pebbles, on top of that dirt and mud.' The men struggled on through this very difficult country, as Moustaquet put it, marching in two long snaking lines 'between two ditches crowned with dense thorn hedges or walls of dry stone'. The Frenchmen admired the enterprise of the inhabitants, who had divided up this unrewarding landscape with so much effort and expense. 'There are only hills or . . . heather-covered rocks.'

Villages were few and far between, but everywhere along the army's route, Huygens noted with satisfaction, people came running out of their isolated farmhouses – 'men, women and children, all calling, "God bless you," and a hundred other good wishes.' He was struck by the fact that even the women were smoking pipes. 'At one spot there were five women saluting [the prince], each with a pipe of tobacco in her mouth, as we very often saw, smoking quite shamelessly, even young children of 13 or 14.' Moustaquet was diverted by the sight. 'We enjoyed studying the way these island people lived, and how addicted to tobacco they all were, men, women, even children.' He couldn't stop laughing when his hostess, 'young and pretty', gave her baby the breast while she smoked a pipe, which she handed to the child when he stopped sucking. 'He took it and put it in his mouth and tried hard to smoke,' commented the astonished Frenchman.

For thousands of soldiers, making camp was an almost impossible task that night. It had been raining for hours and the countryside was a red sea of mud. 'Nevertheless the poor Souldiers being much wearied with the Tent Polls, spare Arms and Other Utensils for War, which they had carried alle Day and some hours after Night, as well as with the badness of the march, lay down to take their repose; and verily the Water ran over and under some of their Legs the major part of the Night.' Some of the men sank halfway into the mud, but dog-tired as they were, 'they slept all Night very sweetly in their Pee, or Campagne Coats'.

Once again the men made their campfires from old hedges, gates, anything they could scrounge, 'else some would have perished from the Cold', and broiled the Dutch beef they had in their snap-sacks, or the chickens they had bought along the way. 'Sundry Captains offer'd any Money for a Guide to bring them to a House thereabout, where they might have some Provision for their Mony, but no Guide could be found, it was exceeding dark and being all Strangers and unacquainted with the Country we could not tell where to find one house.' One way and another, 'we thought this Night almost as long as that in the Storm at Sea,' recalled Whittle, '... we were sure ... that worse Quarters we could never meet.'

At first light the bedraggled and mud-stained army got under way again and toiled on to Newton Abbot. Whittle, zealous as ever, went on ahead and found out that Wednesday was market day in the little town, which consisted of just three streets. There were crowds of people about, so he went straight to the town hall and, pulling the famous Declaration out of his pocket, read it aloud at the top of his voice: 'William Henry by the Grace of God, Prince of Orange . . .', telling the gathering crowds 'of the reasons inducing Him to appear in the Arms in the Kingdom of England, for preserving of the Protestant Religion and restoring the Law and Liberties of England, Scotland and Ireland . . .'

The people flocked round Whittle and, when he had finished reading the Declaration,'with one heart and voice, answered Amen, Amen and forthwith shouted for Joy and made the town ring with their echoing Huzza's'. To save him from being mobbed, some of them pulled the army chaplain into a house, slamming the windows and bolting the doors in a hurry, after which they offered him some food. Whittle answered politely, 'Give me what you will.' In payment for the food, they asked him for a copy of the Declaration, and he gave them three.

Knowing that the prince was not far away, it suddenly occurred to him that it would be a good idea to ring the church bells in welcome, but the parish minister was frightened and hesitated. 'Sir, for my own part, I am ready to serve his Highness any way,' he told Whittle, 'but of my own accord cannot give the Keys; but you know you may command them . . . in the name of the Prince of Orange, and I will readily grant it.' And so it happened. As the bells pealed out, 'the people of the Town were exceedingly joyful and began to drink the Prince of Orange's health.'

Although the people made it plain that the prince and his army were welcome, it was equally clear that they were frightened. Huygens spent the night in the house of a Newton Abbot saddlemaker, and it was there that he was told that the king had published an order-in-council which said that 'commersie' with the Dutch would be considered treason. The saddlemaker explained about the Monmouth invasion, adding, 'If this thing doe miscarry, we are all undon.' Whittle came across the same fears. 'Notwithstanding, some were so couragious as to speak out and say, truly their Hearts were for us.' They told him that they prayed for the prince, but that if the Irish soldiers knew of it, they 'would come and cut them in pieces'.

While the soldiers were 'treated by the Vulgar', their leader was being entertained at Forde Abbey, an attractive Jacobean mansion dating from 1610, four miles outside the town. The Courtenay family who lived there were supporters of William – a young brother was an army officer in Utrecht, and had paid his court to William and Mary, finding them 'with a great deall of Zeall for the Protestant interest and the welfare of England'. But William Courtenay, elderly and disabled by a stroke, had been implicated in both the Monmouth rebellion and the Rye House Plot, and although he had sent his invitation to the prince twenty-four hours after the landing at Brixham, he thought it politic to keep a safe distance himself. 'Even when the Prince spent the night in Courtenay's house near Newton Abbot,' it was reported, 'he gave no countenance to the enterprise either in his own name or by his tenants.' Despite this rather non-committal welcome, the prince 'of his own accord', as Shrewsbury reported, made him a baron in April of the following year, leaving to him the choice of title.

On Thursday, 8 November William with his bodyguard, five battalions of infantry, and two regiments of dragoons, arrived in the small town of Chudleigh, where he stayed the night in an imposing house called Cholwichs, in the town centre. His hostess Bridget Gawler came from the staunchly Protestant Poulett family, like the Courtenays loyal supporters of William. Her husband John was one of the hundreds who had come under suspicion at the time of the Monmouth rebellion. Orders for his arrest had been issued and a guard posted at his house, but he and some other Protestants had evaded arrest and taken refuge in some nearby caves at Black Rock. The intrepid Bridget had managed to get food to them every day, though it hadn't been easy thinking up excuses for leaving the house. The Gawlers were understandably happy to welcome the prince, and it was from the balcony of their house that William made his first public speech in England.

On the same day, Burnet and Lord Mordaunt rode the last nine miles from Chudleigh to Exeter to see what kind of welcome the prince was likely to get. They were not the first of his supporters to reach the city. Only two days after the landing, a certain Captain Hicks, the son of a Nonconformist minister executed for his role in the Monmouth rebellion, had arrived to spread the good news. 'As soon as he came, the Mobile in very great numbers flocked to him to list themselves in the service of the Prince of Orange,' Burnet heard next day. The mayor of Exeter, Sir Christopher Brodrick, strongly objected, and demanded to see his commission. When Hicks could not produce one, he threatened to throw him in jail, 'but the Concourse of People was so great about the Guild Hall, that they would not suffer him to be carried away', and he remained there until next day, guarded by two constables.

It was Mordaunt and Burnet who got him out. Arriving at the West Gate of Exeter, the two men, accompanied by four troops of horse, found it shut. 'Upon which Lord Mordaunt commanded the Porter to open the Gate on pain of Death,' Burnet remembered. The porter hurriedly obeyed and Mordaunt ordered him not to close it again. Then, having heard about Hicks' confinement, he rode on to the Guild Hall, where he soon found that Hicks was 'very nobly provided for' – upon which 'there was a Guinea given to those that waited on him'.

The two men next wanted to know if the mayor intended to give the prince a formal welcome when he arrived next day. Sir Christopher – only recently reinstated with great ceremony – replied courageously that 'he was under the Obligation of an Oath to his Majesty and therefore desired the Prince would lay no commands on him that should be prejudicial to his Conscience'. There would, however, be no resistance. That was good enough for them and they went on to look

for suitable accommodation for the prince. Thomas Lamplugh, the
bishop, had fled the city earlier in the day, and the dean had gone too;
Burnet and Mordaunt inspected his house, the deanery, decided that it
would do very well and went back to report to the prince at Chudleigh.

It rained again on Friday, 9 November, while the army toiled on to
Exeter. The rolling countryside with its trees and hedgerows in soft
autumnal colours and its sticky red earth seemed unfriendly in the
pouring rain to the exhausted troops, but the warm welcome of the
inhabitants was some compensation. As they were marching over the
heath or common near Exeter, about five miles off the city, sundry
'Companies of young Men met them, with each a Club in his Hand,
and as they approached near, they gave sundry shouts and Huzza's,
saying God bless the Prince of Orange and Grant him Victory over all
his Enemies,' Whittle reported. He noticed with satisfaction that when
the column marched past the house of a 'Popish lady' who had been
'cruell to all her Protestant tenants', nothing happened. 'But had the
French King's Army passed thus by a Protestant House, it should soon
have been fired, the People put to the sword or burnt.'

At last the city of Exeter appeared in the plain of the Ex river – a
compact cluster of houses with crumbling towers and walls that would
have been useless against cannon fire, with the grey cathedral rising in
its midst. Huygens, who had left Chudleigh at nine that morning,
arrived soaking wet an hour and a half ahead of the prince, but he had
no chance to explore the city that reminded him of Rotterdam. The
crowds were already gathering for the prince's grand entry and now,
seeing the first Dutchman arrive, they gave him 'many benedictions
. . . even in the outskirts there was shouting and acclamations and
waving with the hats'.

Their enthusiasm for Huygens was as nothing compared with that
which seized the inhabitants when the prince and his army crossed the
Ex bridge and approached the wide-open West Gate. Sir Christopher
Brodrick had kept his word and was absent, but the aldermen thought
better and welcomed William warmly, and the windows were decorated in the streets, and the church bells ringing.

The enormous cavalcade that came clattering into the city that late
Friday afternoon, bridles jingling and pennants flying, was intended
by the prince both as a splendid spectacle to woo the common people,
and a show of military strength calculated to win over any waverers.
'The guards rode, some before and some behind him, with their Swords
drawn, their Colours Flying, Kettle Drums beating and Trumpets
sounding joyfully, all sorts and conditions of Men thronging on each

side the Streets, making great Acclamations and Huzzas as the Prince passed by.'

To emphasize the peaceful nature of this demonstration, the English Earl Macclesfield led the way with a troop of cavalry, 'the most part English Gentlemen, mounted richly on Flanders Steeds, in Headpieces, Back and Breast, Bright Armour'. They were followed by 200 black men, the first these Devon country people had ever seen, brought from the plantations of the Netherlands in America – Surinam – wearing 'Imbroyder'd Caps lin'd with white Fur, and Plumes of white Feathers' on their heads. After them came the same number of Laplanders from the Scandinavian contingent, in black armour with reindeer skins over their shoulders, and armed with broadswords. Just ahead of William there were fifty gentlemen and as many pages to attend and support the prince's huge banner with its inscription, 'God and the Protestant Religion', and then fifty led horses, all 'Manag'd and brought up to Wards', with two grooms to each horse, and two coaches of state. William himself, with Schomberg riding next to him, looked impressive riding on a white horse, in brightly polished armour (an antiquary, Mr Thomas Barrett of Manchester, has stated in a treatise on armour that this was the last occasion on which armour was worn in England), with a 'Plume of White Feathers on his Head' and forty-two footmen running beside him.

After the prince came another contingent of 200 cavalry, 300 Swiss mercenaries armed with fusees, 500 volunteers with two led horses apiece, the Prince's Guards, 600 men armed *'Cap à Pee'* and the rest of the army bringing up the rear. Whittle thought these last rather let the side down: 'The Foot Souldiers did not appear well, because they were sorely weatherbeaten and much dabled in marching in the Dirt and Rain, and look'd very pale and thin after such a hard day's march which made some People conjecture that they were dull sluggish men.'

But altogether it was a splendid show, which took nearly three hours to wind past, and the Exeter people – in holiday spirits despite the rain – showed their appreciation by cheering and lighting bonfires when dusk fell.

Later on that day, there was a solemn service of thanksgiving in the crowded cathedral. When the prince arrived, having refreshed himself at the deanery, he was 'conducted to the Bishop's Seat . . . [and] sat down, with about six of his Life Guard men on his right hand, and many more before him and about him in the Quire', Whittle noted. All went well at first while a Te Deum was earnestly listened to, but when Burnet started reading the prince's Declaration, there was a sudden commotion. 'The Ministers of the Church there present rushed immediately out of their Seats, and busled through all the Croud, going out of the Church.' The congregation stayed put, and when Burnet finished reading the Declaration and shouted at the top of his voice, 'God Bless the Prince of Orange,' they answered, 'Amen.'

FOURTEEN

'NOBODY MINDED THE KING'

The first news of William's landing reached James at Whitehall in about twenty-eight hours. Thomas Bowyer, the Collector of Customs at Dartmouth, had sent off a messenger with an express at noon on 5 November, and the man arrived in London at about four the following afternoon. Not only had he ridden seven horses to death *en route*, it was said, but he himself was so exhausted by his marathon ride that 'he fell speechless at James's feet'. A newsletter reported gloomily: 'It is thought he will hardly recover, but the King's physicians have particular charge to take care of him.'

James at once summoned an extraordinary meeting of the Privy Council. A few hours later a proclamation was issued in which James took the chance of a public reply to William's Declaration. '. . . this invasion of our kingdoms,' he declared, '. . . so unChristian and unnatural an undertaking in a person so nearly related to us,' could have only one object: 'an absolute usurping of our crown and royal authority.' He pointed out that 'many mischiefs and calamities' must follow this invasion by 'an army of foreigners and rebels'. He questioned the sincerity of William's promise to call a free Parliament: 'nothing can be more evident than that a Parliament cannot be free so long as there is an army of foreigners in the heart of our kingdoms.' He himself had already called for a free Parliament – 'so soon as (by the blessing of God) our kingdoms shall be delivered from this invasion.'

As propaganda, this was thin. It was James's own policies, in the view of most of his subjects, which threatened the nation with 'mischiefs and calamities', and it seemed unlikely that the Dutch Protestant prince would do worse. Thanks to William's far more effective public relations, the English had anyhow been taught to mistrust the king's good intentions. James's rhetoric fell on deaf ears – 'the people paid but little attention' – and his promises were disregarded: it was cynically assumed that they would not 'be binding any longer than the emergency which produced them'.

On the face of it, James's position was fairly strong. His fleet under the luckless Dartmouth – still protesting at the 'ill censures and misconstructions . . . of my proceedings' – had been frustrated in yet another attempt to assail the Dutch, and beaten back to the Downs. But at least it was still intact. James sent orders to Dartmouth that he was to pursue the Dutch and if possible attack their fleet at anchor in Tor Bay: should the wind change again, he might cruise to intercept reinforcements.

Meanwhile, the king could congratulate himself on having at least made prompt military preparations for invasion. Over 4,000 of the newly raised troops were still being trained, and about the same number were needed for garrison duty and the defence of London. But even so, he could put in the field against William an army of around 30,000. On the earlier information that William had sailed, Sir John Lanier, commanding the cream of the English cavalry troops, had been dispatched north to Ipswich, to cover a possible landing on the east coast. Now he and his command were hastily summoned south again, and sent off towards Salisbury and William's armies, with orders to report back on their movements as soon as possible. As they clattered through the Home Counties, the main body of the army, under the solid but uninspired command of Feversham, also received its marching orders for the west, complete with baggage and artillery train. James himself proposed to take personal command of the army once he was satisfied that all was well on the London front.

The city of Salisbury, strategically sited on the route William would have to take for London, was picked for the rendezvous, but James's own journey was delayed for some days. The anniversary of Queen Elizabeth's accession – November 17 – was often the occasion for violent anti-popish outbursts, and exactly one hundred years earlier, England had faced and fought off another attempt to reconvert her by force, in the shape of the Spanish Armada. The popish threat now came from Whitehall, and it was the invaders who were seen as deliverers, but this special anniversary might well see an explosion of anti-Catholic feeling, and James's Catholic advisers begged him not to leave London until it was safely over.

There had already been several incidents involving Catholic places of worship. There had been reports of an attack on Sunderland's house. The Benedictine chapel was attacked, and although guards broke up the mob, an even larger crowd gathered the next day, broke in and made a bonfire of its furnishings. The Blackfriars offices of Henry Mills, the king's printer – from which had poured a steady stream of Catholic propaganda for the last three and a half years – had already been attacked three times, 'above 1,000 appearing there last night'. Strong guards had had to be posted at other obvious flashpoints in the City and in and around Whitehall, and the Dutch Minister learned that there were 5,000 troops in London.

Meanwhile, there was an unexpected boost for the king's morale. The day after the bishops' final cruel snub, Lamplugh, the fugitive Bishop of Exeter, arrived at Whitehall to declare his loyalty to the king. James – perhaps bearing in mind Burnet's reported ambitions – at once rewarded him with the vacant See of York. The earliest reports from the west were reassuring too: William had settled at Exeter for the time being, but it seemed that no one of real importance was in a hurry to join him, and there was only a trickle of local volunteers. Better still, an early rising in support of the invasion had been promptly crushed by the determined action of the Duke of Beaufort, Lord-Lieutenant of Gloucestershire. On learning that William had landed, and reached Exeter, Lovelace had at once set out to join him with a troop of seventy armed men. Arriving at Cirencester, they found their road to the south-west barred by a strong detachment of the local militia, called up and posted by Beaufort. Lovelace resolved to force a passage, and in the brief but bloody skirmish that followed, several of his followers were killed or wounded. He himself was taken prisoner and sent to Gloucester Castle, as the *London Gazette* of 15 November jubilantly recorded. Hoffmann noted at this time that James was actually looking quite relaxed again, not at all like a man weighed down with anxiety. But then James was always good at keeping up a brave front.

Lamplugh's arrival was, however, the last of the good tidings. The next day brought shattering news for James. The twenty-eight-year-old Lord Cornbury, Clarendon's eldest son and the king's nephew, had left Salisbury with his regiment of cavalry to join William's camp. His father was bitterly ashamed and exclaimed: 'Oh God, that a son of mine should be a rebel,' but although James did his best to comfort his brother-in-law, assuring him that he would continue to be kind to his family, the news brought disaffection very close to home.

The cavalry regiments sent on to make first contact with William's army had in fact contained a number of the leading army conspirators: Cornbury, commanding the Royal Dragoons, Langston, the Duke of St Albans Horse and Sir Francis Compton, the Royal Horse Guards. Ordered forward to reconnoitre, the conspirators simply headed straight for the Dutch headquarters, according to plan. However, some of the dragoons became suspicious, Cornbury panicked and rode off towards Exeter with a mere handful of troopers. Langston was cooler and luckier, taking his whole regiment with him, but Compton lost his nerve and returned to Salisbury.

As news of William's advance sank in, meanwhile, the bishops began to have second thoughts. Perhaps it might still be possible to bring the king to his senses and preserve the status quo, rather than risk the doubtful outcome of a successful intervention by William, and the strong possibility of bloodshed. Clarendon discussed with some of them the idea of joining forces with the leading peers to address the king, pressing him to summon a Parliament at once. But Halifax and Nottingham were among several influential peers who refused to have anything to do with the Address. And when it was formally presented to James on 17 November, the king was not pleased. He reminded them curtly that he had already refused to call a Parliament, in his Proclamation of 6 November, as long as there were still foreign troops on British soil.

There were advisers to whom he did listen: among them Father Petre and the French ambassador. Father Petre was becoming actively pessimistic, and he urged James to send the baby Prince of Wales to France just in case everything went wrong. 'Then England will realize that she's entering on a war which can last many generations.' Barillon was more bracing, reflecting Louis's anxiety that the Prince of Orange shouldn't have his way. Louis's envoy had been so long in London, and had been such a trusted confidant of first Charles and then James, that both kings often appeared to overlook the fact that their own and French interests might not always be identical: Barillon was like one of the family. And when he too suggested that James should send his son to safety in France – a hostage for Louis XIV, in effect – James was swayed by him, and made one of the most important of the errors that were to cost him his Crown over the next few weeks: he decided to send the infant Prince of Wales, under heavy guard, to Portsmouth, which was under the command of his bastard son the Duke of Berwick. The child's ultimate destination was to be France, and the care and protection of the Sun King. At last on Sunday, 18 November James himself left for Salisbury. Middleton and Barillon went with him.

After a night at Windsor, he reached the city on Monday afternoon. The weather was appalling, with blizzards and high winds. The Imperial ambassador wondered 'how the King and the Prince would ever get to grips with each other in such a hard frost and with this snow . . .' Arriving on horseback, James was met a mile outside the city by Berwick, Feversham and a number of other officers, who accompanied him to the city gates, where, in full regalia and carrying his mace, the mayor, together with the city corporation, gave him a formal welcome.

A newsletter recorded that the mayor preceded His Majesty to the bishop's palace, where the king's volatile people gave him a tumultuous welcome, '. . . in very great multitudes following his Majesty's coach, from his entrance into the City Gate, to the doors of the Palace, with huzzas and demonstrations of joy and satisfaction, the bells ringing all the time.'

But Salisbury's warm welcome was no compensation for the bad news that awaited him. Although men from the three crack cavalry regiments were continuing to straggle back to join the main army, it was still believed that most of them were lost to James. Other officers had defected, there was a growing stream of deserters and morale was at zero. The lack of a strong and resolute command was very obvious. Feversham had never been the most decisive of commanders, and now he changed his plans almost from hour to hour. On 14 November, for instance, he had sent orders to General Kirke, commanding another advanced detachment at Warminster, to fall back on Salisbury; in the same letter he countermanded his own instructions to order Kirke, instead, to Andover; and at nine that night Feversham sent fresh orders summoning him to Salisbury after all. In this atmosphere of confusion and suspicion, discipline was already breaking down. Barillon was struck by the dejected looks of James's officers. 'Even if they aren't capable of treason,' he wrote to Louis, 'it's still obvious that they won't fight with a good heart, and the army is perfectly aware of this . . .' Years earlier, campaigning under the brilliant French Marshal Turenne, James had learned to recognize troops full of fight. Now he was looking at an army that had already given up.

Grim-faced, James summoned his chiefs-of-staff to a meeting. Among them were John Churchill, the Duke of Grafton and Colonel Trelawney. In an attempt to rally loyalties that he knew to be wavering, he told them that he had had a change of heart. He was now ready to summon a free Parliament and to consult the wishes of the people. But if they wished to join the Prince of Orange, he would give them a pass. He paused, studying the faces round the table, which gazed impassively back at him. '. . . No one desired a passport, for they were resolved to go without one.'

Next morning he left early on horseback to inspect his troops. Once more the weather was appalling – his Gentleman of the Bedchamber Ailesbury, who followed him from Windsor that day, arrived soaked to the skin and half-starving, because he had been unable to find 'either meat or bread on the road by the concourse of troops and passengers'.

There was an ominous little incident. The king had been attended in Salisbury by a clergyman, Mr Knightley Chetwood, appointed his

Protestant chaplain. Finding that the chapel in the episcopal palace, where the king was staying, had been taken over by a number of Catholic priests, Mr Chetwood loudly protested and announced that he would give up his appointment. The harassed king reluctantly ordered his priests to withdraw – and Chetwood became a local hero, loudly cheered by the troops whenever he walked through the streets.

James's feverish attempts to assert himself and bring the situation under control in the next few days wore him out to no purpose. Indeed, they actually made matters worse. Barillon commented on his irresolution and the stream of contradictory and confusing orders he gave. Conferences with Barillon always ended in a despairing cry: 'The King your master must save us, or we are lost! It's in his interests to prevent the Prince of Orange becoming master in England!' Under such continual stress, his nerves were rapidly giving way. When Ailesbury went to his bedchamber a few days after his arrival, he found James sprawled in a large chair, 'his nose having bled for some time'. A doctor put an ice-cold key to the back of the king's neck, 'and all was over'. But not for long.

Middleton, who had accompanied the king to Salisbury, reported to Whitehall that James had already had three or four severe nosebleeds that day, and that his physician had finally put him to bed with a dose of 'diascordium', a strong, opiate-based drug. 'He is this morning very well,' Middleton reported the next day. In the circumstances, however, James put off a planned trip to review his troops at Warminster, and later in the day, Thursday, 22 November, the nosebleeds began again. 'The physicians say it is only a ferment in his blood occasioned by too constant and anxious application to business,' wrote an increasingly worried secretary of state. Mary Beatrice shared his concern, and at her commands, he had represented to James in vain that 'the toil he continually put himself to might prove prejudicial to his health, that the detail might be referred to others, by which the despatch might be quicker and he have more leisure to consider of the main and important matters.'

Apart from the nosebleeds, there was certainly plenty for James to be anxious about. The lack of reliable intelligence about what was happening on the other side was a particular aggravation. What was William up to? Nobody knew for sure. 'All avenues and passages are so firmly closed that no mail or expresses can get through,' according to a Dutch pamphlet, 'Missive uyt Engeland'. In one of his reports to Whitehall, Middleton complained that it was very annoying 'to have so little intelligence, since none of the gentry of this or the adjacent counties come near the Court and the commons are spies to the enemy'.

This lack of information was not for want of trying. 'He sent many spies to us,' Burnet reported. 'They all took his money and came and joined themselves to the Prince ... so that he had no intelligence brought him ... and made him think we were coming near him, while we were still at Exeter.'

Barillon found this breakdown of communications quite unbelievable. 'There appears not to have been even the most elementary intelligence in the royal army,' he told Versailles. He had been unable to find out what the Prince of Orange was doing, and 'I do not know that anyone has been sent to his camp and has returned to report.'

Unluckily, this was not the whole truth. In the absence of reliable intelligence, the most alarmist rumours circulated. Ailesbury complained bitterly about the number of false informers 'who came in continually with what they had dreamt, or others instructed , but one and the other were grossly mistaken as to the Prince's near approach'.

In an effort to make up his mind what ought to be done next, James called another council of war. His nosebleed had been successfully stopped by the application of 'sympathetic ash', suggested by a local apothecary, and the need for clear-cut decision was obvious. But he found his officers unable to agree on the advice they gave him. Despite the fact that James's army was certainly overwhelmingly superior in numbers to William's, Feversham argued strongly for withdrawal nearer to London: it would be easier to defend the capital in this way than to maintain the army's present very broad front. Feversham's second-in-command was Churchill, who planned to go over to William when the right moment came. He argued just as strongly that it was madness to turn tail now, and that the army should advance to confront William – perhaps because he was temperamentally incapable of such timid counsels.

With hindsight, Middleton wrote soon afterwards: 'It was lucky that the King's bleeding at the nose hindered him from going thither, where they might have seized him.' Ailesbury, too, was convinced that Churchill planned to deliver the king to the Prince of Orange. 'The bleeding from the nose was the hand of God,' he concluded.

It was Feversham's reasoning that carried the day – probably because it accorded with the king's own growing instincts for flight. Middleton reported that night: 'His Majesty had been prevailed with by the unanimous advice of his general officers to return with the army. Most of the foot and cannon march today. The King has set no day for himself . . .'

When James woke up next morning, Friday, 23 November, Churchill and Grafton were both gone, riding at full speed to join the Prince of Orange. Churchill left a letter behind for his master, probably composed days earlier, in which he attempted to mitigate his apparent treachery: '. . . though my dutiful behaviour to your Majesty in the worst of times (for which I acknowledge my poor service is much overpaid) may not be sufficient to incline you to a charitable interpretation of my actions, yet I hope the great advantage I enjoy under your Majesty, which I own I can never expect in any other change of government, may reasonably convince your Majesty and the world that I am actuated by a higher principle.' Middleton sent a terse note to Whitehall: 'The Duke of Grafton and Lord Churchill are missing, and not doubted but they are gone to the enemy.'

The defection of Churchill – whom James had raised from a pageboy, and relied on implicitly through all the vicissitudes of the last nine years – was a body-blow to James. 'Oh, if my enemies only had cursed me,' he cried in his agony, 'I could have borne it.'

But it was just the start. Hardly had James recovered from this news when he learned that another of his commanders, Colonel Percy Kirke, at Warminster, was refusing to obey orders. 'Villany upon villany,' said a letter from Salisbury, 'the last still greater than the former.'

With the High Command of his army disintegrating around him, it was plain that hopes of a straightforward military solution to James's problems were at an end: he must return to London immediately to see what could be salvaged there, and to keep in touch with news from the north where, in different parts, rebellions had broken out. Princess Anne's husband, the Prince of Denmark, was one of the last of his adjutants left and when James stepped into his coach he asked for his son-in-law. 'He sent word that he would follow His Majesty,' Ailesbury reported, but James, now becoming suspicious even of his next of kin, refused to go without him. George reluctantly climbed into the royal coach to Andover, only to slip away that evening, together with another of the king's commanders, the Duke of Ormonde.

It had been George's habit to greet every desertion of the last days with the words, '*Est-il possible?*' and it was now the king's turn to use this expression. The prince had left a letter in which he justified his flight: 'Whilst the restless spirit of the enemies of the reformed religion, backed by the cruel zeal and prevailing power of France, justly alarm and unite all the Protestant Princes of Christendom and engage them in so vast an expense for the support of it, can I act so degenerate and mean a part as to deny my concurrence to such worthy endeavours for disabusing of your Majesty by the reinforcement of those laws and establishment of that government on which alone depends the well being of your Majesty and of the Protestant religion in Europe?' James was deeply shocked by the last two desertions, but was kind enough to send George his coach and horses later. There was no such consideration for Churchill. Orders were sent off to Whitehall 'for seizing and securing the goods and furniture of Lord Churchill both at the Cockpit and his house at St Albans'.

Utter chaos now reigned at the demoralized Andover base. Dr George Clark, judge-advocate of the army, who called on James there, later wrote: 'I can never forget the confusion the Court was in . . . the King knew not whom to trust and the fright was so great that they were apt to believe an impossible report just then brought in that the Prince of Orange was come with twelve thousand horse between Warminster and Salisbury . . . Everybody in this hurly-burly was thinking of himself, and nobody minded the King.'

The rank and file of the army had up till now remained surprisingly loyal to James, even as their officers melted away, but the confusion was having a disastrous effect on morale, and one observer wrote: 'The foot soldiers were ready to desert, and many did. Some left their baggage and snap-sacks behind them; and the horse, likewise, were in such a hurry to get away that they were ready to spoil their comrades. The whole army was in such a confusion and marched in so disorderly a manner that the country seeing them judged they had been routed in a battle.'

The inhabitants of Warminster, at least, were deeply relieved when the soldiers finally left. According to a newsletter of 22 November, the king had promised that 'his soldiers shall have all the plunder they get', and the population in and around this small town had every reason to believe it. 'The people of Warminster suffered much,' a local called Mr Wansey wrote in his diary, 'by this army of the King's, in eating and spoiling their hay and corn . . . finding their officers gone (that is those of Col Kirke's and Trelawney's) [they] mutinied, when they should have marched and many of them drew away to the Prince of Orange. Some straggled to their own homes.'

James did precisely that. But when he returned to Whitehall, a final blow was in store: his daughter Anne had also disappeared.

The princess's departure had been carefully planned, masterminded by the resourceful Sarah Churchill with the help of Bishop Compton. Just a week earlier Anne had written to William, then at Exeter, to wish him success in his enterprise, 'having on all occasion given you and my sister all imaginable assurances of the great friendship and kindness I have for you both'. She told him that her husband, who was then on his way to join her father, would soon be with the prince, but that she was not yet quite certain of her own plans: 'that shall depend on the advice my friends will give me.' Meanwhile, she sat it out. When Clarendon went to call on her, and explained that he was so shamed by his son's desertion to William that he hardly dared show his face at Court, Anne replied matter-of-factly: people were so apprehensive of popery that she believed many more of the army would do the same thing.

The Sunday evening of 25 November put an end to Anne's long waiting game. Late in the day, Sarah learned from her informants that, according to orders just arrived from the king, the Churchills' property was to be seized, including Sarah's apartment near Anne's – the Cockpit – and she herself placed under immediate arrest. As Pepys related in a letter to Dartmouth, Anne acted at once. She sent for the lord chamberlain, 'who instede of proceeding instantly to the work by way of surprise, for preventing escapes, or removalls of any thinges or persons ... suffered himself in complacence to be delayed by the Princess for half an hour by her express desiring of it from him'. In this half hour, Sarah made good her escape, leaving careful directions for the princess's own flight later that night.

Sarah wrote later that it was the news of the king's imminent return to Whitehall that 'put the Princess into a great fright'. Anne sent for her friend, according to this account, and told her 'that rather than see her father she would jump out of the window'. But there was nothing unpremeditated or impulsive about Anne's next move, other than its speed.

As soon as she left, Sarah Churchill contacted Compton, then in hiding in London, to make the final arrangements for the party's flight, and the princess retired to bed at her usual time. Soon afterwards, Sarah stole back into Anne's apartment in the Cockpit, using a back staircase leading to the princess's water-closet which had recently been constructed as a possible escape route. The two conspirators, together with another lady-in-waiting, Lady Fitzharding, and a servant, crept down the staircase to a waiting coach, in which sat Compton and the Earl of Dorset. They all spent the night at Compton's house in the City, and left London at dawn the next day. Compton, now looking suitably martial in top-boots and a sword, led the party to its first stop at Loughton in Essex, where they were guests of a blustering county justice, Mr John Wroth.

Next day they went on to Dorset's country house, Copt Hall in Essex. Their destination was Nottingham, which the Earl of Devonshire had seized four days earlier, to make it the northern focus of English support for William, with Anne as its figurehead. The party stopped off for refreshments *en route*, at the market town of Hitchin, and at the small alehouse they chose, sitting in a cart outside, Sarah Churchill, who had convinced Anne that Mary Beatrice planned to have her thrown in the Tower, joked that 'but for their flight it might have been their lot'. From Hitchin, Compton's little party rode on to Lord Carteret's house in Bedfordshire, and thence to Nottingham and a royal welcome.

On the day after Anne's flight, Sir Benjamin Bathurst, treasurer of her household, went up to her rooms as usual at half past seven, Pepys later related, 'to enquire after the Princess's health, and finding noebody in the forerooms, went on to the anti-chamber, where he found Mrs Danvers [the lady-in-waiting] dressing herself in order to attend the Princess, as not haveing yet done it.' Bathurst went back to his office, but half an hour later, he heard 'a sudden outcry of women'. When he rushed upstairs to see what had happened, they told him hysterically 'that some or other had carried away the Princess'. Bathurst learned that Mrs Danvers had gone into Anne's room and found the bed unslept in, and all yesterday's clothes, even her stockings and shoes, left behind. Bathurst questioned the sentry at the door, who told them that 'in the dead of the night ... a coach took up two ladies more from that door.'

Clarendon heard the news a little later, when he was walking in Westminster Hall. 'On a sudden rumour all about that the Princess was gone away, nobody knew wither.' He was even told that somebody had 'violently carried her away', and he rushed to the Cockpit where he found all the women still in a state of hysteria. All he could get out of them was that 'last night, after her Royal Highness was in bed, the chamber door locked, and Mrs Danvers in bed in the outer room where she used to lie when in waiting, she rose again, went down the backstairs and, accompanied by Lady Churchill, Mrs Berkeley and a maid of Lady Churchill's, went into a coach and six horses, which stood ready at the street-gate.'

In the confusion of those days, rumours were rife, and for a while Mary Beatrice herself was in danger, as reports that she had kidnapped the princess ran like wildfire through Whitehall. A popular journal reported: 'Nobody knows what is become of [the princess], that all her wearing clothes are left behind and that she is therefore murdered by the papists. That great lamentation is made for the loss of her and some charge the Queen with making her away.' Mary Beatrice made the disagreeable discovery that she herself was a suspect when Anne's women rushed into her rooms and one of them asked her 'in a very rude manner' what she had done with their mistress. She answered calmly that she was sure the princess was 'where she liked to be', and that they would probably hear from her very soon.

They were unwilling to believe her, and the rumours grew. According to one story, the queen had been so indignant when an officer told her that peace would only return to England when all the Catholic chapels were blown up that she gave first him, and then Anne, a box on the ear. Another story – that the night before Anne left Whitehall, she and the queen had a blazing row – may have been closer to the truth. Anne always avoided personal showdowns if she possibly could, and Dartmouth later reported that after some 'expostulations that had passed between her and the Queen', the princess had pretended 'she was out of order . . . therefore she said she would not be disturbed until she rang her bell'.

By the time her servants were confronting the queen next morning, Mary Beatrice had already read a letter Anne had left behind for her, full of hollow protestations. So surprised had the princess been, said her letter, by the news of her husband going away, that she felt she had no choice but to flee herself, 'to avoid the King's displeasure which I am not able to bear, either against the Prince or myself'. She told her stepmother: 'I shall stay at so great a distance as not to return before I hear the happy news of a reconcilement.' It had not been an easy decision: 'never was anyone in such an unhappy condition so divided between duty and affection to a father and husband; and therefore I know not what I must do, but to follow one or to preserve the other.'

She could not resist a dig at Mary Beatrice's supposed responsibility for her father's woes – particularly the priests her stepmother had brought into the royal circle, 'who to promote their own religion, did not care to what dangers they exposed the King'. William's intentions, she had no doubt, were entirely honourable – 'I am fully persuaded that [he] designs the King's safety and preservation . . .' And she ended this last letter she ever addressed to Mary Beatrice with a wish unlikely to be fulfilled: that 'the King's reign may be prosperous and that I may shortly meet you in perfect peace and safety'.

Her desertion was the final straw for the distracted James when he returned to London later that day. 'God help me,' he cried, 'my own children have forsaken me.' Since the defection of the king's daughter was a public matter as well as a personal misery, he grimly gave orders that Anne's servants were to be confined in their rooms 'till they have passed a very strict examination by the Council'.

The normally stoical James found it hard to conceal the fresh distress into which Anne's departure, and the tone of her letter, had plunged him. Anne on the other hand was completely indifferent to his reaction.

When Clarendon a few weeks later mentioned to her husband Prince George, 'with what tenderness the King spake of her when he returned and how much trouble he expressed to find she had left him', George had no comment to make. And in a letter she wrote from Nottingham to her treasurer Lord Bathurst, she made no reference to the astonishing circumstances in which she had left Whitehall. She only asked him 'to give order that the back stairs at the Cockpit may be painted that they may be dry against I come home . . .'

FIFTEEN

DELAY AT EXETER

With a population of 13,000, Exeter in 1688 was fourth or fifth among the cities of England. Its harbour at the mouth of the Ex and its strategic position on the high road to the south-west made it a leading commercial and industrial centre, with tanning and a cloth trade, with the Dutch as its mainstay. It was also the ecclesiastical capital of Cornwall and Devon; and a busy market, its shops and a large number of inns made it the heart of the south-west.

Despite all these claims to importance, Huygens thought it a filthy, down-at-heel place, which didn't compare very well with most of the small towns in the United Provinces. It consisted only, he wrote, 'of badly and slightly decorated houses, of which none have been painted, dirty outside as well as in'. Ten years later another observant traveller, Celia Fiennes, described it as a city with 'well-pitched, spacious and noble streets'. But only the High Street lived up to this description. According to other witnesses, the rest of Exeter's streets were muddy, unpaved and unlit.

The pride of Exeter was its magnificent Gothic St Peter's Cathedral, and it was here that the population crowded on 11 November, the first Sunday since the prince's arrival, to listen for the second time to Burnet, 'some placing themselves in Seats by eight in the Morning'. William sat once more in the bishop's throne, now placed in the body of the church, with 'sundry Sentinels' to guard him. Prayers for the Prince of Wales had been stopped at his orders, and Burnet preached a suitably eulogistic sermon, taking as his text Psalms 107:43: 'Whoso is wise, and will observe these things, even they shall understand the lovingkindness of the Lord.' The doctor, explained Whittle, 'very accurately shewed the loving Kindness of the Lord unto the Prince of Orange, and his Fleet: how he caused the Winds to turn at Tor-Bay ... and then shew'd the upright Design of the Prince to promote the Glory of God, and the good of his Church in England, Scotland and Ireland.'

Moustaquet, who like Huygens had not been much impressed by

Exeter – 'not fortified and rather badly built' – was also present at this service, his first in an Anglican church, and he was surprised to find how closely it resembled a Roman Catholic ceremony. 'The churches have altars, with two candelabras at the side and a basin of silver or vermeil in front, the deacons with their surplice and stole sitting in stalls along the two sides of the nave . . . they have a choir of little boys in surplices . . . all this is exactly the opposite of the simplicity of our reformation. I did not find it very edifying.'

Four days earlier, the cathedral had been the setting for a very different scene. As part of the preliminaries for the docile new Parliament James had originally planned for December, his agents had turned out the old mayor and corporation to replace them with a party of yes-men and Dissenters, with Sir Thomas Jefford as mayor. Lord Bath, the Lord-Lieutenant of Devon, had complained bitterly to Whitehall in October about the consequences of this piece of electioneering: 'Exeter is our London,' he wrote, 'which give laws to all the rest, but it is . . . miserably divided and distracted.' If the king insisted on keeping his puppet mayor and chamber in office, warned Bath grimly, 'Exeter must be made a garrison merely to defend them.' For once the king listened, and while William was disembarking at Brixham, James was dispatching orders for the former mayor, Sir Christopher Brodrick, and the Corporation of Exeter to be reinstated at a solemn ceremony in the cathedral.

Four years' neglect of the local militia could not so easily be undone in a single day, and Bath's warning that it would be unable to put up any resistance to William's armies turned out to be only too accurate. The common people, he judged, had not forgotten their 'ill usage' by the king, and had greeted William with 'great acclamation', he wrote next day to Herbert. But the gentry had stayed away, 'the Clergy as well as the Mayor'. The only persons of importance he had found waiting to welcome him at Exeter were Shrewsbury and Wiltshire, who had made up an advance welcoming party. But despite their promise, none of the other seven signatories, and few of the 'men of substance' they had predicted, had as yet shown up.

With the last of his transports now sailing up the Ex to be unloaded and sent back to Holland, the prince was for the time being virtually isolated: Dartmouth and the English fleet hovering in the Channel made communication with Europe either way highly vulnerable. D'Albeville reported day after day from The Hague that the States-General – and the Princess of Orange – were impatiently waiting for news from the stadholder, but it was certainly not for want of trying that they remained in the dark.

It was a certain Captain Cole who with his cruiser *Pearl* had put a spoke in the prince's wheel. He had stopped and searched a Brandenburg vessel on the way to Holland and discovered a packet of letters from the expedition. They included one from Burnet to his wife, in which he made fun of the wretched Dartmouth and his failure to halt William's expedition. It was noticed that the ship's cook was behaving suspiciously, a more thorough search followed and the result was a priceless haul – another packet of letters, hidden in the cable tier and written by the prince himself, in which he not only announced his safe arrival, but also his plans for the advance to London and a note of the strength of his fleet. This marvellous haul was at once sent by Dartmouth to Pepys, but demoralization in Whitehall by this time had reached such a pitch that no propaganda use was made of it.

As well as his waning contact with The Hague and his European allies, William's intelligence about James's movements was not as yet well organized, and in Exeter as in Whitehall, rumours were soon rife. Hardly had William's troops arrived in Exeter than Whittle heard that the king 'was advanc'd as far towards us as Salisbury, with a very brave army of about thirty-five thousand Men and a prodigious great Train of Artillery – which made the poor country people tremble'.

It turned out to be greatly exaggerated, just like the spiteful item in a newsletter of 13 November: 'Not one person of quality has yet come to the Prince.' The Sunday after William's arrival, in fact, the first gentleman of any local standing had joined the prince, a Captain Burrington from Crediton, and he was soon followed by others of much more consequence. On Tuesday, 13 November Russell dashed off a few lines to Herbert in his execrable spelling: 'Wee are heere in good Condition and the Common Peppel show a greatt desier to serve In the Cause we espouse. Here came to us Saturday night Lord Colchester, Tom Wharton, Ed Russel, Jepson Godfrey and some six others.' He had also heard the good news that eight captains fom Dartmouth's fleet, among them Churchill's younger brother George, were ready to declare for the prince.

Shrewsbury arrived around this time to join William, and Burnet wrote to Herbert three days later: 'Our numbers grow upon us every day. The Gentry of the Country were a little backward at first, but now they come in apace.' There were queues of people waiting at the deanery to pay their respects to the Prince of Orange, 'many coming 20 miles on purpose to see him'. And an Exeter man wrote to a friend in London: 'Now most of the gentry of the country has made visits to the Prince and, as tis said, have resolved to defend the established laws and religion.'

William was badly in need of such adherents, but he was even more worried about his shortage of ready cash. Despite stories of chests full of money, William had only about 400,000 guilders in hand, plus 70,000 of his own personal fortune, by the time he reached Exeter: the storm, the cost of repairing the damage and the long delays in port in Holland had eaten heavily into his reserves. Huygens learned that the money would be just enough to pay the armies until the end of the year. Once settled in Exeter, William took over the local tax-office and its funds, but it was only a stop-gap.

William could easily have solved this problem if his soldiers were allowed the looting and pilfering that made James's standing army so heartily detested. But the prince was determined that his own armies should be models of good behaviour by contrast. He made it a strict rule that his soldiers should pay a fair price for every single thing they needed, including food and lodgings. It was a rule that was ruthlessly enforced throughout the march on London. A newsletter in November reported: 'His soldiers are mighty civil,' and went on to reveal how the prince had given orders that two of them should be hanged for stealing a chicken. 'He told the rest that they had enough money and when they really wanted, it was soon enough to steal.' A soldier was hanged for the same offence at Salisbury, and only the pleas of some English noblemen saved six others from sharing his fate. And the *London Mercury*, later in the year, told of a soldier who was found guilty of stealing some plates from his landlady. He was tried, convicted and sentenced to death. His landlady pleaded for the young man's life, but 'His Highness would not grant it, saying, he came into England to preserve and not to destroy the law.'

Not only were William's armies honest, they were well-behaved too: 'They told me at Exeter that when we were there, the City was more quiet in the night and freer from debauch'd and disorderly people than 'twas before,' reported a proud Whittle.

At first the Exeter shopkeepers were not very happy with the Dutch money the men carried around, but as nobody had anything else, they were obliged to take it. Eventually, as the army chaplain noticed, the throngs of troops billeted in and around the city became quite popular – most unusually for those times. 'The people of the City began now to be more and more inclin'd towards our Army.' These invaders were certainly big spenders. 'Much money was laid out in this city for all sorts of Commodities which the officers and Souldiers lacked.' An order for 7,000 pairs of shoes and 7,000 yards of the good West Country broadcloth which was an Exeter speciality, was especially welcome, although a wicked tongue spread the news that this was simply 'a trick to drill on time, till they could see if any part of England would come into them.'

In fact, even if the Prince of Orange had wished to move on without further delay, it was not within his power. Transport was a major headache. 'The roads are so frightful . . . that none of our carts can get through without horses to drag it,' reported Bentinck on 16 November. 'That's why we're compelled to stay here several days, in order to assemble draught horses and waggons from these parts, and carts from neighbouring provinces, without which we shan't be able to carry either provisions or weapons with us.'

On the same day, in desperation, William issued his first proclamation using the royal 'We'. 'Whereas through the want of Carriages to convey our bagage, traine of Artillery &c from hence to Huniton, wee are necessitated to oblidge all the neighbouring inhabitants to furnish us with their draught oxen and Cariages . . .' it began with a flourish. William offered the sensational payment of '4 schillings' a day for a team of four oxen, six for a team of six, 'hereby commanding the said Inhabitants to be obedient to this Our Order, as they will answer the Contrary at their peril . . .' The response was prompt, and people flocked in with their oxen, draught-horses and waggons from miles around.

The physical condition of William's army was another reason for delay. Even hardened mercenary soldiers at that time were unused to operating in the appalling conditions they had had to put up with on this expedition: the campaigning season, by general consent, was usually considered to be over by September at the very latest, and hostilities seldom started up again much before April or May. William's armies had been tossing about aboard ship in harbour for days – some of them for weeks – on end while his armada was assembled. Many of them had suffered tortures of seasickness during the storm and the three-day crossing; and they had all since endured cold, wet, mud and drenching rain as they floundered through the Devon countryside, with no possibility of dry bedding or adequate shelter for the night. The army was far from peak fighting condition, and many of the soldiers were actually sick men by the time they reached Exeter.

At William's request to the city chamber, a hospital for his 'sik Shouljers' was hastily improvised, and the Blue Maid School requisitioned for this purpose. On 19 November, 156 men were hospitalized. Surgeons and apothecaries were sent for, and vast quantities of bedding, provisions, wood, coal and candles ordered in. The meticulously kept accounts of this hospital – in which patients were listed by their illnesses as well as names, ranks and regiments – show a predictable

crop of diseases brought on or aggravated by exposure: pleurisy, ague,
'feavers', rheumatism, consumption, sciatica. There were many cases
of scurvy, which doctors in those days treated with powerful drugs,
unluckily for their patients, instead of the raw cabbage or turnip which
would have quickly cured them. And chirurgeon John Case dealt with
a wide range of woes, including 'a violent paine in his . . . breast . . .
shortness of breath . . . a great pricking paine and convulsions of all his
Body . . . putrid feavor, a plurisye, a sordid foul ulcer . . . contractions
of the Knees, Hemorhodes . . . and a Crewel Cough'.

This last must have been particularly common: day after day the
apothecary sent over fresh supplies of his Pectorall Water and more
boxes of his Pectorall Pills. Many of these soldiers were still in hospital
when William's army finally left the city, and as late as January 1698
many were still being treated at the city's expense. The total bill came
to £345 7s. 3½d. This was, however, one bill which William failed to
settle, and the 'severall Creditors (who are poor tradesmen)' petitioned
King William's treasury through their MP, Christopher Bale, in vain.
Further petitions to Queen Anne were equally unsuccessful.

As well as having their stock tended, William's officers welcomed the
opportunity to drill and exercise this vast, polyglot army into a cohesive
whole. English and Dutch predominated in its ranks, but there were
also men from Sweden, Switzerland, Greece, Brandenburg, Flanders
and France. And his quartermasters were no doubt equally glad of a
chance to check the army's equipment and uniforms and make good
any deficiencies.

Volunteers were by this time arriving in such numbers that 'every
Regiment of English or Scotch which wanted any Man, was now
compleated'. But there was still a desperate shortage of horses, and the
rolling plains of Wiltshire ahead of the prince, where James's enormous and well-drilled army awaited him, were cavalry country. So
the news that three regiments of the king's cavalry were on their way
to William created great excitement, Huygens reported. They were
those commanded by Clarendon's eldest son, Lord Cornbury, who had
picked the moment when he was senior officer at Salisbury, on 11
November, to order the regiments to march, without revealing their
destination. All went well for two days until they arrived at Axminster,
within six miles of Exeter, where some of the officers became suspicious
and demanded to see Cornbury's written orders.

The young officer took the plunge and addressed the men, asking
them 'if they would fight for the Church of England'. Very few at first
refused, 'but the Confusion of the night . . . together with the vigour of
some Popish Officers among them, put all in so much disorder that the

greater part ... wheeled about'. Cornbury managed to make his escape, but he led in to William no more than a hundred dragoons who, according to those returning to Salisbury, were 'all knaves and rogues'.

It was disappointing that so many of the promised cavalry had remained loyal to the king, but the person of the king's nephew was still an important acquisition to William's side. The prince and the young man had actually met once before, years earlier, when William had almost come to an open breach with Charles II and James over their lack of support for him after Louis XIV seized his principality of Orange. The unfortunate Cornbury, arriving as the representative of these unsatisfactory uncles, had met with the chilliest of receptions from an angry prince. Now William was delighted to see him, and gave him a warm welcome. Schomberg, on the other hand, a professional soldier first and foremost, was inclined to be sniffy: he told the young man bluntly that he 'had done the King more service by going than if he stayed'.

But the arrival of Cornbury was a turning-point for the Prince of Orange. James Bertie, Earl of Abingdon, arrived on the same day, and soon after Sir Edward Seymour made his appearance. Abingdon had been Lord-Lieutenant of Oxfordshire until James turned him out for refusing, in a personal interview, to promise support for the revocation of the Test Acts. Seymour was a staunch Tory who had never been an admirer of William: but as a nobleman of vast wealth and property, MP for Exeter in James's first Parliament, he was one of the most influential men in the whole West Country – Lord Bath being the other. He was also noted for his arrogance: when William welcomed him with the words 'Sir, I believe you are of the same family as the Duke of Somerset,' Sir Edward replied freezingly, 'No, the Duke belongs to my family.'

Despite this unpromising start, Seymour was an important catch, and he contributed some badly needed political expertise as well. He was shocked to discover, for instance, that no effort had been made so far to collect the signatures of those who had come over to the prince and, sending for Burnet, he asked him why no formal association had been drafted, 'signed by all that came'. Till that was done, he pointed out, 'we were as a rope of sand: men might leave us when they pleased'. Burnet told him ingratiatingly, 'It was because we had not a man of his authority and credit to offer and support such advice,' and agreed that it must be put to the prince and Shrewsbury at once. Both men saw the force of Sir Edward's argument, Burnet began work on a draft of the document and, by 17 November, it was ready for the first signatures. Those who signed it committed themselves to 'stick firm' to the defence of the Protestant religion, and 'never to depart from it until our religion, laws and liberties are so far secured to us in a free Parliament that we shall be no more in danger of falling under Popery and slavery.'

But two days earlier, on Thursday, 15 November, William already felt secure enough of his position to give a public reception for the 'Principle Gentlemen of Somersetshire and Dorsetshire' at which – using the royal 'We' – he made a brief and pointed speech. 'You see we are come according to your Invitation and our Promise,' he told them. He saw no need for compliments: 'We expected you that dwelt so near the place of our Landing, would have join'd us sooner . . .' he told them coldly. And he reminded them that although their 'Countenance and Presence' were essential to him, to justify the English support that he had claimed in his Declaration, their military assistance was not, since he had brought with him 'a good Fleet, and a good Army'. But in his great design – 'to render these Kingdoms happy, by Rescuing all Protestants from Popery, Slavery and Arbitrary Power' – they were most heartily welcome to join him. He himself was determined to see it carried out, even if he were offered 'a bridge of gold to turn back', since it was his 'Principle and Resolution rather to dye in a Good Cause, than live in a Bad one'.

As he spoke, other parts of England were rising to join him, in a series of *coups* carefully concerted by a number of the signatories of his invitation. In Cheshire Lord Delamere called the tenants of his huge estates together and told them that he was declaring for the prince. 'They generally applauded his design,' a neighbour wrote to his son in London, 'and have promised cheerfully to accompany him.' Delamere asked them to bring their horses with them, and ordered all the Catholics among them to hand over their arms. Delamere's insurrection closed the port of Chester to the Irish troops James was still hoping for.

Meanwhile another great territorial magnate, the Duke of Beaufort, had also given up James's cause as a bad job, and was turning to the coming man. Beaufort was Lord-Lieutenant of Herefordshire, Gloucestershire and all Wales, and he had at least made an effort to hold the key port of Bristol with a small force of militia. But he appealed in vain for a strong reinforcement of regular troops: finally he gave up on 26 November, writing to Middleton: 'having now no manner of support or Countenance . . . I presume to retire this day into Gloucestershire, hoping to continue to keepe that County and the rest of my lieutenancy . . . from any rising, wch is the utmost in the present Circumstances can be hoped for . . .'

Bristol was thus secured for William by Shrewsbury without any show of resistance. And once Seymour had joined the prince, his rival, Lord Bath, Governor of Plymouth, also abandoned James, writing to tell the prince that 'the harbours of Plymouth and Falmouth will be for the security of your Highness' Fleet, whensover you shall have occasion to command them.' This switch of sides by the west's other great magnate brought William a double bonus: a safe port for the Dutch fleet, should it be needed, and security in the rear while his armies marched eastwards.

The most spectacular of these risings was in the north-east, where Danby had confidently expected William to land. Together with the Earl of Devonshire, he had been working hard for weeks at the organization of simultaneous *coups* at York and Nottingham; and news of William's landing in Tor Bay forced on him a complete change of tactics. But by 22 November he was ready to take York, with its garrison, by surprise.

A meeting of gentry and freeholders had been organized for this day, at which they were heatedly discussing whether or not the city should send a loyal Address to the king promising him their support in these troubled times. Sir John Reresby, as governor, presided, but just as some of them were getting ready to put their names to the Address, a man burst into the hall shouting 'that the papists were risen and had fired at the militia troops'. Everybody rushed out into the street – and Reresby realized, too late, that it was a plot. 'Those that were privy to the design got their horses, which were laid ready for them.'

Danby had been waiting at home with his son Lord Dumblane and other noblemen, 'who made a party with their servants of a hundred horse, well armed and well mounted'. They rode up to the four troops of militia, which had been called out for another purpose but who, in response to excited shouts of 'For a free Parliament, the Protestant religion and no popery', now joined them. Reresby tried to alert the garrison, but one of Danby's lieutenants posted a guard of thirty horse at his door, and soon after Danby turned up in person to tell him that resistance was useless. '. . . He and these gentlemen were in arms for a free Parliament, and for the preservation of the Protestant religion and the Government . . . which the King had very near destroyed and which the Prince of Orange was come to assist them to defend.' He hoped that Reresby would join them. But the governor replied that 'though we agreed in the matter, he could not agree with them in the manner,' after which he was made a prisoner in his own home, while Lord Dumblane was appointed governor in his place.

On the same day, Lord Lumley seized Newcastle, while the Earl of

Devonshire captured Nottingham. By dusk on 23 November all the chief towns in the north-east had been secured for William after, as one eye-witness related, 'such a riding and travelling about at such a rate as I never did see in my life'.

And by this time, too, William's armies were on the move once more, winding along the muddy lanes of Devon and Somerset, past hedgerows thick with old-man's-beard. The prince left Exeter on 20 November, and transport problems compelled him to leave behind most of his artillery and ammunition, in the charge of Sir Edward Seymour, whom he had appointed governor. The 120 pieces of cannon he took with him had to be dragged along the appalling roads by the specially hired oxen, and the army moved at a snail's pace. But its departure was no less impressive for that. 'The Prince marched out this morning with a mighty full and splendid court,' someone wrote in a letter intercepted in Salisbury, where James was still hovering uncertainly. Another report told that William by now had 25,000 'fighting men'. Moustaquet was enjoying himself. Never had he seen an army 'marching so happily and with so much confidence in a season so terrible and through a countryside so changeable'.

The weather that day was indeed wretched, 'and the Roads bad for marching', even if they were a little wider than those leading to Exeter. So it was with some relief that William and 'all his Lords, Knights and Gentlemen' stopped for dinner at 'St Mary Ottrie', after which they rode on once more to Honiton, cheered by crowds who turned out despite the pouring rain. The prince stayed at the Dolphin, a 200-year-old coaching-inn which borrowed its name from the dolphin in the crest of the Courtenay family – William's earlier hosts – who owned it. Huygens, who was staying a few houses away, heard that the prince's vanguard, now as far ahead as Sherborne in Dorset, had run into a troop of James's cavalry in the town. They had told William's officers that they were simply waiting for their paymaster, and left with profuse apologies.

The next day's march was short enough – only seven miles – but once more it was hard going. 'It rained without stopping,' wrote Huygens, 'until 1 o'clock, with a strong wind which made it a punishing march for the soldiers, who waded through mud and sometimes plenty of water too.' As they neared Axminster, it became almost impossible to keep going. 'The rain of that day and the previous one had created such torrents that the army walked for half an hour up to their knees, and in places up to their thighs, in water; some of them slipped and went under.' The prince gave a furious dressing-down to the scout who had been sent ahead to report on the roads. The wretched man protested 'that he had indeed been there, but that it must have been much later that the water had risen so much'.

At Axminster the prince, now a guest at Coaxdon Hall, decided to give his wet and dispirited troops a few days' rest. Some of them were billeted in Coaxdon Manor, to which Charles II had fled after the battle of Worcester, to hide from his pursuers under the ample skirts of a certain Mrs Cogan; where Monmouth had breakfasted on his way to Somerset; and where William's men were now 'feasted without stint of meatie or drinkie'. How the prince was entertained is not recorded, but it cannot have been as well. One of his servants told Huygens that 'His Highness had scolded him worse than ever because . . . he had not had his Breda bottled beer, and when at last he got it, it tasted of salt seawater.'

The little town of Axminster now found itself taking orders from a new master, and footing the bill for some of his expenses. The parish register records a number of sums paid out on the prince's behalf: 'For writing and carrying three hue and crys for soldiers ran away. £0. 0. 8 d. . . . Paid John Dare for himself and his horse, when the great guns were hal'd . . . £0. 1. 6 d. . . . Paid the doctor for a Dutchman who lay sick at the Dolphin . . . £0. 3 s. 6 d. . . . Paid John Seward for riding to Exon for the concerns of the Prince . . . £0. 5 s. 0 d.' Perhaps they were luckier than Exeter in getting this debt settled after the Revolution.

While the prince was at Axminster, news reached him that Churchill and Grafton had deserted James at Salisbury and were on their way to join him. William dispatched Bentinck with 1,200 cavalry and dragoons to welcome them. When they told Bentinck, not only that Prince George of Denmark was to follow them the next day, but that the king's troops in Warminster were also on the point of surrender, Bentinck took his troops on ahead to Sherborne.

Churchill and Grafton, meanwhile, arrived in Axminster, to be greeted by the Prince of Orange with the words King David had spoken to the men of Judah and Benjamin: 'If you be come peacably unto me to help me, mine Heart shall be knit to you: but if you come to betray me to mine Enemies, seeing there is no Wrong in my Hands, the God of our Fathers look thereon and rebuke it.' John Churchill knew his Bible as well as the prince, and promptly answered in the words of Amasal: 'Thine are we, David, and on thy side, thou son of Jesse. Peace, peace be unto thee, and peace be unto thine Helpers, for thy God helpeth thee.'

For William, it was a historic moment: James's trusted second-in-command had joined him. Again the veteran Schomberg was much less impressed, and was later heard to comment that this was the first time in a long career that he had known a commander to desert his colours while the battle was still on.

The next stop was Crewkerne, ten miles away, and at first it looked as if the weather was improving. 'It was mild and nice when we left,' noted Huygens, 'so we hoped to have an easy march. But an hour later rain began falling again, and soon after, it started to blow so hard, with rain and hail, that the march was worse than Thursday's to Axminster, and bitterly cold too.' The roads here were fairly wide, but 'full of loose pebbles and in places made of soft clay'. Crewkerne at least appealed to him – 'very charming and picturesque' – and he lodged in the best shop in town, the house of a grocer selling sugar, spices and linens.

The Prince of Orange rode three miles further on, to Hinton St George, home of the Poulett family, whose guest he was to be for two nights. This sixteenth-century house was impressively ancient, 'yet very stately and of curious building'. Another guest had described it as 'very different from the common style'.

The Poulett family were related by marriage to the powerful Seymour clan, and at the time of the Civil War they had been conspicuous for their loyalty to the Stuart family. The father of William's thirteen-year-old host had distinguished himself in the service of Charles I. But by the 1680s, the family loyalties were wavering: they had entertained Monmouth during his semi-royal progress through the West Country, and at Hinton St George the royal bastard had actually presumed to touch for the king's evil – curing a girl, it was rumoured. In William's slow progress to London, he was to be made welcome in more than one house of this wealthy and influential Protestant family.

The University of Oxford, too, had once been renowned for its loyalty to the Stuarts, unswerving in its allegiance through all the dark years of the Civil War and the Protectorate. But this loyalty had not survived James's cavalier treatment of the Magdalen Fellows, and while William was at Hinton St George, he received another welcome visitor: Dr Finch, Warden of All Souls, came to assure him on behalf of some of the heads of colleges 'that they would declare for him and inviting him to come thither, telling him that their plate would be at his service'. He took back to Oxford the prince's promise that he would be their guest on his way to London.

Churchill and Grafton had brought news of James's crestfallen condition and his violent nosebleeds, both confirmed by later reports. The news was received in William's camp with unchristian glee. 'Much purulent matter comes out,' Burnet wrote to Herbert, 'so much it is generally thought his person is in as ill a state as his affairs are.' Huygens had heard the same lurid account: 'a dirty stinking mess comes out of his nose,' he noted coarsely. Fresh evidence that the royal armies were rapidly disintegrating came in the person of Colonel George Trelawney, who arrived in company with all the officers of his infantry regiment, together with the officers of the dragoons who had been based at Warminster. The trickle of deserters was becoming a flood.

In the circumstances, William decided that he could certainly afford to relax for a while, and he spent Monday, 26 November hunting deer in the park at Hinton St George.

By now, the invasion had turned into a triumphal progress. As the prince and his bodyguard reached the borders of Somerset and Dorset, he was met by a cavalcade of the Dorset nobility, led by John Digby, 3rd Earl of Bristol, whose sister Anne was one of Mary's closest friends. Although the weather had been splendid during the twelve-mile march from Crewkerne, big flakes of snow were now beginning to fall, but nothing could mar the enthusiasm of this welcome, and, escorted by these nobles, William rode on in triumph to Lord Bristol's castle which dominates the town of Sherborne. Huygens thought the town itself 'dirty and muddy, just like all the others we have visited – the drains completely open and in the middle of the street'. Even the peevish Dutchman, however, found the russet-coloured castle, built nearly a century earlier by Sir Walter Raleigh in the shape of an H, 'extraordinarily pleasing'.

The prince stayed at Sherborne for three days, splendidly entertained. While he conferred with the soldiers and politicians flocking to pay court to him, his staff set up once more the portable printing-press which had been idle since Exeter. Its weight promptly cracked the hearthstone in the castle Oak Room – still pointed out to visitors today. Fresh consignments of his Declaration were almost certainly printed here, together with such useful propaganda as his speech at Exeter. A third Declaration appeared and began to circulate about this time, which was also claimed to have been printed at Sherborne with the prince's authority. In it, the prince supposedly declared his entire zeal for the Protestant religion, promising that no injury should be done to anyone, with one exception: if any papist were found armed, he was to be 'intirely delivered up to the descretion of the souldiers'. This open incitement to mob violence seems uncharacteristic of the prince, and he indignantly repudiated authorship. But genuine or not, the Declaration certainly contributed to the general unease and uncertainty which was beginning to grip the country, and which the prince was to exploit so successfully later.

It was at Sherborne that Prince George of Denmark finally surfaced, on 29 November. They had heard days earlier of his defection, and were becoming increasingly worried about his fate. But it turned out that he and the Duke of Ormonde had had to make a long detour to dodge the king's soldiers. That evening he dined with William and all the other Dutch and English noblemen.

After Sherborne, the next stop was the sleepy little town of Wincanton, where William was the guest of Mr Richard Churchey in the Jacobean Old Manor House on Tout Hill. The town was just recovering from the first of the only two armed skirmishes of William's expedition, which had taken place eight days earlier. Major-General Mackay, commanding an advanced guard of the prince's army, had sent on ahead a detachment of fifty men under Lieutenant Campbell to forage for transport. Riding through Wincanton Campbell, who had left some of his men at the outskirts of town, was suddenly confronted by 120 Irish soldiers under Captain Sarsfield. Campbell hesitated to shoot, thinking these might be the troops of Lord Cornbury still on their way to join William. So he blocked the road with his handful of men, shouting, 'Stand, stand, for who are you?' Sarsfield shouted back, 'I am for King James, who art thou for?' 'I am for the Prince of Orange,' returned Campbell. 'We'll Prince you!' roared the other, and gave orders to charge.

Shooting broke out and Campbell's troop, hopelessly outnumbered, was only saved from complete extinction by a passing local miller, who hurried up with the news that the prince's armies were entering Wincanton in force. Sarsfield, who had no desire to be taken prisoner, called off his men and they galloped away, leaving – according to Whittle – fifteen dead, most of them Irish. A newsletter gives quite different figures – nine of the prince's army killed, seven taken prisoner, three wounded: of the king's only 'the gentleman that commanded and three others'. Since Sarsfield survived to confront William's armies in Northern Ireland, Whittle's account was probably the more accurate of the two.

From Wincanton the army train rolled on to Hindon. 'The road was awful,' a weary Huygens jotted down on the first day of December, 'the weather almost dry, but we had a sharp north-eastern wind in our faces.' Near Hindon they were joined by the Duke of Berwick's regiment, which had deserted several days earlier, but got lost on the way to William – 'good-looking, well-mounted people,' Huygens noted. And at Hindon itself, William stayed at the pleasant manor house of Berwick St Leonard, half a mile outside the village, which belonged to the Grobham Howe family, although it was now being rented by the widow of Mr Edward Hyde, Clarendon's cousin.

The now-customary flow of visitors began. It was here that messengers brought news that Devonshire and his fellow-conspirators had secured the north, and that Shrewsbury with his infantry and 200 dragoons was master of Bristol. Other accounts told of the demoralized royal armies straggling back to London in utter disarray, following the flight of their king. In military terms, opposition to the prince had disintegrated: he could consider himself master of the country. In the next few days, the issue would become one of politics. While he pondered his next move, William was delighted to receive a gentleman sent by Princess Anne to announce that she had made good her escape from Whitehall and was now safe under the protection of Compton.

The first overture from James arrived while William was still at Berwick. It was signalled by a trumpeter, sent by Feversham to ask on the king's behalf for three passes: he intended to send commissioners to discuss a treaty with the Prince of Orange. Aernout van Citters, the Dutch ambassador, arrived at almost the same time, equipped with a special passport graciously given him by a now-conciliatory James. He brought the prince valuable information about recent developments in the capital. James had actually issued a Proclamation announcing a Parliament to meet in the New Year, on 15 January. Writs were now being prepared, and some had already been sent out.

According to the prince's own Declaration, this had been the entire purpose of his invasion – to ensure the meeting of a free Parliament. If James were genuinely ready to agree to this, what role would be left for William to play – other than to ensure that elections really were free, and that the Parliament was allowed to sit and deliberate without interference from its king? And what exactly would James's Commission suggest to the prince? What terms was James likely to offer? What concessions was he now ready to make?

On military matters William could still make his own decisions. But these were questions which would eventually have to be settled by the English themselves, and for three days the trumpeter waited while the English around William – who included some of the most hotheaded of the English exiles – discussed whether or not James's commission should be received. Finally he was sent back with three passes.

During this pause in events, Clarendon made his appearance at Berwick. The motives that led the older statesman to William's travelling Court were probably mixed: curiosity, a politician's instinctive gravitation towards the seat of power, the strong loyalty to James which prompted him to see if anything could still be salvaged from the wreckage and a feeling that if it could, he might be well placed to assist: all these, no doubt, played their part. He had urgent personal reasons for being there, too, however. He had been given to understand that his strong and outspoken loyalty to the king had made him *persona non grata* with William. Clarendon was a poor man, with mounting debts, an expensive lawsuit with the queen dowager hanging over his head, and arrears of salary and expenses still owing to him. As brother-in-law to James, and uncle to both William and Mary, there might still be an important conciliatory role for him in English politics. And as the representative of Tory, Anglican England, he was a person to be reckoned with in the Orange camp – for the time being, at least. And as a source of first-hand news from Whitehall, he was particularly welcome.

The prince received him 'very obligingly', the older statesman wrote in his diary, and was complimentary about his son, Lord Cornbury, of whose defection Clarendon had been so bitterly ashamed. Then he pumped the older statesman for half an hour: Why had the king left Salisbury so suddenly? What exactly was going on in Whitehall? When could he expect the king's commissioners? 'And what their business was?'

Clarendon replied that as far as he knew, the business of the commissioners was to agree arrangements for the safe meeting of the Parliament James had summoned. And what was Clarendon's own view? the Prince wanted to know. Why, that if the prince observed the terms of his Declaration, everybody could look forward to a happy settlement, replied Clarendon. 'My Declaration shall be punctually observed,' said the prince impassively.

Clarendon's hopes of this 'happy settlement' rose higher still when he met and talked to Bentinck. '. . . there are not ill men wanting, who give it out that the Prince aspires at the crown,' said the Dutchman warmly, 'which is the most wicked insinuation that could be invented.' Other men might be tempted by three kingdoms: the Prince of Orange would be faithful to the letter of his Declaration.

The old Tory statesman heard other expressions of goodwill to James from a surprising source. Meeting Churchill at dinner, he told him of the king's statement to an assembly of peers in London that Churchill had planned to have him kidnapped and handed over to William. Churchill listened in horror. 'Never would he be so ungrateful to the King,' he protested. 'He had only left him because he saw that our religion and country were in danger of being destroyed.'

But not all those at the prince's Court were eager for a peaceful settlement. When Clarendon called on Burnet, he at once asked loudly what could be the point of the commission? To make arrangements for the safe and easy meeting of the Parliament, of course, replied Clarendon in some surprise. 'How can a Parliament meet, now the kingdom is in this confusion?' burst out Burnet. 'It is impossible. There can be no Parliament! There must be no Parliament!'

SIXTEEN

THE KING'S COMMISSION

The king who faced an assembly of peers and bishops on Tuesday, 27 November was already a loser, prepared to acknowledge defeat and throw his hand in. His Catholic advisers had been excluded from this assembly on the advice of Mary Beatrice's chamberlain, Lord Godolphin, who was emerging as one of the few decisive men in Whitehall. Among the peers were his prominent Anglican brothers-in-law, Rochester and Clarendon, both of whom he had dismissed from office because they were 'not of his mind'. And although James struggled to appear in command of the situation, his indecision and his loss of nerve were painfully obvious to all those present.

What should he do? he asked the peers. Rochester pointed out that in fact there was only one option: to call a Parliament. Possibly the king had left it too late, but there was nothing else to be done. But it was also necessary to open negotiations with the Prince of Orange. Other peers echoed this view, and Clarendon seized his chance to vent the accumulated frustration of many months on the luckless king, roundly blaming his papist policies for his present plight. He was no longer master in his own kingdom: 'the people do now say that the king is run away with his army – we are left defenceless and must therefore side with the prevailing party.' Ailesbury, another of those present, was shocked by his lecturing tone: 'The Earl of Clarendon behaved himself like a pedagogue towards a pupil.'

Halifax, by contrast, was courteous and considerate, but the suggestions he made were just as dismaying. He proposed that the king should dismiss all Roman Catholics from office, make a clean break with France and guarantee indemnity for all those who had declared for William. It was too much for James, according to Van Citters' account of the meeting. 'You talk of nothing but security for others,' he burst out, 'but what about security for me?' One of the peers bit back: 'Your Majesty's weapons are your best security – if you can make use of them. If not – then you will have to compromise.' The more the nation was satisfied, he added, the more secure the king would be. On this unsatisfactory note James broke up the meeting. He must think it over, he told the peers.

He was being backed into a corner, and he knew it. Hoffmann, the Imperial envoy, summed up the options still open to him: 'Whatever turning the events take, it is sure that the King will suffer most, and will remain King of England only on condition that he becomes a shadow of a king.'

Even at the assembly of peers, it was obvious that flight was already in his mind, together with a rising fear of his nephew's true intentions. He had told them that 'he saw he must either retreat or fly beyond seas, but he hoped if he was forced to ye last, God would restore him as he had done his brother.' And he said, darkly, 'that it would appear that the Prince of Orange came for the crown, whatever he pretended; but that he would not see himself deposed: that he had read the story of Richard II.'

This drama of the dissolute king deposed and murdered by his popular young cousin preyed on his mind at a time when he was being battered, as usual, by conflicting advice. A letter addressed to the Earl of Abingdon, in William's camp, reported: 'The King is much divided ... The Protestant Lords advise him to throw himself upon his Parliament ... but the Queen and others advise him to fight tho' he have but 5,000 men to stand by him.' If this failed, there was still time for flight to France, leaving the kingdom 'so embroiled & confused ... that they will not know what to doe; for there will bee no legal way to call a parliament or give Commissions'.

The third alternative was beginning to have much the most appeal for James. Father Petre had fled to France when the king left London, and when James returned from Salisbury he moved Chancellor Jeffreys into the apartments the Jesuit had once occupied, close to his own. His intention, Barillon reported drily to Louis, 'was to have the great Seal within easy reach, so that he could carry it off if need be ... nothing can be done without the great Seal ... It is believed that in this way trouble and division can be created for the Government which will have to be set up.' Lord Melfort was among the Catholic advisers who were urging a tactical withdrawal: 'Several Kings of England first fled, then returned to reign peacefully in their kingdoms. The English will recover from their madness.'

Racked by indecision, the king was 'so confused that he lookes pitifully ... & falls away strangely'. But on the day after the assembly he made a show of resolution. He published a Declaration in which he explained that, 'Considering the Grievances and Distempers of the People, and the present Circumstances of His Majestis Condition', he was pleased

to order the issuing of writs for a free Parliament for 15 January. At
the same time James sent for Halifax and appointed him one of a
three-man commission which was to negotiate with the Prince of
Orange on his behalf: the other two were Nottingham and Godolphin. Halifax and Nottingham accepted the commission reluctantly.
As Burnet wrote to Herbert, they said 'that it was put on them by their
Enemies'.

Halifax had already stressed to James in private audience that flight
would be absolutely fatal to his chances. But he also warned him –
'speaking more home' than even Clarendon had done – that he could
not expect William to accept 'any less concessions than such as would
put it out of his power to do such things as he had done heretofore
against the laws'. He formed the impression that while James had no
intention of making a fight for it – 'no man would engage against all
reason' – he was equally unwilling to make the humiliating volte-face
now being asked of him.

It took a trumpeter three days to reach William's army at Hindon,
to request passes for the three commissioners. The prince was in no
hurry to reply: time was on his side, not on James's, and the delay was
calculated to wear down James's nerve and push him into the decision
for flight that was more and more becoming central to William's careful
and deliberate calculations. Finally, having consulted with 'the Nobility', William sent the men back three days later with passes for the
commissioners and for ten bodyguards each.

None of William's supporters was very happy about this develop-
ment. One of the keenest of them, the veteran politician Sir Robert
Howard, saw Halifax before he left London and warned him 'that
nothing of the sort would be endured, for there was no room left for
trust, and everything must be built upon new foundations'. The many
English political exiles at William's Court had a further reason for
wishing negotiations for the New Year Parliament to founder. They
would have no time to find themselves seats and canvass supporters
before the elections in January; politically, they would still be out in
the cold.

While he waited for James's commissioners, William moved closer to
London, and on 4 December he made a formal entry into Salisbury,
which his father-in-law had left with ignominious speed ten days earlier.
Gone were the days when a mayor and his aldermen could afford to
snub the Prince of Orange, as in Exeter only a month earlier. Now
they waited for him in ceremonious splendour at the city gate, the
mayor in his crimson, ermine and chain, the others in solemn black.
Whittle, who well remembered the Exeter entrance, thought this one

'far more glorious'. Its style was consciously regal. 'First of all marched the Regiment of Foot Guards belonging to Count Solms, with their Colours flying, Drums beating, Hoitboys playing.' The huge crowds lining the streets thought it all a wonderful show, and made 'great Acclamations'. After the infantry, the cavalry came jingling past, 'their Kettle Drums beating, Colours flourishing, Trumpets sounding, the Officers showing their Courtesy to the People . . .' The prince came next, his brother-in-law the Prince of Denmark riding on his right and, at his left, the Duke of Ormonde – the son of the man who had been William's best friend, the Earl of Ossory. 'Never were windows more crowded with faces of both sexes than here,' wrote Whittle enthusiastic- ally, 'never were bells ringing more melodiously than now at Sarum; never were People shouting and echoing forth Huzza's in the Air more than now.'

James had chosen the bishop's palace for his headquarters two weeks earlier, and William did the same. But the bishop himself was absent. The famous Seth Ward, in whose episcopacy Salisbury had gained a reputation for 'excellent Preaching and Divine Service cele- brated with exemplary Piety, Admirable Decency and Celestial Music', was now very old, and his last years had been marred by a long, drawn-out and much publicized row with his dean, Dr Pierce, who had accused him of intolerance towards Salisbury's many Noncon- formists. This endless wrangle had worn him out, and when the prince arrived in Salisbury he was a dying man.

Tension was taking its toll of the imperturbable Prince of Orange, too. He was in a hurry to get the whole business of England settled once for all. Louis XIV had formally declared war on the United Provinces two weeks earlier, and French troops were already pushing into Flanders, where they had fired a dozen villages. Moreover, van Citters had brought ominous news from The Hague: on the death of Fagel, William's old political enemies were once more combining against him. He was badly needed. When his secretary Huygens came to see him at the palace that evening, he found the prince coughing, with a heavy cold. But he urged Huygens to be sure and go to visit Wilton, the home of the Pembroke family, where he himself had stopped that morning on the way to Salisbury, to admire the many paintings there by Van Dyck. Huygens made up his mind to go the next day, only to discover that his horses were stabled too far away. Instead, while the prince held court in the bishop's palace for 'a large crowd of people', the grouchy little Dutchman wandered round the city. He was most impressed by the cathedral – 'very large and with many tombs'. But apart from the main square, with a building like a 'Stadhuis', the city itself did not please him much, particularly the open cess-pools, sometimes four feet wide, that ran through the middle of every street. 'Filthy, like everywhere else,' he noted in disgust.

The day after his triumphal entry, William learned that Halifax, Nottingham and Godolphin had reached Andover and were waiting to be received by him. He sent a message inviting them to join him at Hungerford, which he planned to reach within two days. Again the huge cavalcade took to the road. For once it was a pleasant journey for everyone, Huygens and Whittle both noted. 'The Roads here being good for marching . . . the weather now was favourable . . .' wrote the chaplain, while the Dutchman felt quite at home on these broad plains with their short grass. 'Almost never a house, but enormous flocks of sheep, more than a thousand, with their shepherds, one or two of them, in long white coats with a broad collar round the neck.'

The army's route took it past one of the wonders of the world, Stonehenge, and the men stopped to gape at the ruins of huge stones and wonder what on earth they might be. Huygens suggested that they were the ruins of Old Sarum. Other suggestions were more imaginative. The local vicar, who had joined the march, thought it might be a trophy or monument, 'erected in token of some notable victory'. Others argued that 'these prodigious Stones were brought out of Ireland by Merlin's magical Art, and so curiously fram'd and put together'. A single piece broken off from one of these stones, they told Whittle, 'and put into the Wall of any Well, or cast into the Water, shall, for certain, kill and destroy all the venomous Creatures therein'. Whittle was sceptical, although he had to admit that 'none that saw it could render any satisfactory Account concerning it.'

Along the prince's route, the gentry now hurried to offer him hospitality, and at Collingbourne, the next stop, the prince was the guest of 'Mylady Pyle'. Her chaplain had the audacity to tell one of the Dutch soldiers that it was an 'irremissible sin' to oppose the sovereign, however high-handed he might be. It is unlikely that this remark was responsible for the sleepless night the prince complained of next day.

Heavy snow blanketed Hungerford when he reached it on Friday, 7 December. He found the town in an uproar, buzzing with rumours of lawless Irish troops on the move in its neighbourhood. The previous day a party of James's soldiers had threatened to raid the town, and had been beaten off; and that morning there had actually been a bloody skirmish near Reading – the second and last confrontation between the two armies. An advance guard of the prince's army, 250 men strong, had run into a troop of 600 Irish dragoons. In the sharp encounter that followed, William's men had had the best of it, killing twenty of the dragoons and taking forty of them prisoner. But nerves were taut, and on William's first night at Hungerford there was another panic, among the soldiers camped on the outskirts of town. Some scouts had mistaken a party of vagabonds, travelling on horseback after dark, for enemy cavalry, and they raised the alarm. 'The Souldiers being thus hurried out of their beds, ran here and there to seek the Enemy; Thus were they marching to and fro the whole Night . . .' But when day came and their officers went to have a good look, no enemy was to be seen – 'and so they returned to their Regiments'.

The thirteenth-century Bear Inn, where William stayed on his first night, was jammed with people. He dined privately, with his growing retinue of English noblemen as well as his trusted Dutch advisers, and probably they enjoyed the trout for which Hungerford is famous, while they discussed tactics for the next day's meeting with James's commissioners.

That meeting began early the next day. Halifax, Nottingham and Godolphin were welcomed by Bentinck, and at once asked to see the prince in private. He refused – he would hear what they had to say in public, he told them. There was to be no suggestion that he had made a deal behind the back of his supporters. 'He said he was come upon the business of the Nation,' Burnet reported to Herbert, 'and that he had no private concern of his own.'

This point conceded, once William and his advisers were ready to receive them, the three commissioners handed him two letters, the first a personal one from James, but written by a secretary, and in formal French. The prince was surprised: 'I have had many letters from the King,' he remarked, 'but they were all in English, and in his own hand.' Despite its formality, James's letter was friendly in tone. He had sent the three men, he told his son-in-law, in the hope that 'all obstacles to an agreement' could be cleared away. He asked William to listen attentively to them, 'particularly when they assure you of my sincere disposition to establish a firm and lasting peace'. And he signed it on the same personal note. '*Je suis, mon fils et neveu, votre affectionne Père et Oncle, Jacques R.*'

The other letter was from the three men themselves. They pointed out in it that by summoning a free Parliament, the king had already met the chief complaint which William had given out in his Declaration as the justification for invading England. The commissioners admitted that the king had long hesitated to call this Parliament, but he had now given in, 'seeing that his People still continue to desire it'. The letter went on to say that the king undertook to guarantee the safety of

all those who needed to come to London; and the commissioners were
to discuss with William 'the adjusting of all matters that shall be
agreed, necessary to the Freedom of Elections and the Security of
Sitting'. Finally, the king was perfectly ready to come to terms with the
prince, but must insist that his army stay at a suitable distance from
London.

But as Halifax shrewdly deduced – and reported to Middleton in
London – William had considerable problems of his own: '. . . there is
no kind of Disposition to stopp the march of their Army; the generall
opinion of the Lords and other English being so much against it, that
there is little grounds to hope, that the Prince will go about to Over-
rule it.' Many of these extremists were in favour of a rapid march on
London, when a beaten and disgraced James would be thrown at once
into the Tower of London. The same extremists might be perfectly
happy to see a republic established.

One way and another, in fact, James's removal of himself from the
scene was beginning to seem like the answer to all problems. Halifax
had a curious conversation with Burnet, whom he took aside for a
moment. Did the prince and his followers wish to have the king in their
hands? asked the Marquis. Burnet said no, of course not, they meant
no harm to him personally. What if the king had a mind to go away?
Halifax asked next. 'Nothing was so much to be wished for,' cried
Burnet enthusiastically. William told of this conversation, was
delighted, approving both Burnet's answers.

The talks were broken off by an invitation to the prince to move his
headquarters to nearby Littlecote Manor, which he accepted with
pleasure: he had greatly disliked the 'straitness and inconvenience of
his Quarters' at the noisy, overcrowded Bear Inn. Littlecote belonged
to the Popham family, and its present owner Sir Francis, who had
succeeded to the estate in 1669, was brother of Letitia, married to
William's first important political adherent in the west, Sir Edward
Seymour. Alexander Popham was himself married to a Seymour. He
was absent in Geneva at this time, but a hint from William's entourage
brought a ready welcome. With its splendid high rooms, its formal
gardens and its vistas of rolling parkland, this beautiful Jacobean house
– unique in Wiltshire, as it was made of mellow brick rather than stone
– offered him privacy and distance from the haggling over England's
future. For this, he had determined, should be discussed by the English
among themselves. He chose a number of the lords in his entourage,
the left-wing exiles as well as the territorial magnates such as the Earl
of Abingdon who had recently joined him; to these he added Clarendon's name. And on Saturday afternoon this convention sat down

in the biggest room the Bear could offer to discuss the terms the commission had brought.

The exiles almost immediately proposed that the writs for Parliament should be torn up and, after a long and angry debate, they carried the day. 'Here are people with the Prince will bring all into confusion if they can,' Lord Abingdon commented gloomily to Clarendon. But when a deputation of the lords read out the answer they had agreed on to the prince at Littlecote that night, he deleted the clause about the writs. 'By your favour,' he told them, 'we may drive away the King; but perhaps we may not know how easily to come by a Parliament.' When the lords, meeting at the Bear again the next day, carried the same clause by a majority once again, he struck it out once again. If he turned down James's own proposal of the Parliament which he had declared to be the whole object of his expedition, he would be putting a strong moral weapon in the king's hands. More to the point, he was by this time sure that James's proposals were a bluff: as Burnet wrote that day to Herbert, 'the true designe of this treaty is to amuse the Nation and to stop the Princes March; in which the Court will be deceaved, for wee will still goe on.'

In the circumstances, William decided to wind up the talks, and on Monday, 10 December, James's three-man delegation was handed the reply that he and the English convention had agreed. Elections should go ahead for a Parliament – James had already sent out the first of the writs. All papists were to be dismissed from office, and all proclamations against the prince were to be recalled and his supporters set free. The Tower and Tilbury, with its naval dockyard, were to be garrisoned by the City of London, while Portsmouth – still under the command of James's bastard son, the Duke of Berwick – was to be put in the hands of a commander William could trust to forestall any possible inter-vention by France. The upkeep of the Prince of Orange's huge army was in future to be paid for out of the treasury, and the troops of both the king and the prince were to remain thirty miles outside London. And both men, finally, were to preside at the opening of the new Parliament, either unarmed or each accompanied by the same number of guards.

A messenger left Littlecote for Whitehall at noon on Monday. It was agreed that the commissioners would return three days later with the king's answer. 'If they did not come back,' Huygens learnt, 'it would mean that the treaty is off.' Meanwhile, the prince was determined to continue his advance on London.

He had read his father-in-law's mind correctly. Just before James sent the three commissioners to the prince, he had admitted to Barillon that the negotiations were 'only a feint'. To call a Parliament would be suicide for him, he explained, as it would impose conditions he could not possibly accept. He added that, more serious still, 'I should be forced to undo all I have done for the Catholics, and to break with the King of France.' For the moment he must pretend that everything was normal, 'so that I may gain time to send away my wife and the Prince of Wales'.

By the time William's reply was on its way from Littlecote, he had achieved just that: in a note to Halifax and his fellow-commissioners, hastily scribbled at eight o'clock on Monday night, Middleton told them that 'His Majesty this morning was pleased to declare that he had thought fit to send the Queen and the Prince of Wales to a place where they might be safe.'

The queen and the Prince of Wales would have been on their way days earlier than this if it had not been for the intervention of Lord Dartmouth, who had been keeping an eye on the little prince since 18 November. Finally James sent the baby to Portsmouth with his governess, the Marchioness Lady Powis, for the planned crossing to France. After his unpromising start to life, the baby James Francis Edward was now a strapping child of six months, who stood up well to all these hurryings about the country – Lady Powis had reported to Preston from Portsmouth that 'the Prince doth not only continue in health, but is considerably improved by the journey.'

The king's choice of Portsmouth was predictable. This important naval base had been heavily fortified since the 1670s, and when James came to the throne, he had ordered massive new fortification works to be put in hand. He may already have half-planned it as a future bolt-hole: when Bonrepaus visited it with him in 1687, he was surprised to see that most of the new works were designed to fortify Portsmouth on the landward side. 'I've noticed that he hasn't the slightest intention of making use of his navy,' Bonrepaus had reported to Versailles, 'but that on the contrary, his instincts are to defend himself against his own subjects.' On the first hint of a possible invasion by William, James had at once thought of Portsmouth as a place of safety for Mary Beatrice and the Prince of Wales. '. . . it is the best seaport, and they could live there under the protection of thousands of Irish soldiers,' Hoffmann had concluded.

When the crisis that they had dreaded came, though, it was the Prince of Wales alone who was sent off by a growingly paranoid James. ''Tis my sonne they aime at and 'tis my sonne I must endeaver to preserve,' he told Dartmouth in an agitated little note. The admiral was to assist Lord Dover, the Catholic Governor of Portsmouth, 'in getting him sent away in the yachts as soon as wind and weather will permit for the first port they can get to in France'.

It was a painful moment, and James was no longer capable of coherent thought. A day later he had another note rushed to Dartmouth – 'I have altered my mind as to the delaying it a little' – but on 1 December definite orders arrived: 'Upon the receiving of this you are immediately to put in execution the orders I have already given you and Lord Dover for the sending away of my sonne.'

Dartmouth read these orders with dismay. He had been deeply grateful to James for his continued kindness even after the admiral had failed to stop William in his tracks. But he would not be a party to this counsel of despair. He refused, he wrote back, to be 'the unhappy instrument of so apparent ruin to your Majestie and my country as an act of this kind would be'. James must consider the consequences of his decision: '. . . can the Prince's being sent to France have other prospect than the entailing of a perpetual warre upon your nation and posterity, and giving France a temptation to molest, invade, nay hazard the conquest of England?'

His final advice to James was that he should summon the Prince of Wales back to London: if he left it much longer, the Portsmouth road might be cut off by the Prince of Orange's forces. The following day Dartmouth learnt – quite by chance – that Lord Dover had tried to get the child away behind his back, but had been foiled by the news spreading round the fleet. 'For God's sake my Lord, make no such rash attempt,' Dartmouth wrote to him. Since this was no longer a place of safety for the Prince of Wales, Dartmouth offered to James to take him round by sea, to Margate, within easy reach of the Thames estuary. But he was relieved to learn on the morning of 7 December that the prince was gone, spirited away by Dover and Powis: 'I pray God send his Royal Highness safe into your own arms,' he wrote to James.

The prince had been smuggled out of Portsmouth long before dawn that morning. According to a pamphlet published in Holland, Lord Powis had had a hair-raising journey back to London with him. In the darkness, Lord Powis had lost touch with his bodyguard of forty men, and very nearly blundered into one of the Prince of Orange's army camps. He had wandered around for hours before finding his guard again, and been greatly relieved to hand over his charge in London.

Two days later, the baby prince was once more on his journey. 'Things having so very bad a prospect I could no longer defer securing the Queen and my sonne, which I hope I have done,' James wrote to Dartmouth, 'and that by tomorrow by none they will be out of reach of my enemys. I am at ease now I have sent them away.'

An account of the queen's flight with the infant Prince of Wales reads like the most highly coloured and improbable fiction. The scheme to get them away was dreamed up by a middle-aged romantic, the French Sieur de Lauzun, together with Francesco da Riva, one of the queen's Italian courtiers, in a midnight conference with James. There had been rumours that the queen was once more 'gone great with child', and de Lauzun suggested she should take advantage of these to feign feeling unwell and withdraw to her apartments. At one in the morning Riva, disguised as one of the guards, was to come to fetch her, reaching her rooms by a secret staircase. The queen was to wear very plain travelling clothes and bring as much of her jewellery as possible, hidden about her person. Together they would collect the prince from the room of his wet-nurse, Mrs Dabadie, and be on their way.

When the time came, according to one account, Lauzun had to pull her by force from the bed where she was sleeping with the king. 'I cannot describe her misery when she had to part from the King.' By the morning, Lauzun and da Riva had reached the palace garden with Mary Beatrice wrapped in a huge cloak under which was hidden the Prince of Wales. They picked their way across the muddy garden to a waiting coach in which were two of the queen's attendants and drove ten miles out of London to a ferry across the Thames.

At the other side, the queen and her two companions waited in the shadow outside an inn, while de Lauzun and da Riva went to look for the coach which should have been there. There was a moment of terror when someone carrying a lantern came out and walked towards the queen. With tremendous presence of mind, da Riva ran out straight into the man, who stumbled and fell. In the confusion, Mary Beatrice fled. Even the drive to Gravesend was not without its hazards. At one point they were stopped by country people who suspected them – accurately – of being wealthy Catholics fleeing the country. The coachman saved them this time, by whipping up his horses and bowling away across a field.

At last they reached Gravesend – only to find that the yacht that de Lauzun had hired was lying between two Dutch 'fluyten'. It was four hours before they dared steal aboard, Mary Beatrice carrying the Prince of Wales 'like a bundle of dirty washing'. The crossing was misery. At the best of times the queen was a poor sailor, and it was so rough that everybody was prostrated with seasickness, except the resilient prince. More dead than alive, they tottered ashore at Calais at nine the next morning, and Mary Beatrice was escorted to the house of the magistrate M. Ponton, where she sighed that it was the first time in three months that she had felt safe.

Fifteen years earlier, a shy and ravishing teenager, Mary Beatrice had been received by Louis XIV as a particularly honoured guest, the young bride of the future King of England, when she passed through France on her way to meet her new husband. Now she was a near-penniless refugee in his country. Asking for pen and ink, she dashed off a heart-rending little note to Louis: 'Monsieur, a poor fugitive Queen bathed in tears has not been afraid to expose herself to the greatest perils of the sea to seek consolation and refuge from the greatest and most generous Monarch in the world . . . it is out of her singular regard that she desires to entrust to you all that is most precious to her in the person of the Prince of Wales.'

She was almost at once made aware that she was now the guest of the Sun King. The Governor of Calais had her moved immediately into 'the best house in town', his own being 'exposed to all the whims of the weather', he reported to Louvois, the French minister. But by this time Mary Beatrice was already having second thoughts. She had begun to fret about her husband. Ought she to have abandoned him in his hour of danger? Now that the Prince of Wales was safe, she was determined to go back to England and brave it out at his side. 'She consider'd neither the rage of the people, nor the hazards of the journey, her own safety weighed little with her.'

Charost talked her out of this desperate plan, and saw her safely off on her way to Versailles. No effort was spared to make her journey comfortable. She travelled to Paris over roads swept bare of snow by an army of workers sent on ahead, and all along the road she found food and lodgings miraculously waiting for her 'as if she had been in a Royal Palace'.

She was unaware of the explicit instructions Louis had sent to Calais through Louvois about this valuable hostage: on no account was she to be allowed to leave France again.

SEVENTEEN

FLIGHT AND RESCUE

James's flight in the early hours of Tuesday, 11 December surprised no one. He knew by then that the queen and his son were safe, that William's conditions for a treaty were totally unacceptable and that his army and navy would not lift a finger to save him. There was no alternative, he told Lord Ailesbury, his Gentleman of the Bedchamber. 'What would you have me do? My children hath abandoned me . . . my army hath deserted me, those that I raised from nothing hath done the same, what can I expect from those I have done little or nothing for?'

Ailesbury had spent the evening at Court, crowded that day by many people who sensed drama in the air. There was a general feeling that the end was near: 'Do you come to see the King for the last time?' it was being whispered around. The king kept up a brave pretence that everything was normal. He sent orders in the course of the evening for all his officers to meet him at Windsor the next morning at ten. And when Lord Middleton came up to him at ten o'clock that evening, after supper, to hand over letters from his three commissioners, now on their way back from Hungerford, he told him, 'that's excellent, my Lord. Tomorrow at nine o'clock, you'll have my answer in your office.'

Ailesbury was not taken in, and when James announced at eleven that he was going to bed, the earl followed him to his private apartments. 'I fell on my knees with tears,' he wrote later, 'humbly beseeching him not to think of going.' The king told him, 'That is a Coffeehouse report,' – how could he believe such gossip? Ailesbury replied, 'For the love of God, Sir, why will you hide it from me, that knows that your horses are now actually at Lambeth and that you are to ride on Bay Ailesbury, that Sir Edward Hales is there to attend you, Mr Ralph Sheldon your Equerry, La Badie page of the backstairs and Dick Smith your Groom.' The king, taken aback, said dejectedly: 'I know not who to speak to or who to trust; some would have persuaded me that you was a confederate with him, but I could not believe it.' He listened while the earl did his best to talk him out of quitting. He should go to Nottingham, where the Princess of Denmark was: 'Your Daughter will receive you or she will not. If the latter, and that she retired towards Oxford, all will cry out on her; if she doth stay to receive your Majesty, you will be able to treat honourably with the Prince of Orange.' Or he could go to York, 'where the Earl of Danby is with his broomsticks and wishtail militia, and some raw bubbles he has drawn in who will all run away'; or he could secure Berwick; or he could go to Scotland. But James brushed aside all these suggestions. 'He told me he would speak to me in the morning and so with tears I retired.'

Ailesbury's pleading was not entirely wasted, however. After he had gone, James called in Charles Bertie, Danby's brother-in-law, and asked him hopefully 'whether I thought the Lords and gentlemen in the North would afford him their protection?' Bertie answered that he 'verily believed they would do no manner of hurt to his person'. After this dampening response, James hesitated no longer. Half an hour later, the footman that Ailesbury had posted at the bottom of the private staircase came to tell him that the king was gone.

Before his flight, James had written to the two commanders of his armed forces, Lord Feversham and Lord Dartmouth, blaming the disaffection of his army and navy for his plight. To Feversham he wrote: 'If I could have rely'd on all my troops I might not have been put to the extremity I am in: and would at least have had one blow for it. But tho I know there are amongst you very many Loyal and brave men . . . yet you know that both youre selfe and several of the General officers and others of the army told me twas no wayes advisable for me to venture my selfe at their head or to thinke to fight the Prince of Orange with them.' He had no other choice but to follow the queen and the Prince of Wales, 'to endeavour to secure myselfe the best I can . . .'

The letter to Dartmouth struck the same note of injured majesty. It was not his own mistakes that were responsible for his downfall, but, 'having been basely deserted by many officers and souldiers of my troops, and finding such an infection got amongst very many who still continue with me on shore, and that the same poysone is got among the fleet', he had decided to withdraw 'till this violent storme is over'. Finally, he gave Dartmouth instructions to send the fleet to Ireland, and told Feversham that he had no obligation to make any further show of resistance.

By the time the two men read their letters, James was a prisoner.

Picking the wrong man – as he had so often done during his brief reign
– he had made the mistake of taking along as travelling companion Sir
Edward Hales, former Governor of Dover Castle, who was both well
known and greatly disliked in the area they were heading for, the Isle
of Sheppey. To begin with, however, their chances of a getaway seemed
good. At Sheerness they found the captain of a hoy who agreed to take
them across to France. But first, he told them, he must call in at the
port of Faversham to take on sand: his boat was not ballasted enough
for a sea-going journey. And while they waited for the tide, disaster
struck.

Parties of seamen were roaming around, tracking down wealthy
Catholics who attempted to leave the country secretly. These refugees
often had handsome sums of money or valuable jewellery on their
persons, and the pickings were rich. That day the seamen were systematically searching any boat big enough to make the crossing to
France, and when they came shouting on to the hoy, their leader, a
Captain Amos, immediately recognized Sir Edward. He had no idea,
though, of the identity of the man with him – 'extremely plain in
habit', wearing a dark cloak, 'an ill pair of boots', a short black wig
and a patch at the left corner of his upper lip.

Hales tried bribery, discreetly giving Amos fifty guineas, with the
promise of another hundred if he could call off the seamen. The captain
agreed to do his best, but before he left to summon help, he warned
them that his men could be quite rough, and that if they had anything
valuable on them, it would be better to hand it over at once without
any more resistance.

James made a show of obeying, but secretly hung on to a 'great
diamond bodkin' that belonged to Mary Beatrice, and his coronation
ring. The men's suspicions had, however, been aroused by the sight of
this 'ugly, lean-jawed hatchet faced popish dog', who they thought
might even be the infamous Father Petre, and they decided to search
him more thoroughly. One man actually felt the bodkin in his pocket,
but when James very coolly produced a pair of scissors and some keys,
gave up. Others were more persistent. They even forced James to undo
his breeches and 'examined [these] for secret treasure, so indecently as
even to the discovery of his nudities'.

When Amos at last returned with a coach in which he meant to take
the two men to Faversham, he found the king, he later remembered,
in a terrible state: 'pale looks and violent trembling'. He had been left
in the charge of a man called Edwards who took an immediate dislike
to him. The ferryman had carried Hales and Sheldon ashore on his
back, across the mud of low tide. But Edwards stopped him when he

went to get the king. 'Hang him, the old Jesuitical Dog,' he cried brutally. 'Let him walk out himselfe and be damn'd.'

They were taken to an inn, the Queen's Arms, in Faversham, where James was at last recognized. The mayor, Captain Southouse, came to see him, and James immediately asked if he would allow him to leave for France. Once more, he had picked the wrong man. Southouse had been turned out of his commission in the reign of King Charles II, and had actually been imprisoned as a suspect during the Monmouth rebellion. He pretended now to go along with James's plans and, at his suggestion, made arrangements with one Rich, chief boatman of the customs house. The king was to be ready at midnight, he told him, but within a 'quarter of an hour, there was a thousand of the mob got about the house, that his Majestie's voyage was quite abandoned'.

Meantime, James had at least succeeded in getting a message off to Lord Winchelsea, the Lord-Lieutenant of Kent. Winchelsea was a Protestant, but he was also a loyal monarchist, so James hoped for an early rescue. His stay in the Queen's Arms was certainly disagreeable enough. News that the King of England was now a prisoner in the local pub spread like wildfire through the town, and it was soon besieged by an excited crowd, while the seamen kept him under close guard inside. They followed his every move, 'and were so indecent as to press near him in his retirement for nature'.

He had plenty of other reasons to be upset. 'The East Kent Gentlemen came in a great body, and before his face (for he was in ye window) read ye Prince of Orange's Declaration,' recalled a local lawyer named Napleton – at which the crowds roared with approval; and that evening a messenger came into town on purpose to tell him that the Governor of Sheerness intended to surrender the fortress and the ships there to the Prince of Orange, 'which seemed to afflict him'. Rallying himself with an effort, James said piously that he would agree to anything to avoid bloodshed.

At nightfall Lord Winchelsea at last arrived, with a small escort. Forcing their way through the mob, they managed to get James away to the house of the mayor, where he could be lodged with a little more comfort and privacy. But the party of seamen, who were beginning by this time to feel rather protective towards their important prisoner, came crowding along too, to take up their guard again.

In the mayor's house, another local lawyer, Dr St Johns, looked after him, and Mr Platt, 'an honest inn keeper at Canterbury and Ensign in the Militia', served as his Page of the Backstairs. Life began to seem slightly more normal again. But the nightmare days spent cooped up in Faversham, with a baying mob outside his windows, had completed

James's mental disintegration. Firmness, resolution, decisiveness all vanished: instead, he clung to the one stable element in his universe, the Catholic religion. He began to see himself in a new role: that of the suffering martyr-king. His audience of simple seamen were deeply impressed: 'his discourses were very grave & pious & shew'd a great sense of Religion.' He spent hours in prayer, and refused to drink any wine between his meals. He asked for a Bible, and combed it for suitable texts. Maccabee 1:10 struck him as most appropriate: 'For I repent that I gave my daughter unto him, for he sought to slay me . . .'

The Prince of Orange was more and more cast in his mind as executioner, another Herod, who not only sought 'the life of the young child to destroy him', but planned to have James done away with too. 'He thought there was but one step between his prison & his grave.' Even if he escaped actual martydom, '. . . he would forsake Sceptre & Crowne, & all the world's glory for Christ's sake; & he had that inward peace & comfort which he would not exchange for all the interest of the earth.'

It was perhaps no coincidence that when on Friday, 14 December, Ailesbury finally turned up to rescue him and found the king 'sitting in a great chair, his hat on and his beard being much grown,' the earl was struck by his resemblance to his father Charles I in a painting of his trial.

Ailesbury had been one of the twenty-seven Lords Spiritual and Temporal hastily summoned, on the initiative of the Archbishop of Canterbury, as soon as it became known in London on the morning of 11 December that James had fled. The peers gathered at Whitehall to consider this unprecedented situation. Not only had their king fled and his administration disintegrated; he had also gone without naming a regent to govern in his name. And, in a final burst of petulance, he had burnt the writs for the election that were still sitting on his desk waiting to be dispatched, and had thrown into the Thames, as he drove over it, the Great Seal of the kingdom, which legalized any act of government.

There were already ominous signs of mob unrest in the streets of London; and the country's armies and navy were still, in theory, mobilized to attack the Prince of Orange.

With Sancroft in the chair, the peers constituted themselves an *ad hoc* temporary administration, and at once made several emergency decisions. Orders were sent off to Lord Craven – as Lord-Lieutenant of Middlesex, he was responsible for law and order in London – to call out the militia. Messengers were despatched to Feversham and Dartmouth, telling them to stop all further acts of hostility against the Prince of Orange. And Skelton was summoned to the Guildhall to be told that he was no longer Governor of the Tower of London – a Lord Lucas was nominated in his place.

The most important item on the agenda, however, was what message was to be sent to the Prince of Orange, and here the council found it much harder to agree. The initiative in summoning the peers had been taken by Rochester and Bishop Turner of Ely, together with the Archbishop of Canterbury, putting up a last-ditch struggle for what they saw as the principle of hereditary monarchy. They still hoped against hope that James might be restored, suitably chastened and prepared to bow to the dictates of a freely elected Parliament. The first Declaration drafted by Rochester, Turner and two others, which called on the Prince of Orange to help secure 'Our Religion & Laws in a Free Parliamt', added the phrase, 'of his Matys calling'.

The debate was heated and tempers rose. But the king's 'old friends' failed to carry the meeting with them. Others were convinced that only the Prince of Orange could save the day, and Bishop Turner suspected that 'many Others had even then a Secrett purpose if they could to Depose ye King'. The result was a compromise. The Declaration they finally agreed on, and which was sent off to William as well as being printed for public circulation, contained no invitation to him to present himself in London and take over. It simply pledged those who signed it 'to assist his Highness with their uttermost endeavours in the obtaining of a Free Parliament . . . and in all things endeavour to promote his Highness' generous Intentions.' It also signalled that there was in being once more a semblance of government, which would do its best to preserve 'the Peace and Security of the Cities of London and Westminster, by taking care to disarm all Papists'.

It seems not to have occurred to them that it might be the papists themselves – a panic-stricken minority – who would be most in need of preservation. As Ailesbury walked home late that afternoon, after a splendid dinner offered by the Lord Mayor of London, Sir John Chapman, the first bonfires were already being lit. They were the signal for a wild outburst of anti-popish feeling. Unrest had been building up for days in London, fed by rumours of the Prince of Orange's advance with a large army, the queen's flight, the disappearance of the Prince of Wales and reports of troops of soldiers on the loose, abandoned by officers who had deserted to the Prince of Orange.

At daybreak on 11 December, news of the king's flight had spread rapidly through the streets. Everybody downed tools, all normal activity came to a halt, knots of people gathered and swelled into crowds, and soon excitable crowds of 'the Mobile' were surging around the streets looking for action. The city's Catholic chapels had been closed down at the beginning of December, since they had so often been targets for mob violence. But there were still plenty of obvious popish targets, including the embassies of Catholic countries, where masses were still said. As darkness fell, crowds began drifting purposefully towards one after another of these. Wild House, the official residence of the Spanish Ambassador Ronquillo, was stormed and broken into; a scrambling mob plundered it of all 'its rich furniture, plate, money and three coaches to the value as is computed of £100,000', while others raged through the building, looting and burning books, and all the fittings of the ornate chapel. The houses of the Residents of Florence, Venice, Tuscany and the Elector Palatine were broken open, looted and set alight; 'whilst some pluck'd down and threw out all the Pictures, Goods and Furniture out of the Windows, others without and below set them on fire'. The diplomats fled, clutching a few treasures. The minister of Tuscany managed to retrieve a box James had given him for safekeeping just before his departure – it turned out to contain nine volumes of his memoirs.

The *London Mercury* was one of a handful of newspapers that had sprung into brief life at this time, after years of censorship. On Saturday, 15 December, it dedicated its whole front page to the riots. 'Tuesday Night last and all Wednesday the Apprentices were busie in pulling down the Chappels and spoiling the houses of Papists; they crying out the Fire should not go out till the Prince of Orange came to Town.' In a letter, the writer added dramatic details: '. . . having levelled them, they carried all the frumpery in mock procession and triumph, with oranges on the top of swords and staves . . .'

As the night skies over London became lurid with many fires, the premises of James's printer, Henry Mills, were once more attacked and gutted by the mob, and hundreds of reams of paper went up in smoke.

Astonishingly, the house of the French Ambassador Barillon, in St James's Square, survived intact. Barillon was quite popular in the neighbourhood – at least he paid his bills promptly, unlike the Spanish Ambassador – and he had taken the precaution of asking for a large guard to be placed on his house.

Less lucky was the lord chancellor, Jeffreys, detested by one and all for his role as James's stooge in the trial of the Seven Bishops, as well as the man responsible for so many executions during the Bloody Assizes after Monmouth's rebellion. He had shaved off the bushy eyebrows which today would be a cartoonist's delight, blackened his face with coal, rigged himself out as a common seaman and hurried to Wapping, hoping to take ship for France. But a former solicitor in the

Chancery Court happened to spot his familiar face peering from a tavern window. He was hauled off in triumph to the lord mayor, with a huge and angry crowd surging round the hackney coach in which he cowered.

They 'threatened to dissect him, saying "now we have the greatest rogue of all"'. The sight of this mob and its victim caused the lord mayor, it is reported, 'to fell down in Paraletick Fit' – he died the next day – and it was the assembled peers, with some of the Privy Counsellors meeting in the council chamber at Whitehall, who gave orders for Jeffrey to be sent to the Tower of London under a strong guard.

By this time there was a general feeling throughout town that the Prince of Orange was the man of the moment: only his arrival could save the situation, now fast deteriorating. When Ailesbury was roused from sleep at one in the morning next day by the door-keeper of the council chamber, and summoned to an emergency meeting of the peers, he was fully prepared to learn that the prince was on his way in to London. Instead, he was at once taken aside by Sancroft, who shispered stunning news into his ear: there was a report that the king had not left the country at all. Instead, he was being held prisoner down at Faversham.

Since the report was still only hearsay, the meeting broke up. But the peers were called back again in the afternoon to hear a seaman confirm it beyond any doubt. He had recognized the king, whom he had known as Duke of York when he took part in a seafight with him. The council listened in glum silence to his report, and when he left 'there was a silence of a good quarter of an hour, each looking on the other.'

It was Ailesbury who broke the painful pause. There was only one thing to be done, he pointed out, and that was to bring the king back to London. Nobody could disagree. James was, after all, still their king.

A delegation of four was chosen to go down to Faversham and escort him back to town: Ailesbury, Secretary of State Middleton, Feversham, as captain of the Life Guards, and the king's Treasurer of the Household, the Earl of Yarmouth. Ailesbury was to go on ahead, while the others followed with a troop of 250 Life Guards.

It was already late in the evening when he set off, trundling away towards Kent in a coach and six horses. He was stopped continually by 'clamourous watch and ward men', but even worse was the weather. 'Such a night was hardly known for rain, wind and darkness – Thursday December fourteenth 1688.' Huge crowds at Deptford Bridge let him get through, but at Dartford, where about 2,000 people were amassed, it took two hours of arguing before he was allowed to go on. 'The constable, an honest man, told me that I should run great danger in the night time, especially for that the way was filled with plundering mobs,' and he kindly offered the earl a bed in his own house, which the exhausted Ailesbury was delighted to accept. But he hardly slept a wink because of the crowds roaring drunkenly outside until, at five in the morning, they broke up hurriedly at the news that Feversham and his strong detachment of guards were on the way.

An hour later, Ailesbury was on the road again, this time on horse-back, with a bodyguard of twelve Horse Grenadiers and a corporal. The journey was uneventful till they got to Rochester Bridge, where a number of men were busily hacking down the central arch of the wooden bridge. When he asked them why, they shouted at him 'to hinder the Irish Papists from cutting their throats and of their wives and children, for all that Dartford was on fire and the streets ran with blood'. He managed to stop further destruction, but terror of the Irish seemed to be spreading fast. At the next stop, a post-house in Rochester, he went to call on an old friend, and found him 'half dead with fear, in night gown and night cap. He told me he had not been in bed for three nights for fear of having his throat cut by the Irish papists.' And as they journeyed on through Chatham and Sittingbourne, he saw crowds of people everywhere apparently dazed with fear, the women 'crying at their doors on each side, with their children by them, choosing rather to be murdered there than in their beds'.

Here too Ailesbury managed to calm them down, but by now he was so tired that he was nodding off on horseback. Despite all these hold-ups, he still made good time, covering the last thirty-eight miles of his journey in just five hours. By one p.m. on Saturday, 15 December he was in Faversham, where Lord Winchelsea at once took him to the king.

A cross, tired James rose to greet him and took him to the window 'with an air of displeasure, indeed quite contrary to what I had expected'. And a minute later he burst out resentfully, 'You were all kings when I left London.' This was too much, even for the devoted Ailesbury, who answered angrily, 'Sir, I expected another sort of welcome after the great dangers I ran last night by repairing to you.' 'I suppose you meant well as to your particular,' replied the king. Ailesbury, still very angry, told him bluntly that since he had left without leaving a commission of regency, 'the City of London might have been in ashes but for our care and vigilance.'

Eventually the king calmed down and said he was glad to see him. And with a devoted courtier once more fussing about him, James was beginning to recover his spirits. When the exhausted Ailesbury asked him if he would like his dinner served with the usual ceremony, he said yes. The earl noticed that James was wriggling his shoulders round a lot, and found that he was still wearing the same shirt he had been seized in, four days earlier. 'I hope you can give me a clean one,' said the king, wistfully. His wish was granted when in the middle of dinner the Yeoman of the Robes, Mr Tomlinson, appeared with some of his staff, and a supply of clean linen for him. 'Now I can give YOU a shirt,' he said merrily to the travel-stained earl.

As the party got ready to leave after dinner, Ailesbury stopped to ask James's unofficial bodyguard of seamen, still camped in the ante-room, why they had guarded him so fearfully. 'My Lord, that no one should touch so much as a hair of the King's head,' was their answer. 'You won't recognize me when you see me next,' the king told them merrily; and in fact he looked a new man when he reappeared in his normal periwig, washed, freshly shaved and in clean clothes. From Faversham they went to Rochester, where the king was guest of Sir Richard Head, and where James decided to send a friendly invitation to the Prince of Orange: could they meet in London on Monday and talk things over?

With an escort of 120 Life Guards, who had cheered him loudly when they set eyes on him, he rode next day to Dartford. There he swapped horseback for a coach, in which he travelled with Ailesbury and his two secretaries of state, Preston and Middleton. They reached Blackheath, where the king, who had sneaked out of his capital in disguise not a week earlier, now found himself being welcomed back, so it seemed, with open arms. 'Vast numbers of persons out of the City and suburbs came out on horseback, and the road filled with spectators on foot with faces of joy,' according to Ailesbury.

An unobtrusive return by barge up the Thames had been planned for the king – it had been feared that his appearance might trigger further outbreaks of anti-Catholic violence. But when two City gentlemen rode up to the coach to beg the king to ride through the City instead, he was only too pleased to change his plans. 'The balconies and windows beside were thronged, with loud acclamations beyond whatever was heard of . . . in fine the joy was so great and general, that if there had been any foreigners in the streets and subjects of a despotic King or commonwealth . . . they would imagine that they had been all mad.' A newsletter confirmed this rather extravagant account: 'The King was welcomed with all the usual demonstrations of loyalty, bonfires, bell-ringing, the people shouting, "God Bless your Majesty."'

According to other accounts, however, most of the crowds looked on in silence, and it was only a few idle boys who did all the shouting. Barillon, making a professional assessment of the general mood, concluded that 'at heart, most of the people were for the Prince of Orange.'

The *London Mercury* of two days later reported that James got down from his coach outside Somerset House to pay his respects to the queen dowager, and then went on to Whitehall, where 'the Court was thronged with the Nobility'. Archbishops, bishops, lords and courtiers jostled in the halls, some of them no doubt brought as much by curiosity as by loyalty. And Catholics, who had been in hiding, reappeared, relieved. The *Mercury* made no guess at their feelings – but in the next column their reporter told how London was making ready for the reception and quartering of the Prince of Orange's forces. 'Several Goods of Lodgers were yesterday removed out of St James and the Cloyster is making ready for the Lodgings of Marshal Schomberg.'

The question that everybody was asking at Whitehall now was no longer if, but when, the prince would come to town. And on the day Ailesbury left to collect the king from Faversham, the Lords Spiritual and Temporal had the embarrassing task of writing a little note to William: 'We think it our duty to acquaint your Highness that upon information this day brought to us that his Majesty is at Faversham in the county of Kent, we have ordered four lords to attend his Majesty's person and secure him from the Insolence of the numbers of People who may press to come neer Him upon this occasion . . . I hope this that we have done will have your Highness' approbation . . .'

EIGHTEEN

THE IRISH FRIGHT

The Prince of Orange was dining with his second-in-command, Marshal Schomberg, at Abingdon on Tuesday, 11 December when they were suddenly interrupted. A businessman had come post-haste from London to tell them that the king had left his capital, and was now presumably on the way to France, following the queen and the Prince of Wales. The messenger was a pawnbroker and had learnt of the king's flight quite by chance. The previous evening he had been approached by a number of Irish officers wanting to trade their possessions for cash. 'He thought that this meant something was going on,' Huygens had learned, 'and he went to Whitehall next morning at 6, where some friends told him that the King had gone down river at 4 o'clock, giving orders that the gates [of the palace] should not be opened till 8 o'clock.'

No news could have pleased the prince more, and Clarendon, who was also at the dinner, noticed that 'he could not conceal his satisfaction at the King's being gone.' Huygens, too, noted that 'the tidings created so much joy at Court as you can imagine.'

Although confirmation of the report only reached him at eleven that night, the prince instantly changed his plans. He had been on his way to Oxford and had sent the Prince of Denmark on ahead to meet his wife Anne. Early next day he sent a letter of apology to the chancellor and the city fathers. Having received news of the king's departure, he was obliged to go to London 'with all the speed imaginable, to prevent such disorders as may happen in this conjuncture'. That day his army marched on to Wallingford, seven miles closer to London.

If the prince had hoped to be able to prevent 'disorders' he had miscalculated, but it was hardly his fault. On receiving the king's farewell letter the commander of the royal armies, Lord Feversham, had committed the folly of disbanding his troops at once. William heard the news at Wallingford, and was livid. 'The soldiers were all running up and down not knowing what course to take,' he raged at Clarendon. But that was only the start.

After the wild 'popish' night of 11 December, when the mob had torn down and burnt Catholic chapels and property all over London and elsewhere in the country, a semblance of calm had returned to the capital. The Council of Lords Spiritual and Temporal had ordered detachments of horse and foot to mount guard at St James's Palace, and sent 300 men armed with cannon to Whitehall. The queen dowager, taking a leaf out of Barillon's book, asked for thirty cavalry men to protect her at Somerset House. More of the big guns were dragged from the Tower and planted in St James's Park, at Charing Cross and at the Hyde Park entrance to Piccadilly. The council also rushed out a Proclamation forbidding anyone to pull down and deface buildings, 'especially those of Foreign Ministers', and giving orders for the militia to be called out: if necessary, they had instructions to shoot.

To appease the irate Spanish Ambassador Ronquillo, whose embassy was now a heap of smoking ruins, the Lords offered him a first £6,000 to tide him over, and moved him and his retinue into luxurious apartments in Whitehall, 'towards Satisfaction of the Damage'.

All these measures had been effective, and apart from an isolated skirmish between some soldiers at Lincoln's Inn Fields, London on the evening of 12 December was calm again. But not for long. In the small hours of the night, long before daybreak, a rumour went flying through the sleeping metropolis 'that a great number of Irish' had got together and were heading for town. In a hurried letter to Dartmouth, warning him not to repeat Feversham's folly, the chamberlain, Lord Mulgrave, put the blame squarely on James's commander who, 'disbanding the army, hath increased our miseries, for he did not disarm any of them, and the Irish and Roman Catholics (as we are informed) are in a great body about Uxbridge who burn, kill and destroy all they meet with'. Mulgrave was badly misinformed, but he was by no means the only one, and the whole story of the Irish panic is the strangest episode in the history of William's 'conquest'.

In London the rumours at once produced total panic. 'About two this morning, an alarm was spread through the City and suburbs of "Rise, Arme, Arme, the Irish are cutting throats,"' someone reported. 'In half an hour there was an appearance of above a hundred thousand men to have made head against any enterprise of that nature.' By common consent, the streets were lit up by candles blazing at every window, and Ailesbury, sound asleep, was roused in the middle of the night by an agitated servant who told him 'that they were bawling before my house because it was not illuminated'. He hastily corrected this omission and slept on.

At the height of the panic, nine of the lords had a hurried conference in the council chamber. Very sensibly, they dispatched a number of reliable scouts to ride round the city and find out exactly what was going on. The scouts came back to report that not an Irish soldier was to be seen. Hundreds of copies of an official Declaration to this effect were printed and sent round and, soon after daylight, peace returned to the capital.

Elsewhere the panic lasted far longer, as Ailesbury was to realize on his way to Faversham to collect the king. All along his route he had spotted weeping women and children, and grim-faced vigilante groups armed against the Irish menace. He happened to have some copies of the Lords' Declaration, and had it read to the people at a number of places with a calming effect. But few towns were so promptly informed of this official announcement, and in many places mass hysteria gripped the entire population.

Perfectly intelligent, responsible people were taken in by the alarming rumours, which flew like wildfire all over England. It was always a case, though, of 'reports of reports', like that from the Mayor of Wigan to his opposite number in Preston: 'At five this morning an express came from Warrington with letters from Newcastle, Chester and four other towns that 8,000 or more Irish and Scotch had committed a massacre at Birmingham and were marching northwards . . . They burned Stafford . . . on Thursday night . . . All Cheshire is in consternation and so are we. Warrington Bridge is barricaded.'

Another letter told how Yorkshire had yielded to the Irish panic. 'It was proclaimed in Settle market this day that the Irish and Scotch had burned Halifax yesterday and were expected at Skipton . . .' And on 14 December, Major Holdsworth found the rumours convincing enough to write from Chesterfield: 'The Papists and Irish to the number of 3,000 are coming towards these parts and have burnt and fired Birmingham and are for to come to Darby, Ashburn and Uxitor this night . . . All shopps are shutt up and all risen with such armes as they have.'

The most vivid description of this brief reign of terror comes from Ralph Thoresby, a cool-headed nonconformist businessman and antiquarian of Leeds, who had once lived in Holland and was following the progress of the Prince of Orange with great interest. Thoresby, like most people, was completely taken in by the first rumours of 'the flying army of Irish and massacring Papists, who with unheard-of cruelty burnt and killed all before them'. So appalling were the reports from

Nottingham that stolid Yorkshire Leeds took fright. Within the day, the town had 7,000 horse and foot assembled, all ready for the 'defence of their lives and liberties, religion and property, against those barbarous and inhuman wretches'.

Leeds was beginning to breathe easily again when, so reported Thoresby, 'all upon the sudden at night [their fears] were raised to the height upon a most dreadful alarm: "Horse and arms, Horse and Arms – the enemy are upon us – Beeston is actually burning and only some escaped to bring the doleful tidings."' Everybody now panicked and fled – 'some men with their wives and children left all behind them (even monies and plate upon the tables) and ran for shelter to the barns and haystacks in the fields.' Other braver souls put candles to burn in their windows, or took up arms and marched to the bridge and in the direction of Beeston, where they soon discovered that it had been a false alarm, 'taken from some drunken people, who cried out horribly murder, murder'.

One of the few who kept their heads was Thoresby's heavily pregnant wife. He had hastily thrown some valuables into a chest and ordered her to lower it into the well if the worst came to the worst. Before she obeyed his orders, Mrs Thoresby climbed up to the attic to look across towards nearby Beeston – only to discover that not a flame was to be seen.

After this fright, the citizens had only just got home to bed when another alarm was raised by frantic knocking at everybody's doors. 'Fire – Fire – Horse and Arms – For God's Sake!' This time the horror stories came from Halifax, supposedly in flames, and once more the armed volunteers sprang hastily to their posts. 'I could see nothing but paleness and horror in the countenance of all men,' remembered Thoresby. 'But no enemy appearing near, and watch being set at several passes, I lay me down again, but with my clothes on.' When he woke up, he was understandably 'rejoiced to see the light of another day'.

Like many others, Thoresby later came to the conclusion that the Irish panic – so general, experienced from one end of the country to the other – must have been fabricated by someone with an axe to grind. The 'barbarous and inhuman wretches' of Catholics who had terrorized the entire nation were, after all, as Ailesbury reflected, 'not twelve hundred in the whole Army, and these lurked and hid themselves out of fear'. James's biographer Clarke pointed out that the much-dreaded Irish troops, just dismissed by Feversham, were mostly objects of pity, 'not generally knowing where to get a meels meat or a nights lodging and lyable themselves to be knocked on the head in every town they came to . . .'

Everything points to the likelihood that the Irish panic was carefully engineered to raise terror and confusion, and even if the Prince of Orange was not himself secretly responsible, which many people believed at the time, he certainly lost nothing by it. On the contrary: what the Irish panic produced was a universal yearning for firm, decisive government again, and a return to normal life, after weeks of rumours, jitters and uncertainty. And only one man could supply this. 'All the Lords and city have invited the Prince of Orange,' a Londoner recorded, 'which we all pray may come quickly that a stop may be put to the fury of the rabble who have done great mischief.'

The delegation bearing this invitation was only one of a stream of people now flowing into the little town of Henley-on-Thames, where William was the guest of the Bulstrode family at their mansion of Phyllis Court. His host and hostess – another William and Mary – must have received him with mingled pride and grief, since their eldest son had volunteered to join the prince's army and had been killed at Lovelace's side during the rising at Cirencester. Other visitors included the Irish author and journalist Daniel Defoe, later one of William's most ardent admirers.

At Henley the prince made no statement of his intentions. But he was already beginning to take over an administrative role, as two orders showed. One was to Churchill, ordering him to round up and re-marshal an army of the disbanded troops as soon as possible. The other was a warrant for Feversham's arrest, to which William added thoughtfully that if he were found to be with the queen dowager at Somerset House – he was her chamberlain – the warrant could be held over for the time being.

Before anything else could be decided, the lawyer Nappleton arrived from Feversham bursting with his news for the prince: his father-in-law had been stopped and was now in safe custody at Faversham. If Nappleton expected anybody to be pleased with the news he had travelled so eagerly to bring, he was doomed to disappointment. 'The foolish men of Faversham have thrown us into an uneasy aftergame,' Burnet wrote crossly to Herbert. Later on, Nappleton hinted that he should be rewarded for his action, only to be rudely disillusioned by Burnet: 'Mr Nappleton, how can you expect a reward for doing something that might have spoilt all our measures?'

For the Prince of Orange, James's sudden reappearance on stage at this point was an acute embarrassment. The king's withdrawal had been central to all his calculations. But he remained impassive as usual, and continued his journey to Windsor, where he arrived on Sunday night to establish himself in the castle and wait for the next move. It was James's – letter suggesting a meeting in London arrived the next day, carried by Feversham. After some thought, William dispatched his kinsman Zuylestein to Rochester with his reply. It was brief and chilling: William asked for time to consider the king's suggestion, but he refused to enter the capital until it was cleared of James's troops. Meantime, he suggested, the king should remain at Rochester. James, already back in Whitehall when Zuylestein tracked him down, offered to have St James's Palace made ready for his son-in-law and pressed hard for the conference. Zuylestein committed William to nothing, and left him.

As for James's messenger to William, Lord Feversham, he had hardly handed over the king's letter at Windsor when he was arrested, on William's warrant of the day before. Huygens saw him later that day, looking 'miserable and confused'.

William's fury at Feversham's action in disbanding the army was not only on account of the riots and unrest it had produced. He needed James's well-drilled armies intact to use against France in the near future, and also for possible use against the Catholic rising in Ireland, that an exiled James was certain to encourage relief when a letter arriving from Spithead the same day assured him that at least the English navy would not fall into French hands.

The prince's earliest contact with the English navy under Dartmouth had been made at the end of November. A young naval officer, George Byng, had come to see the prince at Sherborne, and revealed that a large number of his fellow-officers, as well as ordinary seamen, were ready to declare for him. The prince sent him back to his ship with a letter for Dartmouth: 'My Lord, the Protestant religion and the liberties of England being now at stake, I cannot believe you will contribute towards the destruction of either. I therefore . . . invite you earnestly to joyne the fleete under your command with mine . . . I expect and desire . . . that I may speedely receaue the news of your compliance, which will make me your affectionate friend . . .' But when Byng got back to Spithead, Dartmouth was at sea again, and in the end a fortnight went by before William's letter could be successfully smuggled into the Admiral's cabin for him to discover on 12 December. By this time, James had fled and, almost simultaneously, Dartmouth received instructions from the temporary Council of Peers to cease all hostilities against the Dutch fleet. But Dartmouth's mind was already made up: 'with the unanimous concurrence of the fleet,' he had written to the Prince of Orange his conclusion that it was 'not only a just but commendable act to join with your Highness'.

Dartmouth had been one of the most devoted of James's servants –

an outstanding example of the kind of intense personal loyalty that
James could still command, even at this last stage, and even with his
deplorable record as monarch. In a letter to Feversham of the same
date, Dartmouth burst out, '. . . my owne heart has been allmost
breaking. Oh God what could make our master desert his kingdom
and his friends . . . God in his infinite mercy restore him to his throne
with comfort again . . .' Like Ailesbury, Dartmouth was ready to blame
all of James's errors and misfortunes on the evil advice of those around
him: 'it cannot be the effects of his owne thoughts but of womanish or
timorous councells . . .' and if he surrendered his command now it was
in the hope – as he made clear to everyone, including the Prince of
Orange – that matters could be so arranged as to leave James on his
throne.

The submission of Dartmouth and Feversham left William master of
the military field, and it had been a walkover. England was his without
a single battle. But the political obstacles which lay ahead were far
more formidable, and the first headache was James's unexpected
reappearance in London, and his invitation – on the face of it so
reasonable – to a conference. His son-in-law had no intention of
meeting him face to face, and no intention of agreeing to a conference
– James in London would still be king in his own capital. At the same
time he was anxious to avoid using his military muscle to force a
solution: he was determined instead, as he had consistently been since
the very start of the whole enterprise, to involve the English politicians
in the decision-making.

So on Monday morning, the future of their king was discussed in his
own castle, at the invitation of the prince, by a number of peers led by
Halifax. Tempers rose as they argued. If James's flight had produced
confusion, his unexpected return threatened chaos. Armed conflict
might be unavoidable: even civil war was not out of the question. The
London crowds had given him a warm welcome. If king and prince
were to be in London simultaneously, who knew what might happen?
The peers had no difficulty agreeing that James must not be allowed to
remain in Whitehall. The question was, what was to be done with
him? Clarendon arrived towards the end of their discussions, and was
astonished by their hostile tone towards the king.

Some of the suggestions made were extreme: Delamere said savagely
that he ought to be locked up in the Tower: as far as he was concerned,
James was king no longer. This proposal was formally seconded by
another of the revolutionaries, the hot-headed Lord Mordaunt; at least
two other peers agreed. But the Duke of Grafton objected, and kind-
hearted Shrewsbury, backed by Churchill, argued against such rough

treatment. Should he be exiled? Perhaps to Breda? It was pointed out that Mary would certainly object strongly to this. Should he be kept under close guard, prisoner in one of his own houses? Windsor or Hampton Court? 'All spoke against his going to any of his own houses . . . [They] would not do anything that might look like treating him as a friend.' Finally, it was agreed that he should be sent to a private house and kept there under guard while his fate was decided. And somebody proposed Ham, a pleasant Thames-side villa belonging to the Duchess of Lauderdale.

Sent to learn their decision, William asked for it to be put in writing: in 1688, it was unwise to trust the word of English politicians. The request sobered them. 'Lord Halifax then told the Prince there had been very free debates, which would not be very fit to be talked of; whereupon his Highness enjoined secrecy.'

His next question was even more disconcerting. Who should tell the king of their decision? Some of the prince's Dutch officers? suggested Halifax: Count Solms? William shook his head. It was the joint decision of all those present – the English were to do their own dirty work. 'By your favour, My Lord,' he told Halifax smoothly, 'it is the advice of the peers here, and some of yourselves shall carry it.' In the same breath, he named Halifax, Delamere and Shrewsbury. Once more Halifax found himself charged with a painful and embarrassing mission. The three men left at once, arriving in Whitehall after midnight.

The king had already gone to bed, after a busy day in which, like his son-in-law, he had had lengthy discussions with the few lords that remained faithful to him. But if his 'old friends' looked for signs that he was ready to mend his ways, they had looked in vain. All the Catholics had come hopefully flocking back, it was reported, 'with Mons. Barillon at the head of them; and this day there were thirty or forty at His Majesty's dinner, and no other priest but a Jesuit to say grace . . .' Proving yet again his inability to learn from experience, James had also 'expressed much dissatisfaction at what the Lords had done in his absence'.

It had been, so Ailesbury reported, a 'melancholy' day. The king dined and supped in public, but the exuberant mood of the night before had evaporated: 'all conversation was dry.' Just before he retired, he was confronted with a gruff von Solms, who came to tell him that he had orders to take command of all the royal posts at Whitehall, Somerset House and St James's. Surprised, the king asked why it was not possible for the prince to stay at St James's Palace, while he remained at Whitehall with his own guards. The count replied curtly that those were his orders, and James had to look on helplessly while his own trusted guards were replaced by a strong detachment of William's Dutch guards. Ailesbury, an indignant witness, commented bitterly: 'At midnight the Dutch Guards were posted . . . and the King's Guards dismissed and treated like a pack of rogues.'

James was in bed and asleep when the final humiliation came. Halifax, Shrewsbury and Delamere, accompanied by Lord Middleton, were led in by a Page of the Backstairs to announce that the Prince of Orange wished him to go immediately to Ham. The king protested. The Duchess of Lauderdale was in Scotland, he said, and 'the house was cold and moist and uninhabited – he chose rather to go to Rochester'. The three lords answered that those were their instructions, but that they would consult the prince and return by eight with his answer. William, concealing his satisfaction, gave his permission.

It was raining heavily the next morning when at eleven o'clock James walked to the royal barge moored at Whitehall steps. The prince's delegates had insisted that he should go by river to Gravesend, rather than by coach through the City – they were afraid of trouble, after the enthusiastic welcome James had had two days earlier. As it was, the king made an impressive and graceful exit. 'All the loyal nobility and many others, and the foreign ministers came to pay their last respects,' and there was hardly a dry eye among those present. 'Such a melancholy farewell was never seen.' Huygens later heard that the king, by contrast, was perfectly composed and not the least emotional as he got into the barge. He himself organized the seating arrangements in the crowded boat, which sped off to shoot past Westminster Bridge so fast that Ailesbury 'offered many prayers to God Almighty', consoling himself that if he drowned now he would perish in 'a righteous cause and not forsaking my King and Sovereign in his bitter affliction'. While Ailesbury brooded, James enjoyed an excellent picnic that his resourceful chef Patrick Lamb had provided, and chatted easily with the commander of the Dutch Foot Guards in charge of him. This Colonel Wycke was a nephew of Sir Peter Lely, the Restoration Court-painter and, before they set off, he had apologized to the king 'for the employment they had given him'. James – the saintly martyr-king on his way to execution – smiled kindly at him and told him 'he did his duty and he wished all his own had done the like'.

Hundreds of Londoners lined the river to watch their king disappearing, this time for good, and Clarendon summed up the mood: 'It is not to be imagined what a damp there was upon all sorts of men throughout the town. The treatment the King had met from the Prince of Orange, and the manner of his being driven, as it were from White-hall . . . moved compassion even in those who were not very fond of him.' Burnet had the same impression: 'Compassion has begun to work, especially since the Prince sent him word to leave Whitehall.'

While James travelled down-river in his twelve-oared barge with its accompanying flotilla of smaller boats filled with guards, William prepared for his own entry into London. He left Windsor to stop for an early dinner at Syon House, in Brentford, as the guest of the Countess of Northumberland. Then, hearing that James was definitely gone, he got into his coach once more for the last stage of his journey. Huygens had gone on ahead and was as usual unimpressed by the state of the roads – 'so dirty as I've hardly ever seen before'. But in London itself he was struck by a more festive mood, the crowds shouting and singing, and 'a mass of people with orange ribbons on their hat or oranges on sticks'.

For the last mile or so of the prince's journey, and through the tiny hamlet of Knightsbridge, the route was lined with the prince's own guards and men from the London militia. At Knightsbridge his procession was swelled by 'a great number of Persons of Quality in their Coaches and six Horses, and a great Train of Gentlemen on Horseback; the People huzzaing and loudly rejoycing all along as he came.'

Ahead of the prince marched four regiments of foot, two of them the Scotch regiments under Mackay; around him, his own guards; behind, a regiment of dragoons and a body of foot. Immediately ahead of William was a grand coach with six white horses, in which sat his kinsman the Count of Nassau, and Schomberg's son. But he himself chose to ride in unostentatious style, in a small 'Callash' drawn by four bay horses.

At Hyde Park Corner, he was officially greeted by the Sheriffs of London and Middlesex, who surrendered their white staves of office to him, and it had been expected that he would ride along the road to St James's. Despite 'the excessive rain which fell this day . . . almost . . . without intermission', every window was filled with people, and such huge crowds had turned out to line the streets 'that many were forced to run through the dirt up to the middle-leg'. But William chose to disappoint them and 'he who loved neither shows nor shoutings, went through the Park.'

The bells of London were ringing as he reached St James's Palace. As soon as he entered, according to a newsletter, 'the Flag was put forth upon the round Tower, and his Highness wellcom'd by the discharge of the Cannon.'

The Court that evening was crowded. The diarist John Evelyn was among those who couldn't wait to set eyes on this legendary personality and see how he would behave on such an extraordinary occasion. 'All the world go to see the Prince,' he wrote in his diary, '. . . there I saw severall of my Acquaintance that come over with him. He is very stately, serious and reserved.'

But despite the huzzas, the ringing bells, the crowds and the bonfires lit that night, Reresby observed that 'thinking men of the City seemed displeased at the King's being forced to withdraw himself a second time.' King James was not yet forgotten.

NINETEEN

'FALLEN FROM THE CROWN'

On 25 December 1688 London was covered with snow, and it was bitterly cold. It was none the less one of the busiest Christmases the capital had known for years. In Westminster there was a steady coming and going of politicians, and the Court of the Prince of Orange was crowded with people come to welcome, to thank, to petition or simply to gaze.

William had been in London for a week now, and had settled into St James's Palace, where his study overlooked the park and the frozen lake on which the Londoners were skating. Not normally very sociable, he had grasped the importance of being accessible, and he had adopted – for the time being, at least – the English Court's habit of keeping open house most of the day. 'This day the Prince dined at St James's publick and at the table with him about 40 of the Peers of England and others,' reported the *London Mercury* of 20 December. 'His Royal Highness was very chearful and his Habit of a Cinamon colour, English Cloth, very richly lac'd with Gold Lace.' He was ready to receive all comers – friend or foe – and when Ailesbury came to greet him, he invited this Jacobite of the first order to stay and dine. Ailesbury was surprised to find him quite chatty: 'He entertained me ... with discourse, very much for one that was normally taciturn.'

On Christmas Day William went to St James's Chapel, where Dr Burnet 'preach'd before his Highness from a Text suiting the day'. The English clergy cheered up when they heard that the Calvinist prince had attended an Anglican service, and were greatly reassured to learn, a week later, that he had received the sacrament from Dr Compton. There had been fears that he might be more Presbyterian than Anglican, while others felt that 'a Calvinist would be as unsuitable a Head of the Church of England as a papist'. What was also noticed, according to the *English Currant* was that on Christmas Day, the prayers for King James, his queen and the whole royal family were still being said as usual in the royal chapel.

On the same day, the prince also called on his ageing aunt, the

Catholic queen dowager at Somerset House. She was unwell, and received him lying in bed. She had been talking for months about packing her bags and returning to her native Portugal, but the prince assured her that she was most welcome to stay, and that no difficulties would be made about her continuing to have her Catholic chapel and chaplain as before. Was there anything else he could do for her? he asked politely. And did she still play her favourite card-game, basset? The queen dowager seized her chance. Well no, she had been unable to play for some time, since her 'banker' was in prison. When he asked who this banker was, she told her nephew that it was Feversham, her chamberlain, who was so devoted to her that he was often nicknamed the king dowager. The prince took the hint, and next day the earl, still in custody at Windsor, was released.

While the royal family socialized in London, James had settled in Rochester where he arrived on 19 December after a night at Gravesend. He was once more the guest of Sir Richard Head, who had made him welcome on his way to London a few days earlier, and although the devoted Ailesbury – still in attendance – thought it no more than 'an indifferent good house', the king seemed perfectly happy, and often chatted to his Dutch guards and their civil Captain Dorp. He was surprised to see so many of them attending his daily mass, but when he asked one of them how he could have joined the prince's Protestant army, the man answered: 'My soul is Catholic, Sir, but my sword is for the Prince of Orange.' Brooding over this, James exclaimed to Dorp that his Dutch troop was at least two-thirds followers of his own religion, 'so cried out against'; but it was explained to him that while the Dutch fleet only accepted Dutch Protestant subjects, anyone could join the Republic's army, and that among the lower ranks there was no religious discrimination.

So polite were his guards that they seemed more like attendants than jailers. And in fact, they had had clear instructions from London not to intervene if James made any move to escape. 'But he doesn't want to go,' noted Huygens irritably. In the inner circle of William's advisers, no news was more impatiently awaited than news of James's second, and final, flight.

Unobtrusively, William began to apply pressure. The house in Rochester backed on to the Medway, but no guards were seen to be posted in the garden. A letter from Mary Beatrice, in which she urged him to follow her, was intercepted and read – and then hastily passed on to him. When James asked for passports, they sent him twice the number he asked for. Still he hesitated. Then while he was at supper on 22 December, he was handed 'an express from London, from one of the Lords that was admitted into Councils that the Prince of Orange held, with his advice that the King would not be safe if he stayed in the realm,' according to Ailesbury. He does not mention the name of this gentleman, but Reresby soon afterwards had a fascinating conversation with an anonymous Court lady, who told him that it was Halifax who sent the king a private letter 'after he had spoken to the Prince, threatening some ill design against his person'. The marquis was convinced that the prince's party had decided to imprison the king, according to her. Whether William actually considered this as a last resort, or whether Halifax felt that he would be unable to resist pressure from his more extreme supporters to do so, we have no way of knowing.

But for James this suggestion, echoing his own fears, was the last straw. Late that night he called his bastard son the Duke of Berwick into his rooms, together with Secretary of State Middleton, for a discussion. Finally, Ailesbury was summoned, and after telling him to shut the door, James broke the news that he was leaving: '. . . if I do not retire, I shall certainly be sent to the Tower,' he said fearfully, 'and no King ever went out of that place but to his grave.' But he made one formal statement which deeply impressed his listeners: 'I call God to witness I had no desire of retiring,' he insisted. 'I retire for the security of my person. I shall always be in readiness to return when my subjects' eyes may be opened.' He hugged Ailesbury, then left through a back door out into the garden: on the river at its end a rowing boat was waiting with Berwick, his groom, Mr Biddulph and three servants.

In spite of a freezing east wind, they managed to make the mouth of the Medway by six the next morning. In the darkness they couldn't find the *Henrietta* – by coincidence, this was the yacht that brought William of Orange over on his first visit to England in October 1669 – which was to take him to France, and they took refuge on another ship till daylight revealed that the *Henrietta* had slipped her moorings in the gale, but was not far away. With the king aboard, she set sail for France. The 'Protestant' wind made it a lengthy and disagreeable crossing, with only a moment of light relief – when the captain served up some bacon he had fried in a pan so ancient that he'd plugged the hole in it with a terry rag. The king said cheerfully that it was the best feast he had ever had. At daylight on Christmas Day he landed at Ambleteuse, near Calais.

Among those in London to whom his departure caused little concern was his daughter Anne. 'People who were with her . . . took notice, that when news came of the King's being gone, she seemed not at all moved, but called for cards and was as merry, as she used to be.'

As usual, James's timing was disastrous. His continued presence in England constituted the most formidable obstacle to William's plans, and the prince had been consulting closely about possible expedients. One such – strongly favoured by the Whig lawyer Pollexfen – was that James should be talked into agreeing to a 'cession' of the Crown in his son-in-law's favour. When it became known that the king had been detained at Faversham and was returning to Whitehall, Bishop Lloyd of St Asaph, almost the only 'Williamite' of the higher clergy, was commissioned to sound out Turner, the most solidly pro-James of their number. Lloyd's report to William was discouraging: Turner said serenely that he believed His Majesty was now 'willing to do all that could be required of him, and even to be reduced to the state of Duke of Venice . . .' Lloyd concluded that only James's Catholic advisers could bring him round to the idea of a 'cession'.

During James's second stay at Rochester, his 'old friends', led by Turner, Rochester and Clarendon, actively canvassed political support for him, and sent urgent messages begging him not to leave until his supporters had had time to get up an Address to him. To the last and most pressing of these messages, James replied that he would hear it in the morning – and left that night.

His flight was a body-blow to his supporters. Francis Gwyn, secretary of the Council of Lords Spiritual and Temporal, wrote to Dartmouth that the king had blundered for the second time. 'He went away first from London on the very day the Commissioners were to return with the proposals of a treaty, and this second time of his going from Rochester was on the day the Lords were to meet, and a great part of them would have been for an application to him in relation to a Parliament.' It was all up with him now, Gwyn thought: 'Neither he nor his (if the child be so) are like ever to set foot here again.'

James's brother-in-law Lord Rochester had the same reaction. 'I am very confident if the King had not again withdrawn himself, the Peers would have sent to him before they had made any address to the Prince,' he stated, but that was probably exactly what Halifax and other supporters of the prince hoped to forestall by their grim warning to the king. It is doubtful anyway if anybody could still have saved James, by that time. The French King Louis XIV certainly did not believe it possible. As early as August, after he learned of William's invasion plans, he instructed Bonrepaus to find out 'what plans the King of England has for the safety of his own person, in case he finds himself deserted'. And when news of the prince's landing arrived in Versailles, Louis remarked, '*Le Roy d'Angleterre est un homme perdu.*'

With James's flight and his arrival in France as a penniless refugee, Louis XIV not only gained a pensioner for life: he lost a valuable ally. From now on, he could count the English, as well as the Dutch, among his most staunch enemies. The new mood in London became plain when within twenty-four hours of James's departure, Barillon was coolly given his marching orders. That same day, Sunday, 23 December, the French ambassador had delivered to the prince, from his master, a letter which, according to the *London Mercury*, was written in 'insulting terms, containing little besides Threats, what he designed to do to Holland as also against the Protestant Merchants in his Kingdom, in case any Violence is offered to the Papists in England'. Next day Barillon departed with his retinue, 'having some of the Prince's Troops to conduct him safe to the Sea Shoar'.

The letter from Louis XIV came as no surprise. Over Christmas the English newspapers were filled with rumours of war from Paris. 'The French Preparations are almost incredible,' reported the *London Mercury* on 24 December. 'That King designing three armies in the Spring, of 40,000 men each, one in the Lower Rhine, another in the Palatinate and the Third against Holland . . . That King also designs to have Eight Men of Warre in the Channel and it is conjectured, will shortly declare a War against England.' Much more alarming to William was a story that the French king was planning to invade Holland with 50,000 men soon after 12 January and, according to the *Mercury*, had ordered 25,000 coats, 'lined with lamb skins with the wool on', 'Ice Sledges, and several thousand sliding-shoes, to invade Holland, in case of a frost'.

Not surprisingly, the Prince of Orange was in a hurry to get 'the Business of England' sorted out, and the kingdom back to normal as soon as possible. On Christmas Eve he summoned all the peers in town and asked them to consider how a free Parliament could be procured, as the only way to a peaceful settlement of its problems. Sancroft – shattered by James's flight – did not appear. A general hardening of attitudes towards their errant king was noticeable, and the mood of the gathering was brisk. It was moved that the letter James had left with Middleton should be brought and read aloud. Godolphin said smoothly that he had seen it and could assure them it would give them no satisfaction – and the question was dropped. Clarendon attempted to revive the question of the legitimacy of the Prince of Wales, and proposed a new enquiry into the circumstances of his birth. But by common consent this embarrassing topic had now been shelved. 'I did not expect at this time of day to hear anybody mention that child who was called the Prince of Wales,' said one of the peers, cutting him short. 'Indeed I did not, and I hope we shall hear no more of him.'

Long wrangling discussions then followed, but the peers finally reached agreement that day. At four o'clock on Christmas Day they came to see the prince at St James's with two Addresses that ninety of their number had signed. 'The first gave his highness most humble and hearty thanks for his coming over,' reported the *English Currant* of Wednesday 26 December, 'and rescuing the Nation from Popery and Slavery and pray'd his Highness to take upon him the government both Civil and Military, until a free Parliament could assemble to settle and secure Religion, Laws, Liberties etc.' In the second Address they came to the point and asked the prince to issue writs for Parliamentary elections, to be held on 22 January.

While the lords had been debating, William had quietly convened the next best thing to a House of Commons available, and the following day at ten they gathered at St James's. He had invited all the 'Knights, Citizens and Burgesses' who had sat in any of Charles II's Parliaments – but not that of James's heavily Tory one – together with the lord mayor, aldermen and common councillors, to consult with him at the palace: a gathering in which the Whigs had a heavy majority, and James few friends. To the 160 men who assembled before him, William said that after the peers, it was now their turn to tell him what they wanted him to do. They retired to the House of Commons, where Francis Gwyn brought them copies of the Addresses of the peers, 'which the Assembly caused to be read and afterwards Debated the same, Paragraph by Paragraph'. This makeshift Commons wasted no time in voting its agreement with the peers. When the Irish landowner Sir Robert Southwell queried the prince's authority to act without a distinguishing title, he was overruled by England's foremost barrister, the octogenarian Maynard, who replied briskly 'That the Assembly wou'd lose a great deal of Time, if they waited till Sir Robert cou'd conceive how that was possible'. The resulting Association was signed by almost everyone present: on 22 January England would have a Convention Parliament to settle the question of the succession. The Prince of Orange would 'endeavour to secure the peace of the nation, until the meeting of the convention in January next'. He would also 'take care to apply the public revenue to the most proper uses that the present affairs require'.

This was a matter of some urgency. When on 29 December William went to the treasury to inspect the accounts, he discovered that there was no more than £60,000 in it, according to the *Orange Gazette*. Despite this, he ordered that every member of James's household should receive six months' salary, and that the king's forces should be paid up to 1 January, after which they could consider themselves dismissed. The City of London rose to the occasion and arranged a loan to the treasury of £200,000, with only the prince's word as security.

While election campaigning got under way all over England – the extreme cold and perpetual snow made it very hard going – heated debates began about the crown. Who was to wear it, and on what authority? Four parties almost immediately formed. One was in favour of recalling James and, as Burnet put it, 'treating with him for . . . securities to religion and the laws'. Another party – a small minority, mainly High Church – were for calling James back with no strings attached at all. A much larger group of Tories argued that by his ill administration, James had made himself incapable of exercising his sovereign authority, so that he must have a guardian or regent. The largest party of all were those, mainly Whig, who held that by his flight, James could be considered as having abdicated the throne, which thus became vacant. And the question which divided *this* group was who was to succeed James: Mary, William or both.

Nobody could talk of anything else, as the debate raged on. And certainly at Court, opinions were strongly divided. Burnet learned this after Halifax had proposed that the Crown should be given to the prince, and that only after him should the two princesses succeed, first Mary and then Anne. This suggestion, Burnet noticed, 'made a great impression on Bentinck. He spoke of it to me, asking my opinion about it, but so, that I plainly saw that was his own; for he gave me all the arguments that were offered for it.' Bentinck, never one for petticoat power, doubtless echoed William's own feelings when he said he thought sovereign power should be in one person only – 'a man's wife ought only to be his wife.' And making William king, he suggested, would be no more than a fitting reward for what he had done. Burnet, very angry, burst out that it would be 'an ill return' to the princess for her generosity to the prince three years earlier, and it would give a most disagreeable impression of the prince too – 'insatiable and jealous in his ambition'.

The two men sat up till dawn going over all the various possibilities, but Burnet felt that Bentinck was still only half convinced, and he was not amazed, a few days later, to hear the Dutchman remark in Herbert's bedroom – the admiral was sick at the time – that it would be better to give Mary the title of queen consort rather than queen. Herbert listened in horror and sat up in bed to declare emphatically, 'I would never have drawn my sword in the Prince's favour if I could have suspected him of acting in such a way towards his wife.' Bentinck hastily withdrew the suggestion, coming back the next day to assure Herbert that the prince had no intention of insisting on this point, but that he would be content with a joint monarchy, as long as the administration was in his hands. Discussions in the palace, however, were academic. It was the electorate and after them the Convention Parliament, together with the Peers, that would decide.

The strength of support for James, despite his irresponsible behaviour, was a continuing anxiety for William. Sancroft behaved as if the prince did not exist, as did most of the bishops. Through Dijkvelt William made a discreet overture to Clarendon, a declared partisan of the king. '. . . He told me he was sure the Prince came over full of intentions to show great kindness to me,' noted Clarendon, 'and he was sure I might have any employment I had a mind to, as soon as the Prince was settled.' Even after Clarendon had made it plain that he would be true to James, Dijkvelt continued to press him to use his influence with the clergy: the prince was disappointed that they had not made their application to him, as he had expected and hoped. Clarendon remained unmoved: Burnet – calling on the same errand – had no better luck. Much too late in the day to be of any service to him, the bishops had decided that their first loyalty was to King James.

With the future of the Crown under discussion, some rather odd ideas were put forward, and bizarre arguments invoked. One pamphlet proposed to make William king solo – 'the Princess of Orange will share in all the glory of a crown without the trouble of it.' Another urged that the impostor should be returned to his natural parents, and that then the succession of the Crown should be secured with six noblemen as sureties. The most imaginative proposal was that the monarchy should be abolished and the country run by a Privy Council of forty lords and forty members of the House of Commons, to be chaired by the prince. The councillors of this second Commonwealth should be paid £1,000 a year – 'a trifle', according to the proposer, 'there is more spent in some monarchies upon hawks, hounds and whores'.

Nobody was taking such ideas seriously when the debates began in earnest on 21 January, and the Convention House of Commons got down to brass tacks. Sir Edward Seymour had confidently expected to be made Speaker, but it was an open secret that this unpopular nobleman was no great admirer of the prince, although he had joined him in Exeter, and was even beginning to hanker after James's return. 'No Seymour, No Seymour,' was the slogan Huygens heard being chanted, and instead the veteran Henry Powle – 'a very honest man' and a brilliant lawyer – was elected, while Halifax was chosen Speaker for the House of Lords.

The next question the Convention Parliament had to answer was if the throne was vacant. The Whigs found no difficulty in arguing that James deserved to be removed from the Crown, and had in fact forfeited it. But the Tories found it harder to deal with the notion that an unsatisfactory king might be removed by Act of Parliament – and the Tories were in a majority in the House of Lords, where James's party was known to be strong. Day in and day out the old arguments were rehashed in the House of Lords. The Prince of Wales featured in some of these discussions, but never for long. A half-hearted attempt to propose James's abdication in favour of his son was swiftly countered. ' 'Tis the opinion of the House that there is a legal incapacity as well as natural,' the Convention was told. And it was clear that most people took it for granted that he was not the king's son. Others considered the fact that he was in France as the clinching argument: 'If he dies, France will find another for you.'

The main debate, of course, turned on the question of what were the consequences to himself of James's flight, and there were two schools of thought. One, represented by the Earl of Pembroke, likened the king leaving his country to a man running out of his house when it was on fire, 'or a seaman's throwing his goods overboard in a storm, to save his life'. Such acts, maintained Lord Pembroke, could not be considered as renunciations of his house or his goods. The other school saw the fact of the king's flight without establishing a legal administration during his absence as a formal abdication. Sir William Temple, an old friend of the Prince of Orange and one of the advocates of his marriage with Mary, pointed out that the king had 'quitted the government without assurance of anything. He has suppressed the Parliament writs, he has taken the great seal . . .' to conclude in a solemn *coup de grâce*: 'Here is an apparent end of government. The King has fallen from the Crown.' Huygens, who followed the debate with interest in spite of a nasty attack of gout, complained sourly: 'The arguments between the two houses about the King's vacancy of abdication took a long time.'

It was the last school that carried the day – together with a rising sense of urgency, prompted by news that Ireland might be in arms for James any day now. John Reresby who had come down from York to sit in the Convention Parliament and had been struck by the changes in the capital – 'the street filled with ill-looking and ill-habited Dutch' – was there for the final vote on 28 January. By it they asserted 'that King James the Second, having endeavoured to pervert the government of this kingdom, by breaking the original contract between the King and the people, and, by the advice of Jesuits and other wicked people, having subverted the fundamental laws, and having withdrawn himself out of the Kingdom, had abdicated the government and that the throne was thereby vacant.'

The Lords followed the example of the Commons two days later, but it was a near thing: the vote was only carried by a majority of three. Several of James's party had a last-minute change of heart and stayed away: one of them was actually ill, while William's supporters lugged in the half-mad old Earl of Lincoln – who said he came to vote as Lords Mordaunt and Shrewsbury told him – and the crippled Earl of Carlisle. The general feeling of the House was perhaps summed up by the Earl of Thanet, who told Clarendon that he thought the House had done ill in making the monarchy to be 'elective', but that 'he thought there was an absolute necessity of having a Government; and he did not see it likely to be any other than this.'

To celebrate the nation's deliverance from this tyrant, it was decided that Sunday, 31 January should be proclaimed throughout the country as Thanksgiving Day. In some places, the thanksgiving was a little over-enthusiastic. At Gloucester a fine stone statue of James – put up by the loyal mayor only a couple of years earlier – was thrown to the ground and smashed, while pieces of it were 'most scornefully & degrediously put into a wheelbarrow, and Ruggeld downe to ye Key; and there throwne into ye River Severne'. The city's cathedral organist and choirmaster Stephen Jefferies caused an even greater sensation when before a huge congregation he played *Lilliburlero* with great flourishes on the organ at the end of the service. Despite a furious ticking-off from the cathedral authorities, he played it again at the end of evensong – with such spirit that the young ladies in the congregation jumped up and started dancing.

But such rejoicing was by no means universal. Reresby – no lover of the Prince of Orange, admittedly – observed that the celebrations were not half as enthusiastic as he had expected. 'So mutable are the minds of Englishmen that they are never very long fond of anything.' As for the MPs, they were in for a rude surprise when they trooped off to St Margaret's, to hear Dr Sharp preach on this important occasion. Just two days after James's abdication had been solemnly voted a legal fact by Parliament, the minister not only said the prayers for the king, he also declared to the assembled parliamentarians that the deposing of kings was a wicked, popish doctrine. 'Exception was taken that Dr Sharp in his prayer before sermon ... prayed for the King, by which you may guess at our temper,' Lord Mulgrave wrote to a friend. There was talk of throwing the insolent cleric in jail, but in the end it was decided merely 'that he should have no thanks for his sermon'.

Burnet, taking the pulpit later that day in the same church, preached a much more acceptable sermon, taking as his text the 144th Psalm: 'Happy is that people that is in such a case: Yea, happy is that people whose God is the Lord.' According to the *Orange Gazette*, his sermon was 'so affectionately Divine and Learned, applicable to the present Conjuncture, that he was highly Reverenced and Applauded.' Unlike Sharp, Burnet was warmly thanked by the Commons and it was recommended that his sermon should be printed.

With the question settled of whether there was actually a Crown to be offered, the two Houses of Parliament next took a week deciding to whom it should be offered. The divisions in the house broadly paralleled those in the country, but by the end of the week, the view that a joint sovereignty was the most acceptable solution was slowly gaining ground. Danby had other ideas. The earl was a disappointed man: he had organized the rising in the north, only to find himself of little account at William's Court in London, and he now decided to approach Princess Mary himself, and to tell her that if it were her wish, he was certain he could persuade Parliament to set her alone on the throne.

Mary's sister Anne, too, was beginning to take a different view of the matter. She wanted it to be made clear that it was she herself, or her children, who would succeed directly to Mary, and she gave the impression that she was beginning to regret her support for the prince, whose candidacy for the throne looked like triumphing. 'The Princess of Denmark was very sensible what a mistake she had committed to leave her father to join the Prince, who was now endeavouring to invade her right, and to get priority of succession before her,' Reresby was told.

To the public debate a new voice was added: that of the press. In the absence of a government to enforce the strict censorship of normal times, no fewer than eight newspapers sprang into being before Christmas, among them the *London Mercury*, the *Universall Intelligencer* and the *English Currant*. Much more readable than the staid official *London Gazette*, they were invariably pro-William in their account of public events and the proceedings of the Convention. So, too, were many of the pamphlets printed around this time, though few were quite such blatant propaganda as '*The Character of His Royal Highness William Henry Prince of Orange*', which appeared while the Convention Parliament was in session, and lyrically assured its readers that the prince was 'benign ... affable ... of ... sweet temper'. 'Women and

Wine, the two great seducers of mankind, never could entice him to the least frailty,' asserted the author, who went on to praise the 'charming dispositions of his Mind'. The pamphlet was printed 'With Allowance' – in other words, with formal authorization, which could only have come from the prince himself, thus making him, as a modern historian has pointed out, the first ruler in European history to systematically court public opinion by enlisting the power of the press.

But through all these weeks of feverish public debate, one person remained conspicuously silent: the prince himself. 'The Prince all this while seemed not much to concern himself,' Reresby noted. Certainly he made no effort initially to influence the course of the debate. But his air of disinterest was only a front. In private, William seethed with anger and frustration at the snail's pace of this leisurely decision-making, while threatening France was arming and the worried Dutch were hurrying to prepare their defences.

He spent his days restlessly waiting for the decision, and Huygens noticed a significant change: he had given up any effort to please – or even charm – the English. John Evelyn noticed, one day in January, how morose the prince's manner had become. '[He] showed little countenance to the noblemen and others, who expected a more gracious and cheerful reception.'

Huygens also found him increasingly snappy, and he made no attempt to hide the fact that he was suffering from homesickness. He asked his valet, who came to collect some letters one evening, if he didn't suffer from it; he wouldn't be the only one, said the prince wistfully. Dutch businessmen and politicians who came over to London for discussions with him were disturbed by the change in him. 'His Highness does not look as he did before,' one of them told Huygens. 'He has obviously got a lot of worries and upset, and he told me how horrible it all was, he said so at least twice.' The prince's temper was not improved by a burglary at his dressing-room one night, in which a silver teapot, a gold spoon and a pair of boots disappeared. A few days later he was again a loser – but this time through his own fault: he lost 300 guineas to the queen dowager at the comfortable basset games which were once more filling her evenings at Somerset House.

Now and then the mask slipped, especially in his letters to Holland. 'If you knew the life I lead,' he wrote on 11 January to his army commander Waldeck in the Republic, 'you would certainly pity me. The only consolation is, that God knows its not ambition that governs me.' Earlier he lamented, 'If I were not so scrupulous by nature, I shouldn't have hesitated to wind up this whole business at once.'

Finally, in the first week of February, his patience ran out. He summoned Danby, Halifax and Shrewsbury to his study at St James's Palace, and told them bluntly that 'he had not come over to establish a commonwealth or be a duke of Venice.' He rejected the idea both of a regency or of being a prince consort to Mary; 'no man could think more of a woman than he did of the Princess,' he told the three astonished politicians, according to Burnet, 'but he was so made that he could not think it reasonable to have any share in the government unless it was put in his person, and that for the term of life.' If these conditions were unacceptable, then he would go back to Holland, 'and meddle no more in their affairs'.

It was a gamble, but it was a fairly safe gamble. As Halifax had shrewdly remarked weeks earlier, the prince 'might be what he pleased himself . . . for as nobody knew what to do with him, so nobody knew what to do without him.'

Moreover, the prince had two factors in his favour. Princess Anne, under pressure from the Churchills, who had grasped that William as king was the only feasible option, was at last ready to accept that he should be king for life, not just until the death of Mary. The prince, for his part, had conceded that Anne and her children should take precedence of any child of William's eventual second marriage if Mary died before him: it was taken for granted that Mary was unlikely to produce a child.

The second factor was far more important. Mary had now replied to Danby's proposal that she should be made queen in her own right, and she left nobody in any doubt about her views. 'She made him a very sharp answer,' Burnet recorded. 'She said that she was the Prince's wife, and never would be other than what she should be in conjunction with him and under him.' She would take it 'extremely unkindly if any, under a pretence of their care of her, would set up a divided interest between her and the Prince'.

The die was cast, and Parliament bowed to the inevitable. They wrung one last concession out of the prince before voting: that William and Mary should be joint monarchs. But the administration was to be in his hands, and when the king was in the country, the queen would not have the great sword of state carried before her when she went to chapel.

That was good enough for William, and for the Convention. On Wednesday 6 February Parliament voted William and Mary joint sovereigns – the Lords with seventy-four for and thirty-eight against, the Convention with 251 for and 183 against. It was, so Bentinck pointed out to Huygens, just three years to the day since James II was proclaimed king, an event that nobody cared to celebrate that year.

TWENTY

KING AND QUEEN

Far from being ambitious for the English crown, Mary was greatly dismayed to learn that she was to wear it at all, and the news that it had now been formally offered to her husband and herself filled her with gloom. She was happy at the thought of seeing her husband again, but she had put down roots in the Republic during her eleven years of marriage, and she had come to love her quiet, orderly life among the friendly Dutch. In her journal she noted that she had cried bitter tears at the news, and wondered 'if I ever should be so happy in my own country'.

On reflection, she was ashamed at this self-indulgence: 'I checked myself and was angry at so much mistrust of God's mercy.' But she couldn't resist confiding something of her shrinking dread of this upheaval to Kramprich, the Imperial ambassador. She was only going, she told him, because it was what the prince wanted. She added – as the well-trained wife of one of Europe's leading statesmen – that she hoped the prince's expedition 'would be to Europe's profit and would give the Emperor satisfaction'.

Whether she liked it or not, however, the departure for England of the Prince of Orange had inevitably pushed Mary into the limelight. Politically, she had no official status, but as the wife of the prince-stadholder at this critical time, all eyes were turned to her during his absence, and she lived with the uncomfortable knowledge that she was now a public property. Not for long could she indulge in the luxury of seclusion.

As soon as official news of the prince's landing reached her, according to one of d'Albeville's dispatches from The Hague, she sent for the deputies of Amsterdam, Rotterdam, Dort and Haarlem to give them a full account: 'how happily the Prince had escaped the English fleet; that the hand of God appeared in it, for that if they had met such a numerous fleet they would have sustained a great loss; that he as happily landed . . .' A steady stream of callers came to her Court at The Hague.

Whatever her feelings, she had to maintain a public façade of cheerfulness and calm, because whatever she said or did was likely to be noticed, commented on and reported back to England, where it might influence events or be used by one political faction or another. Towards the end of November, for instance, thousands of copies of the depositions of witnesses to the birth of the Prince of Wales were circulated in Holland and, according to d'Albeville, they made a powerful impression: 'they begin now to believe him truly the King's son . . . Pensioner Faguel has declared to some foreign ministers that he believes it . . . it must do the Prince a great deal of prejudice and dishonour to have said anything of it in his manifesto . . .' Mary had already had a copy delivered to her by d'Albeville and, if she read it at all, it must now have been obvious to her that the Prince of Wales was no more a 'supposed' child than she was herself; but nothing of this could be allowed to appear in her manner, or her references to the subject. Nor could she allow her feelings for her father to show – even when the general feeling for him was beginning to be one of sympathy: 'Those of the States declare openly that no King was ever so ill served and so betrayed.'

The worst thing for Mary, though, was the lack of news. Storms in the North Sea, intercepted posts and the breakdown of normal postal services meant that news trickled through patchily, often only in the shape of rumours, and occasionally through very odd channels indeed. In mid-December (by the continental calendar) everybody in the Republic was on tenterhooks for news from England, expecting to learn any day that the king had fled, was a prisoner or even dead, and their stadholder already proclaimed king. The princess was no better informed than any of them. Out of the blue one day, she received a call from one of the leaders of the Jewish community, who came to tell her that he had learnt from good sources that James had called a Parliament for mid-January. According to d'Albeville, 'the Princess was extraordinarily surprised, and asked if it was her father or her husband that called the Parliament.' She went at noon to pass on the news to the States-General, who were equally puzzled: did this mean that James was once more in control of the situation? There were many such days of uncertainty.

Most painful of all was the silence of the prince himself. During the weeks of the expedition, William found time to dash off notes to Herbert, he wrote fairly often to Waldeck and, by the beginning of December, he could certainly have found ways of getting a letter safely conveyed to her. None came, and she was reduced to brooding about her last, emotional meeting with him: 'I confess that the last words the Prince had said to me, about my marriage and his death, had sunk so deeply into my mind that I could not root them out; I imagined to myself that they had been uttered in a sort of prophetic manner, which made me suffer more than I can ever express.'

At the same time, Mary was playing political wife for William. The most important guests she received were the Elector Frederick of Brandenburg and his wife Sophie Charlotte. The Brandenburg alliance had made the prince's expedition possible, and William had impressed on her the importance of giving the couple the red-carpet treatment whenever they came to The Hague, especially since their visit on 12 December would be seen as a public demonstration of their support for him. So, for the three or four days they were there, Mary exerted herself to pay them 'all the honours and civilities imaginable', sitting up with the electrice 'at play and conversation till three in the morning'. To her relief, she got on well with the electrice – 'a good face and agreeable' – though she was rather shocked by her evident lack of interest in religious matters. The elector pleased her less – 'a strange man to look on'. The Brandenburgs themselves were charmed by the princess: 'Mary's beauty equalled her mental gifts,' Sophie told her mother.

A month later, in the New Year, the Brandenburgs returned for a longer visit. By this time the prince's compaign was a *fait accompli*, her father was safely – if ignominiously – retired to France and much of the appalling tension of the last few weeks had lifted. Now she threw herself with a will into the role of hostess and, rather to her surprise, she found that their visit cheered her up enormously. In the circumstances, there could be no public festivities, so she laid on a splendid round of private entertainment, 'treating them at my severall houses', where they dined, played cards, chatted and sat up so late 'that it was ever neer two before I got to bed'. One evening she gave a small private dance for them, but she herself pointedly sat out the dances, saying 'that she could not dance since her father was in such distress' – a remark that, repeated to James in France, brought tears to his eyes.

There were excellent political reasons for making much of the Brandenburgs, and it was what the prince would have wished, but all the same she felt guilty afterwards at having enjoyed herself so much; 'I took so much care to be civil to them that I gave myself no time for anything else.' She had been going to prayers in her private chapel four times every day, and in this zeal she had conformed to the public mood: 'there was never so much praying in these countries as is now daily for the success of the Prince's enterprise . . .' But during the Brandenburg visit she went only three times a day. She needed these prayers badly as a source of strength and courage during this, the longest and heaviest ordeal of her life.

Uncertainty about what was happening in England again became the order of the day from the moment of the prince's arrival in London when, according to the Polish envoy at The Hague, Moreau, he had imposed a postal blackout: as late as 28 January, according to Moreau, neither the princess nor the States-General had heard from him. There were good political reasons why William should not have communicated with his wife: in the delicate negotiations going on in London about the succession, he was determined to leave Mary out of the discussion at this point, and not be seen even to consult with her. But the States-General were avid for news, so in mid-January they dispatched to London a three-man delegation of MM. Odijck, Witsen – the Burgomaster of Amsterdam – and Dijkvelt. The departure of the latter removed from Mary the last of the trio of trusted advisers recommended to her by William: Fagel had died after a long illness on 28 December and Waldeck had left to take the field again.

Many other once-familiar faces at her Court – English political refugees from James – were now back in London too, and soon after William's departure Mary had also lost one of her closest women friends, Bentinck's wife Anne. She had been seriously ill most of the summer, and five days after her husband landed in England with the prince she died quietly between eleven and twelve at night. She had been conscious up to the last, though unable to speak, and Mary, deeply affected, had 'stayed with her till her last sigh, and with bitter tears left the body'. Bentinck's secretary Thomer had asked her if she would take care of the now-motherless Bentinck children in their father's absence, which 'the Princess, still bitterly weeping, said amidst her tears that she would do'. During the prince's absence, long reports from Bentinck were often the only reliable accounts Mary had of her husband's progress.

The interminable state of suspense was finally ended on 10 February, when Herbert turned up once more at The Hague, accompanied by a childhood friend of Mary's, Sir Edward Villiers. Herbert had come to take her to England and brought with him a letter from the prince at last, asking her to join him as soon as possible, and giving her careful instructions about how she was to comport herself in England. On 27 January (O.S.) Pepys had ordered two yachts to sail for Holland on this important mission, the *Fubbs* – Charles II's teasing nickname for his favourite mistress, the Duchess of Portsmouth – and the *Isabella*, named by James for his daughter who had died in infancy. Sir John Berry had also been ordered to provide a naval escort at Goeree, to accompany the admiral and the princess safely back to England. News of her imminent departure spread rapidly through The Hague, and Kramprich wrote: 'They're having great difficulty keeping people away from court. Everybody wants to see the Princess for the last time. The Princess has not been able to get through it all without being upset and shedding tears.'

Next day a sizeable delegation from the States of Holland came to take a solemn leave, with – as the *Orange Gazette* put it – 'all the Veneration and profound respect they could possibly perform'. The Dutch were devoted to the wife of their stadholder-hero, who had plainly felt so much at home in their country, and had even attempted to learn a little Dutch. They wished her 'many happy and Prosperous Days', assuring her that 'nothing in this world could afflict them with greater sorrow than to be deprived of her Royal Presence, were they not comforted that She was going to be seated in a more Exalted Sphere.' They hoped she would never forget her Dutch friends.

Mary, very much moved, thanked them from her heart for their good wishes. It was impossible, she told them, 'that any change of Fortune should be able to make her ever forget that State and Country where she has met with such Returns of Kindness'. She would always 'consider them equally with the same tenderness as she had for her own Countrymen'.

All this was said, according to the *Gazette*, 'with such moving and obliging Sweetness, that the Lords were in a Transport shedding Tears for Joy'. The States' delegation was only the start of a long procession of people wanting to say goodbye. A committee of the Provincial States followed, led by Fagel's temporary successor, Michiel ten Hove, a committee of the council, the lords of both courts of justice and, finally, representatives of the Earldom of Holland.

A day later it was the turn of the States-General themselves, and on 17 February the Stadholder of Friesland, Count van Nassau – recovering from a serious illness which had nearly killed him – came to take leave of his cousin, accompanied by many of the lords and ladies of his Court.

It must have been almost with relief that on 19 February Mary drove out of The Hague for the last time, in a simple carriage and pair, to go to her favourite palace of Honslaersdijck. She hoped to have sailed the same day, from Scheveningen, but weather conditions were dire. 'The wind had not only been contrary,' reported the *Gazette*, 'but great Mountains of Ice appeared on the coast, whereby 'twas judged unsafe to put then to sea, but rather tarry for a favourable Opportunity.' Some of the company suggested she might like to go back to The Hague, but Mary refused with a shudder; anything rather than go through all those agonizing farewells again. From the *Isabella* she wrote to one of her ladies-in-waiting: '. . . they accuse me of obstinacy in staying here with a contrary wind, but if only they knew what I suffered yesterday, nobody would be astonished that I prefer to wait for the wind here than to go back, because truly it is so great a grief for me to leave a country where I have been so happy . . .'

The two yachts finally set sail on 20 February, escorted not only by the British squadron but by a number of Dutch warships as well. Mary's mood see-sawed: 'The joy of seeing the Prince again, strove against the melancholly [about her father] and the thoughts that I should see my husband owned as the deliverer of my country, made me vain' – till she remembered from whom he had delivered her country – 'alas poor mortal.'

By the evening of Monday, 11 February (21 February, N.S.) the yachts were slipping past Sheerness, and on Tuesday morning, Mary was at last reunited with her husband at Greenwich, where he had travelled to meet her. It was not a happy meeting. Her first reaction was how ill he looked – 'he had a violent cough upon him and was grown extreamly lean.' The moment they were alone, they both burst into tears – 'of joy to meet and of sorrow at meeting in England, both wishing it might have been in Holland'. Both of them bitterly regretted the loss of the freedom they had known in Holland, and would never be able to enjoy in England, a fact brought home to them when they prepared to go out and join the company again: 'we durst not let ourselves go on with these reflections but dryed up our teares lest it should be perceived . . .' Their official attitude was to be one of confident optimism.

That was certainly the mood of the London crowds, according to the lengthy account of Mary's arrival published that week by the *London Mercury*. The prince had been attended down at Greenwich by a large number of the nobility and gentry in their own barges, and at about four in the afternoon this flotilla got back to Whitehall. On their way they were saluted by 'thousands of small and great Shot from the Ships', and the great guns roared out as they passed the Tower of London. By this time there were hundreds of small boats to escort them, and the river banks were 'each side lined with thousands of people who by great Shouts and Acclamation expressed their Joy'.

The crowds burst out in a last loud hurrah when Mary landed on the Privy Stairs of Whitehall to a welcome from her sister Anne, who led her into her new apartments facing the Privy Garden. The reporter of the *Mercury* ran out of adjectives at this point – 'to express the joy of their long'd for happy Meeting would but blur this Paper.' In the evening the bonfires – London's traditional way of celebrating – blazed so fiercely that 'several persons came to the Town thinking the City had been on fire'.

The Palace of Whitehall that evening was packed with people, ostensibly there to congratulate the princess on her safe arrival. Curiosity was probably an even stronger motive for most of them. Certainly it was a piquant and unprecedented situation – the beautiful young princess taking possession of the Court from which her soldier-husband had just driven out her misguided but unfortunate father. And all eyes were upon Mary: what did she really think of it all?

There was no possibility that she would please everybody, and she knew it. If she looked down in the mouth, it would be assumed that she secretly disapproved of the whole proceeding; if she looked cheerful, she would be denounced as an ambitious and heartless woman, devoid of all natural feeling. Anticipating this dilemma, William had sent her explicit instructions in his letter: on no account was she to seem anything but perfectly happy, 'that nobody might be discouraged by her looks, or be led to apprehend that she was uneasy by reason of what had been done'. But in her anxiety to get it right, Mary overplayed her part. The old-fashioned Evelyn was deeply shocked: 'She came into Whitehall laughing and jolly, as to a wedding, so as to seem quite transported.'

On the morning of her arrival, the prince had moved from St James's, which had been the home of her childhood, to Whitehall, where she now occupied Mary Beatrice's apartments. Picking up the palace gossip, Evelyn heard the next day that 'she rose early . . . and in her undress . . . before her women were about, went from roome to roome to see the convenience of White-hall, lay in the same bed and apartment where the late Queen lay.'

Later on in the day, William and Mary were proclaimed king and queen, 'with general acclamation and general good reception', and once more Mary's reactions were studied with curiosity. Evelyn noted with great disapproval that there seemed to be no kind of reluctance to accept her father's crown, not even any regret 'that he should by his mismanagement necessitate the Nation to so extraordinary a proceeding'. Dartmouth thought that 'she put on more airs of gaiety . . . than became her or seemed natural.'

But 'put on', it seemed, was the *mot juste*, and even Burnet, who knew her well, was taken in by it, and perplexed by this apparent heartlessness: so much so that after a day or two he tackled her about it, asking 'how it came that what she saw in so sad a revolution as to her father's person, made not a greater impression to her'. Mary meekly accepted the implied rebuke, and explained that she had simply been doing what she had been asked, but 'that she might perhaps go too far, because she was . . . acting a part which was not very natural to her'.

William had obviously worried that dejected looks in Mary might also be taken to indicate her resentment of the subordinate role she had been given. But here at least Mary felt no difficulty in carrying out her instructions. Describing the occasion when 'we were proclaimed and the government put wholy in the Prince's hand', Mary noted in her journal how sincerely happy she was for William at these terms, although, as she realized, 'many would not believe it' and think any cheerfulness she showed a sign of 'ill nature, pride and the great delight I had to be Queen'. It was more and more dawning on her that the worst of her trials might still be to come: 'My heart is not made for a kingdom and my inclination leads me to a retired quiet life . . . Indeed, the Prince's being made King has lessened the pain, but not the trouble of what I am like to endure.'

On Ash Wednesday, 13 February, the London crowds massed in Whitehall in drenching rain to see their new sovereigns arrive at the Banqueting Hall in Whitehall to be proclaimed. The ceremony itself was impressive. The magnificent hall of Inigo Jones, with its exuberant Rubens ceiling, was filled with the Peers in their crimson and ermine and members of the Commons when William and Mary entered and took their seats under the canopy of state. Halifax presided as speaker of the House of Lords.

Forty years earlier – almost to the day – an English king had been beheaded in this very hall because he attempted to assert an excess of authority at the expense of Parliament. Now his grandson listened impassively to the conditions on which he himself had been offered the throne: the Bill of Rights, by which the power of the monarchy would in future be severely limited. Its three main provisions were a catalogue of James's iniquities. Never again would a King of England be allowed to keep a standing army in peacetime without the consent of Parliament; or rule for months and years on end without a Parliament in session; or suspend the law of the land. The Glorious Revolution, as it has been called, was a *fait accompli*. The age of constitutional monarchy had been formally ushered in. The brief ceremony was, in its way, as decisive a moment in English history as the signing of the Magna Charta nearly five centuries earlier.

Two months later, the bells of London rang out again, this time for the coronation of William and Mary. Feverish preparations had begun weeks earlier, when the Lord Great Chamberlain had sent for the detailed guidelines laid down for the previous coronation, that of James II. On a copy neatly headed *The Method of the Preparations for the Last Coronation*, he made a number of marginal notes. There could be no improving on the ceremonial itself – James, a stickler for tradition and ritual, had seen to that – but a number of changes had to be made, all the same, and some of the trappings of the occasion needed renewal or replacement. Two new States, or canopies, for instance, would be needed for Westminster Hall: 'Those that are, very old & unservice-able', he noted.

The fact that it was a double coronation, not simply that of a king and his consort, was another complication, as well as adding enor-mously to the cost. When James was crowned, for instance, 'The Queen went first with Her Traine And then the King and His Traine followed'. This was surely incorrect for the coming ceremony – 'Quere,' he wrote, 'now whether they should not goe together, under the Canopy, being both sovereigns.' Scaffolding had to be ordered for the stands outside Westminster Hall and the Abbey; James's cipher removed from hundreds of pounds' worth of the royal plate and replaced by the elegant new double cipher of William and Mary; and the royal jeweller, Robert Vyner, kept working flat out to get the regalia ready in time. He had to produce two heavy coronation crowns and two Crowns of State instead of one, two orbs instead of one, and four sceptres instead of two, as well as plenty of gold, 'ex-traordinary wrought into . . . banners, enamelled Georges, enamelled badges, Garters, chains, etc.'

Their coronation day, 11 April 1689, started early for the new sovereigns. At seven a.m. they left Whitehall Palace by the Privy Stairs to go the few yards up river by barge to the House of Lords. Here it took almost three hours to get them both dressed and ready in their ceremonial finery. Both wore shirts of fine linen 'to be opened in the places of anointing'. Over that another shirt of red sarcenet, a surcoat of crimson satin 'made with a collar, for a band, both opened for the anoyinting and closed with ribands'. For the king there was a pair of under-trousers and breeches over them, 'with stockings fastened to the Trousers, all of crimson silk', a pair of linen gloves, linen coif, a sleeveless surplice. 'A close coat of cloth of Gold reaching to the heels, lined with crimson tafta and girt with a broad girdle of cloth of Gold to be putt over . . . a stole of cloth of Gold to be put about the King's neck' all added up to many pounds' dead weight of tradition. Mary's was a feminine version of the same elaborate splendour. As well as her two crowns, there was also for her 'a circlet or diadem set with 2,725 diamonds, 71 rubies, 59 sapphires, 40 emeralds and 1,591 large pearls, all valued at £126,000'.

At ten a.m., bowed down with all this finery, William and Mary at last appeared to walk in slow procession to Westminster Abbey, over yards of blue carpet. To the fury of many in the crowd their route was lined with William's drab Blue Guards, instead of the familiar splendour of the English guards in their blazing scarlet and gold.

The significant changes the Lord Chamberlain had made concerned Mary's role, crowned as equal with William. Like him she was handed a sword of state; like him she was raised into the throne and presented with the Bible, the spurs and the jewelled orb. There was one other change. Where James and his predecessors had sworn to uphold the law made by their ancestors, William and Mary swore to govern according to 'the Statutes in Parliament agreed upon and the laws and customs of the same'.

However glorious the day's ceremonies, it was not the happiest of days for the couple who were its stars. William – nearly a head shorter than his statuesque wife – looked pinched and ill, with an asthmatic cough he could not control. So many pressing matters waited for his attention that he grudged every minute of the time given up to 'these foolish old popish ceremonies' as he later irritably called them. He had left Huygens hard at work decoding particularly important dispatches from the States-General, about the new treaty with the emperor. And, just before his departure, an express had brought news that was no less dismaying for being so long anticipated: James had landed in Ireland with an army of French and Irish troops.

As for Mary, wilting in the heat of the Abbey's thousand candles and the weight of her robes, the news dashed all hope of enjoyment in what ought to have been a day of triumph. Instead, there was the dreary realization that it was all to be gone through again. Once more, her husband would confront her father on the battlefield; once more she would be torn between love and loyalty to both; and once more, no sign of this most natural of conflicts could be allowed to appear either in her looks or behaviour. Nor was any reconciliation possible in the future between her and her father – even if he survived. Today's ceremony sealed the rift. Others might make their peace with St Germain. Her loyalty could only be to William, and to England.

But her heart was not so easily overruled by reasons of State. Some days later she wrote to Sophia of Hanover: 'You must not doubt the sincerity of my feelings when I say I cannot forget my father, and I grieve for his misfortune.'

EPILOGUE

Whig historians firmly styled the revolution of 1688 as Glorious; more recently it has been termed a *coup d'état* based on appeals to religious bigotry and treachery. Even William's severest critics, however, cannot dispute that his reign saw initiated the slow but steady transfer of real power from monarchy to Parliament. Thus were laid the foundations of two British institutions still admired and envied the world over: constitutional monarchy and Parliamentary democracy. This process of transfer was a remarkably pacific one. As a result, Britain was spared the bloody excesses of the French Revolution and the violent birth-pangs of other European democracies in the mid nineteenth century.

But however beneficial it may have been for the nation as a whole, the revolution was deeply traumatic for its leading actors and actresses – as indeed for hundreds of those who either abetted or resisted it.

For William and Mary, as they foresaw only too clearly at their first meeting in England after the revolution, life was never again to be tranquil, unclouded, straightforward. Gratitude is the rarest of human sentiments, and if William expected it from those who had hailed him as their deliverer, he was soon undeceived. The Tories, consciously or not, considered him little better than a usurper of the hereditary monarchy; while the Whigs would have liked to see the powers of the Crown still more drastically curtailed. Even in the best and most faithful of his ministers, like Shrewsbury or Nottingham, William could never count on the kind of singleminded devotion James had enjoyed: the wrench of loyalties had been too great. Those who served him, on the whole, did so because it suited them. Ironically, much the most useful and dependable minister turned out to be that great survivor Sunderland, who after a decent interval returned to England, politics and the Protestant fold.

Suspicious of his new subjects, forced even to mistrust many of his ministers, William naturally fell back on the solid affection and loyalty of his Dutch friends and servants – thus supplying the English with yet another grievance. The faithful Bentinck especially – on whom William heaped honours, wealth, estates and the title of Earl of Portland – almost immediately became the most unpopular man in the country, and the butt of savage political satire.

Even with the Dutch, William's relationship was clouded by the revolution. Their stadholder, they felt, had shifted his allegiance: their interests would always now come second to that of their old trade rivals. The English had more solid grounds for grievance: in the teeth of their obstinate insularity, William successfully involved them in his own Grand Design – that of European resistance to the hegemony of Louis XIV's France. 'Hee hath such a mind to France, that it would incline one to think hee tooke England onely in his way,' quipped Halifax shrewdly, soon after William became king.

The only section of William's new people by whom he was whole-heartedly worshipped was the English Protestant colony of Northern Ireland, the scene of James's bid to regain his Crown in 1689. Jacobite prospects, together with those of the Irish Catholics, were dashed by the Battle of the Boyne, which turned William into the Protestant folk-hero of Belfast and Limerick.

From the glare of the English political arena at Whitehall – and from the filthy smog of central London – William was glad to escape to the calm and order of the new country homes Mary prepared for him. One was the pretty little villa at Kensington they bought from Lord Nottingham, the other was Wolsey's former palace of Hampton Court: under Mary's direction, both were enlarged, modernized and adroitly converted by Christopher Wren, with gardens in the Dutch style.

But the hours that the couple were able to spend relaxing together were severely limited. After the Irish question had been temporarily settled, it was the Wars of the Grand Alliance against France that called for William's attention. And for months on end, every year, Mary became a public figure, compelled to preside over a squabbling, irresolute and often disloyal council while William risked his life on distant European battlefields, or spent weeks in negotiation. She missed him desperately, and there were no children to console her, no friends or family to whom she could turn for solace: certainly not her sister Anne. Perhaps the father they had driven out and the half-brother they had wronged came between the two women: at all events, the first warmth of their reunion cooled rapidly, not helped by William's haggling over Anne's allowance. The final quarrel came when Churchill – now the Earl of Marlborough – was disgraced by William for corresponding with the exiled King James. Anne naturally sided with Marlborough's wife, her great friend Sarah, and the breach between the two sisters became public and irrevocable.

Five and a half years of such accumulating stress wore down Mary's resistance. 'I believe that I am becoming old . . .' she wrote wearily to a friend in the spring of 1694, 'with the chagrin and inquietude one has so regularly every summer.' She was only thirty-three, but when she fell ill with smallpox on 21 December of that year, she shut herself up alone in her study and, with a chilling resolution, spent the whole night going through her papers, burning many of them and setting her affairs in order before she at last called in her doctors. Death may have come as a deliverance from a life she found almost intolerable.

William's grief amazed everyone. In her sickroom he repeatedly broke down in floods of tears: he told Burnet that 'from being the happiest, he was now going to be the miserablest creature upon earth. He said, during the whole course of their marriage, he had never known one single fault in her.'

Her father survived her for little more than six years. After his final flight from England, James joined his wife in the Palace of St Germain-en-Laye which Louis XIV generously placed at their disposal. The Court of Versailles, on the whole, was unimpressed by the royal fugitive. 'The more I see of this King,' exclaimed the Duchesse d'Orléans, 'the more excuses I find for the Prince . . .'

James's first hopes of regaining his kingdom were crushed in 1689, first in Ireland, at the Boyne, and then in Scotland, when the Earl of Dundee and his Highlanders, raising James's standard in Scotland, were overwhelmed in the Pass of Killiecrankie. James made two more abortive attempts at a comeback. That of 1692 was foiled by the decisive defeat of the French navy at La Hogue, under the eyes of James and the French High Command. '*Ah, mes braves Anglais*,' exclaimed James in a tactless burst of patriotic pride. And the failure, finally, of a Jacobite rising in 1696 put paid to his last hopes.

Perhaps James was secretly relieved at this excuse for giving up all further effort. He had returned from La Hogue to St Germain just in time for the birth of another child – their last – to Mary Beatrice: a pretty little baby girl, whom they christened Louisa as a compliment to their generous patron, and always called 'La Consolatrice'. James used to say pathetically that he now had one daughter who had never sinned against him. He actually invited his eldest, Mary, to be present at her birth – 'the most Christian king had given his consent to promise you . . . that you shall have leave to come and, the queen's labour over, to return with safety . . .' There was no response to his invitation.

This late and last child grew up a joy indeed to her parents: good, intelligent, charming and devoted to them both. She was also the final refutation of the cruel revolution slanders: she and her elder brother James Francis Edward were so alike they might have been twins.

The last years of James's life were spent in peaceful domesticity with his wife and his two children, surrounded by the faithful courtiers – Middleton among them – who had followed him into exile. He still hunted as often as he could, but there were no more mistresses to torment Mary Beatrice. Instead, he grew more and more devout, saying piously that he looked upon the Prince of Orange as one of his best friends, 'because that Prince . . . was made use of by Almighty God . . . for chastizing him'. All the same, when one day in chapel he heard the anthem, 'Remember O Lord what is come upon us . . . Our inheritance is turned to strangers, our house to aliens', he had a terrifying seizure, blood gushing from his nose and mouth as at Salisbury, and he never fully recovered. He died in September 1701, perfectly resigned, gently urging his wife to share his happiness. Her own distress was so great that his doctors forcibly removed her from his deathbed. Before this, however, she witnessed Louis XIV make a *grande geste* that actual treaty obligations forbade him: he promised the dying man to recognize his son as King of England.

From the time of Mary Beatrice's arrival in France, Saint-Simon later wrote, 'her life . . . had been one continued course of sorrow and misfortune'. Not the least of her trials was her abject and humiliating poverty, despite the generous allowance made to her by Louis XIV. She sold all her jewellery and pretty trinkets and went without any luxury for herself, but it was never enough to feed the huge army of Jacobite hangers-on at St Germain who had no other means of support.

According to the terms of the Treaty of Rijswick in 1697, she was to have been paid an annual jointure of £50,000. First by William and then by Anne, this sum was withheld: not until 1714 did she finally receive the niggardly sum of £11,750, and never another penny. The death of her adored daughter Louisa in 1712, from smallpox, and the banishment from France of her son completed her desolation. In May 1718 she died of cancer, thanking God for her deliverance from this life. 'She is bound to be in heaven,' wrote the Duchesse d'Or-léans. 'She never kept a penny for herself, she gave everything to the poor, she used to support entire families, she never spoke ill of anyone . . .'

The leading actor in this family drama, William of Orange, died only six months after his father-in-law. After Mary's death he pressed on doggedly and alone with his life's great work. Slowly the English came to terms with their continental obligations, Parliament voted its

support for the Grand Alliance and, as commander-in-chief of the
English armies, Marlborough was already earning a formidable reputation on the battlefields of Europe.

With national feeling at last united behind him, William began
making preparations in the New Year of 1702 for a season's intensive
campaign against the French armies mobilizing in Flanders and on the
Rhine. He did not live to direct it. Riding in Hampton Court Park on
a February afternoon, he was thrown when his horse stumbled on a
molehill, and broke his collarbone. The fracture never mended properly
and a chill developed into pneumonia. He died on 8 March, surrounded
by his closest friends and holding Bentinck's hand.

From exile in early 1689, James had addressed a last passionate
appeal to his countrymen, hoping that they would agree to 'Liberty of
Conscience for all . . . & that those of my own persuasion may . . . have
such a share of it, as they may live peacefully and quietly as Englishmen
& Christians ought to doe, & not to be obliged to transplant themselves
. . .' These modest hopes were not realized – although the worst fears of
the Catholics were. 'Our own imprudence, avarice and ambition
have brought all this upon us,' wrote one of the English Jesuits to his
superior at Rome, '. . . for us there is neither faith nor hope left.'

Successive Acts of Parliament in William's reign transformed Catholics once more into the harried and persecuted minority of Elizabethan times. They were barred from Court or political careers, from
professional life, from keeping up any kind of aristocratic state and
from inheriting or buying land. England became a mission field once
more, and priests had a price on their head – £100, a huge sum in
those days. Mass was said furtively, in the domestic chapels of the fast
dwindling number of Catholic noble families, in backstreet mass houses,
or inns with a tolerant landlord; and James's vicars-apostolic were
hunted from one hiding-place to another like common criminals. All of
them were a prey to informers; and not the least of Catholic sufferings
was the fact that the most zealous of these were invariably apostates or
renegade priests.

Not until nearly a century later was a tiny measure of relief finally
granted to Catholics. And only in 1829, 140 years after William and
Mary were proclaimed king and queen, was the full political emancipation of British Catholics entered into the statute books.

William had solemnly assured the emperor that he would undertake
to see Catholics 'put out of fear of being persecuted on account of their
religion'. It was a promise he failed to honour. For the Roman Catholics
of Great Britain, James's Indulgence was tragically long in coming.

BIBLIOGRAPHY

I. Manuscript Sources
British Museum
Additional MSS; Egerton MSS
Nottingham University Library
Portland MSS
Exeter Public Record Office
Miscellaneous papers, broadsheets and MSS

II. Contemporary Newspapers
The London Gazette; The Universall Intelligencer; The English Currant;
The London Mercury; The Orange Gazette; Public Occurrences Truly
Stated; The London Courant

III. Printed Sources

Ailesbury, Thomas Bruce, 2nd Earl of: *Memoirs* (Roxburghe Club, 1890)
Arundell, Baron James Everard: *The History of Modern Wiltshire* (1829)
Ashley, Maurice: *The Glorious Revolution of 1688* (London, 1966)
–: *James II* (London, 1977)
Avaux, Jean-Antoine de Mesmes, Comte d': *Négociations depuis 1679 jusqu'en 1684*, 6 vols, Paris, 1752.

Bathurst, Lt. Col. The Hon. Benjamin: *Letters of Two Queens* (London, 1924)
Baxter, Stephen: *William III* (London, 1966)
Bentinck, Mechtild, Comtesse (ed.): *Marie, Reine d'Angleterre, Lettres et Mémoires* (The Hague, 1880)
Bloxam, the Revd J. R.: *Magdalen College and King James II*, 1686–8 (Oxford 1886)
Brown, Beatrice Curtis: *The Letters of Queen Anne* (London, 1935)
Browning, Andrew (ed.): *English Historical Documents 1660–1714* (London, 1953): *The Life and Letters of Thomas Osborne, Earl of Danby* (Glasgow, 1951)
Bryant, Sir Arthur: *Pepys, the Saviour of the Navy* (London, 1949)
Burnet, Gilbert: *History of his own Time, with notes by the Earls of Dartmouth and Hardwicke, Speaker Onslow and Dean Swift, to which added other Annotations* (2nd ed. enlarged, 6 vols, Oxford, 1833)

–: *The Expedition of His Highness the Prince of Orange for England* (Somers Tract, IX, London 1813)

Burnett, David: Salisbury: *The History of an English Cathedral City* (Tisbury 1978)

Calendar of State Papers, Domestic Series: James II, Vol III: June 1687–February 1689 (London, 1972)

Campana di Cavelli, Marchese de: *Les Derniers Stuarts à Saint-Germain-en-Laye* (London, 1871)

Carpenter, Edward: *The Protestant Bishop* (London, 1956)

Carswell, John: *The Descent on England* (London, 1969)

–: *The Old Cause* (London, 1954)

Chapman, Hester: *Mary II, Queen of England* (London, 1953)

Childs, John: *The Army, James II and the Glorious Revolution* (Manchester, 1980)

Churchill, Sir Winston S.: *Marlborough, His Life and Times* (2 vols, London, 1933)

Clarendon, Henry Hyde, 2nd Earl of: *Correspondence* and *Diary* (London, 1828)

Clarke, J. S.: *Life of James II* (London, 1816)

Dalrymple, Sir John: *Memoirs of Great Britain and Ireland* (3 vols, Edinburgh, 1771–88)

Daniell, The Revd. John F.: *The History of Warminster* (London, 1879)

Dodsworth, William: *An Historical Account of the Episcopal See and Cathedral Church of Salisbury* (Salisbury 1814)

Doebner, Dr (ed.): *Mary of Orange, Memoirs* (London, 1886)

Dunning, R. W.: *A History of the County of Somerset* (Vol. IV, Oxford 1978)

Echard, Laurence: *The History of the Revolution, and the Establishment of England in the Year 1688* (London, 1725)

Ellis, Henry: *Original Letters Illustrative of English History*, 2nd ser. (London, 1827)

Erlanger, Philippe: *Louis XIV* (London, 1970)

Evelyn, John: *Diary*, ed. E. S. de Beer (Oxford, 1955)

Eward, Suzanne: *No Fine but a Glass of Wine* (Salisbury, 1985)

Foxcroft, H. C.: *A Character of the Trimmer* (Cambridge, 1946)

–: *The Life and Letters of Sir George Savile, Bart, First Marquis of Halifax* (2 vols, London, 1898)

Fruin, Robert Jacob: *Prins Willem III in zijn verhouding tot Engeland* (1889)

–: *Verspreide Geschriften* (The Hague, 1901–2)

Green, David: *Queen Anne* (London, 1970)

Green, Emanuel: *The March of William of Orange through Somerset* (London, 1892)

Gregg, Edward: *Queen Anne* (London, 1980)

Groen van Prinsterer, G.: *Archives de la Maison d'Orange–Nassau*, 2nd ser. (The Hague, 1861)

Haile, Martin: *Queen Mary of Modena, her Life and Letters* (London, 1905)

Halifax, George Savile, 1st Marquis of: *Complete Works*, ed. J. P. Kenyon (London, 1969)

Haswell, Jock: *James II, Soldier and Sailor* (London, 1972)

Hatton, Ragnhild (ed.): *Louis XIV and Europe* (London, 1976)

Henning, Basil Duke: *The House of Commons 1660–1690* (London, 1983)

Historical Manuscripts Commission, Reports of: Various: particularly I, VII and XI; Dartmouth, Downshire, Eliot Hodgkin, Finch, Le Fleming, Leyborne-Popham, Lindsey, Ormonde, Portland, Rutland.

Hoare, Sir Richard: *The History of Modern Wiltshire* (London, 1843)

Hoskins, W. G.: *Industry, Trade and People in Exeter 1688-1800* (Exeter, 1968)

–: *Two Thousand Years in Exeter* (Chichester, 1960)

Hunter, Revd. Joseph (ed.): *The Diary of Ralph Thoresby FRS* (2 vols, London, 1830)

Huygens, Constantyn: *Journalen* (Utrecht, 1876–7)

Japikse, Nicolaas: *Correspondentie van Willem III en Hans Willem Bentinck* (The Hague, 1927–37)

–: *De Geschiedenis van het Huis van Oranje–Nassau* (The Hague, 1937–8)

–: *De Verwikkelingen tussen de Republiek en Engeland van 1660–1665* (Leiden, 1900)

–: *Prins Willem III, de Stadhouder-Koning* (Amsterdam, 1933)

Jones, J. R.: *The Revolution of 1688 in England* (London, 1972)

Jonge, J. C. de: *Geschiedenis van het Nederlandsche zeewezen*, Vol. III, ii (The Hague, 1837)

Kenyon, J. P.: *Robert Spencer, Earl of Sunderland, 1641–1702* (London, 1958)

–: *The Stuart Constitution* (Cambridge, 1966)

–: *The Stuarts* (4th ed., London, 1969)

Kerr, R. J. and Duncan, I. C. (eds.): *The Portledge Papers*

Klopp, Onno: *Der Fall des Hauses Stuart* (Vienna, 1877)

Krämer, F. J. L. (ed.): *Archives de la Maison d'Orange–Nassau*, 3rd ser. (Leiden, 1907–9)

–: *Maria Stuart, gemalin van Willem III* (Utrecht, 1890)

Kroll, M. (ed.): *Letters from Liselotte* (London, 1970)

Macaulay, Thomas Babington, Lord: *The History of England, from the Accession of James II* (Everyman ed., London, 1966)

Mathew, David: *Catholicism in England* (London, 1948)

Mazure, F. A. J.: *Histoire de la Révolution de 1688 en Angleterre* (Paris, 1825)

Miller, John: *The Glorious Revolution* (London and New York, 1983)

–: *James II: A Study in Kingship* (Hove, 1977)

Morris, Revd. John, S. J.: *Catholic England in Modern Times* (London, 1892)

Newton, Robert: *Eighteenth-Century Exeter* (Exeter, 1984)

Ollard, Richard: *Pepys* (Oxford, 1984)
Oman, Carola: *Mary of Modena* (London, 1962)

Packe, Joyce: *The Prince It Is That's Come* (Newton Abbot, 1984)
Page, Dr William (ed.): *The Victoria History of Somerset*, Vol II (London, 1911)
Perkins, Angela: *The Phyllis Court Story* (Oxford, 1983)
Pinkham, Lucille: *William III and the Respectable Revolution* (Cambridge, Mass., 1954)
Plumb, J. H.: *The Growth of Political Stability in England 1675–1725* (London, 1967)
Powley, Edward B.: *The English Navy in the Revolution of 1688* (Cambridge, 1928)
Pulman, George: *The Book of the Axe* (Bath, 1969)

Read, C. and Waddington, F.: *Mémoirs Inédits de Dumont de Mostaquet* (Paris, 1864)
Reresby, Sir John: *Memoirs 1634–1689* (London, 1875)
Rowse, A. L.: *The Early Churchills* (London, 1969)

St Maur, H.: *Annals of the Seymours* (London, 1902)
Sidney, Henry: *Diary and Correspondence* (London, 1843)
Sidney, Philip: *Memoirs of the Sidney Family* (London 1899)
Somers, Baron John: *Collection of Tracts* (London, 1813)
Somerville, D. H.: *The King of Hearts* (London, 1962)
Strickland, Agnes: *Lives of the Queens of England*, Vols 6, 7, 8 (London, 1885)
Sweetman, George: *History of Wincanton* (London, 1903)

Temple Patterson, A.: *Portsmouth: A History* (London, 1976)
Turner, F. C.: *James II* (London, 1948)

White J. F.: *The History of Torquay* (Torquay, 1879)
Whittle, John: *An Exact Diary of the Late Expedition* (London, 1689)
Winn, Colin G.: *The Pouletts of Hinton St George* (London, 1976)
Wolf, John B.: *Louis XIV* (London, 1968)
Worth, R. W.: *History of Devonshire* (London, 1866)

Zee, Henri and Barbara van der: *William and Mary* (London, 1973)

IV. Articles

Beddard, Robert: 'The Guildhall Declaration of 11 December 1688 and the Counter-Revolution of the Loyalists', *Historical Journal*, 1968, XI, 3, pp. 403–20
Boyer, Richard E.: 'English Declarations of Indulgence of 1687 and 1688', *Catholic Historical Review*, 1964, I, pp. 322–71

Couldrey, W. G.: 'Memories and Antiquities of Paignton', *Transactions of the Devon Association,* 1932

Drabble, John E.: 'Gilbert Burnet and the History of the English Revolution', *Journal of Religious History,* 1984, xii

Frankle, Robert J.: 'The Formulation of the Declaration of Rights', *Historical Journal,* 1974, XVI, 2, pp. 265–79

George, Robert H.: 'The Financial Relations of Louis XIV and James II', *Journal of Modern History,* 1931, p. 111

Goldie, Mark: 'Edmund Bohun and *Jus Gentium* in the Revolution Debate, 1689–1693', *Historical Journal,* 1977, 20, 3, pp. 569–86

Gwynn, Robin D.: 'James II in the light of his treatment of Huguenot refugees in England, 1685–1686', *English Historical Review,* 1977, Vol. 92, pp. 820–33

Hosford, David H.: 'Bishop Compton and the Revolution of 1688', *Journal of Ecclesiastical History,* July 1972, Vol. XXIII, no. 3

Jones, Clyve (ed.): 'Journal of the Voyage of William of Orange from Holland to Torbay, 1688', *Journal of Army Historical Research,* 51, (1973) pp. 15–18

–: 'The Protestant Wind of 1688: Myth and Reality', *European Studies Review,* July 1973, Vol. 3, no. 3

Jones, George Hilton: 'The Recall of the British from the Dutch Service', *Historical Journal,* 1982, 25, 2, pp. 423–35

Kenyon, J. P.: 'The Earl of Sunderland and the Revolution of 1688', *Cambridge Historical Journal,* XI, 1955

–: 'The Birth of the Old Pretender', *History Today,* June 1963

Miller, John: 'Catholic Officers in the later Stuart Army', *English Historical Review,* 1973, Vol. 88, pp. 35–53

–: 'The Glorious Revolution: "Contract" and "Abdication" Reconsidered', *Historical Journal,* 1982, 25, 3, pp. 541–55

–: 'Militia and the Army in the Reign of James II', *Historical Journal,* 1973, XVI, 4, pp. 659–79

Reitan, E. A.: 'From Revenue to Civil List, 1689–1702: The Revolution Settlement and the "Mixed and Balanced" Constitution', *Historical Journal,* 1970, XIII, 4, pp. 571–88

Sachse, William L. (ed.), 'Da Cunha's Account of the Condition of Catholics in the British Isles in 1710', *Catholic Historical Review,* 1963, Vol. xlix, pp. 20–46

–: 'The Mob and the Revolution of 1688', *Journal of British Studies,* pp. 23–40

Schwoerer, Lois G.: 'Press and Parliament in the Revolution of 1689', *Historical Journal,* 1977, 20, 3, pp. 545–67

–: 'Propaganda in the Revolution of 1688–9', *American Historical Review,* 1977, Vol. 82, pp. 843–74

Slaughter, Thomas P.: '"Abdicate" and "Contract" in the Glorious Revolution', *Historical Journal,* 1981, 24, 2, pp. 323–37

Sydenham, M. J.: 'The Anxieties of an Admiral: Lord Dartmouth and the Revolution of 1688', *History Today,* October 1972, Vol. 12

Tanner, J. R.: 'Naval Preparations of James II in 1688', *English Historical Review*, 1893, 8, pp. 272–83

Varwell, P.: 'Notes on the Ancient Parish of Brixham, Devon, and on some of its Ancient People', *Transactions of the Devon Association*, 1886, Vol. 18

Walker, R. B.: 'The Newspaper Press in the Reign of William III', *Historical Journal*, 1974, XVII, 4, pp. 691–709

Windeatt, T. W.: 'The Landing of the Prince of Orange at Brixham in 1688', *Transactions of the Devon Association*, 1880, Vol. 12

V. Local Histories

We have relied heavily on publications of local history societies, pamphlets, newspapers and other ephemera.

INDEX